THE ROGUE KING

INFERNO RISING

THE ROGUE KING

INFERNO  RISING

ABIGAIL OWEN

Entangled Publishing, LLC
2614 South Timberline Road
Suite 109
Fort Collins, CO 80525
Visit our website at www.entangledpublishing.com.

Amara is an imprint of Entangled Publishing, LLC.

Edited by Heather Howland
Cover design by Bree Archer and Kelley Martin
Cover images by
Shutterstock/Satyrenko
Getty Images/ Spondylolithesis and greenleaf123
DepositPhotos/Photocreo
Interior design by Heather Howland

Print ISBN 978-1-64063-531-9
ebook ISBN 978-1-64063-532-6

Manufactured in the United States of America

First Edition August 2019

AMARA

To Heather.
For loving this series and
believing in it as much as I do!

THE DRAGON CLANS

GOLD
King: Uther Hagan
Location: North Europe
Based in: Store Skagastølstind, Norway

BLUE
King: Ladon Ormarr
Location: Western Europe
Based in: Ben Nevis, Scotland

BLACK
King: Gorgon Ejderha
Location: Western Asia/Northern Africa
Based in: Mount Ararat, Turkey

GREEN
King: Fraener Luu
Location: Eastern/Southern Asia
Based in: Yulong Xueshan, China

WHITE
King: Volos Ajdaho
Location: Eastern Europe/Northern Asia
Based in: Kamen, Russia

RED
King: Pytheios Chandali
Location: Central Asia
Based in: Everest, Nepal/China

PROLOGUE

The scent of raw meat, tinged with putrid rot, curled around Serefina, filling her nostrils and awakening a memory she would have sooner forgotten.

At least he'd waited to confront her until after closing, when she was the last person left in the place. Her hands shook even as they slowed in the mundane task of clearing one of the handful of linoleum-topped tables in the small, rural Kansas diner where she worked. Where she pretended to be just another human and not who and what she truly was.

A prize sought by every creature.

Legend held that the man who captured a phoenix would be blessed. Unable to put a foot wrong. Every choice the right one. Every action leading to greater fortune. Except legend had it wrong. The man had to capture the phoenix's heart.

The man who'd come for her would never have her heart. She knew who stood directly behind her, bringing that nasty smell inside with him where the rancid fumes mingled with the grease that hung heavy in the air.

Pytheios.

The Rotting King of the Red Dragon Clan. The man who had once deluded himself into thinking he could mate Serefina and take her parents' throne. But she'd chosen another, a different clan's king, and for her sins, Pytheios had murdered him.

Zilant. Her destined mate, and her one true love.

So she'd run.

Disappeared.

Pytheios had hunted her ever since, needing her at his side to legitimize his reign as High King. Thankfully, he had no idea of the secret she'd taken with her that fateful night all those centuries ago when she'd escaped, pregnant and terrified. And so alone. A secret concealed not ten miles from here. A secret she'd guard with her life.

Pytheios would *never* find her daughters.

"You didn't think you could remain hidden forever, did you?" Pytheios's charred voice rumbled behind her. Smug bastard.

The skin on the back of Serefina's neck crawled at his mere presence. She didn't question how he'd finally tracked her down. Five centuries of hiding from him were five more than she'd expected to get.

Now her daughters must find their own way without her there to guide them. Protect them. Teach them. *Please let me have prepared them enough.*

Serefina didn't bother trying to figure out how to save herself from the attack she knew was coming. Before Pytheios had killed them, her parents had been living proof that the dragon king who mated the phoenix would become the High King and rule wisely and well, leading to an era of prosperity.

The Red Clan had ruled over all dragon shifters during her parents' reign. The five other dragon kings would have no choice but to bow down to Pytheios if he brought her back as his mated prize.

But he wasn't destined to be her mate. Her fire would consume him, as it would any dragon shifter other than Zilant, whether she liked it or not. Zilant's brand hadn't yet appeared on her neck, but all that meant was that she hadn't died with her mate. No other man could *ever* have her.

Pytheios might try anyway, or at the very least take her. Imprison her. Use her.

So yes. There was no doubt in her mind; today was the last day of her life. But could she save the fire inside her, and the magic that came with it, to perform one last desperate act to protect her daughters before the final blow came?

Acrid bile burned her throat as it rose from the pit of her stomach. She forced it down. Now was not the time to allow fear into her heart. Fear could wait for those last precious seconds of life, when she'd fought until she could no longer move, when she'd done everything she could. Maybe not even then.

Not fear for herself. Fear for the four precious women she'd be leaving behind.

If not for them, death would be a welcome relief. Then she could finally join Zilant in the afterlife where he waited for her.

Serefina closed her eyes, reaching for the power that had lain dormant inside her for too many years, stoking an inferno, the flames licking her insides with a pleasant warmth she'd almost forgotten.

"Turn around," the monster behind her commanded. "Now."

Frustration lined the edges of Pytheios's words, and she smiled. Even now, she could defy him. She took some small consolation from the thought.

Slowly, as if careful not to spook a wild animal, she pivoted. And blinked. The years had not been kind to her enemy. When she'd seen him last, his body had already started rotting, having passed into that age when an unmated dragon's body broke down, becoming susceptible to disease, deterioration, or insanity. Sometimes all of the above. For Pytheios, disease had taken his body in the form of skin decay.

The flesh hung from his bones as though gravity had dragged at him so long, the tissue lost elasticity. His eyes were sunken into his head, the reddish-brown irises, the hallmark of a red dragon, now milky and faded with age. Even the king's brand, the symbol of Pytheios's house, appeared faded where it marked the flesh on his hand between his thumb and forefinger.

How was he still alive?

Despite his now-decrepit appearance, she knew she'd never overpower him physically. She'd be willing to bet he no longer did his own fighting, though, and likely hadn't in a while, which might make him slower, easier to surprise.

Serefina lifted her chin, ready to buy herself time. "You look like shit."

His lips pulled back in what she guessed was supposed to be a smile. "How very…American. You are as lovely as ever." He sniffed the air. "And you smell like ambrosia."

Again, she had to hold down the bile threatening to spew from her. Serefina focused the fire inside herself, the gathering power undulating under her skin. If she wasn't visibly glowing yet, she would be any second. She directed a small amount of energy into a single thought that she sent to her daughters.

The time has come.

They knew what those words meant. They knew what they had to do. Since the day of their birth—a day of joy devoured by a despair so deep she'd hardly been able to push her babies out of her body—Serefina had been preparing them for this eventuality.

Pytheios, still so arrogant he hadn't yet restrained her, continued his demands. "Time to give me what you denied me more than five hundred years ago."

"My duty was to Zilant, my destined mate," she spat. "You will *never* be my king."

Pytheios's neck worked as though he were swallowing back his rage, the column of his throat moving like a serpent was trapped inside. "I no longer need your submission or your body."

An icy shard of terror pierced her heart at the words and the sneer curling his lip. What did he mean?

"I'll take your power *and* your life."

Take her power? Could he? She'd never heard of such a thing, but his threat lent urgency to her next steps.

"I'll die before I give you an ounce of my power," she snarled. Fisting her hands, Serefina threw her arms wide. Her skin came alive with dancing flames, and her vision changed to one alight in a reddish glow.

Before she could use her strongest gift—the ability to transport her body anywhere with a single thought—Pytheios leaped forward and wrapped his hands around her throat. He squeezed hard enough to cut off oxygen, but not enough to kill. As a dragon, her fire didn't harm him...couldn't harm him unless he tried to force her to mate.

Serefina wouldn't risk teleporting him with her. She needed to reach her daughters ahead of him — alone. But she'd learned a few tricks in the centuries she'd been hiding. In a simultaneous move, she brought her hands up to strike at the back of his thumbs, dislodging his grip from her neck, while at the same time kneeing him hard in the balls.

Pytheios dropped to the ground, clutching his groin, and she sprinted for the door. She didn't make it more than three steps before he reached out and snagged her by the ankle. Serefina went down hard, slamming her head into a tabletop as she fell. Ears ringing, she turned on her attacker like a feral animal. She kicked him in the face, not that she'd ever damage a dragon's harder bone structure, but the move surprised him into releasing her.

Serefina scrambled to her feet and rushed outside into the gravel parking lot. In the struggle with Pytheios, she'd lost her fire. She closed her eyes, gathering the necessary force from deep inside. She had seconds at best.

As her enemy's bellow of frustration sounded from inside the diner, the fire ignited, pouring out of her skin. With another small burst of power and a whisper of resolve, she disappeared.

But not before the long blade of a hurled knife pierced through skin and bone, lodging in her spine with a sickening thud. Agony screamed through her body, even as her legs went horrifyingly numb.

Serefina accepted the pain, let it fuel the fury whipping the blaze inside her, and pictured the small clearing behind the unassuming house where she'd kept her family for the last twenty years. The image formed clearly in her mind—rickety white siding that needed replacing, dirt-covered screens, and the field with its tall, dry grass almost silver in the light of the full moon. Her daughters would be gathering out there now. Waiting for her. Probably terrified.

Using more energy than she'd wanted to expend, she accessed her gift of teleportation and pulled her body from the diner parking lot through the silent darkness of empty space, to appear in that familiar field in less than a heartbeat.

She hit the ground hard, crumpling to her knees, which no longer functioned. The knife had done its job, severing nerves and removing control over her own body. No matter. She could do what she had to do from the ground.

"Mother!" Her daughter Kasia's voice pierced the sweltering night air.

Serefina raised her head to find all four of her daughters gathered about twenty feet away, their faces pale and stricken.

There wasn't enough time.

The house where they lived was located only ten miles from the diner. Pytheios would eventually see the fire she was about to unleash, and not be far behind. She had only a few minutes to complete her task, if that.

Serefina focused on her children—grown women now, each as different from the other as the moon from the sun, each a reflection of both their darkly exotic mother, born of the red dragon king and a phoenix, and their blond-haired, pale-blue-eyed white dragon king father.

A cry of agony burst from her lips as she forced the crackling energy inside her to manifest. All around her, the grass burned, tinder to her flames, catching quickly. Her body began to shift, long, gloriously soft feathers bursting from her arms for the first time in her life. It was a bittersweet sight—the one time a phoenix ever turned into the bird was when she passed her powers to her daughter—or daughters, in Serefina's case—either in death or by choice.

She couldn't send her babies away without a final message, so she spared another precious ounce of her energy. *"I love you all, and I am so proud of you. You are women worthy of our phoenix legacy, but don't let history control you. Find your own way in this world."*

A colossal roar reverberated across the land behind her. Her daughters ducked, covering their ears. Pytheios, in his true form, lured by the flames, was coming for her.

No time.

She ignored the anguish racking her body, focusing on what she had to do with all her might. Her last act as a mother was the most important thing she'd ever do on this earth.

Picturing each of the four separate locations she'd predetermined ages ago, Serefina directed her gaze to the youngest of her quadruplets.

Tears streamed down Angelika's heart-shaped face. Her pale blond hair whipped in the wind. "I love you," her sweet daughter mouthed. And then, she was gone. Forced to another place, a safer place, by her mother's will alone.

Serefina's core trembled, her power depleting exponentially, but she pushed through, focusing next on Meira. More angular and serious, with her bouncy strawberry blonde curls at odds with her personality, she held her body rigidly, dark eyes closed as though unable to watch her mother's last moments. Another burst of power, another push, and Meira was gone.

Her strength faltering, breath coming in panting bursts, Serefina felt smaller now, lighter, as her bones became hollow. Most of her had completed the shift, but she didn't care about that. She refused to succumb to the dark spots dancing before her eyes.

Skylar came next. Her midnight hair, so like Serefina's own, hung in a long braid over her shoulder. Even from here, those glacial blue eyes, her father's eyes, so filled with defiance, pierced Serefina's heart. Again, she focused her resolve and her waning control, and Skylar disappeared.

Flames poured off Serefina's body, raising her dark curls around her head and eating up every inch of the land around her. The one tree in their yard exploded with a thunderous clash of sound and light as it ignited. Divergent with the blaze, a deep cold ached in Serefina's bones, spreading insidiously through her body from within.

Did she have enough fire left in her? Enough for one final act?

Kasia stood before her, calm and steady. Dark red hair waved around her, lit with gold from the flames that crept nearer and nearer to her, but not yet licking at her feet.

Serefina looked closer. Was that fire in her child's eyes? Was the power of the phoenix already passing from mother to child? Serefina knew she had mere moments until her body would be consumed by her own flames. She had to get Kasia away before that happened, or Pytheios would take her.

The blistering flames around her swayed and danced as a draft of wind pushed down from above, and the shadow of a massive beast high overhead loomed.

Pytheios.

Had he seen all four of her daughters? A crimson claw reached for Kasia, who dove for the ground. Her brave girl didn't even scream, instead looking to her mother, waiting for the deliverance she trusted would come.

Serefina reached out to Kasia, her hand now a wing of deep red and gold feathers, and shoved every last ounce of the raging storm inside her at her daughter, and with iron will forged in fire and pain, she sent her child far away from the monster above her, to a safer place.

Finally, she could let go. Let death consume her, sending her home. To rest. To peace. To Zilant.

The furious roar of the dragon was the last thing Serefina heard as her body disintegrated to ash, starting at the tips of her wings and working toward her center, the fine powder drifting away in the wind.

I

Brand pulled his 1970 Plymouth Hemi Cuda into the empty parking lot and rolled into the space nearest the frosted glass door sporting a tiny sign. MEDICAL SERVICES.

Right place. The fact that it appeared deserted didn't faze him, not for this kind of facility. With a flick of the key, he cut off the deep rumble of the souped-up classic car's engine but didn't get out immediately.

"Why the hell am I here?" he muttered under his breath.

The fifth place he'd been sent in the last year looking for gods knew what—having visited the traitors in South America, the Huracán Enforcers in California, a witch in Alaska, and a chimera in Toronto. Now Cheyenne, Wyoming.

The Blood King was searching for a woman. That's all Brand had pieced together, though suspicion had started to itch at him.

He pulled out the satellite phone he carried with him when working for the king and punched in the private number he never stored in the device's memory, just his own. Immediately a low male voice answered.

"Have you met her?" came the immediate question. No intro or greeting necessary. The man on the other end already knew who he was and why he was calling.

"No. I'm parked outside." *And this is a colossal*

fucking waste of my time.

He'd traveled halfway around the world on a goose chase for something that didn't exist. Brand kept that last bit to himself. Ladon Ormarr wouldn't appreciate having his obsessive quest questioned again. Not that he'd rip Brand's insides out next time they crossed paths or anything, but Brand needed the other dragon to stay on his side. Serving as a mercenary for Ladon, the Blood King of the Blue Dragon Clan, doing every job no one else would take, was all for a purpose—survival and revenge.

Ladon was a major key to a plan centuries in the making—one that involved killing Uther, the King of the Gold Clan. Something that had turned out to be a lot tougher than Brand had ever expected, so Brand had no intention of pissing off his only ally.

"Call me when you've seen her."

Click.

Brand stared at his phone and held back his irritation with effort. Looked like Ladon had zero intention of letting this fixation go.

Fine. He'd get this over with, get paid regardless, and move on to trying to figure out how to get to Uther before he died of old age.

Brand swung himself out of the car and stalked into the facility.

And immediately froze.

Smoke. The noticeable scent of it hung heavy in the halls of the private medical clinic tucked discreetly into a series of warehouses in Cheyenne, Wyoming. The campfire aroma had a sweet undercurrent, sort of chocolaty, and was strong enough to mask the antiseptic smell that inundated most medical facilities.

Brand stopped inside the doors and studied the flavor of the odor, letting it wash over his senses of smell and taste, trying to identify the source. Only a handful of creatures dealt in fire. A dragon shifter himself, he should be able to easily identify this one.

The fact that he couldn't pinpoint a species landed on the "pay attention" scale of his give-a-shit-o-meter.

That small suspicion that had been creeping up on him grew deeper roots.

Brand controlled his reaction, determined to give no outward sign of his tension. He'd trained himself long ago to never respond so others could see. Reaction was weakness that could be exploited, and weakness for a rogue dragon meant certain death.

Instead, he walked up to the receptionist, a woman who gave a low growl deep in her throat. Polar bear shifter. He'd expected no less at this clinic. From what he understood after checking this place out, Dr. Oppenheim dealt only with special cases. Supernatural medical needs. Having reinforcement in the front office in the form of a large predator shifter was only smart.

The polar bear wouldn't have been able to help the growl or the way her canines elongated in her mouth. Predators didn't like it when more dangerous predators showed up. Dragons were as dangerous as anything supernatural got, and they didn't play nice with others.

Strike that. They didn't play. Period.

Brand ignored the growled warning. He'd already

sized her up in one glance. This woman was an alpha and unmated, which could make her dangerous. Good thing he didn't care.

He whipped out the credentials he used in situations like these. "My name is Brand Astarot. I'm a private investigator."

The lie about his job tripped easily off his tongue. He'd been using the PI cover for his own purposes for a long time. It tended to open doors faster, or at least give him a reason to be in unusual locations and circumstances. "Dr. Oppenheim should be expecting me."

The bear shifter took a moment to force her teeth back to human size. "My apologies, Mr. Astarot," she murmured. "We don't get much traffic during daylight hours."

Not completely at ease, she eyed his form, taking in his six-foot-five, muscled frame, the breadth of his shoulders, her gaze finally dropping to his right hand.

Every dragon shifter sported a brand signifying the clan and king he owed allegiance to—Blue, Gold, Red, White, Green, or Black. Even in the Americas, supernaturals knew to check.

Brand had no such mark on his hand. Which left only one option—he was a rogue dragon, abandoned or exiled by his people, or one who'd deliberately left his clan.

A rogue who hadn't already been hunted down and killed by his own kind tended to be batshit crazy and unpredictable with it. Crazy wasn't his style.

Yet.

But the receptionist didn't know that, and the

general perception was a tool he relied on to stay alive.

"We don't get many dragons in here, either," she finally said.

Reading between the lines, and knowing his extremely secretive people, he doubted this clinic got any. Dragons had their own healers. "I understand."

She nodded, then picked up the phone. "Dr. Oppenheim? A private investigator named Mr. Astarot has arrived. Shall I have him go on back?"

After a long silence, a calm voice answered. "I've been expecting him. However, our patient is about to supernova again."

Supernova?

Dr. Oppenheim continued. "I guess if he's investigating her, he'd better see what he's dealing with."

Even the shifter grimaced. She hit the button to hang up and pointed at a set of double doors to her right. "Through there. End of the hall."

Brand paused at the doors. "What does supernova mean in this context?"

She grimaced again. "Let's just say we're lucky we have a fireproof room, or we would've burned down twice in the last month."

Fire. The same symptom he'd been tracking all over the damn planet. Brand couldn't see Ladon bothering with any of the lesser fire creatures, and he was too smart to mess with a hellhound. He'd initially assumed Ladon was searching for a dragon mate. A queen would stop the aging process for the king, as well as help solidify his claim to the throne. As a new king, Ladon could use all the support he could get.

But no. The scent mingling in the smoke wasn't dragon. This was something…different. And if his suspicions were right, something impossible.

Adrenaline-fueled curiosity mixed with a certain amount of dread as Brand made his way down the long corridor. About the length of a football field, the walls were painted white, matching the white tile floors, all illuminated by overhead lights that gave off a low buzz that aggravated his sensitive hearing and cast a bluish hue over everything.

He passed several doors with various labels. Normal ones like exam rooms and surgery. A few not-so-normal ones. He held in a sneer as he passed a room geared toward newly made werewolves— no windows, dragonsteel bars that he'd bet were electrified, magically warded, or both. Not that a dragon's first time shifting was any easier, but they had their own process for that.

He reached the end of the hall just as a woman with dark gray hair tipped in neon green stepped out of a room. She wore a white lab coat, so he figured this had to be the doctor.

"Mr. Astarot?" She held out her hand, which he grasped as he nodded. "I'm Dr. Oppenheim. Mariska has been under my care for the last five weeks or so."

Mariska? Sounded Russian. A good place to hide if she was what he suspected.

Brand tucked a spurt of uneasiness behind a poker face that never lost him a game. "All I've been told is to come see this woman."

"We didn't want to discuss particulars over the phone, in case someone was…listening in."

Brand narrowed his eyes, taking in the slightly too eager light in the doctor's eyes. His experience dealing with liars and manipulators lit up a warning with big red lights. He'd bet his hefty fee for this job that this Oppenheim person knew what her patient was already.

Did that mean Ladon knew, too? "Can you give me the particulars now?"

Her green-tipped hair swayed as she nodded. "She's almost at the end of another bout. I think you should witness the worst of her symptoms. Then we can talk."

At that, Dr. Oppenheim turned and hit a button beside the door. The entire wall was instantly rendered transparent, like glass, and Brand got his first view of the reason he was here. Sort of.

A woman huddled on the floor in the middle of the room with her back to him, naked, her body consumed by angry red flames that sparked at the tips.

"We had to remove all the furniture, because when she goes, she melts everything but the walls, which are magically warded to withstand even dragon fire." The doctor sent him a significant glance, which meant she knew what he was, though he had yet to identify her species. Some kind of healer, possibly a minor deity or demigod with the ability?

Suddenly, the woman on the other side of the glass clutched her stomach and moaned, low and long. An answering pain radiated through Brand's body.

What the fuck?

He swallowed back a groan. "Is she hurt?"

The doctor flicked him another glance. "You could say that. She experiences episodes that start with a loss of vision, followed by discomfort, which builds to what she describes as a full-body migraine at the height of the fire."

Brand nodded, even as his thoughts spun.

No dragon or any other fire creature he knew of suffered when they loosed their fire or shifted. And why the hell had her moan affected *him*, the painful burn spreading deep into his bones?

Brand breathed in, steadying himself. He possessed a massive level of self-control thanks to the power of kings that flowed through his blood. He was the only one left from his bloodline, but the authority of his ancestors still filled his veins. He sought that control now, having to reach for it, struggle to find it.

As he watched, the fire pouring off Mariska's body grew, crawling over the floor and up the walls almost as though it were alive. She crumpled to the ground, curling into a ball. At the same time, a series of keening sounds burst from her.

His control slipped another notch as pain pulsed through him, stronger than before. On the edge of something sharper, but not quite there. Brand slammed his hand on the wall and leaned into the pain. In the same instant, instinct dragged at him. He needed to be in that room to... Fucking hell. He didn't know what. Help her? Instinct screamed at him to *help* her.

"Mr. Astarot?" Dr. Oppenheim's concerned tones barely penetrated the haze that had taken over his body. Brand couldn't tear his gaze from the woman separated from him by a wall.

She trembled now, body visibly tensing and

releasing. Low moans tumbled from her lips and slid down his spine like electric shocks.

"Why does it take so long?" he groaned around his own escalating situation.

"We don't know." The doctor put a hand on his arm. "But I'm more concerned about you right now."

Instinct chose that instant to take over every cell of his body. He needed to be in that room. Now. He shook the doctor off.

"Step back," he growled, his voice already dark and smoky, even though he wasn't shifting.

"Wait!" Dr. Oppenheim yelled.

But she was too late. Brand burst into the room and ran at the woman sprawled in the middle of the floor. He dropped to his knees in front of her. "Let me help you."

She jerked back. Her eyes, blazing with flame to the point he couldn't see their color, darted around as if she were searching for him in the dark. Right, she couldn't see. Her mouth dropped open, but he couldn't tell if it was from fear of him or from panting through what looked like waves of razor-edged agony. He knew the feeling.

"I know I can help you." He had no idea *how* he knew, but he did. "Will you let me try?"

She sucked in a sharp hiss, her face contorting. Then she nodded, wincing as if even that small movement was unbearable.

Urgency moved him around behind her, where he dropped to his knees, banding an arm around her waist and pulling her up and against him, his thighs bracketing hers. The softness of her bare skin registered in his fogged mind, and the edge of his own pain dulled.

Interesting…

Flames licked at his body, the heat intensifying. Thankfully, his control of fire kept her from burning off his clothes. Maybe he could try to contain her fire? He sensed her need for more touch, needing it, too, but didn't want to take advantage.

"I've got you," he whispered in her ear.

He ran a hand down her arm, and she sighed, seeming to ease, if only a fraction, at his touch.

Then she clenched as another pulse shot through her—he knew because an answering pulse shot through *him*—and she dropped her head back against his shoulder. A scream that pierced his heart poured from her lips, and the fire burst around them before he could get a handle on it, the reverberation of the explosion ringing in his ears, the power behind it shaking him.

Then, before he could process what was happening, the flames sucked back into her body, a river of angry color disappearing into her skin, like water down a drain, swirling around them both, until all that was left were the two of them in a room gone deadly quiet.

The pain in his body evaporated, leaving behind only a dull ache. Meanwhile, her skin glowed, like a white-hot poker just removed from the kiln.

What the hell just happened?

He glanced down into her face and registered how the woman in his arms was beautiful in a way that snatched the breath from his lungs—long red hair spilled over his arm. Delicate features, high cheekbones, eminently kissable mouth. She reminded him of a tiny bird. One who needed protecting from the world. Who might snap if he held her too tight.

And glowing, like an angel.

"Fuck me," Brand spat. Mariska—and he doubted that was her real name—was a phoenix. A creature destined to mate a dragon king, making him the High King of the dragon clans, and, according to legend, bringing peace to their kind.

Total crap in his opinion, and not Brand's primary concern.

This was why Ladon had sent him, because he knew Brand was the only dragon who'd bring her back to him. Because Brand needed Ladon more than he'd need a phoenix. Being a rogue no longer scared him—he knew how to survive that way indefinitely—but he did need the power of a clan behind him in order to take out Uther. He'd waited centuries to kill the King of the Gold Clan.

Giving this phoenix to Ladon would open that door.

The woman in his arms stirred, eyelids fluttering open to reveal eyes so pale blue they reminded him of blues found deep in glacier ice. Eyes like a white dragon. Hypnotic.

"You," she croaked.

The lingering dull ache disappeared as an unaccustomed stomach-clenching sensation of trepidation sank to the bottom of his gut. "You know me?"

She gave a trembling smile. "That was a damn idiotic thing to do, you ass. I could've killed you."

Then she went limp in his arms.

*H*e's real.

Kasia's first thought as she pulled herself out of a deep and dreamless sleep was for the man... The man she'd seen in almost every vision she experienced when she went up in flames. A year of seeing his face with more and more frequency. A year of not knowing his name or who he was. A year of hiding and waiting in total isolation since her mother sacrificed her life.

Now she'd finally met him.

While in the midst of what she could only describe as an almighty full-body migraine, blind and incapacitated with pain...and naked as a newborn. That had to have made quite an impression.

The sensation that came with her visions, that seemed to be tied to them, like a physical manifestation of the intense power being released inside her, was something she couldn't control, or stop, or even ignore. Almost like unlocking the visions in her head required peeling back her physical self to let the magic loose. No sight, to clear the way for her mind's eye, followed by the anguish of being stripped raw, turned her body into an open gateway.

You'd think the fire would be enough, but apparently not.

He'd held her through it all, his surprisingly gentle touch both soothing her pain and bringing her to the end of her tussle with fire much faster than she could've done on her own.

Leaving me lying naked in his arms.

The heat of a rare blush crept up her chest and neck and into her face. Then, as the lethargy of exhaustion receded more, realization struck hard.

No way should he have been able to survive her fire. Who the hell, or more specifically *what* the hell, was he? And could she trust him? Or did she need to run?

"How are you feeling?" The deep tones of a smooth male voice washed over her. He had an accent she couldn't quite place—not quite American, not quite British.

A small part of her mind hummed in appreciation. She liked his voice, which reminded her of bottomless pools of water in a cave. Dark. Sinfully beautiful. Her visions were silent, so until today, she'd never heard him speak.

Stop stalling, she told herself sternly. *Face the man.*

After all, he'd done a bang-up job helping her through that vision, though *how* was a mystery.

Kasia stifled a miserably embarrassed groan. Slowly, she forced open her eyes, noting the darkened sky outside the window. How long had she been out? Obviously, they'd moved her to her usual room while she was unconscious. Dressed her, too, thankfully. A hospital gown, but that was better than naked, which was how she always ended up.

Finally, she moved her gaze to the man seated in the chair beside her bed. Despite seeing images of him, she still had to swallow around a suddenly dry throat at the man in the flesh. His face was all hard angles with surprisingly sensual lips that kept him off the edge of too hard. In combination with dirty blond hair, almost light brown in color, that brushed his collar, and an unusual golden-eyed gaze pinned on her now, he gave off a don't-fuck-with-me attitude that couldn't be missed.

He wore what she'd come to think of as his standard uniform—jeans, black T-shirt, probably those steel-toed boots he wore in every vision. An aura of control practically rolled off him, clotting the air and swamping her senses. Of their own accord, her eyes dropped to the tattoo on his arm, the pine trees around his wrist in clearer detail here than in her visions. If her body weren't still wrung out, she'd be tingling all over by now.

He stared back steadily, as if waiting for her to make the first move.

Kasia grabbed the remote for her hospital bed and raised the head so she could address him more upright. Anything to lessen the disadvantage she was already starting with where he was concerned.

"Who are you?" she asked, keeping her gaze steady on his, trying to project a calm she was far from feeling. As always, her voice came out scratchy following the fire, and she swallowed around her sore throat.

He raised his eyebrows. "You tell me. You recognized me in there."

Kasia shrugged. "I don't know. Not really."

"But you know me." Not a question, and a tone that indicated zero tolerance for stalling.

She sighed. "Yes. Sort of." She quickly considered how much to tell him. "I have visions."

His brows scrunched over his eyes. "Visions? The doctor didn't mention anything like that."

She flicked a glance at the door. "Probably because I didn't tell her. When the pain comes and I light on fire, I see things. Glimpses, mostly. Nothing makes sense, and I can't hear."

That intent stare narrowed, hardened. "And you've seen me in these visions?"

She fought back a shiver. Guess he didn't like that little fact. Too late now. "Yes."

He thought about that, and she waited him out. Eventually, he crossed his arms, the muscles stretching the limits of his T-shirt and drawing her gaze again to the tattoo on his arm. Curiosity peaked. Maybe now she'd get to see the rest of it? She'd wondered...

"My name is Brand Astarot."

Brand. Uncompromising. The name suited him.

His frown deepened. "Dr. Oppenheim thought I might be able to help you figure out who and what you are."

Why did she get the impression that he wasn't comfortable with that statement, like a suit that didn't fit him quite right? Was he lying about why he was here? If he was, why?

"I see." She eyed him closely. He hadn't stated what his specific job was in that introduction. Something she found concerning. "Is that all you are?" She'd learned to ask the question lately, though certain species were more sensitive than others at being quizzed about their origin.

Not Brand. His expression didn't so much as twitch. "I'm a dragon shifter."

Panic slammed through Kasia so hard she would've swayed if she'd been standing. To hide her shaking hands, she clutched the blanket, pulling it up around her as if she were cold.

Damn. Damn. Double damn.

The scent of fire in the room made more sense now. She'd assumed the lingering odor to be her own, a remnant from her fiery vision, but it had a woodsier, earthier undertone to it, not sweet like hers.

Why didn't I see this coming?

Despite wanting to hyperventilate, she did her best to keep her reaction under wraps, deliberately relaxing back against the pillows like she thought his being a dragon was a good thing, and not the most terrifying answer he could have given her. "Makes sense with the fire, I guess."

She glanced away, plucking at the front string from her gown as she stalled for time to think, to formulate some kind of plan. She had to figure out how to get him out of here without suspecting anything, then she could disappear.

Kasia cleared her throat. "So how does this work?"

Brand rooted around in a well-used backpack she hadn't even noticed on the tiled floor beside him. He pulled out a tablet and pushed a button to turn it on. "We start at the beginning, and I decide where we go from there."

Fan-freaking-tastic. Another round of lies.

She'd already given a false name and a false history. After a year of hiding in a cabin buried in the wilderness of Alaska, not being able to control her fire, she'd come here in a desperate attempt to get help. Horrible idea. It had just landed her with one of the bad guys.

Except her visions told her otherwise. If she went on only what she'd seen in those flashes, Kasia would have trusted Brand without hesitation. The memory of how he felt earlier, arm around her,

solid chest pressed against her back, his hands
on her, touching her without *actually* touching
her, threatened to take away all her logic and
experience, which screamed at her to run fast and
far away from this man.

Which version of Brand was real?

Kasia rolled her shoulders. "Didn't you already
get this info from Dr. Oppenheim?"

He lifted his head, intense gaze back on her,
making her want to shift in the bed. "Are you going
to be difficult?"

Was that…teasing…in those dark gold eyes
of his? Awareness prickled through her until she
slammed on the mental and hormonal brakes.

What the hell was she thinking? Brand was
as perilous as it came in relation to what she was.
She had more important things than inconvenient,
unwanted attraction to deal with right now. She
needed to focus on escaping. "That depends."

Her edginess made her snippier than she meant
to be, and the barely-there twinkle disappeared
behind a scowl. "I'm here to help you."

Kasia scrubbed a hand over her face. "Sorry."
She dropped her hand to her lap. "But what I need
is a doctor to help me figure out how to control my
visions and everything that comes with them. Unless
you have some mysterious magical cure, I don't see
what you can do."

He leaned back, expression showing he was
clearly unimpressed. Immovable. "They can't help
you until they know what you are."

Shoot.

She'd lied about not knowing what she was in

the hopes that the clinic wouldn't need the info. She couldn't very well tell them she was a phoenix when her mother was supposed to have been the last, and most had believed her dead for centuries. Pytheios had seen her that awful night, though, had tried to scoop her up. So at least he knew of her existence.

Was Brand here on Pytheios's behalf?

She needed to get him out of there, and fast. Sticking to her original lies was her best bet. "What questions do you have?" she huffed.

Thankfully, he let her rudeness go and got straight to it. "Your name is Mariska?"

"Umm…yeah."

He glanced up from the tablet. Despite his blanked-out expression, she got the impression he wanted to shake her. "You really want to start out by lying to me?"

She stared back, unspeaking, mind spinning.

"I'm trying to help you," he pointed out again.

She pursed her lips, then sighed. "My name is Kasia."

"Last name?"

"Not important." Not worth the risk of stating it in case he recognized the name and connected it to her royal bloodline.

"How long has this been going on?"

Kasia, already having answered these questions for every healer and doctor this clinic had brought in, rattled off the dates easily enough. "Everything started September eighteenth of last year. At first the fire was small. Just my hand or my fingertips. With those, the visions were quick, a flash. The longer the flames last, the longer the vision."

"And the pain?"

"Similar to the fire—smaller vision means less pain." Like less of her had to clear out of the way. "Though I still lose my sight, like a warning."

He took notes using a stylus to write on his tablet, making no comments. "When did it start getting worse?"

"About six weeks ago. Luckily, I was at a lake, so I was able to control it with the water." Burning down her hideaway in the Alaskan wilderness would've sucked.

"How'd you end up here?"

Kasia had to tread this one carefully. "My mother told me about this place."

He glanced up at that. "How did she know?"

"She was a shifter." Of a sort. Not a total lie.

His eyebrows popped up. "What kind?"

Kasia tipped up her chin. "A bird." Close enough.

Another penetrating stare landed on her. Kasia tried not to fidget, holding his gaze with effort, feeling like a schoolgirl caught telling tales.

"Lying again?" he asked.

Was Brand clairvoyant, or did he already suspect what she was? Phoenixes were exceptionally rare and not the only fire creatures out there. Kasia concentrated on keeping her breathing slow and even, despite the way her heart was jumping around inside her chest like a dang jackrabbit, adrenaline and fear dueling within her.

"My mother's dead."

Gods, it hurt saying that truth out loud. Her mother was dead. She and her sisters scattered to the winds, never to see one another again. Kasia was completely alone in the world, her only goal to remain hidden. That was, if she could get this freaking fire thing under control. Her mother may have tried to train them before they came into their powers, but she'd said nothing about explosive fireballs and the sensations that came along with them. Meanwhile, only a year on her own and she'd already walked right into the hands of the enemy. How had her mother hidden them for over five hundred years?

"I'm sorry," Brand said.

She doubted that.

"Tell me more about the vision you had in the lake. Did you see anything in particular?"

Interesting. He was the first to ask that. Would it hurt to tell him?

Kasia plucked at that drawstring again. "I saw caverns. All gray rock. Eyes reflecting in the dark, in the back of the caves. You were standing next to me, and we were talking to another man."

Brand didn't move, didn't glance up, but still seemed to move closer. "What did he look like?"

"Dark hair. Kind of Mediterranean-looking. Greek, maybe? Blue eyes. Intense... Oh! And a scar running down the left side of his face." She shivered. There'd been a chill in that other man's eyes that struck her to the bone. She got the impression he wasn't someone you wanted as an enemy. "Similar build to yours, maybe a bit shorter and leaner, and he wore a tailored suit." She particularly remembered that, as it had seemed an odd choice of fashion for a cave.

Brand stopped writing, but he still didn't look up. "Got it." He went back to making his notes. "Other family?"

She glanced away, looking anywhere but at his hand. The one without a brand.

Come to think of it, in every vision, and even now, he wore his hair on the longer side. To cover the mark of his family at the nape of his neck? Regardless, the man was a rogue.

Shit. Much worse than she'd thought.

"What?" she asked when she caught his stare.

"Your family?"

"No. Grandparents on both sides died before I was born." Pytheios made sure of that. "My parents were only children as far as I know. Both dead. It's just me left."

She was proud she didn't hesitate over that last statement. She may have screwed herself by landing in this situation, but no way would she ever give up her sisters or put them at risk.

"Okay. That doesn't give me much to go on tracing your family. I'll need any records you can provide. Birth certificates, pictures, official documents."

Kasia winced. "That'll be a bit of a problem."

"Why?"

"Everything was destroyed in a fire when I was five." A lie her mother had told the humans whenever they started requiring that kind of proof—be it for travel, driver's licenses, school records, or whatnot— faking their lives as normal people.

At that Brand put his tablet down to stare at her. "You're telling me you have no information on your background and family history."

"Yes. I'm sure that makes your job harder."

He snorted an unamused laugh. "More like damn

near impossible."

Kasia pretended to be disappointed, drooping back against the bed. Now if she could get him to leave. "Well…thanks for coming anyway, Mr. Astarot."

"Brand. And I'm not leaving. Not yet, at least."

She turned her head to look at him. "But you just said—"

"Your situation makes any normal human means of investigating your background pretty useless. However, I happen to have access to several supernatural methods."

Dammit. "So, there's hope of finding out what I am?" She continued to play out her role of not knowing until she could get the dragon shifter out of here.

He leaned forward, elbows on his knees, and she got the impression he was…amused. "I'm not giving up on you yet."

Why did it feel as though his words carried a double meaning? She attempted a smile that she hoped appeared appropriately grateful, or whatever. "So, I'll hang out here, exploding every so often, until you get back?"

Best news she'd had all day. He'd leave, and she could disappear.

"Nope."

She jerked her gaze to his. "Nope?"

He shook his head. "I'm certain I can contain your fire if or when you…explode…next."

Was that a secret grin? Better not be.

"So…I'm coming with you?" she asked slowly.

He stood, stuffing his tablet into his backpack. "Get some sleep. We'll leave in the morning. Better to travel in the daylight."

Kasia blew out a long, silent breath of relief. Regardless of how short the absence, he'd still leave. She just had to play this out until he did.

Brand stood and slung his backpack over one shoulder. When he made to walk away, she put a hand on his arm, surprised when his muscles bunched under her touch. Even more surprised when her wrung-out body warmed at the contact.

She swallowed. "What time?"

He stared at her hand still gripping his arm. "I'll be back at six a.m."

Had his voice roughened?

He pulled away from her grasp then almost seemed to relax, shoulders dropping a hair. The guy appeared to have a serious issue with touching. He glanced at her hospital gown. "You might want to wear something else."

Never had she been so aware that she was naked beneath the flimsy material. She had to keep herself from glancing down to see if her nipples were visibly beading. "Right."

That wouldn't be his problem, because when he came back tomorrow, she'd be a ghost…long gone and far away from there.

II

As soon as Brand left the room, Kasia counted out the minutes, figuring at least ten would mean he had time to clear out of the facility. Longest damn ten minutes of her life, which was saying a ton, given how old she was in human terms.

Not like waiting and watching as her mother sacrificed herself, those last few moments spent separated by a field of moonlight and fire. Witnessing her mother die while fighting for her children's lives didn't slow down time, it sped it up.

Then came waking up alone in a cabin in the middle of the Alaskan wilderness. Of the four sisters, Kasia needed human contact the most. Waking up alone—Maul, the faithful hellhound her mother sent her to, didn't exactly count as human—day in and day out had been a slow form of torture.

Finally, the minute hand pointed to the three. Kasia hopped out of bed, adrenaline already pumping. With shaking hands, she yanked on the darkest clothing she owned, jeans and a navy tank top, and stuffed her hair into a baseball cap. She needed to blend into the night as much as possible.

Going up on tiptoe, she felt around on the closet shelf where she'd stashed her wallet, which contained a myriad of fake IDs, prepaid credit cards, cash, and other untraceable necessities when trying to stay off a hunter's radar. She also grabbed a wire hanger from inside the closet. She was going to need transportation.

With more haste than care, she stuffed those and extra clothes into her backpack. Then glanced around one last time. Another empty room. Not for the first time she wondered if this transient existence resulted in an empty life. Was she going to be running forever?

A quick check of the hallway showed no one nearby. If she was going to go, now was the time. She wanted as much of a lead as she could get before anyone discovered her absence and raised the alarm.

Kasia closed and locked the door to her room, stepped up to her window, then paused and bit her lip. The doctors and staff had been nice to her here. She couldn't let them think she'd been taken.

After a moment's debate, she gave a low growl of frustration with herself, then hustled to the bedside table where she'd seen a pad of paper and pen in the drawer. She scrawled a note and left it under her pillow. They'd find it when cleaning the room.

Guilt assuaged, Kasia returned to the window and studied the layout. Her room faced the back of the building—a paved lot, industrial trash bins, loading docks, with pools of yellow-tinted glow cast by a series of lights attached to the building roof.

She grimaced at the thirty-foot drop from the third-floor room where she stayed when she wasn't on one of her flaming benders.

"You can do this," she muttered with less conviction than she would've liked. "Thirty feet is cake."

She may have inherited her mother's ability to teleport, but erratic aim and limited distances were the best she could do so far. As in, she'd never made it more than ten feet, and who the hell knew where she'd end up. Frustrating, but she'd get better eventually. She did her best to ignore the mental image of slamming into the ground and snapping her leg bones. She could already hear the crunch.

Kasia gave herself a shake. "Quit stalling, you wimp."

Then she scowled. Talking to herself had become more of a thing in the last year of solitude, a gap filler for her sisters' constant chatter. That time of isolation, especially in the winter when she'd hardly left her cabin, nearly had her doing a "Here's Johnny!" a la *The Shining*. Clearly residual effects lingered.

Focus.

Closing her eyes, Kasia thought about fire, picturing the red and gold flames licking through her. Immediately, a pleasant warmth bloomed inside her belly. At least she could control the fire when it didn't involve her unexpected and uncontrollable visions.

The warmth spread until she could no longer contain it. With a snap of her fingers, Kasia gave the flames a way out, holding her palm face up, almost cradling the dancing light in her hand. Then she pictured herself standing on the pavement outside, below her room. She stared hard, aiming all her concentration at that spot.

"Now," she whispered.

In an instant, a blink of silence, she disappeared from the room and reappeared outside in the back lot.

Too high.

"Shit."

She hung in midair for a millisecond before gravity took hold of her rematerialized form and yanked her down. Flailing, she hit the ground hard and with a sad lack of dexterity. Kasia grunted as her knees buckled, and she tumbled forward on her hands. Her backpack flipped up and smacked her in the back of the head.

"Ow." Thankfully no witnesses were there to laugh at her shame.

Please don't let anything be broken.

No sickening crunch was a good sign. A quick check showed the only battered parts were her knees. Her jeans sported new rips on both sides, and she'd bet money the right one was bleeding if the sharp sting was anything to go by.

"That's going to leave a mark," she half groaned, half grumbled.

But she didn't have time to examine the wound. With a scrambling motion, she shoved back up to her feet, brushed her hands off on her jeans, and teleported as quietly and quickly as she could, in ten-foot hops aiming for the corner of the building where the lights didn't reach. She just hoped she was disappearing fast enough that the cameras she was sure had to be out here didn't catch her.

She cautiously poked her head around the corner, checking for anyone else skulking around random buildings in the dead of night. Sticking to the shadows, she continued to teleport down the ridiculously long side, passing several other buildings as she went, pausing every so often to listen or check an alleyway off to her left.

At the next corner she paused again, before cautiously taking a peek. Parking lot. Good. Bright lights, not so good. Worse, only one car sat there. Some kind of ancient American muscle car men seemed to drool over, but also tended to be obnoxiously loud.

Seriously? No other options? She scanned the area. Not one other vehicle.

Why couldn't she have stumbled across one of those electric things that ran blessedly silent? Didn't fate realize she was trying to escape unnoticed? Still, beggars couldn't be choosers.

The car was parked directly in front of the doors leading into the medical clinic, so Kasia took her time searching for any sign of someone coming out of the building. She couldn't do anything about the cameras except hope she was gone before anyone caught her. As sure as she could be that she'd have enough cover and time, she extracted the wire hanger from her backpack, then hurried through the harsh parking lot lights to her getaway vehicle.

Untwisting the wire hanger, she formed it into a *J* and slipped it between the driver's side window and the rubber seal. It took a few tries, but she managed to jimmy the lock. She slipped inside the car and bent over to reach under the dash.

The good thing about these older cars was how much easier it was to access the lines to hotwire the suckers. After stripping back the coating, she touched the ends together. The engine roared to life, vibrating the car under her ass.

"I still got it, Mom." She sent the words out into the universe, hoping her mother, who'd taught them all these survival skills—skill sets that changed over the centuries from riding horses and scaling walls to hotwiring cars and hacking computers—was somewhere smiling down.

After twisting the ends of the wires together, Kasia popped up in her seat, shoved the car into reverse, and got moving. She didn't relax until she'd made it to the highway and could open up the massive engine.

With a grin, she patted the dashboard. "You may be loud, but at least you're fast."

And in mint condition. Another stab of guilt had to be shoved aside for whomever loved this vehicle. She'd have to find some way to get it back to the clinic. Later. For now, her one goal was putting distance between herself and Brand Astarot.

Despite her apparent success, Kasia kept checking the skies, because that freaking dragon shifter might catch up to her any second. She ignored the dull ache of disappointment that settled in her chest as she lumped him in with all of his kind.

I wanted him to be one of the good guys.

Her visions had never shown her what Brand was. And, okay, so maybe she'd developed a bit of a crush on the nameless guy she saw over and over. Along with a minor obsession with finding out what the rest of the tattoo on his right arm looked like.

More than a crush, she mentally argued with herself. Another new habit from her year of solitude.

After all, his was the face she pictured every time the visions came over her, whether or not he was in the images flashing through her mind. The things she'd pictured him doing to her... Kasia gave a little hiss of frustration and shifted in her seat as her body reacted to her thoughts.

Damn, she was in trouble. Those same visions that made her feel safe around him, protected, were tainted by the fact that dragon's blood ran in his veins. Granted, a dragon king's blood, her father's blood, ran in her own veins, but that didn't make Brand any safer to her. With Pytheios still alive, and most likely the puppet master over the five other dragon kings, just as her mother had feared, she couldn't trust any of those shifters. Even when the Rotting King died, she still might not trust them. No matter what her heart told her.

So she kept going. Hopefully, he wouldn't find out about her vanishing act until she was long gone and in the wind.

Talking to Kasia's doctor had taken longer than Brand would've liked, but getting Dr. Oppenheim to destroy all records relating to a phoenix had been critical. At least she'd agreed in the end. All it took was a painfully large transfer of cash into her account from one of his own. He had plenty to cover it. The solitary mercenary life had padded his pockets over the years. The King of the Blue Clan was his most frequent customer, and for good reason, but he'd still make sure Ladon reimbursed him later as part of his payment for this task.

Brand would rather have threatened the good

doctor until she wet herself and never pulled this fuckery again. She was clearly the person who betrayed Kasia and leaked to all who might be interested that the facility was treating a possible phoenix. The problem with his preferred plan was getting out of here easily. He needed to be able to walk out that door unimpeded, or Kasia would never go with him.

He *needed* her to go with him. Everything he'd done in his life, every single step, every job, every horrible act, had been calculated to move him closer to one goal, and one goal only.

Revenge.

Revenge against Uther, who'd killed Brand's entire family to take the gold throne. The Red King, Pytheios, might control the other five kings, but Uther had done the killing. Revenge also burned inside him for every dragon who'd helped that bastard or who'd looked the other way while it all went down. Helping Ladon take the throne from Thanatos, the previous Blue King, had been a big step in that goal.

Now, giving Kasia to Ladon, the only ruler he trusted, was the key to the next step, the one that would deliver Uther to him, eventually. Brand could do only so much as a rogue. Being exiled made him persona non grata among all dragon shifters. Half the time he was watching his own back. Bringing Ladon a phoenix would be big enough that the Blood King would finally let him become a member of the Blue Clan. With a clan behind him, revenge was that much closer.

So he'd paid the doctor off.

Brand strolled down the long hallway, into the lobby, and out of the medical clinic, intending to grab the duffel bag with his clothes that he had stashed in the trunk of his car earlier. The smug doctor had offered him a room to sleep in so he could stay close to the prize he'd just paid several arms and legs for. But as soon as the doors whooshed open on a cool blast of early autumn air, he stopped dead in his tracks and stared at the empty parking spot where he was damn sure he'd left the Hemi Cuda.

"Where the fuck is my car?"

Cold logic followed hot on the heels of instant anger.

Kasia. Shit.

Her campfire and chocolate scent lingered in the air out here. He'd know that aroma anywhere after being surrounded by it while she went up in flames in his arms. The question was, had someone else come and stolen her out from under his nose? Or had she pulled a runner?

Either way, he had to confirm she was gone before he went off half cocked. With another expletive, he hauled back inside. The polar bear shifter looked up, her raised eyebrows frozen at half mast as she processed his expression, which Brand had no doubt was grim to the point of scary.

"What happened?" she asked.

He appreciated that she skipped straight to the point. "Send someone to check that Kas...um... Mariska is still in her room."

Rather than pick up the phone, she grabbed a walkie-talkie, relaying his instructions to whoever was on the other end. Less than a minute later, his fear was confirmed.

"She's not here," the male voice came back. "Smells like smoke in here."

Damn it. That could mean any number of things. Brand grabbed the walkie-talkie from the bear shifter's grasp. "Do you see any ashes in the room?"

"Who is this?"

Rather than answer himself, Brand held down the button and shoved the device in the bear shifter's face. She didn't even blink. "Just answer him, Jace."

"No ashes," the guy called Jace came back.

"Are all her clothes there?" Brand barked his next question.

"There's a hospital gown on the bed. A few clothes still in the drawers and closet. I'm not sure if anything is missing."

So she'd taken the time to get dressed, but a kidnapper would probably have her do that, which meant he was no closer to knowing for sure what happened.

"Any other scents?" Brand asked.

"Not that aren't normal for this place."

Brand glanced at the receptionist, who understood his silent question. "Jace is a wolf shifter," she said.

Which meant a sense of smell that would catch even subtle scents.

The receptionist snatched the walkie-talkie back. "She came in with a backpack. Do you see it anywhere?"

"Looking." Another minute later. "No backpack."

Brand leaned his weight onto his fisted hands

on the top of the desk and debated his next move. Taking her backpack likely meant she'd run. Since he was the only new variable in her world, that meant she'd run from him.

Why?

Brand racked his brain, going over and over the conversation they'd had when she'd woken up. How she'd acted. Sure as shit, she had no idea of Dr. Oppenheim's duplicity, or she would've been terrified. Had he done or said anything that would've scared her badly enough to leave these people who were supposedly trying to help her? He didn't think so. That had to mean she was running from what he was—a dragon shifter.

Didn't a phoenix seek out dragon shifters?

As creatures who dealt with fire, dragons were uniquely equipped to be a phoenix's mate. As the biggest, baddest shifters on the planet, they were also natural protectors for the delicate creatures. Not that he knew for sure, since no one had seen a phoenix in over five centuries.

Then again, no one seemed entirely sure about what happened to the last phoenix all those years ago. Rumor had it, she'd picked the wrong mate— Zilant Amon, the King of the White Clan, rather than Pytheios—and both Zilant and the phoenix had died during the mating process. Some said she'd killed the White King with her flames and taken her own life out of sorrow.

Didn't matter. He needed to track Kasia down. Double time.

Brand had no doubts Ladon hadn't been the good doctor's only call, and other paranormals would want to claim a phoenix for all sorts of reasons. To try to ally with a dragon king by bringing her to one, or as insurance against dragons. Some might believe the myths that possessing a phoenix would make them invincible or bring them unimaginable fortune. Vampires, in particular, believed that if they ingested a phoenix's blood they'd absorb her powers.

No matter the reason, everything that crawled, slithered, ran, or flew would be after Kasia now.

If that phoenix was the ticket to his revenge, losing her would cost him his head, regardless of his history with the Blue King.

Brand didn't stop to dwell on the underlying dread twisting up his insides that came dangerously close to concern. Concern for *Kasia*? No way. He didn't worry about anyone but himself. He didn't know the phoenix. Didn't plan to.

The question was, could he track her from the sky?

Brand threw his backpack on, then hastily pulled a business card out of his wallet and tossed it at the bear shifter. "Call me if you find her or if she comes back."

"Where are you going?" she called out after him.

"To track her down," he yelled back.

If he could.

The bigger problem would be controlling his dragon once he found her. He didn't think he'd hurt her, but unleashing the feral creature he could turn into was always a risk. Especially when he was already angry. Pissed didn't begin to cover the emotions pumping through him.

Then again, someone getting to her first was a

bigger risk. With no choice left to him, he'd have to try.

"We'll keep searching from here." The polar bear shifter's voice followed him out the door.

Luckily the parking lot was as deserted as it had been when he'd arrived earlier in the day. The space was also large enough, though he might knock out a few power lines in the process. The wide-open field across the way was better, but he didn't have time to run out there.

He closed his eyes, took a deep breath, and called forth the dragon from within. In a silent rush, his body changed. His soul stayed in place as his physical form shifted around his essence — everything human about him, including his clothes and backpack, absorbed into his new shape as he grew to massive proportions. He hunched forward as legs and arms adjusted and aligned to stand on all fours. Eyes open now, his perspective changed, allowing him to see over the tops of the buildings.

His sight sharpened, and he could make out details on the cars on the highway miles away. He unfurled the wings tucked against his back, and before the full transformation had completed, Brand launched himself into the air, his claws gouging long marks in the pavement with the force of his leap.

He finished the details of his shift as he flew — golden scales both malleable and hard as diamonds, long tail trailing behind him like a rudder, razor-sharp teeth, spiked ridges along his back.

In this form, his sense of smell honed to a greater degree, and that chocolaty campfire scent of Kasia's, blending with the unique combination of leather, metal, and gas from his car, provided a trail that was practically a blinking neon sign.

The creature half of him, the half currently in charge, relished her aroma. A concerning wave of possessiveness coursed through Brand, something he couldn't control. Something that came from pure instinct.

Thoughts like those weren't useful. He needed to focus. A deep breath revealed no other scents mingled with those of the woman and the vehicle, which added to his reasoning that this wasn't a kidnapping.

I can't believe she snuck out under my nose and fucking stole my car.

No way would he admit that under the teeth-grinding frustration, a small spark of respect for her ingenuity lit inside him. The woman was no easy mark, and he'd been an arrogant son of a bitch to have assumed she would be.

She'd seemed so helpless and naive, lying in that hospital bed pretending to have no clue about who and what she was. Had that grateful, batting lashes gaze all been an act to stroke his ego merely to get him out her door? Had he been a fool to admit his species to her? Not to mention what it meant for his reputation as a skilled mercenary if this ever got out.

He'd find out when he caught up to her.

If he caught her before someone or something else did. How the hell had she lasted this long without protection?

Gaining altitude quickly, Brand made sure he went only as high as the scent trail would allow. Not as high as he preferred, unfortunately. He pushed himself as fast and as hard as he could without losing it, and hopefully without being seen by humans, or worse, anything else hunting his quarry.

Thank the fates for a moonless night.

Kasia hummed along to another country song—the only station she could get out here in the middle of nowhere, though it didn't come in quite right, going fuzzy on her every now and then, but she needed the noise to help her stay awake. The Montana border was still hours away, but she was making decent time despite doubling back a few times and changing directions.

The headlights lit up the patch of road in front of her, the highway only a two-lane road this far away from larger cities. At this early hour, long before dawn broke, she'd passed hardly a soul. If she could make it to Bozeman, she'd drop this car and borrow another, but that was hours of driving ahead of her.

The only warning she got that she was being followed was the flick of a shadow in the headlights. Before she could react, a massive golden dragon slammed down on the road in front of her about half a mile out. She almost expected the ground to shake with the force, but the act was near silent.

Dammit.

She gritted her teeth and tightened her hands on the wheel. Rather than stop, Kasia hit the gas, pushing the car to go faster. He wasn't taking her without a fight, that was for damn sure.

The dragon's deep golden scales glittered in the oncoming headlights. He didn't budge. But he did growl, his tail slashing back and forth.

"Move, you scaly bastard," she muttered.

But she didn't let up on the pedal.

He lowered his head and let loose a growl of warning, which she responded to by stomping harder on the gas.

"Get out of the way!"

She had no intention of playing chicken. If he didn't, she'd ram this car down his fire-breathing throat. The hell with it. She didn't want to go back to that cabin in Alaska anyway. Maul would miss her, but he'd be the only one.

Only the dragon didn't move. *Okay, then.* Kasia braced for impact.

At the moment she should've slammed into him, the beast heaved himself into the air, and she zoomed past, fishtailing underneath him from the force of the wind his wings caused.

He must've backed up, because he landed on the road in front of her again.

"You want another go, you oversized flying iguana?" she shouted, and bore down on him.

And again, he hopped out of her way only to land in her path.

Damn. Kasia held in a scream of fear-tinged frustration. They could keep this up all night, getting them nowhere fast. He wasn't going to let her go.

With a growl of aggravation, though not defeat, Kasia stomped on the brakes. The tires squealed in protest, and the unpleasant odor of burning rubber followed her as she skidded the car to a stop broadside of the dragon, only a few feet away. If she rolled down her window, she could reach out and touch him.

The terrifying creature moved around the car, his movements more of a glide, like golden water flowing around her. He lowered his head to gaze in at her with an eye the size of her entire thigh. He snorted, and smoke trailed from his nostrils as he glared at her.

Please let this be Brand, and not some other phoenix-stealing dragon shifter.

Kasia glared back but raised her hands off the steering wheel in a gesture of surrender. He backed up, and she slowly exited the car, grimacing a bit as she straightened her knees, the scrapes from her landing earlier having stiffened up.

Once outside, she raised her gaze up, way up, as the dragon lifted his head. Was she completely nuts to think he was glorious? Impressively large— at least forty feet high—the sheen of his scales gave him a metallic appearance, as though hewn from spun gold. Even so, she could make out the definition of his muscles underneath. Hell, even his muscles had muscles. Deadly-looking spikes rose from his head, like a crest, meeting at the back of his neck. They stood out down the length of his spine to the tip of his tail, which sported larger spikes, like a mace.

Her mother had told them all sorts of facts and stories about dragon shifters. She'd conveniently left out how sexy and powerful they could be in this form.

As that thought registered, Kasia gave herself a mental slap. What was she doing drooling over this asshole who'd hunted her down?

It's official. I've lost my mind.

"Brand?" she asked, needing to know.

He didn't move or make a sound, staring at her long and hard, muscles trembling as if he was not quite in control himself…or holding himself back.

Kasia raised her eyebrows, then opened her mouth to ask again, only a subtle change in his form caught her attention. It took another few moments of staring before she realized he was shifting.

No bones crunching or grunting. No sound whatsoever. No naked skin, either, as he slowly reformed into a fully clothed man, though she had no idea where the garments came from. They appeared to flow out of him, along with a backpack, as he shrank to his human size in a silent rush. Limbs shifted positions and proportion, spine straightened to stand on two legs rather than four, scales disappeared, and wings tucked into his back, almost like they were absorbed into him.

She let out a puff of relief. Definitely Brand.

Then she caught the hard glint in his eyes and revised that thought. Maybe relief was the wrong sentiment; perhaps dread would've been a better choice. Kasia lifted her chin, matching him glare for glare as he stalked toward her, only to give in at the last moment, taking a small step back, brought up short by the car behind her.

Brand didn't stop when he got to her, instead invading her space. He leaned one hand against the car and stared down at her. Kasia held her breath and tried not to register the heat of his body close to hers or the amber and obsidian flecks that graced the depths of those tawny eyes. Eyes narrowed at her in smoldering anger. If she hadn't seen him in her visions, she would've been nervous that he'd shake her or something, his gaze had gone so savage.

Kasia waited, unblinking, for his next move.

"Get in," he growled. His voice was lower, smokier. Was that from his shift? And why was she noticing that inconsequential detail right now?

Frustration—with herself for her reactions as well as getting caught—surged back to the fore, joining the dread that refused to dissipate. She had no choice but to follow his instructions. It's not like she could outrun him. She'd just have to outthink him and escape. Again. Only better.

Followed by his unfaltering stare, Kasia scooted along the car, away from his body, then moved around to the passenger side and got in.

Brand took the driver's seat in total silence. After a year of it, Kasia wasn't a fan of silence, but she didn't break it. He sat there for a long moment, running his hands over the steering wheel, almost in a caress.

Realization struck. No way. She couldn't have. "I took *your* car?"

His jaw hardened. "You did."

Kasia grimaced. Of course she did. Because apparently the fates had it in for her. "At least I don't have to worry about returning it now," she quipped, though he didn't strike her as the type to appreciate her "look on the bright side" comment.

He wasn't. "I suggest you don't talk to me for a while."

He didn't even glance her way. Instead he put the

car in drive, turned it to head in the direction she'd just come from, and started them back on the road.

She ignored the no talking edict. Too much needed to be said. "Where are you taking me?"

"Away from here. Airport."

Airport? Hell no. "You know what I am?"

He flicked her a brief, unreadable glance. "Do you?"

Right. All those lies at the clinic. "Yes."

His hands gripped the steering wheel tighter, knuckles showing white, even in the dim interior lights of the dash. "I do, too."

So much for her cover story. Back to that airport issue. "Are you going to try to mate me?"

Would he be that stupid? Or did he assume mating a phoenix worked the same as mating a human? Mating a human had its own level of danger, resulting in the woman's highly gruesome death if she wasn't destined to be the dragon's mate, not to mention the dragon losing part of himself as punishment. Mating a phoenix, however, added a whole extra layer of complication. If she didn't choose him, the dragon was the one consumed by the flames, not the phoenix.

Did Brand know that?

"No. I'm not going to mate you."

So not that stupid. "Then why the airport?"

"Because dangerous things walk the earth. Things that would love to capture a phoenix. The sooner I get you to a clan, the better."

That word—what she was—hung in the air between them. Like a gauntlet thrown down. Like a challenge. Like an unbreachable wall.

Kasia frowned as she processed his statement but also the subtle shift in his tone. Was he…*worried* about her? "Where are you taking me?"

"Scotland. To a man named Ladon Ormarr."

Ormarr. That wasn't one of the names her mother had listed as a line of kings, was it? Kasia tried to pull the memory from her mind but couldn't quite reach it. "Which clan does he rule?"

Another flick of a glance. "Blue."

Kasia slumped down in her seat. So Brand *was* taking her to a dragon king. "Is he mated?"

"Not yet." Now his tone carried an edge of darkness.

"I see," she replied quietly.

Less than a year on her own, and already she was to be slaved out to the first dragon king to find her. At least Brand wasn't taking her to Pytheios. She could be grateful for that small mercy. But who was to say that this Ladon guy was any better?

Can't be worse.

She hoped.

Wait. She bit her lip. "What if I have a vision on our way there? They're coming on faster lately. I might crash the plane."

He gave an unconcerned shrug. "I can control the fire if one comes on. Just give me warning so I can get you somewhere out of sight."

On an airplane? Sure. Easy. And what about the pain? The passengers would hear her screams, no matter how hard she tried to keep them in.

Not that she wasn't going to try to get out of this *before* they were airborne.

Kasia turned her head toward her window, staring out into the inky darkness, but not seeing. A strange disenchantment threaded its way through the alarm and anxiety sitting in her stomach like giant boulders. Silence, her old enemy, settled between them, heavy and still.

After a while, she closed her eyes and pretended to sleep, but used the time afforded her to tick over different plans to escape. First, she needed to figure out how he'd tracked her down so fast, so she'd know how to fool him next time. She'd wait and observe.

For now.

III

After hours in the car, they'd bypassed Cheyenne and driven to Denver, leaving Brand's car in the airport parking lot. Maybe he'd get it later? They'd arrived in time to hop a plane to Barcelona, stopping through Toronto on the way.

Dragons couldn't fly across oceans. Her mother had always appreciated that fact. Apparently the farthest they could fly before they needed to land, rest, and feed was about two hundred miles, which didn't quite allow them to island-hop the Atlantic.

Kasia suspected there was no way he would've risked taking her across Alaska to Russia where, last she heard, Volos was King of the White Dragon Clan. According to her mother, Pytheios controlled Volos. If Brand was trying to get her to Ladon, he couldn't risk another king snatching her away.

The only good news so far was that she hadn't had a vision. They'd left at seven in the morning and had arrived, vision- and plane crash-free, at nine in the morning local time, and despite his assurances that he could control her fire if one *had* come on, she'd been a bundle of nerves the entire flight, leaving her exhausted.

But did they stop then? Nope. When he couldn't get a flight to London that day, Brand had hustled her to the airport parking lot. She stopped dead as he approached a familiar vehicle.

"Is that…?"

The Hemi Cuda sat shining in the sun.

His lips tipped up in a grin. "A demon owed me a favor. It's enchanted to show up wherever I need it."

She had to close her mouth, which hung open. "Handy trick. Why didn't you just summon it, or whatever you do, when I stole it?"

He dumped his duffel and her backpack in the trunk. "It doesn't work like that. I can summon it only when it's parked, turned off, and doesn't have anyone inside it." Another rare grin had her tummy fluttering in response. "I didn't want the demon able to hijack me along with the car."

Because you had to watch out for those sneaky demons. Hysteria wanted to bubble out of her in a laugh, but she held it back. "Good thinking."

She shut up after that.

When they drove over the Pyrenees, she hadn't missed how tense Brand had gotten in the mountains, but he didn't say a word.

He'd relaxed more once they left those peaks behind, making their way across France, heading for the Chunnel. The man was a machine.

Kasia stared outside her car window and tried not to let the combination of weariness and nerves make her sound whiny. "How much longer?"

He didn't even spare her a glance. "Not long. I don't want to be on the road in the dark if we can avoid it."

"Plus, sleep and food are always good ideas," she muttered.

Evil things came out to eat you at night. Even her mother had taught them that. Kasia had ignored that edict in order to escape from Brand, which turned out to be an exercise in futility. She knew they were damn lucky to make it this far. That didn't make her any less grumpy.

After several turns, taking them west of Paris, and another hour of driving, the lights of a small town glowed white on the horizon. The creak of the leather on the steering wheel brought her gaze to Brand's hands. He was white-knuckling that wheel again, or at least his version of it.

"Something got you worried?" she asked.

His chest rose and fell on a breath, but he said nothing.

"Because you're holding that wheel like you want to strangle it. What'd it ever do to you, anyway?"

Immediately, his hands loosened up. "I don't like this."

"What? Slaving me out to your king?" she asked. "Me neither. Let's part ways now."

Brand ignored her, staying eerily silent the rest of the way to the small town, eyes darting from side to side. He didn't speak even when a questionable-looking motel came into view—run-down, trashed out, neon sign not even attempting to blink, and mostly uninhabited based on the lack of cars gracing the small lot.

Nor did he speak as they parked, grabbed their bags, and checked in. Kasia didn't bother to protest the single room he procured. No point in beating her head against an immovable object. She'd only give herself a headache. After moving the car to outside their door, they finally settled in.

Kind of.

Kasia plopped down on the foot of one of the double beds with threadbare covers and watched as

Brand prowled the room, checking every nook and cranny. Not that there was much to scope out. She didn't say anything, though, because she'd be doing those checks herself were he not here.

His presence filled the room, crowding her, putting her on edge. She hadn't been able to escape him for going on thirty-plus hours.

"Is there a specific something you're concerned about finding us?" she prodded when he went to the window and cracked the curtain to stare out into the night for the sixth time.

He kept his focus outward. "Not specific, no."

"Just any garden-variety monster?"

That caught his attention, and he glanced at where she sat. "We're not monsters, Kasia."

She snorted inelegantly. "Wrong. I grew up on terrifying stories of what hunted me."

Brand let the curtain slide back in place and gave her a hard stare. "You don't look terrified."

She raised a single eyebrow. "I'm not exactly a damsel who faints at the first hint of danger."

"Good to know."

Was that a quirk of a smile lifting one side of his mouth? No, she had to be wrong.

He crossed to stand in front of her and leaned a hip against the dresser, on top of which sat the silent, boxy TV from the 1990s. He considered her for several long, uncomfortable moments, during which she did her best to stare steadily back without blinking or dropping her gaze. Hard to do when that look, even when impersonal, heated up parts of her that made her want to squirm.

Allowing herself those fantasies before she met

him was messing with her mind way too much. No more of that in the future.

"What kinds of monsters?" he asked.

It took her a second to figure out what he was asking. She shrugged. "All kinds. But dragons are the worst."

"Who says?"

"My mother." She glanced down at her feet. "Your kind killed her and her mother."

"A dragon killed two phoenixes?"

If she didn't know better, she'd say he was pissed.

She hitched a shoulder. "Red dragon. Big guy. Named Pytheios, I believe. Ring a bell?"

"You're saying the High King killed a phoenix." Skepticism laced his voice.

Kasia snorted her derision. "As I understand it, he's not truly the High King without a phoenix for a mate."

"Apparently with no phoenixes around, he was the only option." Brand didn't blink or move, but his eyes went from molten gold to flat tawny yellow. She had been right. He was pissed. "Rumor had it that the last phoenix mated the wrong man and they both died during the process," he said.

A sharp ache took up residence in her heart. Heavens, dragons had gotten that so wrong. "No," she insisted. "My parents mated, though the bond hadn't solidified."

The brand hadn't shown up on the back of her mother's neck, the final step in the process, and something that could take minutes or even months to happen. No one knew what triggered that brand or why the timing mattered.

"And Pytheios killed your father?"

She sat up straighter. "Yes." Though her mother had refused to tell them exactly how, claiming talking about it to be too painful.

His gaze turned speculative. "And because the bond wasn't in place, she didn't die."

"Yes." Once mates were branded, if one died, they both died.

Another heavy silence settled between them. "Is that why you ran from me?" His words came out almost…kind.

Kasia lifted her gaze to find him regarding her more curiously than kindly. Maybe she'd imagined the kindness. "One of the reasons, yes."

He crossed his arms. "Are you going to run again?"

No. The thought punched through her. Kasia paused, trying to figure out why her gut reaction would be adamantly against leaving this man when logic told her she should run at the first opportunity. Not that she'd tell him that.

"I haven't decided," she murmured instead.

If he could find her, so could others. Possibly others who'd be worse.

"Why's that?" he asked.

She gave him a direct look. "I'd rather the devil I know than the devil I don't." Did he flinch? Before he could comment, Kasia kept going. "I have mixed feelings about it. Some tell me to trust you, and some tell me not to."

"Trust me?"

She almost laughed at the deep doubt in those two words, not that she blamed him. "Yes."

"Word to the wise…"

She felt that gaze again, almost like a caress, and her skin prickled. What was wrong with her?

"Don't give your trust too easily in this world. More often than not, people like me are out to harm you or use you."

"Aren't you trying to stop me from running away?" she pointed out. "You might want to work on your sales pitch."

Brand frowned, and she got the distinct impression he'd surprised himself with his honesty, and not in a good way. Interesting.

"Besides," she continued. "Dr. Oppenheim wasn't out to harm me or use me, and I don't think you are, either. Your king, maybe, but not you."

"Dr. Oppenheim called my people with info on you. That's how I found you." Brand flattened his lips, clamping them over what she suspected would be tougher words. "I'm sure we're not the only people she called."

Despite the small flare of disappointment about the doctor, Kasia leaned back on her hands and swung her feet, even while she watched him closely. "I do know *some* things about you." She stood, intending to make her point, though now she was uncomfortably aware of how close that move brought her to him in the tiny space. Why'd they make this room so small? "You want to know what you were doing in every vision I've had of you?"

His shoulders stiffened, his biceps stretching out his T-shirt a little more. "What?"

"Protecting. Sometimes me, sometimes others. Big ways. Small ways. But always protecting."

Brand jerked, though his expression didn't change one iota.

Kasia kept pushing. "Look at how you handled our first meeting. Your instinct was to help me."

Now he scowled. "My first instinct was to fuck you. Long and hard."

They both froze, gazes locked, as his harsh words lingered in the air between them. If he'd meant to shock her, prove her wrong, all he'd managed to do was give her ideas. Ones that aligned way too closely with those fantasies she'd indulged in about him all year long.

Wrong, wrong, wrong ideas, but her body tingled in all the right places. However, he'd also hit on the fact that confused her the most. He was a dragon shifter, a creature she had to avoid, someone she *shouldn't* put her trust in regardless of the visions.

After a long, uncomfortable stretch of silence, she realized how carefully he was holding himself. From touching her? She cleared her throat.

"You won't hurt me," she insisted.

"You're right. I'm going to take you to Ladon, then you're no longer my problem."

Kasia managed to contain her flinch as his words struck closer to her heart than she expected, the ache sharper than it should be given their short acquaintance and the roles each had to play.

The man must have no heart to so easily sell her off to the highest bidder. Had every single vision she'd had about him been wrong? Because he obviously didn't give two shits about her. Even if she decided to give this Ladon guy a chance, Brand's callousness about using her for his own ends, whatever those were, formed a pit in her stomach that wouldn't go away.

With no warning, the room disappeared, leaving Kasia in a void of darkness, and a backlash of pain jolted her body, like electricity passing through her nerves—heat, then sting. A sensation she'd become all too familiar with this year.

Not now. Please not now.

Another zap raised the fine hairs on her arms. *Aw, hell.*

She held still, staring into the nothing. "Um, Brand...?"

"Yeah?"

She scrunched up her face. "We have a problem."

A beat of silence greeted her statement. "Don't tell me you want to take me up on that fucking long and hard offer, sweetheart. Because I don't think—"

"No," she cut him off. "A different problem."

A rustle reached her ears as he moved her way, his silence suddenly feeling serious. "What problem?"

Kasia held up her hand, warmth already telling her a flame danced from each of her five fingertips.

"What? *Now?*" Brand demanded.

The apprehension in his voice might've been funny if it hadn't reflected her own. It seemed even big, tough, tattooed dragon shifters got nervous when a woman was about to leap into the freefall of a full-body migraine, only to explode into flames and see visions.

Another wave of torture shuddered through her. "Mmm hmm," she managed around a whimper. "And fast."

A low grunt reached her ears. "I feel it," he said.

Brand could feel her pain? That made no sense.

"How fast?" he asked, before she could question him.

Another stab, and she wrapped her arms around her middle, rocking through the sensations throbbing through her body. Soon everything would hurt—her skin, her brain, her teeth, her insides. Every noise, even a puff of wind, only adding to the agony. "I hope you're right about being able to control the fire," she choked out.

Kasia wasn't even positive she managed to get all those words out intelligibly, because her body took over, sending her into that hazy space between pain and panic.

Vaguely she heard Brand swear a cocktail of curses that would have made her laugh had another wave not hijacked her system. He certainly got creative with the F word.

Without her being aware of his movement, he pulled her down to sit beside him on the edge of the bed. Gently, he turned her toward him and took her face between his hands.

The storm of sensation swirling inside her calmed, just a bit.

How did he do that?

"That's it," he murmured. "Just breathe."

She tried to do as he said. Her world narrowed to a pair of work-roughened hands against her cheeks, steady and comforting.

Then another wave washed over her, and she lost the moment, closing her eyes as she struggled for control. Vaguely, Brand's groan reached her. She tried to hold her own cry in, but it slipped out from between her lips just the same.

"I've got you," he said between what sounded like gritted teeth.

His hands smoothed down her neck to her shoulders, and just like at the clinic, his touch reached inside her and soothed part of the sensations overtaking her body, dulling them. As the wave crested and fell, she desperately locked onto his presence again, taking strength from whatever it was about him that gave her relief.

"More," she managed to squeeze out between panting breaths, wrapping her hands around his wrists, not to pull him away, but to hold his touch to her.

I'm so fucked, she thought she heard him mutter. "Don't kill me for this."

What?

He pressed his lips to hers, soft at first, then harder. Kasia gasped as relief swirled through her body along with a sudden blazing need. She opened herself up to him in an instant, and Brand slipped his tongue inside her mouth, tangling with hers in the most delicious way.

At the same time, a pulling sensation captured her attention.

Wait. Was Brand drawing her fire into himself?

But she didn't have time to process the implications, because he deepened the kiss, obliterating her agony. Whimpering, Kasia threw herself into a sensation unlike any she'd ever experienced. Maybe the pain had addled her perception, but something about Brand's kisses, being in his arms, felt...right.

Or maybe that was all her X-rated fantasies about the man in her visions kicking in.

Pleasure washed over her, each upsurge growing in intensity. Her body in charge, she hooked an arm around his neck and swung a leg over his lap, straddling him. He grasped her by the hips, helping her rub against the hard rod of his cock. A secret corner of her mind delighted to find him equally into this, into *her*, in a way that pushed all the right buttons. Though, maybe not in the way she wanted, the way she'd pictured all those times. What she wanted was nothing between them.

No clothes. No questions. No secrets.

She didn't have time to explore that bit of idiocy, though. With a low groan that sounded more like a growl, Brand backed off, slowing her down, and she opened her mouth to protest, only to gasp as a lance of pain returned.

"I don't want you to regret going too far when you're like this," he said.

She shuddered with her need to run from the pain and return to the pleasure, rubbing against him again, her hardened nipples brushing against his chest through their clothing. "It hurts if you don't."

"I know. Me, too."

Him, too? A dull throb returned, and she let that question go. Instead she took over, kissing him, licking at his lips, toying with his tongue.

Again, the ache receded as wonderful desire eased through her blood.

He lifted the hair off the back of her neck, where a mating brand would show if she mated a dragon, and pressed a kiss just to the side of that spot. That touch sent a sweet warmth rolling through her.

A tingling kicked off at the base of her spine, building and spreading. Usually her vision came on with the worst of the pain, but this was different, better.

She threw her head back and let out a long, keening moan as everything inside her opened up, clearing the way for the images that would come next. Flames erupted from her body in what should have been a conflagration of spectacular proportions, but Brand contained her, his mouth on hers and something both soft and rough wrapping around her like a cocoon, holding the fire inside.

At the same time, images flashed through her mind, like flipping quickly through a picture book, or akin to an old-timey movie, all herky-jerky and hard to decipher. Except this time, instead of pure anguish and terror that usually came with the overwhelming rush, Brand's touch morphed the pain into a sensation more akin to being buffeted by roaring waves on the ocean, at the mercy of a crushing force greater than herself.

Finally, the vision ebbed as she came up from under the pressure. She blinked as her sight returned, and any remaining flickers receded back into her body. Succumbing to the aftermath, Kasia's muscles went limp. Exhaustion filled every limb.

She recognized something had her cradled. Forcing her heavy eyelids open, she gasped, arrested first by the golden flames reflected in Brand's eyes, and then by the massive golden wings folded around both of them.

She should be terrified out of her mind—she lay

in the grasp of a dragon. But strangely, terror wasn't part of her current state of emotional being. Instead, she wrapped her arms around Brand's neck and laid her forehead against his shoulder, though he tensed underneath her touch. She ignored him as she slowly caught her breath.

A glance down revealed she was still dressed. Relief punched from her lungs in a sharp breath. Somehow, he'd kept the fire from disintegrating her clothes. At least she didn't have to worry about ending up naked anymore. Thank goodness.

The soft rustle of sound, like the creak of a well-loved leather jacket, and subtle shifting of his body had her directing her gaze upward. He unwrapped his wings from around them, and she tipped her head back to watch in fascination as they seemed to fold back into his body.

"How'd you do that?" she asked, her voice rough and scratchy yet again. Those damned out-of-control flames.

"Do what?" Though his arms still encircled her, he held her more loosely, as though trying to put distance between them that wasn't there.

"Only have wings."

He tipped up one shoulder, shifting her grasp so she dropped one hand. More space between them. "Some dragons can control their shift—both what shifts and the size of it. My wings helped contain the explosion."

Why did she get the impression that detail about shifting only a portion of himself was important, like a rare ability or something? Had Mother ever mentioned it?

He held up a hand, and his fingernails transformed before her eyes, becoming golden claws before he fisted his hands and turned them back into nails. "In my full form, I'd be much larger than this room, so I had to limit my shift."

"Very cool."

He choked out a surprised laugh. "Of course you'd think that's cool."

"Who wouldn't?" Granted, she should be totally wigged out about now—sitting in a dragon's lap casually discussing his shifting abilities after having just shared an intimate, surreal moment. Not to mention the sexual fulfillment bit. Embarrassment, at the very least, should be involved in her current state of mind. However, about six months ago Kasia had given up trying to act like she thought she should.

Brand shook his head, sobering. "What did you see?"

Kasia forced her mind to the flashes she'd witnessed. After the fact, she always had to replay her visions in her mind, drag them from a memory both hazy and patchy, the agonizing sensations in her body during the initial visions doing a bang-up job of keeping the majority of her attention. Her version of a VCR tape in rewind was always hit-and-miss.

This incident had been fast and brief, the images equally brief.

She latched on to a flash of the motel in which they were staying, seen from outside and across the street, she'd guess. Followed by another picture of at least five men bursting into their room. Brand fighting. Her screaming as they dragged her away—so eerie to watch without the sound. And fire. Lots of fire.

She tightened her grip on him, more reflex than conscious thought. "We have to leave. Now."

She made her sluggish muscles obey and shimmied off his lap. Though landing in a heap at his feet had been a close call, requiring him to scoop her up and deposit her on her less-than-steady feet. Thankfully, they hadn't unpacked, and she snapped up her backpack, which lay on the ground, teetering with the move.

Her urgency must've carried through to her voice and actions. She expected more argument or questions before he acted, but immediately Brand followed suit, grabbing his own backpack, as well as his duffel bag and car keys.

"Wait." He stopped her as she reached for the door handle.

He moved her to the side and cracked the door. He checked the parking lot beyond, sniffed the air. Now she saw why he had picked a place with the room door facing outside and on the first floor, rather than an interior hallway or on a different floor. Easier getaway.

As they neared the car, a low growl sounded from the darkened parking lot across the road.

She met Brand's gaze across the top of the car.

"Move," he said.

But before she could reach for the handle, Brand spun away, facing two men who'd come up behind him. At the same time, an arm wrapped around her waist. Kasia thrashed as she was lifted off her feet.

Whoever had her managed to tuck her under one arm like a football and run.

"Brand!" she yelled.

She tried to curl around the arm holding her to see if Brand had followed, but he was busy dealing with the two men.

One thought entered her mind. She couldn't let this guy get her into a car. Her mother had always told them that. *Death is better than letting them take you.*

All that physical training her mother had insisted on kicked in, instinct taking over.

Rather than try to grapple with the man's iron grip or reach the ground with her feet, Kasia twisted then pushed her feet off his ass, which threw off his balance. Her would-be kidnapper tripped over her limbs, and they both tumbled to the ground.

Gravel tore up the exposed skin of her shoulder as she came down hard.

Ouch. That was going to leave a couple of marks. No time to worry over that, though. Not while the brute was pinning her down with his bulk.

Kasia kicked out, and he gave an *oomph* as she connected with his sternum. He moved just enough for her to roll out from under him. She hopped to her feet, but so did he. They faced each other.

"Don't make me do this the hard way," he warned.

She took in his appearance—hard face, all angles, dark hair cut military style, and big. Really big. "Does that line work with all the girls?" she asked.

Slowly, she started moving away. If she could keep him distracted, she could get some distance. Maybe enough to light a fire and teleport her ass out of here.

She took another step.

He shook his head slowly. "I can't let you do that."

"I won't go with you. So one of us is fucked here." Another slow step back.

He lunged at her...

...just as the Hemi Cuda skidded to a halt between them, Brand at the wheel.

How'd he get away from the other two?

"Get in!"

She reached for the handle, and again missed as the car suddenly jumped forward. Military dude on the other side ran at her, and Brand hit the gas, opening his door to hit the guy and tossing him a good twenty feet away with the force of impact.

"Kasia!" he yelled as he slammed his door shut.

She ran for the car, and this time she managed to get in. The second her butt hit the seat, he gunned it.

"Fucktastic," he muttered as he glanced in the rearview mirror.

She whipped around and gasped at the sight that greeted her. Three wolves sprinted after them at full speed. And, unless she was seeing things, the gleam of several other pairs of eyes reflected in the darkness behind them. Brand hit the gas, opening up the engine, and they flew down the narrow country roads at speeds she didn't want to contemplate.

A few minutes later the wolves gave up the chase. Damn, they were fast. Kasia lapsed into silence, too tired to talk anyway, letting him focus, letting him do his thing, as they blasted down the deserted back roads of the French countryside. She didn't miss the fact that he constantly scanned the area around them or checked the mirror to see if they were being followed using eyesight a hundred times more powerful than most other earthly creatures. A handy ability she had to admit to envying.

"Is that what you saw before they attacked?" he asked again, finally. "Wolf shifters?"

"Yes and no." Kasia told him of the images, of the men crashing into their room, dragging her away as he tried to fight them off.

"Men, not wolves?" he asked. "Or dragons?"

"I didn't see any dragons, but everything was from inside the room. I'm guessing most dragons can't control the shift like you can?"

He tossed her an inscrutable look. "Anything else?"

Kasia closed her eyes, trying to force the memories to be clearer, to move slower through them so she could take in the details. "Yes."

"What?"

"I did see one wolf. Dark gray, I think, though it was hard to tell because he was in shadow. He didn't join the fight, just watched from the other side of the road."

Brand's shoulders stiffened a hair. "But no dragons?" he asked again.

"No. No dragons."

He let out a low breath. "I thought I scented wolves when we crossed the Pyrenees." He shook his head, talking more to himself now. "Fucking wolf shifters. They won't be able to keep up with me if I take to the air. That's something at least."

"But if they get to you as a pack, they could overpower you, kill you even." She couldn't keep the worry from her voice.

He cast her one of those sideways glances that took in way too much. "Is that what you saw?"

"You fought hard…"

When she didn't go on, his glance turned annoyed, eyes narrowed. "Don't treat me like I'm glass, princess. I'm far from it."

"I'm not a princess." The protest popped out automatically. Kasia had been born and raised poor, among common hardworking people. She'd be damned if she ever claimed royalty on purpose, no matter her bloodline or future prospects.

"Might as well be," he taunted.

Little did he know… Kasia faced forward. "I'm not the princess type."

"Better get used to it, because a phoenix will always become a queen."

Kasia slid him a sideways glance, as the tone more than the words struck her as off. Why did he sound bitter about that?

Time for a shift in subject, because she suspected neither of them would agree about what her future held. "So we're going to fly?"

"No."

"No?" She tried to keep the relief from her voice. Flying wasn't her thing, and crossing the Atlantic in an airplane had been more than enough.

"Dragon shifters from other clans would be worse than wolves if they found us. I can fight off wolves—even a pack. At least one that small."

She ignored his subtle jab about the pack. Harder to ignore how his mouth kicked up at the corner in a barely-there smile. Did he think he'd just won a point?

Silly dragon.

"Well...if they do catch up to us, take out the red one first," she advised. "At least, that's what I'd recommend from what I saw in the vision."

That arrogant smile disappeared. Ha! Score one for the princess.

Brand continued as though she hadn't spoken. "We need to stay off the grid, and that means out of the sky as much as possible, despite the wolves."

Good. Avoiding flying via dragon shifter was high on her priority list. "What do we do, then? I assume you have a plan?"

Brand kept his gaze forward, his expression unreadable. "You're not running anymore?"

She shook her head. "Not from you, at least." If he could track her, and wolf shifters could track her, then her existence was more widely known than what she could handle on her own. Apparently, thanks to the doctor, her cover was completely blown. She doubted she'd ever be safe on her own again.

Her words came back to haunt her. Better the devil she knew than the one she didn't. There was a reason previous phoenixes had mated dragons.

Protection.

After all, her grandmother had mated one. So had her mother, once. Not that she'd talked much about their father. She'd claimed to love him so much that she couldn't talk about him without it hurting.

Kasia had always tried to balance the lifelong, soul-deep love that her mother held on to even centuries after losing her mate with her mother's equally dogged hatred of the shifters who destroyed him. She'd built dragons up as terrible beasts out to use them, fuck them, and control them.

But now Kasia's choices had narrowed.

"I guess you'd better get me to your king," she said to Brand.

"Right." Brand grunted the word, but she didn't have time to analyze whatever emotion laced that one syllable.

She had her own concerns to worry over, because she'd just changed the entire course of her future with one impossible choice.

Could she trust Ladon, the dragon Brand was so loyal to that he'd risk his life to get her there? She'd just have to pray to every god, fate, and being she'd ever heard of that Ladon Ormarr proved to be a better man than she feared, better than Pytheios at least, and ignore the queasy pit in her stomach that told her mating the King of the Blue Clan wasn't a path she should follow.

No other paths appeared to her now.

With a deep sigh, Kasia dropped her head back against the seat. The adrenaline of their preemptive escape was dissipating, and the lethargy that typically followed her fight with her visions started to permeate her limbs once more, weighing them down like sandbags.

"We need to find a place to hide for the night," Brand said, the words reaching through the sleepy fog overtaking her.

"How exactly are we supposed to do that?" They were in the middle of nowhere, essentially stranded.

"As soon as we've gone far enough, I'll pull off,

then fly low for a couple miles. See if I can find a place from the air that's harder to access by ground where we can sleep."

Kasia forced herself to focus through the blur of exhaustion taking over her body, to think about the important part of what he'd said. Right. Scrounge up a hard-to-access place between here and the Chunnel?

"Easy-peasy," she murmured. Then she scooted across the bench seat and snuggled into him, which suddenly seemed much comfier than the headrest or the side of the door.

Brand tensed under her touch, cast her a sharp glance, and swore.

What? Did she slur her last words? Kasia barely processed his reaction. She was too warm and cozy right where she was. Sleep was overtaking her too quickly.

Her eyes drifted closed, and she thought she heard him sigh.

"Sleep, sweetheart. I'll make sure you're safe." Brand's words found their way to her down a long tunnel.

"I know you will," she mumbled. Then she let oblivion take over, as the darkness enfolded her into its soft warmth, and she let go.

B eing a dragon came in handy sometimes. The roaring fire he started in the old, but functional, fireplace with just a puff of breath had warded off the chill of the seaside air throughout the night. Not that he needed it, and likely Kasia didn't, either, but he wasn't risking her health.

A glance over his shoulder showed her to still be dead to the world, but at least she wasn't as off-color as earlier. Those visions…holy shit.

Why he felt the pain, too, or the fact that his touch took it away, for both of them, was nothing but bad news. Would another dragon have the same effect on her? Or did it have to be him?

Brand scrubbed a hand over his face. That was a dangerous line of thinking. He needed to get her to his king and get the hell out. Instead he was stuck here, waiting for daylight.

After several hours of driving, he'd taken to the air—pushing aside the pit of anxiety in his stomach at leaving her alone and defenseless, asleep in the car when wolves were on their tail. He'd located a remote house along the beach, a bit rough with sparse furniture that'd seen better days. The building had gone unused in the last year or two, if he had to hazard a guess. Perfect for their needs.

He'd hidden the Hemi Cuda on the side of the road among the trees and lifted a sleeping Kasia out. Her red hair spilled over his arm in a waterfall of flame, and he gazed down at her face, long lashes fanned out over pale cheeks, kissable lips relaxed in repose. A spark of need ignited deep in his chest.

The woman trusted too easily. No one ever just *expected* him to do the right thing. He was a fucking mercenary, after all—he'd do any job for the right price, the right connections. People of all sorts paid him to do what they couldn't do themselves, and that set the expectations. Even then, trust was never a part of the deal. He watched his back. His clients watched their backs.

But Kasia?

She expected his help as though he were a decent person who would give it without hope or thought of reciprocity or a separate agenda. Even when she was well aware he had a separate agenda, though he hadn't shared specifics with her.

He shook his head, still staring down into that arresting face.

If she insisted on believing in him, she was in for disappointment. Kasia was meant for a king, something Brand could never be—not as a rogue dragon. Something he didn't want to be, either way.

As soon as he took her to Ladon and got credit for bringing the king a phoenix, she was no longer his concern, just like he'd told her.

Clutching her in his talons, he'd flown them both to the beach house he'd found and settled in for the rest of the night. Him standing guard through the long hours. Her on a rickety twin bed with a lumpy old mattress, rusty springs that creaked with every twitch, and no sheets or blankets, but still more comfortable than the hard ground or the seat of the car.

Now, fingers of light reached over the house, reflecting against the ocean water as the sun did its best to wake the greens and browns and grays of the French seaside around him.

Brand ran a weary hand over his eyes and finally dialed Ladon's number into the satellite phone. He hadn't wanted to risk contact while darkness prevailed. Daylight meant that vampires, at least, among a few others, were removed from the equation. It made it harder for dragons as well.

A deep male voice answered on the second ring. "I expected a call earlier."

Brand said nothing. He didn't make excuses, nor did he apologize. Both showed weakness, and in his line of work, he couldn't afford weakness.

"What did you find?" Irritation laced the king's voice.

Brand ignored it. "Nothing of interest." No way would he risk revealing exactly what he'd found, even over a sat phone. Too dangerous. Plus, Ladon and his warriors were too far away to ask for help quite yet.

"Was the woman there?" Ladon asked.

"Yes."

"And?"

"She was an Ifrit who couldn't control her fire," Brand lied for anyone listening in. "Her people will help her figure it out."

"Dammit." The sound of a fist hitting a table told Brand exactly how important this was to Ladon. Understandable, given the legend. If Ladon mated a phoenix, dragons worldwide would recognize him as the High King. The Red King might have an iron grip over the clans now, using the other kings like pawns in a game of chess, but if Ladon were the High King, dragon shifters would rise up.

That would throw a spanner in the works. Right now, though, he needed an excuse to see Ladon face-to-face, to bring Kasia to the king, hopefully without anyone knowing. "If you're looking for a specific woman, we should discuss it. I can find her more easily if I know what I'm looking for."

Silence greeted that offer. Ladon Ormarr leaned toward scary smart, and Brand had never requested a face-to-face before in all the centuries they'd known each other, long before Ladon took the throne. The request was the biggest hint he could throw. Did the other dragon catch it?

"When can you be here?" the king finally asked.

"I have another case to wrap up first. I'll be traveling and out of touch."

Another pause. "I understand," Ladon said. "Shall I expect you in about a week?"

Brand mentally calculated the odds. He suspected at some point they might have to abandon the car and go on foot. "I think a day or two should do it."

"I'll see you then." Irritation had left Ladon's voice, replaced with a neutral tone that couldn't quite hide the undercurrent of satisfaction.

Yeah. He knew.

"I'll send a car for you when you arrive." Which probably meant coming himself with a handful of warriors.

"Sounds good."

Brand hung up and stared at the yellow and black device, unseeing for a long moment, then dropped it onto the splintered kitchen table. With a heavy sigh, he walked to the open window, leaned against the sill, and gazed out at the slowly stirring land beyond, the rhythmic sound of the surf soothing.

That was that. Kasia was the king's now, assuming Brand could get her all the way to Scotland in one piece. That was a big fucking if.

Now an odd sort of discontent settled like an ache in his chest. Absently, he rubbed at the spot.

"A beach cabin? Guess that's better than another cabin in the woods."

Kasia's soft voice floated across the chilly morning air. Brand didn't startle. He'd already felt her stirring, as though his instincts were now tied to her, aware of her. He wondered at the comment, but didn't answer.

"So it's official? You're going to hand me over to Ladon?" she asked.

He glanced over his shoulder to find her watching him with eyes gone distant. After crossing the room, he dropped to the bed, sitting at her feet, and leaned back against the wall, closing his eyes. Damn he was tired. "That's the plan. You already knew that."

"Then what?" she asked.

He turned his head, trailing his gaze over the perfect oval of her face, darkly lashed eyes only highlighting the rare coloring, those ripe cotton candy lips.

"Then what?" she repeated. "You leave?"

He steeled his reserve. "Then I serve the Blood King."

For once, her expressive eyes gave nothing away. What did she feel about that? Because he felt as though someone had just skewered his gut with a shard of ice at the thought of leaving her. Why? He had no damn idea.

"Blood King?" Kasia finally asked.

Brand grimaced. That had been a stupid slip. "His throne was hard won."

"You mean many people died in taking it?"

Many didn't begin to cover it. Not only had the fighting been rough—not that he'd been there; a rogue had no place in clan wars—he'd heard Ladon executed a good number of the people in power almost the second the fighting ended.

Brand didn't blame him. After five centuries under Thanatos, Ladon would know who was loyal to the old king and who wasn't, regardless of whether their brands changed or not. But how did he explain that to Kasia?

"So you're going to dump me with a man called the Blood King. Nice."

"No choice."

"Why no choice?" she asked.

His tone should've cut short any further questions. However, Brand couldn't say he was all that surprised when she pushed to sitting, her hair a sexy tangle about her face. She watched him with total expectation that he'd answer.

Brand crossed his arms. "I have my reasons."

"Bullshit."

He glowered at her and snapped his mouth shut so hard his teeth clacked. Only she didn't act remotely cowed, tipping her chin up to return his glare.

"It's not smart to piss off a dragon."

She lifted a single eyebrow and snorted—a very dragon sound. "Like you'd hurt me."

There went that trust thing again, like a quiver of arrows unloaded into his heart. Only now, it just pissed him off. "You don't know that for sure."

She rolled her eyes. "Remember all those visions? You always protecting me? I *do* know that for sure."

Brand grunted. Her visions had, in all probability, saved his life last night, and hers. But, at this precise moment, he could do without those damn visions.

She continued to watch him from where she leaned against the headboard of the bed, expectation clear in the stubborn tilt of her chin and her unblinking stare.

"What other choices do you think we have?" he demanded.

Her brows drew down in a frown that reminded him of an angry kitten. "There are always options."

"Not always. Trust me." He should know. How had she survived this long when she was this naive?

Kasia's stare shifted subtly from snapping with anger to speculative, and Brand held it, refusing to give away any more of himself than he'd already revealed. After another moment, she dropped her gaze. He tried not to notice how she pursed those lush lips.

"Will you promise to stick around until I make up my mind if I'm staying with the dragons?" she asked.

Brand blinked. He hadn't considered that she had a choice to stay or not. "If you don't stay, where will you go?"

The corners of her mouth turned down. "I'll cross that bridge later, if I have to."

"You'll burn that bridge."

He meant to caution her, but Kasia appeared unimpressed. And stubborn. That darn chin was a blatant challenge where he was concerned, a dare he had trouble turning down, making him want to shake her—or kiss her into submission.

"This strikes me as a life-changing decision," she pointed out. "I'm not making it on the assumption there are zero other options."

"What if there *are* zero options?" he pushed.

"Then I'll make new options. If a phoenix is in such demand, I'm guessing all sorts of people or creatures...or whatever...would be interested in helping me."

"More would be interested in using you." Hurting her. Taking her. Enslaving her.

"I get that."

"Do you?" She was too flippant for his peace of mind.

"Yes, Brand. I'm not an idiot, nor do I own a pair of rose-colored glasses." And now she was talking to him like an infant. "But I was also raised to stand apart and make my own way in this world."

She looked away, lips pressed together in a flat line, eyes going vague like she was suddenly somewhere else. "I refuse to end up just like my mother," she murmured, more to herself than to him.

"What does that mean?" he asked.

"Alone. Scared all the time. Missing her mate. A piece on the board of someone else's game." She took a deep breath. "So maybe I have a different perspective, one you've never considered."

He crossed his arms and tried not to notice how her eyes followed the movement. He'd caught her gaze on his tattoo a couple of times over the last thirty-six hours. "Like other options?" he asked.

She seemed to drag her gaze back up to his face with effort. "Exactly."

They shared a long look, one filled with unspoken things, things he wasn't even sure she was communicating to him, or he to her. Things that tightened his body and made him ache in an unfulfilled kind of way.

Time to put some distance between them. Metaphorically speaking. He got up and offered her a hand. "We should get back to the car."

The second they walked out the door, Brand froze. "Kasia," he said slowly. "Can you light on fire without the pain?"

She turned her face up to him, frowning, but he ignored her, his senses tuned to the area around them.

"Can you?" he prodded when she didn't answer.

"Yes."

He nodded. "When I tell you to run, head straight down the beach."

"Shit," she muttered. But that was it. That fast, she was ready to go.

"And if something gets to you before I do," he said, "light the bastard up."

IV

Pytheios leaned back in his chair as he considered the people gathered around the table at which he sat and waited on the last arrival in silence. Near silence, except for Nathair. His brother's incessant need to keep his hands occupied resulted in a rhythmic clicking sound as he solved a human-made cube puzzle, a toy he carried everywhere.

Pytheios barely heard the sound after so many years as his constant companion. Instead, he considered with satisfaction their current location.

The Alps. One of the Blue Clan's last outposts. Now his.

He'd sacrificed many red and green dragons—more green really—in order to wrest this stronghold from Ladon Ormarr, driving the Blue Clan to their only remaining home deep inside Ben Nevis mountain in Scotland. Gaining this location also gave Pytheios a base from which he could both blockade and attack that bloody bastard currently on the blue throne.

He couldn't say he particularly cared for *this* room, which was essentially a cave located deep within the mountain. From the opening to this system of caverns, which looked out to the west, he could see Mont Blanc, the tallest mountain in the range, but not from this windowless room with its solid gray rock walls smoothed by time and dragon fire.

Not remotely like his ancestral home in the

Himalayas.

His home was almost entirely forged from a glass as hard and durable as diamonds, allowing light to penetrate even the most interior of rooms. The origin of all dragon-kind, his people had been living among those peaks for tens of thousands of years, long before humans evolved from apes.

Pytheios held in a derisive snort at that thought.

Other than as a source of female mates, humans were worse than useless. Though tell that to the dragon shifters in the colonies. In America, still the Wild West as far as dragons were concerned, they lived among the humans, worked beside them. Still, the number of suitable mates found there had supplied Europe and Asia steadily since the colonies had been established. Human women who showed dragon signs were hard to find. He'd let those lawless slaves over there continue to interact with humans and continue to supply his dragons in Europe and Asia with mates.

Mates.

Smoke coiled around him as fury rose to the surface. The others in the room shifted nervously. Even his brother stopped that clacking sound, but Pytheios ignored them.

Five hundred years and he was still dealing with that bitch phoenix—Serefina.

Serefina's mother had ruled beside the previous King of the Red Clan for centuries and had decided to pass the power on to their daughter—the only way for a phoenix to claim her powers was for her mother to die or to choose to give them up to her daughter. Serefina was meant to be Pytheios's mate, making him the next High King of all dragon shifters.

But Serefina defied her parents' wishes, generations of tradition, and her unspoken promise to Pytheios. She had chosen another—Zilant Amon the White King—denying Pytheios the title that was rightfully his.

Worse, succession would have made Zilant the king of both his White Clan and Pytheios's Red Clan—because mating Serefina made him both the phoenix's mate as well as the mate of the former Red King's daughter.

No white dragon was going to rule his clan. Pytheios had made sure of that.

He'd gone after her parents. Killing the king and his phoenix had been easy, since the mother had already chosen to pass her powers to her daughter. Then he'd made Serefina's new mate pay. Killing Zilant Amon had been a pleasure. He'd never liked that arrogant ass of a leader—someone who thought the clans should live in equality, that the colonies should govern themselves, and that mates should find each other without being overseen by a Mating Council. Pathetic. How Zilant became King of the White Clan was something Pytheios never understood.

Serefina, that traitorous bitch, disappeared before he could do anything to her.

Fuck her. *He* was the High King of the dragon clans and didn't need some pathetic flaming bird to prove it.

He'd spread lies through the clans explaining the deaths as a result of her mating the wrong man, and then he'd taken over as King of the Red Clan. And he damn well hadn't needed a phoenix then. Look at how he'd put men loyal to him on the throne of each of the other clans. Look at how he, and he alone, decided the laws and fates of his people.

Until this Ladon Ormarr had stolen the blue throne, Pytheios had managed without the magical creature at his side.

Dragons didn't need a phoenix, shouldn't need her. *He* just needed one, and not as a mate. Not anymore. He had other plans for those pitiful creatures.

Hopefully, Jaakobah had good news for him today. Time was running out.

He glanced around the faces at the table. The only piece of furniture in the dark space was an oblong table hewn from pine, the chairs built to match. Primitive, but functional. Three of the five people he trusted most, which wasn't saying a whole hell of a lot, stared back at him. Correction, two stared back at him, while one stood off to the side and clicked away at his game.

No one spoke, though Merikh, the youngest of this inner circle, glanced away as their gazes crossed paths and adjusted the purple silk tie at his neck.

Irritation spiked. Pytheios had been told once that he possessed an intimidating stare. Didn't all kings? The members of his Curia Regis—his King's Council—should be able to hold his fucking gaze, though. Especially his son.

"I apologize for my tardiness, my king." A tall man, skinny to the point of appearing emaciated, with his cheekbones jutting out from under his skin and pale red hair pulled back in a neat ponytail at the nape of his neck, entered the room. He was dressed in his typical attire of a collarless suit with intricate detail—this one white with blue embroidered birds and flowers—and not appearing at all hurried. "I received important news that delayed me."

Pytheios vibrated with the effort of containing his impatience when after that, the man called the Stoat, though never to his face, proceeded to take his sweet time in selecting one of the two remaining chairs and seating himself, the protesting squeal of the wood against the stone floor a particularly painful accompaniment.

Jaakobah always had loved to play to a crowd.

"And what is this news?" Pytheios finally asked, knowing the man would never get to it without prompting.

Jaakobah laced his perfectly manicured hands and leaned against the table as he faced Pytheios as though his king weren't waiting for him. "The woman we believe to be one of the phoenixes that you witnessed last year left the medical facility where she's been staying."

Pytheios leaned forward. "With Uther?" *They had her?*

"I'm afraid not."

"Wait," Merikh interrupted. "You sent *Uther*?"

Pytheios ignored him. "They let her go?" He controlled the scowl that wanted to pull at his face, his skin too painful to allow the expression.

Dammit. Jaakobah had received news of the woman's existence only two days ago. Uther should have retrieved her if she proved to be whom they thought. How could she already be gone?

I should have gone myself. Why the hell did I entrust something so important to someone else?

But he already knew the answer. Because the energy it took to fly drained his waning powers, and Uther would remain loyal for once—bring the phoenix back untouched. Pytheios had ensured that with a promise of immortality that had nothing to do with mating a phoenix. Not only that, but he'd agreed to remove Volos from the white throne and give Uther reign over both the Gold and White Clans.

Pytheios had no intention of keeping that promise, but for now he needed Uther to stay in line.

However, for the chance of capturing a phoenix, he should've weighed the pros more heavily against the cons.

"No. She left on her own." Jaakobah pulled out his cell phone and messed with it for a moment, swiping until he reached the desired screen.

"She left a note." He then turned the phone to show Pytheios.

A handwritten note lay on white sheets and read, "*I have not been taken, but have left on my own. Do not share my information with anyone who asks*."

They'd missed her? Pytheios stood, leaning his hands on the table and working to control his rage. Beneath his hands, the stone table started to bubble and melt under the heat he generated. "She knows she's being followed."

A statement, not a question, but Jaakobah dipped his chin anyway. "I believe so."

"And Uther?"

"Had not made contact with her yet as far as I know. He arrived after she disappeared," Jaakobah hastened to confirm in his nasal tones.

Which meant she wasn't running from them. So who or what had scared her off?

"There's more," Jaakobah murmured.

Pytheios gritted his teeth. "Yes?"

"She's relocated to this continent. I managed to get word that a pack of wolf shifters is on her trail. Uther is tracking them now. They thought they'd caught up to her somewhere in France."

Dead silence settled over the room as Pytheios absorbed those words. He rubbed the fingertips of his left hand together, wiping away the stone from the table now cooling on his fingertips, as he considered the news.

Wolf shifters. Useless creatures, but still, the Federation of Packs might pull together against him if it meant keeping a phoenix for themselves. He'd need to take them out of the equation.

To his right, Jaakobah's expression revealed nothing more than a calm patience. Despite his habit of grandstanding, the man never showed any other fucking emotion than calm patience, which just added to his off-putting oddness.

While that unchanging expression came in handy for a person privy to many of Pytheios's own secrets, every so often, Pytheios had the urge to force those angular features into a different alignment. Fear, shock, pain, pleasure. All would be acceptable over nothing.

Like now, for instance. News such as what Jaakobah had just shared should include some sort of emotion—a cringe, maybe, or a frown, even trembling fear at what Pytheios's reaction might be would be better than nothing.

Slowly, he said, "You're telling me a pack of mutts reached the phoenix before I could?"

Jaakobah gazed back steadily with those pale reddish-brown eyes. "Not exactly."

Pytheios narrowed his eyes to slits, and even Jaakobah stiffened. "You know I hate playing your little guessing games. Spit it out."

Again, no change in expression. The man merely bobbed his head in acknowledgment in that birdlike way of his. "According to my sources, she disappeared before the wolves could get to her."

"Disappeared?" The others in the room shifted in their seats at his tone. Pytheios ignored their discomfort. At least the wolves hadn't gotten to her first. "How?" he demanded.

Jaakobah shrugged. "Undetermined. All I know is she was able to evade them at a motel in France."

"I suggest you determine it."

Another dipping head nod.

Could Serefina's daughter teleport like her mother? Pytheios's own experience with phoenixes, though limited to only two in his lifetime, suggested each new generation developed her own gifts, unique to her and specific to helping the dragon clans under her care and rule. A teleporting phoenix would make this damn tricky. Serefina couldn't have hidden from him as long as she had without that ability.

"And find out if she has help," he added. Because if teleporting wasn't her gift, then no way was she doing this on her own.

"Understood," Jaakobah murmured.

Pytheios flicked a hand. "Step outside and wait for my summons."

The pale man's eye twitched, the most emotion he'd shown yet. "Of course."

Once the door closed behind Jaakobah, Pytheios shifted his gaze to the woman at the far end of the table who had yet to speak. Rhiamon, his witch. She was critical to his plans for Serefina's daughters. "What about the other three?"

He'd seen more than one woman in that field the night he killed Serefina. Even now, the shock of that discovery reverberated through him.

A phoenix giving birth to more than one child was unheard of. Were they all phoenixes? Or had she gone and slept with human men over the years? Hard to tell, since phoenixes were immortal, achieving adulthood at about the same rate as dragons, but their aging stopped around the human equivalent of twenty-five years.

He hadn't had much time to determine how old they were, as they had disappeared from that field one by one, Serefina's powers having grown over the years to allow her to teleport others, even without touching them.

No matter what, he had to find them before anyone else got their grubby hands on them. All he needed was the power inside them, then they could die.

He'd hunted down Serefina and killed her too quickly, before he'd had a chance to take those powers from her. He'd let his rage get ahold of him. He'd intended to keep her alive until Rhiamon could work the spell that would siphon Serefina's powers, giving them to Pytheios. The strike of his blade in her back had been intended to kill her slowly, giving him time, but she'd died too fast, before the spell had been completed.

However, discovering her daughters had given him hope. He just needed one. One to suck dry. One to reverse time and claim immortality to continue his reign. The flesh falling from his bones would heal, and *he* would possess the power a phoenix bestowed on the clans. Then *he*, Pytheios, the High King, could be the one to bring his people peace, without a phoenix at his side.

"I have not located the other phoenix," Rhiamon murmured.

Unlike the Stoat, Rhiamon's frustration with her lack of progress over the last year practically screamed across the table. At least to Pytheios.

After centuries with the witch at his side, Pytheios knew the signs. Her curls, lustrous though they'd faded from blond to white, almost vibrated with her ire, and her still-vibrant green eyes snapped. Plus, her habit of tapping a single long fingernail against the table in a slow cadence was a dead giveaway.

Pytheios allowed himself to soften, probably imperceptibly to everyone but her, as he addressed her frustration. "You are already overburdened, my pet. Your efforts in the tower drain you."

Plus her efforts keeping him alive well past when his body should've collapsed. "Not to mention keeping yourself alive, Mother," Merikh added.

A carbon copy of Pytheios in his younger years—

tall and broad with black hair and the reddish-brown eyes that signaled his red dragon heritage—Merikh had thankfully inherited the dragon shifter genes rather than his mother's magical gifts.

He'd also inherited his mother's propensity to fuck anything that so much as breathed in his direction, every woman an easy target thanks to his pretty-boy good looks and calculated charm. A weakness Pytheios had zero patience for.

Rhiamon patted her son's hand, and Pytheios noticed for the first time how paper-thin her skin had become. He was running out of time. If the witch died, he would soon follow…that or he'd have to mate to extend his life. Mating a phoenix was something he refused to do, and relying on a weak human turned his stomach.

"Do you know why your mother keeps herself alive?" he asked Merikh.

The younger man's gaze shifted from his mother back to Pytheios. "Because she believes in your vision," he finally answered.

Displeasure sifted through Pytheios like hot sand through an hourglass. This boy, because Merikh could hardly be termed a man given his shortsighted tendencies and lack of analytical judgment, was his son. What a waste.

"My lowest servant believes in my vision," Pytheios scoffed.

Merikh flinched, hatred slipping over his features before he managed to check his reaction.

Good. Hatred was something Pytheios could work with.

Perhaps the time had come to implement a

secondary plan. Taking a phoenix's power had just become a thousand times easier than the last five centuries, given he had four to choose from. However, making Merikh a carbon copy of himself could be a handy tool in the future—another weapon he could use in this fight to rule dragons like they needed to be ruled. Like he'd done with the boy's mother, Pytheios would twist his son to suit his purposes. He'd make him stronger, smarter. He should've started to do so long before.

He smiled. "Your mother keeps me alive because no one could rule dragons like I can. As the oldest of the living dragons, my experiences both in war and in peace are invaluable. No other king has the guts to make the tough decisions I do."

"You are the King of Kings, Father."

Pytheios continued as if Merikh hadn't interrupted. "And the dragons of your generation are pathetically inept for the position." Deliberately, he injected his voice with cold cynicism.

Merikh glared across the table but said nothing.

After a long, uncomfortable stretch of silence, Rhiamon twitched her shoulders to face Pytheios and redirected the conversation. "If you'd allow me to kill those women—"

He held up a hand, and she clamped her lips down on any further words. They'd had this conversation before.

"Until we determine which of Serefina's offspring is the phoenix, all remain alive." Until they took her power. That process would kill her, anyway.

Pytheios ignored Rhiamon's moue of displeasure. His new plan to mold Merikh in his image would soothe those ruffled feathers. She'd assume he was grooming her son for the crown, that assumption another string he could pull to keep her in line.

"I thought the plan was to kill every phoenix?"

Pytheios flicked an annoyed glance in his brother's direction. His mother's late-in-life oops leaned against the smooth stone wall. His dark brown hair flopped over one eye, giving him a childlike appearance. He didn't raise his gaze, staying focused on the Rubik's Cube he solved then disordered in rapid succession.

"It was, when the phoenix in question was Serefina," Pytheios agreed.

Only Rhiamon knew about the need to take her powers first. He didn't bother to keep the impatience from his tone.

"What changed?" Nathair persisted as the *click-click-click* of his toy clattered on. He didn't look up, nor would he.

But Pytheios didn't keep him around for his eye contact or lack thereof. He had other uses for his only sibling, so he stated his reasoning succinctly. "Five hundred years without a phoenix, and the clans are mine, with the exception of the Blue. Even then, my right to rule as High King could be questioned."

The Rubik's Cube slowed down. "So, you're going to use one of those phoenixes?" Nathair asked slowly.

"I'm going to mate one, then add her to my collection of useless relics in Rhiamon's tower." A necessary lie to keep his Curia Regis in the dark as to his true plans. "If the phoenix's presence pays off, and the clans find peace, then she can stay up there until my reign is unquestionable. I'll kill her when the time is right. If we don't see a noticeable difference, she'll go the same way as her sisters, sooner rather than later."

Nathair's hands stopped altogether as he absorbed that plan, running the idea through the impressive matrix that was his brain.

Pytheios waited. So did the others.

"Won't that kill you? Once the mating bond is in place, if one mate dies, so does the other."

Pytheios shared a smirk with Rhiamon.

"No." The witch's finger stopped tapping the table. "I've found a way to protect him from the effect."

Again, his brother considered that in silence.

"Too many variables," Nathair finally declared.

Pytheios allowed himself a small smile. That comment basically meant his plan was sound enough to fool the others. Otherwise, Nathair would voice any big obstacles. "Let me handle whatever variables get in my way."

Nathair shrugged and went back to his toy.

"Bring Jaakobah back in," Pytheios instructed Merikh.

Once both men were seated again, Pytheios turned to Jaakobah. "We don't know where she went?"

"No, my king."

"Can we follow the wolves? Or learn what they know? How they found her?"

Jaakobah dipped his head. "I believe both are possible."

"Do it." For a brief moment, Pytheios considered going after her himself. The Alps were close to

France. But the location put him too close to the Blue Clan. Better to risk Uther and the Gold Clan rather than his own neck. He would give the man another chance to get it right and bring him a phoenix.

"Get Uther on it," he ordered.

Pytheios stood, and the others took his cue and filed out of the room. All except the witch. Rhiamon waited until the door closed behind the others. Then she stepped closer, her cinnamon scent swirling enticingly around him.

"Did you have to be so hard on Merikh?" she asked.

Irritation joined his rapidly rising desire. "He's too soft."

"He's a boy."

"He needs to learn to be a king."

Satisfaction lit her eyes as the implication sank in. Good. One more way to control her magic.

"You need to work off some of that anger." She gave him that siren's smile that had even his decrepit old body sitting up and taking notice. "I have a surprise for you in my chambers."

She didn't touch him, knowing his skin wouldn't handle the contact. But if that hint was what he expected...

In silence, he followed her to her rooms. Rhiamon opened the door, and he stepped inside only to halt at the sight of an animal strapped to the stone wall with thick chains of dragonsteel, and, probably, Rhiamon's own spells.

"A hellhound," he murmured, satisfaction lacing the words.

"A fine gift, my lord," she said, moving forward. "He's young and strong. His fire will feed your flesh."

In lieu of a phoenix, they'd been siphoning the powers of other fire creatures for years to keep his condition at bay and keep the witch alive as well. Soon they'd have to start draining dragon shifters of their fire. If he mated a human, Pytheios could have arrested the aging process that affected all dragon shifters eventually.

He stood, silent and watchful in the center of the room while Rhiamon chanted her spell. As her chanting grew louder, the hellhound started to whimper, but his witch silenced it, like a mute switch, with a flick of her hand. Seconds more, and the creature opened its mouth in an eerily silent howl of agony, its body shook, and fire poured from it into Rhiamon.

She turned to Pytheios and cradled his face in one hand, her other hand on his arm, and where she touched the skin turned noticeably younger, healthier. She kissed him, and the fire she'd consumed from the hound flowed into him.

As she continued to drain the creature behind them and feed that energy into Pytheios, he reached for the bottom of her skirt and worked it up. He trailed a hand over the exposed skin of her thigh and up to her ass, still firm despite her age.

Finally, she finished the process. A glance revealed the charred, dried husk of the massive dog's body still hanging from the chains. Excellent. A hellhound's fire would buy him more time.

"Turn around," he commanded her.

Rhiamon chuckled low in her throat, even as

she obeyed, turning in his arms and bending over to place her hands on the bed nearby. He flipped her skirt up over her back.

But before he could sink into her heat, she turned to pin him with a demanding glance over her shoulder. "My son will be king?"

Pytheios lowered his pants. "*Our* son will be king. One day." The lie slipped easily from his lips. Keeping the witch happy was just one more step closer to immortality.

She'd learn the truth too late. After she did to a phoenix what she'd just done to that hellhound.

V

"*R*un."

The word punched from him. Even through his tension, a spurt of pride filled Brand at how she didn't hesitate. Just took off down the stairs and over the path to the beach.

As she ran, Brand worked into his shift. He couldn't take on vampires in his human form—they were stronger, faster...and headed his and Kasia's way. He needed the dragon. Luckily, the closest vamp to him was far enough away to give him time.

Curse that fucking doctor in the States. She'd screwed Kasia with her big, fat mouth. He'd go back and snap her neck when this was over.

As his form realigned, even as his perspective blurred and changed, he kept his gaze trained on Kasia's form as she got smaller and smaller.

Damn, she was fast.

At first, nothing followed her, but they were out there. The coppery scent of blood in the air had been a dead giveaway. It followed those creatures wherever they went.

Sure enough, a dark figure wearing a duster, of all things, and running faster than human speeds, sprinted out of the dunes. Where was the other one, though? There were definitely two.

Adrenaline pumping as the vampire closed in on his phoenix, Brand urged his shift to move faster. The second his wings formed, Brand took to the skies.

Except another figure jumped from the roof and

managed to catch him by the leg, dragging him back down. Brand's heavy bulk hit the ground, spraying up sand. He turned and snapped at the vamp, but missed, because the fuckers were fast.

Kasia's scream pierced the air. The other vampire must've reached her.

Brand's control was tenuous at the best of times. He lost it.

With a roar, he stoked the fire and aimed it at the creature keeping him occupied. While they weren't affected by sun—unless you counted how shitty their pale skin looked in the daylight—fire was one of the few things that could kill them.

Every blast of flame missed. The cottage, all weathered wood, caught a direct hit, though, and went up in a fireball.

Fuck. That'd bring humans down on his ass in a hurry.

He wasn't going to catch the vamp this way. Instead, he took off again, but this time turning his body in a circle while blowing a torrent of fire, so his opponent couldn't yank him back down. As soon as he gained enough altitude that he couldn't be reached, he took off after the vampire that had Kasia pinned to the ground.

The asshole had its fangs in her wrist, not budging as she thrashed and beat against it.

No. Brand blasted a roar of challenge, but it didn't let up. A flash of movement directly below him caught his attention. As he expected, the second vampire was racing down the beach to help his compatriot.

A piercing wail rent the air. The vampire that

had Kasia went up in flames, his long coat catching. Good girl. The thing flew back from her, writhing on the ground in agony as it perished.

The second vampire also let out a scream, increasing his speed to get to his partner. Brand took advantage of his distraction and dove.

The vamp looked up just as Brand's shadow alerted him, but it was too late. Brand caught him up in his talons and pushed back into the air. Using the razor-sharp tips designed to pierce through diamond-hard dragon scales, he ripped the fucker in two. That copper scent filled his nostrils, but he dropped the halves, flinging fire after them. No need to leave evidence for the humans to find.

Immediate danger handled, Brand deliberately landed a half mile away from where Kasia stood on the beach. He needed to get control first. As soon as he hit sand, he tried to shift, but the dragon side didn't want to let go. Not yet.

The stench of death and the need to protect the woman still on the beach were too much. Brand had to force himself into human. He needed to be able to check on Kasia, and as a dragon that wouldn't work.

Finally, he managed to calm enough to regain control, then he sprinted over the dunes to find Kasia waiting, watching in the direction he came from, cradling her wrist.

Only instead of gratitude, as he ran up to her, she shoved him in the chest with shaking hands. "You used me as bait, asshole."

She hissed, face twisting with pain as she yanked back her wrist to cradle it.

Brand held up both hands. "I needed time to shift to deal with them. I knew they'd go after you."

She continued to glower at him.

"Good job lighting one on fire." He reached out to take her hand, needing to check the wound.

Only she jerked away. "I'm fine."

"I'm sorry." Where the hell had that come from? Brand had a policy. No apologizing. Ever.

Kasia huffed. "I guess I get why you did it." She shoved him with her one good hand. "But you scared the shit out of me, Brand."

He lifted a single eyebrow. "I'll try not to do it again."

She rolled her eyes at the dry tone of his voice. When he reached for her hand this time, she let him tug it closer. Two small puncture wounds directly over her veins had already clotted up. "Doesn't look too bad. Do you feel woozy? Weak?"

He checked her color, which wasn't too pale.

"No." She tugged her hand away. "I lit on fire before he got too much."

"Good." He hesitated, wrestling with the urge to say more, to offer comfort. Again, a foreign notion. "We'd better get going."

"Ya think?"

He ignored her sarcasm. "The sooner we get to the Blue Clan, the better."

That was for damn sure. Wolves. Vampires. And Brand was still worried about dragons. What next? The fucking boogeyman?

She expected him to immediately shift, but he didn't.

"When I'm in dragon form, I don't…" A warning lingered in Brand's words, but he trailed off.

"Don't what?"

He rolled his shoulders. "I don't always have control."

She gave him a sideways glance, trying to figure that one out.

Brand sighed. "Sort of like a dog that seems nice but then snaps."

Oh. That explained her impression the night he caught her. "Are you dangerous?"

"I can be, if I'm angry enough."

Awesome. Dragons already made her nervous. "If you go all Cujo on me, what's the plan?"

"I don't think I will."

She put her hands on her hips. "*I don't think* is not good enough."

Suddenly he pulled out that infuriating half smile of his. Somewhere between teasing, egotistical, and charming. "I guess it's a good thing you're a fast runner, then."

"Ha. Ha."

He winked. The damn man actually winked at her. "Keep back."

"Wait—"

They still didn't have a plan, but too late, he'd already started the shift.

She'd seen him in both forms, but this was the first time she'd witnessed the transition to dragon. The strangeness alone, of seeing the man she knew…the man she'd trusted with her life…silently disappear, folding in on himself and expanding as something completely different, should have her mind reeling. Instead, mostly she was impressed and a tiny bit awed. Her mother had told her of it, of course, but her descriptions left a lot to the imagination, and Kasia's imagination had been sorely lacking in this area.

Kasia stiffened as, once done with the transformation, he lowered his head, his huge golden eye on level with her.

"Are you going to eat me?" she asked.

He shook his head.

That was something at least. A small amount of her trepidation eased. On a whim stoked by simple curiosity, Kasia reached out, flattening her palm against scales that were surprisingly supple, more like a snake's underbelly, but hard at the same time, and reflective, like liquid gold lay trapped inside each scale.

She could feel him.

Feel Brand's...presence, or maybe his soul. He was in there, though she understood that the animal version of him was more in charge in this form, raw elemental nature. He slowly blinked then cocked his head and sniffed at her, his warm, smoky breath puffing against her skin. A peculiar sense of...safety...slid through her. A treacherous idea to entertain.

I shouldn't trust this.

Despite that logical thought, tense muscles she hadn't even realized she was clenching released, loosening up, and she grinned. "Has anyone ever told you that you're hot as a giant lizard? And I don't mean because of the fire."

He snorted, though she wasn't sure if the sound indicated a laugh or derision.

"Dragon." His voice boomed, echoing inside her head, and Kasia slapped her hands over her ears in a futile attempt to make it stop.

"That's right, you're telepathic now," she muttered more to herself. A handful of centuries learning dragon facts had not prepared her for the up close and personal encounter.

"Only when I'm in this form."

She cringed as the sound of his voice sent splinters of pain through her head. "Yeah. I know. Turn down the volume, raptor boy."

"Sorry. I'm used to communicating with much larger creatures this way." His voice came over more softly, and, when no splitting headache followed, she dropped her hands. He nudged her gently, as if cuddling away the hurt he'd caused, or maybe apologizing, but was the Brand-half doing that, or the dragon-half?

She didn't take him for the cuddly type.

Then she gave him a narrow-eyed stare. Her mother had said the dragons' ability to talk with their minds was like a baby monitor, only going one way. But just in case…

"Can you hear my thoughts, too?" If he could, she was out of here. No creature was getting that kind of advantage over her.

"No. I can only project."

Well, that was something at least. She definitely did not need him in her head. Put aside the plethora of secrets she'd locked inside, tucked away safe and sound, what if he heard her growing obsession with kissing him? Actually, strike that. Her fantasies had passed kissing months ago, and that was before the flesh and blood man had been available, so to speak.

Brand was planning to abandon her once his job was done, and she'd be in another dragon's bed then. More importantly, she had to protect her sisters and determine her place with Ladon. If she decided to stay with dragons, then she needed to be mated, or she'd always be at risk of Pytheios getting to her.

Either way, getting attached to Brand was a horrible idea.

"So how is this supposed to work?" She waved a hand at his massive form.

"I was thinking you'd ride on my back," came the dry retort.

Kasia gave him an uber-patient look. "I know that. How do you suggest I get up there, Godzilla?"

Those scales weren't rough like tree bark. She'd be slipping and sliding all over the dang place. She hadn't told him about the teleporting thing yet, so that was out as an option. She might trust him with her life, but her secrets were hers alone. Besides, with her lack of control, she might impale herself on a spike accidentally.

"Oh." Brand lowered his body to the ground for easier access. *"Climb up and hold on."*

"Right," she muttered. "Easy as all that."

The climbing up part wasn't as difficult as she expected. The spikes helped, but the holding on part? She was practically doing the splits, his neck was so broad, and she was afraid she'd slip right off him. She glanced around, searching for a handhold of any sort. Maybe a place to wedge her feet.

"Hold on to what?" she asked.

"Scoot back and watch out."

As soon as she did, a series of extra spikes rose from where they'd lain flat against the back of his neck and shoulders, the last ending where she sat between his shoulder blades. Kasia had to inch backward farther and duck to the side to avoid being skewered as he raised them. Then she settled herself between two protrusions and wrapped her arms around the one in front of her, which thankfully wasn't razor sharp, except maybe the tip, which rose well above her head, out of her reach. *No impaling today, please.*

This would work.

"Ready?"

Not really. "Yup." She tightened her grip as Brand rose to his feet, bumping her all around as his weight shifted from side to side. Then behind her he unfurled his wings, which spanned at least eighty feet, double his height, if she had to guess, and were beautiful in the sunlight that penetrated the thinner membranes at the tips and along the edges, giving him an iridescent glow.

"My knight in shining scales," she quipped.

"I'm no knight any more than you're a princess," came the immediate denial.

Huh. Little do you know.

Kasia barely held in a squeal of terror as he brought his wings down, heaving them into the air. She tasted the metallic tang of blood as she bit down on her lower lip too hard.

Flying was really not her thing, and definitely not

this violent takeoff.

Quickly, Brand gained altitude, tipped in such a way that she was grateful for the spike at her back which sort of held her on, though she also maintained a death grip on the one in front. Eventually he leveled off, and Kasia breathed a sigh of relief at the easier position for her, though she didn't loosen her grasp. At least the spike partially protected her from the winds, though she could feel the skin of her face vibrating.

"Can you hear me?" she called.

"Dragons are equipped to hear in the wind. Our ears are formed to cut down on wind noise and hone in on any other noise we choose to monitor."

That answered that. Wind rushed through Kasia's hair, and she wished, not for the first time, that she'd brought extra hairbands with her, because her long strands would be a knotted mess by the time they got where they were going.

Plus, despite the early autumn months, the temperature could only be termed as frigid up this high. She may contain and release fire, but that fact hadn't seemed to alter her comfort levels with the cold. Or lack thereof.

She'd had enough of the cold in that damned solitary cabin in Alaska this last year anyway—a thought that reminded her of Maul. She hoped he wasn't looking for her. She'd told him to stay at the cabin and wait, but she didn't control the hellhound. He had a mind of his own.

"Aren't you worried about people seeing you from the ground?" she yelled over the rush of the wind around her, the words snatched from her mouth as they came out.

"We can camouflage. Though it's not as foolproof in daylight."

She knew about that in theory, though she'd been under the impression that some colors of dragon were better at it than others. Her mother had worried about it endlessly in terms of Pytheios coming for them. "How does it work?"

"Our scales along the bottom reflect whatever is above us."

"Like a chameleon? That's a handy trick."

He didn't comment one way or another, and Kasia clutched his spike, trying her best not to think about the drop. All that nothing followed by hard ground. At the moment, the view below reminded her of a patchwork quilt—the green earth dotted with trees, broken up by roads, rivers, ponds, hills, towns that appeared tiny, the vehicles like ants, the people indistinguishable. And just ahead, the blue-gray of ocean dotted with whitecaps.

"How high are we?" she asked.

"Around twelve thousand feet. You'll need oxygen if we go much above that."

Right. Oxygen. Because breathing was important. "What about you?"

"Dragons are built for flying. I can go as high as forty thousand without a problem, though I shouldn't stay up there long."

"What happens if I fall off?" The question popped out before she could stuff it back in and swallow it down. She grimaced, hating to show fear of any sort.

"Don't fall off."

"Anyone ever called you an ass to your face?" she muttered.

"Only you."

Oh, he'd heard that? Damn. Laughter lurked in his smoky tones. Kasia pulled her gaze off the ground, trying not to think about it. Instead she returned to his comment about not being a knight.

"So, you have a thing against knights?"

"Pretty boys who run around slaying dragons to save the fair maiden?" He let the sarcasm dangle for a moment. *"Nah. I'm just not one."*

"What are you, then?"

Silence greeted her question. His modus operandi, she was coming to learn.

Undeterred, Kasia set about wondering aloud. "I can't see you doing everyday stuff like going to a day job and cooking dinner. Which means you're into something more unusual. My guess is dangerous. Your PI gig was a total lie to get access to me, so that's not it. Not exactly, at least."

Shoulder muscles shifted below her, and she smiled, knowing she was getting close.

"Are you a warrior?"

Silence continued, thick and, unless she missed her guess, annoyed.

Kasia smiled to herself. Brand reminded her of her younger sister, Meira. When Meira didn't want to reveal secrets, she simply said nothing. The funny thing was, saying nothing became her tell. Her silence meant she knew something, so Kasia and Skylar would pester her endlessly until Angelika would step in and shoo them away.

Kasia buried the silly, fond memory in the black

hole that opened up inside her at the thought of the sisters she missed dearly. Would she ever have a chance to tease Meira like that again? Phoenixes were immortal. Maybe hope wasn't a total waste of time.

"No." She continued her solitary debate aloud. "I guess a warrior doesn't make sense, because you work for Ladon. He's a blue dragon, while you're a gold dragon. His other warriors would never allow that, would they?"

Suddenly, Brand tipped his wings, banking hard. Unprepared for the move, Kasia didn't manage to hold in her squeal of terror as she clung to his spike like a barnacle and tried not to fall to a gruesome and terrible death.

He leveled out.

After gathering her courage and her dignity, Kasia glared at the long spiked neck in front of her. She let go of him with one hand long enough to poke one shiny scale by her leg with her finger. Not that she expected him to even notice it, but it made her feel better.

"Hey," he protested.

Huh. He did feel it. Interesting that his scales were that sensitive. "Warn me next time, you giant gecko. I'm not strapped in."

"Sorry." His tone said otherwise.

"Strike a nerve, did I?" She asked this sweetly, knowing that he'd catch the intended sarcasm.

Silence again.

Kasia adjusted her seat, in case he tried that crap again, and remained undeterred. She could be stubborn, too. "What were we discussing before your acrobatic maneuver?" She pretended to think about it. "Oh, that's right. Your job."

A low growl of frustration rumbled beneath her, and Kasia grinned, though she managed not to chuckle, which would undermine her goal. "You're a gold dragon and work for a blue dragon... Are you a spy? I guess you could be part of some inter-clan exchange program? Or maybe you're just his errand boy?"

"I get things for him." Irritation laced his words.

Score! Progress from the silent peanut gallery. But what did getting things mean? Some kind of mercenary? That would account for the hard light in his eyes and the tendency toward grim silence.

"What kind of things?" she pressed.

Silence returned. *Grrrr...*

Kasia debated what a rough customer like Brand would get for a king. Not hard to imagine a multitude of things. "Money, maybe, though I understand most of the clans are relatively wealthy."

"Some more than others."

Implying Ladon's wasn't? Good to know. She tucked that little tidbit away for later use. "Weapons?"

A put-upon sigh reached her through that strange mental link.

"Secrets?"

He twitched beneath her. *"I'm not trusted enough for secrets."*

Another score for her. "Why not?"

Silence.

Damn. That line of questioning could have proved interesting. Although, come to think of it, didn't *she* count as a secret? Seemed like Brand had a bit of a chip on his shoulder. "What else? Resources, I guess? People? Not slaves, I hope. Female mates, perhaps?" She gave a little gasp as a thought struck. "Do you kill people?"

"I get him things he wants. Like a phoenix, so he can fuck her and bring peace to the clans."

Kasia stiffened but then stopped herself as logic prevailed. Rather than take offense at the snapped-off remark, she considered what hitting that sore spot meant to him. Had he killed people for the king and regretted it? Or was it turning Kasia over to Ladon that had him so grumpy?

If she'd been brave enough to let go, she would've held up her hands in surrender. "Okay, okay. You're touchy. I can take a hint."

Another snort and a wisp of smoke trailed back to her from his nostrils. *"If you could take a hint, you would've stopped talking a while ago."*

"If you weren't touchy, you would've answered my questions to begin with." She deliberately injected a carefree insouciance into her tone. "Such a fuss. When I become Ladon's queen, I'm going to find out anyway, you know." She tossed the words down between them, curious to see how he'd react.

This time when he rumbled his annoyance, she let him hear her chuckle.

"We're here." Based on the relief in his voice, she'd guess he was offering up a silent thanks for that.

Kasia leaned over to try to spot the car, then jerked upright, immediately regretting the action. "Is it safe?"

"I don't see anyone or smell anything that has me worried. We should be cautious, anyway."

"Okay."

"Hold on. I'm going to spiral down."

He tipped his wings, and she gripped his spike with both arms and legs, fighting the pull of the forces that seemed to want to rip her off his back.

Hold on? Clearly the man had never ridden one of his kind.

Brand landed in a clearing not far from where he'd left the Hemi Cuda. Conscious of his passenger, he lowered his belly to the ground and waited for Kasia to climb off. He didn't miss the slight tremble to her steps. Was that from holding on so tightly? Or fear? Or being close to him?

He didn't think she was afraid of anything. Look at how she'd handled both the wolves and the vampires.

Once she stood well back, he shifted, completely aware of her wide-eyed gaze as she watched.

"What?" The question slipped out of him when she didn't stop staring, even after he was done. That gaze affected him like a physical touch even from forty feet away.

She blinked, then seemed to shake herself out of her thoughts. With a shrug, she turned to walk through the brush. "Nothing. I just find the whole shifting thing interesting."

"This way, princess."

She paused, glanced at where he pointed, and dropped the branch she'd held out of her way before marching off in the right direction.

Brand stayed where he was, watching her walk away, and needing a moment to get his fucking act together. The mouth on that woman. She'd test the patience of a saint with all those probing questions and one-way conversation that somehow still managed to get him to share facts he'd rather not.

He'd been a total asshole to throw that mating thing at her, but she just wouldn't shut up. Brand had no intention of opening up to Kasia about the life he'd been forced into at an age when he should've been safe and protected. He didn't want her to know the things he'd done to survive, many of which still haunted him at night. Even though she shouldn't, Kasia still looked at him with trust, and a weird kind of faith, in her eyes.

A part of him—a squishy part he'd had no idea even existed until now—didn't want to give that up quite yet.

Though the comment about Ladon should've shut her down, it didn't. She'd got her own back, though, shoving the fact that she'd be queen, mated to another man, down his throat, and fire had burned up his gullet at that thought.

A violent reaction had roiled inside him, the animal part of who he was wanting to rage against her words. For a couple of seconds, he'd had to struggle for control rather than let the beast completely take over and fly them far away from clans and kings.

The conflicting needs to give her away or to keep her clashed within him—a dual reaction to the woman that was baffling at best, a growing cancer to his well-laid plans at worst.

"This doesn't seem like a great time to stop for a daydream, reptile boy." Her voice drifted through the brush. "Which way?"

How many euphemisms for "dragon" could she come up with? Gritting his teeth while at the same time stuffing a reluctant laugh back down deep before it could get out, Brand joined her in the woods and took the lead. He was going to have to do something about that mouth of hers.

Unfortunately, with the uncharacteristic reactions she was pulling from him, Brand suspected his solution might not work in his favor given his intention to get her to another man.

Without a word, he got them back to the car, got in, and turned the key.

Click.

The car battery didn't even make an effort to turn the engine over. Brand frowned and checked that he hadn't left the headlights or interior lights on all night to burn the thing out. No. All lights were off. At the same time, his radar kicked into high gear, his senses on alert for any sign out of the norm.

But, as from the air, he could detect no other creatures. He tried the key again.

Click.

"Do you think my hot-wiring job shorted out?" Kasia asked.

Before he could stop her, she dropped to lie across the seat and look beneath the dash, her hand inconveniently on his thigh. Brand gritted his teeth and lifted an arm to give her room. Having no other place to put it, he held his damn hand in the air like he was being robbed. Meanwhile her head and her hand were way too close to a part of his anatomy that sat up and took notice.

Unaware of the growing bulge in his pants, Kasia's muffled voice drifted up to him. "I don't see any problem. It should work fine."

She sat up. Did she pause as her eyes came level with his crotch? Yeah, she noticed, because she jerked the rest of the way up, trapping his free-floating hand between the small of her back and the leather seat of the car, her face inches from his.

Neither of them spoke, and neither seemed able to pull away. Kasia bit the corner of her lip, just the smallest flash of teeth dragging at the plump pink flesh. Brand held in a groan, even as part of him pushed to close the distance between them. He ignored that instinct.

He could hear her heart racing, her gaze both expectant and wary. "The hell with this," she muttered.

Before he could react, she closed the distance between their mouths, placing the softest, sweetest kiss against his lips. Had she tried for a hot, tongue-heavy kiss, he might've been able to push her away.

But this kiss…

Hell. She called to something deep inside him.

Mine, that voice whispered.

But she wasn't his. Even as she pressed up against him, she lay out of reach—tantalizing, tormenting, unattainable.

Kasia lingered over the kiss for an agonizing second before pulling back, but only barely. Their breath mingled as Brand scrambled for the control that was swiftly slipping from his grasp as need urged him to take.

Possess.

How could he fight both himself and the animal nature driving him?

"What was that for?" he grumbled. But he didn't move away. Couldn't.

A small shrug of one shoulder. "Maybe I like how you taste."

Holy fuck. Instantly images of her tasting every other part of his body exploded into his mind, and his dick did a fantastic impersonation of an iron rod, pressing painfully against the zip of his jeans.

"We can't." That's all he could manage. That infamous control of his was threadbare and ready to snap.

Kasia tipped her head, and her long hair brushed against his forearm. Her hot, glittering gaze lowered to his mouth. "You don't want to? Or you can't? There's a difference."

Brand sucked in a breath to answer her, then froze as another scent—both foreign and familiar— filtered through his senses.

Dammit. How could he have been so dumb? "Get out the car. Now!"

Before she could react, he shoved his door open and grabbed her by the wrist, dragging her across the seat and out behind him.

Fuck. Not again. He just couldn't get a break with this shit.

"What is it?" she asked as he moved to the back.

"Wolf shifters," he ground through clenched teeth. "Same ones as before."

With fingers usually nimble, even in a fight, he wasted precious seconds fiddling with the lock to the trunk. Finally, he got it open. He flipped open his handgun case, checked the mag, loaded a round in the chamber, and handed it to her. "Clear off. I'll hold them here."

"What? No—"

"You're not bait this time. I am. You can't be caught. That's what's important here. Got it? I'll try to follow, so don't shoot me." He gave her a lopsided smile.

She opened her mouth, but before she could argue, he pointed her in a direction away from the scent strongly invading his nose. "Run."

To her credit, though her face had paled, Kasia didn't ask any more questions, refuse to leave him, or go into hysterics. If anything, she steadied, her gaze clear and intent.

"Don't get killed," she offered. Then she turned in the direction he pointed and took off at a dead sprint.

Brand didn't follow, no matter that every atom in his being screamed at him to not let her out of his sight. However, the scent of wolf shifter—which to a dragon shifter comprised an unpleasant combo of rotting goat and dog breath—had grown so strong he was choking on it, which meant the wolf shifters were too close. Brand wouldn't have time to shift, and he needed to give her time to get away by keeping their focus on him.

He turned to grab another gun, but he'd taken too long getting her away. A massive rust-colored wolf with a white streak of fur over one eye shot out from the trees, jaws ready to snap around Brand's jugular and rip it out.

Brand got his arm up in time to take the brunt of the attack. Razor-sharp teeth sliced through flesh and blood. Brand let out a hiss of pain, pretty damn sure the thing struck bone.

Putting the extra strength that came with his dragon behind the move, Brand spun with the momentum of the wolf and flung his arm. The wolf released his grip, soared through the air, and slammed into a tree with a yelp.

But Brand didn't look to see if the thing limped away or not. A low growl had him focused on another wolf, this one pale gray, standing fifteen feet away, hackles raised and teeth bared in a near-silent snarl.

Blood dripped down Brand's wrist over his fisted hand in warm rivulets, the metallic scent thick on the breeze. The wolf in front of him twitched its nose, but it didn't move, holding its place. Why was it waiting?

"I don't have all fucking day," Brand sneered.

Sure that the two wolves couldn't be alone, he needed to draw out the others before they could circle him and coordinate a pack attack, or worse, go after Kasia.

Brand dropped into a forward roll, grabbing a knife from where it lay hidden in the ankle of his boot in a smooth, practiced motion. As he came up, he used the thrust of his forward trajectory to hurl the knife at the wolf. He didn't wait to see if his aim was true, pivoting immediately to face another mutt who charged at him from the right.

As the animal leaped for him, Brand whipped out his long tail and caught the creature midair. He hurled it away, slingshot style.

But he fucked up. He knew it the second a screaming pain ignited in his calf. He went down on one knee with another dark brown wolf ripping at his leg, snarling sounds spewing from it as it tore into him. Only Brand's thick jeans and boots kept it from doing worse damage.

Using his good leg, he smashed the heel of his steel-toed boot into the snout of the wolf gnawing at his leg with rabid intent. He had the satisfaction of seeing blood gush from the animal's nose as it dropped to the ground, out cold.

He needed to shift, to turn these bastards to ash, but he didn't have time.

Before he could get up, another mutt came at him from the back, going for his neck. Brand managed to evade the deadly jaws and drove his elbow back into the wolf's soft underbelly. It backed off with a hacking cough.

With one of the five wolves he knew of out of commission, the others, including the two injured ones, backed off to regroup, and Brand took advantage of their hesitation, running for the car as fast as dragging one bloody pulp of a leg allowed. If he could get to the shotgun in his trunk, that'd help him keep the shifters at bay. In their wolf forms, they couldn't operate weapons.

Brand didn't make it.

The dark gray wolf must've guessed his intention, as it busted out from behind a tree on the opposite side. The animal beat him to the car and jumped, landing on the trunk lid and closing it with a doom-filled *click*.

Fuckwad.

Brand skidded to a halt ten feet away, but a crunch of pine needles told him he was out of time, with more wolves behind him. He spun and charged the two wolves at his back, wrapping up the rust-colored one—who'd apparently survived being thrown into that tree—in a bear hug and driving it backward until it finally lost its footing and fell. He let it flop to the ground, landing on its back. Brand brought his boot down on the animal's hind leg with a satisfying crunch, and the thing howled in pain as the bone snapped.

Kasia'd told him to take out the red wolf. Fucking check that off the list.

Brand spun around, taking stock of his surroundings, but only the dark gray wolf remained in view. *Where the hell are the others?*

With no time to gloat over his minor victory, Brand faced off against the one wolf in sight and stopped cold, fear crawling up his spine at the sight behind his attacker. Every muscle tensed, and the instinct to protect shuddered through him, igniting the fire in his gut.

Kasia stood at the trunk of the car, fiddling with the lock.

Fuck.

With brutal effort, he forced his gaze back to the wolf, not wanting to alert it to her presence. She was supposed to be running, not helping him. And where were the other two wolves?

Fisting his hands, he took an aggressive stance, determined to keep the wolf focused on him. "You're not getting your hands on her."

The beast snorted. *"You're outnumbered, rogue."*

Brand showed no surprise that the wolf chose to speak to him through that mental link shifters all claimed when in their animal forms. Wolves usually chose to use that to coordinate their pack attacks, not to address their enemy. He didn't miss that rogue comment, either. Thanks to the lack of a brand on his hand, the wolves knew he was on his own rather than waiting for his clan to show up and help. He needed to get in the air. Now.

The telltale *shunk-shunk* of a shotgun being cocked, followed by another *click* as the safety was turned off, had the wolf swinging around, snarling and snapping.

Brand grinned. By her stance, feet set and the stock of the gun firmly in place at her shoulder, Kasia knew her way around the weapon. Damned if that woman wielding a gun to defend him wasn't sexy as hell.

Her gaze remained hard and steady on the animal standing between them. "If you don't want to die, I suggest you and your friends clear out. Now."

The wolf tensed, but not as though it were about to leap. Instead, it closed its mouth and cocked its head. Confused?

At the same time, the two missing wolves materialized from the woods. The light gray wolf, younger than the others now that Brand got a better look at him, though not juvenile, went to check its downed companion with the broken leg. The black wolf took up position beside their leader. There was no doubt in Brand's mind the dark gray wolf with white around his muzzle and eyes was the leader, not with the way all the others seemed to be taking their cues from him. While the black wolf's posturing remained aggressive—head lowered, muscles tensed and ready to leap, yellow eyes glaring—the dark gray wolf lifted his head and pricked his ears.

Brand, mid-process of creeping around them to reach Kasia's side, stopped and watched more closely. After a second, Kasia's eyes widened, and the barrel of the gun dropped a hair, just slightly, but enough that Brand caught it.

The wolf was talking to her with that telepathic link. What was it saying?

She shook her head no. Paused. Did it again. Another pause. "Then you know why I can't."

What the fuck did that mean? Can't what?

Another long moment, she readjusted her aim, raised the muzzle, and narrowed her gaze. "Like I said, if you don't want a round to the chest, leave."

The wolf's posture went defensive, the fur on his back raising and his fangs making another appearance. It turned its head to glare at Brand. *"This isn't over."*

Brand matched the creature glare for glare. "Didn't think it was."

Rather than shift into their more vulnerable human forms, the wolves dragged their injured partner off by the scruff at the back of his rust-colored neck. The brown wolf he'd knocked out, they managed to revive, though his gait reminded Brand of a drunk doing his best to walk straight and failing.

Brand kept his gaze trained in the direction they

disappeared, listening and scenting the air until he was sure they were gone. He stayed still, his injuries throbbing and needing to put on a calm front for Kasia, dictating that he had to hold still when what he wanted to do was stalk back and forth. Agitation poked at him like an itch that wouldn't quit.

Wolves didn't give up that easily. No way would five of them, even with two injured, have been that intimidated by a shotgun. So what the hell was going on?

Finally satisfied that they were alone, Brand turned to find an off-color and shaking Kasia staring off into the woods after the wolves, gun lowered but gripped in white hands. He tamped down on the rumble of concern trying to escape up his throat.

Ignoring the shafts of pain in his leg, he approached her slowly, like he would a wild animal, not wanting to spook her. "All right?"

Thankfully, she gave him a wan smile. "Now is probably a good time to tell you I'm a piss-poor shot."

"He was fifteen feet away. I think you could've hit him."

She huffed a laugh. "Maybe, but there was no way I could've held off all three. I'm great with mechanics, I even have a degree, but never did do well with weapons."

Gently, he retrieved the gun from her grasp. She gave it up almost as though she didn't notice. He pushed the safety and put the gun back in the trunk. Unfortunately, he didn't have time to dole out hugs.

"Can you fly?"

"Fly?" she repeated, a little too automaton for him.

He hooked his functioning hand around the back of her neck, his bloody arm still aching, and pulled her close, so he could look into her eyes, take up her total focus. "I need you here with me, ready to roll. Can you do that?"

Somehow, just touching her calmed the burning fury inside him, bringing him…not peace exactly…more a quiet stillness. How did she do that?

Kasia took a deep breath. Then another. Then nodded. "Yes. I'm ready."

He gave her a half smile. "Good girl."

Kasia rolled her eyes at his patronizing words, and Brand relaxed, knowing she was with him. He had his doubts that her bad aim was what had shaken her so badly, but no other explanation presented itself. Except that odd conversation with the lead wolf that he caught only her half of, and that wasn't much.

He'd ask her later. Right now, he had to get her out of here. He'd almost lost her today. Twice in less than an hour.

"Let's go," he urged.

VI

Angelika fidgeted, kicking up the rocks along the mostly dry stream bed where she waited. Mud coated the bottom of her white tennis shoes, probably ruined now. Not her best attire-related decision, but then again, she hadn't expected to come along. Especially when all the pack did was keep her far from the action, far from her sister.

What was the point of bringing her, anyway? She couldn't even help them if she wanted to, since she'd inherited no powers upon her mother's death. No, Angelika had remained annoyingly, frailly human. Had everything gone to Kasia? It would make sense, since Kasia was the oldest.

Sure, they needed her to identify Kasia, but she could do that when they brought her sister to their home. Not that she would've waited there with any less worry.

Jedd, whom she'd dubbed her personal bodyguard when he'd seemed to assign himself that role over the last year, stood off to the side in a position where he could watch her closely and wait for the others to return.

He stood tall, broad shoulders back like a soldier at attention, all senses tuned to their surroundings, ready for anything. His Spanish ancestry showed through in swarthy skin, dark hair and eyes, and the aura of a warrior. Even his hair screamed "no funny business," cut military close, a tad longer on top. She teased him by saying the way it stood straight up made him look like a fuzzy teddy bear that needed a cuddle.

He should be with them.

As the most skilled fighter, they needed him. Especially given what they were up against. She'd tried to make him go, but he'd insisted on staying with her. Guilt snuck in under the fear and worry for her sister. She didn't want any of the wolves who'd taken such good care of her dying or being injured protecting her and her sister.

Angelika tossed a rock at the slowly meandering water a few feet away, but the plop was unsatisfying.

"Where are they?" she muttered.

"Worry never solved anything," Jedd threw over his shoulder, not turning his gaze away from the woods.

Angelika lobbed another stone at him and snickered when she inadvertently struck her mark, the rock thudding as it struck the middle of his back.

Jedd still didn't turn. "Not funny."

Deliberately, Angelika lowered her voice. "Worry never solved anything," she huffed in her best well-meaning, but slightly superior Jedd impersonation.

He merely shook his head, though she suspected his shoulders shook with a silent chuckle.

"You know telling someone not to worry is like telling the sun not to shine, don't you?" she prodded. "It's just going to keep shining anyway, because that's what it does."

"You're saying that worry is your main function in life?" Heavy skepticism laced his naturally gruff tones.

"After five hundred years of running and preparing for the worst?" Another rock made a *ploop* as it dropped into the stream. "Yeah. I'd say that's a good way to put it."

Jedd opened his mouth and started to turn her way but stopped and returned his total focus to the woods beyond. "They're coming."

Before she could ask any questions, he lifted his head to sniff the air, then took off at a sprint, leaving her by the stream. A useless bystander, yet again.

Silence descended over the surrounding woods. The animals, insects, and breeze all stopping at once. Even the stream didn't make any noise, as the water moved so slowly. Angelika jumped to her feet and waited, eyes anxiously scanning the trees.

After what felt like an interminable wait, finally six men, including Jedd, appeared from the direction he'd run off. She desperately searched the woods behind them, but no one else appeared, and Angelika's heart dropped to the soles of her feet.

Then she absorbed the rest of the scene. Hunter and Rigel appeared unharmed. Cairn supported a nasty-looking broken nose with blood covering his front. But the more urgent issue was Rafe.

Jedd and Bleidd supported the stocky scrapper between them. He held his leg up, his face contorted in pain. Even from this distance, she could see that it didn't hang quite right.

Shit.

Someone had been seriously injured trying to rescue her sister. Angelika would never be able to repay these wolf shifters for their kindness at the rate she was going.

Shoving that thought aside, she rushed forward. This, at least, she could help with. Her mother had taught each of her daughters survival skills. They all learned how to shoot a gun, though Kasia never had liked them. They all learned how to tend a garden and milk a cow. They all learned to work computers and how to beat a lie detector. The lessons changed over time as the world and abilities needed to survive in it changed. In addition to those essential skills, each of them had learned other individual skills suited to her personal proclivities and temperaments.

For Angelika, that meant nursing school.

"What happened?" she asked as she rushed over to them.

"Bastard brought his boot down on my leg," Rafe grated through clenched teeth.

They lowered him to the ground, and the white streak in his rust-colored hair fell forward over one eye.

Angelika crouched beside him. "The dragon?" she asked, tossing a glance up at Bleidd's grim countenance.

He smoothed a hand over his thick beard, unconsciously smoothing the two gray stripes at the chin. "Yes."

Bleidd crossed his arms, feet set. "He was a tough son of a bitch. We didn't give him a chance to shift, but even in human form, he was strong."

"And he could shift only parts of his body. Did you see what he did to Hunter with that tail?" Rigel showed his relative youth in the eager awe included in that statement.

"It's a miracle he didn't skewer me with one of those wicked-looking spikes," Hunter muttered darkly.

Then Bleidd caught her expression and waved a hand at both Hunter and Rigel.

He needn't have bothered. Worry already had her in its grip. *A dragon who can hold off five warrior wolves in human form has my sister?*

Hunter grimaced. "Sorry."

Angelika rolled her eyes. "Don't worry about me."

She had so many questions that wanted to burst out, but Rafe and Cairn needed her help first. Angelika put aside her needs for the moment. She ran a practiced eye over the man panting in agony on the ground. She could detect no signs of blood or major trauma beyond the obvious. He was breathing okay and lucid.

"Any issues other than the leg?" she asked, just to be sure.

"No."

"Good." She glanced up at the others, who stood around them in a circle. "Anyone have a knife?"

Jedd, who'd remained silent up till now, placed one in her outstretched hand, metal handle first. She immediately went to work exposing the wound, cutting a straight rip up the inside seam of Rafe's black combat pants and peeling the rest back, folding it up around his knee, so she could get a better look.

The bone had not pierced the skin, though the off-kilter lump showed how it had snapped. "Hunter, help me stabilize the leg."

The jokester of the group dropped to his knees beside her. He wasn't laughing now.

"Hold him here, and here." She pointed but needn't have bothered, as Hunter was already reaching for those spots. She'd have to remember these guys, like the military, were trained to deal with injuries in the field.

"I'll find you something to use as a splint," Jedd said.

He loped off to search for long, straight branches. While he did that, Angelika got started on her neurovascular observations, checking for sensation changes and perfusion below the fracture site.

"Wiggle your toes for me?"

Rafe did so with a grunt of pain.

"Good. Looks like a clean break." She glanced up at Bleidd. "Doc should be able to reset the leg. What about his accelerated healing?"

"I've got that," Jedd said. He took out an instrument that looked like an EpiPen and stabbed it into Rafe's upper arm.

"What was that?" Angelika asked.

Jedd shrugged. "A scientist in America invented it a few decades ago. It'll slow his healing down for a few hours. Whatever it is has saved a lot of pain over the years."

Bleidd pulled out a cell phone. While he talked in a low rumble to whomever picked up, Angelika focused on splinting the leg using the solid sticks Jedd brought and belts each of the guys provided.

She squeezed Rafe's shoulder. "Don't put any weight on it. Got that?"

"Not likely to try," he managed to joke through white lips.

Angelika nodded, happy to see Rafe held onto his sense of humor, and levered to her feet.

"You're next," she said to Cairn.

He held up his hands, backing away. "No need, Nurse Ratched. I already set it myself."

Angelika grinned. "Come here, you big baby, or I'll think you're scared of a little girl."

Hunter and Rigel both laughed and earned themselves hard stares from Cairn's swiftly swelling eyes. He was going to sport a helluva set of shiners for the next day or so until his body healed.

"Wouldn't want to ruin that pretty face," Rafe tossed up from his prone position.

"All right," Cairn huffed.

He stepped closer and allowed Angelika to press gently on either side of his nose, gritting his teeth as she did so. She didn't have an otoscope on her, so she couldn't check the nasal cavity for obstruction, but he seemed to be breathing okay.

"I think your pretty face is safe." She winked. "But have Doc check you out to be sure."

"Yes, ma'am," he muttered.

"And get some ice on that face, too." She pivoted to run her gaze over Hunter and Rigel. "Any complaints from you two?"

Both of them shrugged. "He tossed us around a fair bit, but nothing we couldn't handle," Rigel said.

Angelika knew better than to push it. After a year living with the shifters, she'd come to learn they didn't appreciate coddling in any variation. So she nodded, then turned to Bleidd. "What about you?"

The leader of the wolf shifters shook his head.

She hadn't expected him to be injured, anyway. The man was too damn smart to come off the worst in most any encounter. Although a dragon shifter was a whole different kettle of whatever came in kettles these days.

"What's the plan to get him out of here?" she

asked, nodding at Rafe. "He shouldn't be jostled too much if we can help it."

"Helicopter."

She nodded. "I've done everything I can to set him until they get here."

"Thank you." Bleidd glanced at the men gathered around their pack brother, then took her by the arm and pulled her to the side.

Not that the action did much given their supernatural hearing. But the men knew better than to deliberately listen in. Another thing she'd learned about wolves since her mother sent her to them.

Showing up in the middle of a pack of wolf shifters had been a huge shock. Though Bleidd had not been surprised. Apparently, he'd agreed to help one of Serefina's daughters when the time came. Granted, he'd been a younger wolf at the time he'd made that agreement.

"We found your sister," he said. No fluff, no sparing her feelings.

Angelika blinked as she pulled herself out of nurse mode and back to the reason they were all here in the first place.

"The dragon didn't want to give her up?" Given Rafe's condition, that conclusion was an easy one to reach on her own.

Bleidd shook his head. "He didn't, but that's not why we don't have her."

Angelika frowned. "Why don't you have her, then?"

"She insisted on staying with him. Pointed a shotgun at my chest, actually." His lips tilted with an amusement marked with something more. Respect, unless Angelika missed her guess.

"Sounds like Kasia. Was she afraid of you?" Angelika had been worried about that happening.

Kasia could be a little too quick to trust sometimes, but even she probably knew better than to immediately fall in with wolf shifters who pinned her down in the middle of France. "I should've gone with you. If she'd seen me—"

He shook his head. "I told her you were with us."

Pain ebbed into her heart, but not from rejection. Kasia hadn't rejected her, Angelika had no concern about that. She knew her sister too well. "She didn't want to put me in danger. Is that it?"

He shrugged. "With the dragon listening to her side of it, we couldn't have a detailed conversation. But yes, I think that was part of it."

Angelika didn't miss the qualification. "What's the other part?"

"I got the impression that she is going with the dragon shifter willingly." Bleidd watched her with the steady gaze she'd come to expect from him. One that usually soothed her jumbled mess of emotions, especially after her mother's death. But not right now.

Hands on her hips, Angelika lowered her chin, staring at the leaf-covered ground but not seeing. "I guess we wait and watch, then."

"Yes." Bleidd gave her arm a squeeze and walked back over to the men, leaving her to her thoughts.

What are you doing, Kasia?

Taking Kasia's hand, Brand tried to lead her away but had to stop when she jerked on his arm.

"You're hurt!"

"I'll be fine." He brushed off her concern, more worried about getting their asses out of there double-quick.

Those wolves could come back.

But she stubbornly dug in her heels. Literally, her sneakers sank into the soft dirt. Kasia grabbed his injured arm, inspecting the wound closely, and *tsk*ing to herself as she did. Brand, meanwhile, held on to his patience, and his inappropriate reaction as her gentle touch stirred things inside him—things like a yearning he didn't fucking need.

He yanked his arm back, and she snapped her narrowed gaze up to his, mouth hanging open on a squeak of protest. He refused to feel like he'd kicked a puppy or squashed a butterfly. She was tougher than she let on.

"Dragons heal fast. The bleeding has already stopped," he said.

"Right." A wall of indifference slammed down over her eyes as she took a step back from him, putting a distance there that should make no difference to him. "Lead on."

Brand spun on his boot heel and marched off through the trees to the clearing where they'd landed earlier. The one where he'd shifted last night when he'd scouted the area for a place to stay while she slept peacefully in the car.

Those wolves could've taken her then.

He gritted his teeth and shoved aside the disturbing thought that did him no good now.

"Can you even fly?" She was laying on the sarcasm with a trowel and a heavy hand now.

"Worried about plummeting to your death?" he flung back.

"Yes."

Well, now he felt like a total dick. "I'll be fine." He repeated his earlier words.

"And the leg?"

She'd noticed that as well? He'd been doing his best not to limp.

She glanced down at where his jeans were plastered to his skin with blood, saliva, and probably knitting into the skin as it healed. That'd be painful as hell when he finally fixed it.

"I don't need a leg to fly." Mostly.

"No. Just to land." That smart mouth again. He could think of better uses for it.

"By the time we get to where we're going, it'll be strong enough for a landing." He hoped.

"Good, because I don't relish the thought of being smooshed like a bug under a dragon who rolls on top of me when his leg buckles." Her tone implied that she thought him a moron but that she was done arguing.

Fine by him.

Kasia stood to the side, and he took the hint and shifted. But he didn't take into consideration his emotional state—fury and a kick-to-the-balls type of worry for her had been roiling inside him like a festering cauldron since she cocked that shotgun. The second he was fully formed, Brand lost all control of the feral beast that lurked inside.

He lowered his head to fix her with a furious

gaze and snarled.

Color drained from her face, leaving the freckles across her nose and even her shoulders to stand out in stark relief. "Brand?" Her voice shook slightly.

Brand didn't move. Couldn't move.

Don't run. If she did, she'd trigger his predator instinct, not that he'd hurt her, but he'd chase and scare the shit out of her. Only he couldn't get the thought through the haze of anger holding him hostage.

Thankfully, she held her ground, watching him closely, muscles quivering. "Brand," she tried again.

Then she gasped as he lunged for her. Only he didn't pounce or bite. Instead, he snaked over to her and rubbed his snout against her side.

"Whoa!" she said as the animal he turned into—still out of control, still driven entirely by elemental needs—communicated his concern and anger through physical touch that she'd put herself in danger. Something Brand had held himself back from doing when in human form, able to apply logic.

"Um? What's going on?" Clearly having a massive, horned creature snuggle Kasia up was a disconcerting experience.

Only Brand still couldn't speak. Not while he was like this.

After a minute, she patted his snout. "Are you okay?"

Brand snorted. Was *he* okay? Gods, the woman scored a zero on self-preservation.

Brand did his best to wrest control over his body from his more instinctually driven self, but the dragon wasn't done. He wrapped around Kasia, lying on the ground and tucking his tail so that she was surrounded. Protected.

He should have protected her, not sent her off alone. The realization struck home like a hard punch to the chest. An assortment of reactions swirled inside him—shock, irritation, and not a small amount of guilt for not having watched after her the way he should have.

But mostly shock.

It almost seemed as though the man he was and the animal he became had split. Not that the dragon and he were separate creatures. Hell, they couldn't be separated. He *was* the dragon. But the animal side of his nature wanted to claim Kasia, while the logical man knew giving her to Ladon was a crucial step in the revenge he'd sought for so long. He needed that dragon clan in his corner.

The day he'd watched as Uther beheaded his mother and father and murdered his brothers, Brand had sworn he'd kill the man—somehow, someday. He'd been only ten at the time. Using a secret tunnel, he'd managed to escape. The second he'd left his family's mountain in Norway, the mark on his hand disappeared.

He'd gone to the Blue Clan, the closest to them, and begged asylum only to be turned away by King Thanatos. That's when he'd met a boy of similar age and together, they'd agreed: when they were old enough and strong enough, they'd take it all back and make those who'd betrayed them—belittled them and stolen their riches—pay.

Granted, things had taken a little longer than expected. Centuries longer.

Now here he stood with a phoenix. Was he going to have to fight his own needs, Kasia's insistence on making a choice, and the gut-level drives of the powerful creature locked inside him?

Suddenly, Kasia reached out, placing a hand against his snout, her touch warm, even through his scales. "I'm okay," she whispered. "I promise."

He lifted his head and gently nudged her, almost in thanks, even giving a low purring sound of satisfaction, despite Brand's struggle to stop himself.

They needed to get out of there. Those wolves could return at any second, or more vamps, or dragons, or any other damn thing. But the wolves were his primary concern right now. They'd already proved to be ingenious when it came to sneaking up on a dragon shifter. Not an easy thing to do. He still wanted to know how he'd missed them twice. Vampires were harder, their scent subtler, and they traveled in smaller groups. But wolves he should've known before he'd even gotten to the car. Finally, he managed to rein in the animal, allowing his more logical human nature to take charge again.

Or had her touch soothed the savageness inside him?

Fuck-a-doodle-doo. Nothing he could do about it right now.

But at least he had control. Brand uncurled his body from around her, then lowered himself to the ground so she could climb on.

"We need to go. Now."

Neither of them said anything until they were airborne and had gained altitude. As soon as he leveled off, she started with the questions he had no doubt were building up since the wolves left.

"I thought you said it was dangerous to fly right now. Other dragons," she called.

The wind snatched the words from her mouth, but his heightened hearing caught every sound. *"My car has been identified, and apparently everyone after you knows you're with me. Those damn wolves have caught us twice. The vamps followed us. We're not safe on the ground any more than we are in the air. But we need to clear out of this place faster than driving will allow."*

"So now what? We fly to Ladon's?"

"No. We make it to a place I know is…safe." *Mostly* safe, he amended in his head. But she didn't need to know that the best place he could think of to take them didn't come with that guarantee. "The guy there is someone I trust."

You trust someone?

Brand wasn't entirely sure he caught those words, they were so faint, like an echo bouncing off mountain walls. *"What?"*

"I didn't say anything."

Huh. Now he was hearing things? *"While we're on the subject of trust… Next time I tell you to run, you fucking run."*

"I did," she said.

Her innocent act didn't go over well, and Brand rumbled a frustrated growl before he could control it. *"Did your mother not teach you how to run in a straight line?"*

"I never did have a good sense of direction," came her dry retort.

He snorted again. *"Funny."*

She shifted her position on his back. From guilt, he hoped. "I wasn't going to outrun the two sentries they sent after me. I figured we had a better shot together than apart, so I circled back."

Grudgingly, he had to give her that point. *"I had hoped all the wolves would be too occupied with me."*

"Mother told me wolves go after the biggest threat as a pack, so I guess that was a solid assumption."

"Not this time." Brand was still kicking himself in the balls. First for missing the wolf shifters' presence, then for assuming they'd focus on him.

"Don't get too down on yourself."

Brand frowned. He'd kept his voice completely neutral. How had she guessed that he was blaming himself? Probably that overprotective act he'd put on a second ago.

"They must've thought I wasn't a threat, or they wouldn't have risked their people to follow me," she said.

"You sure proved them wrong." He gave a mental chuckle as the memory of her pointing that loaded shotgun at the lead wolf struck him again.

Kasia's husky chuckle sent a bolt of need through him. Fuck. How could he go from furious to torqued up that fast?

"Bluffed them, you mean," she said.

"The means don't make a difference, as long as you get results."

"I guess." She sat silently for a little while, blatantly thinking hard. Brand wished he could see her face, her posture, to figure out what she was worrying over.

"Do you think wolf shifters could protect someone like me?"

Brand rumbled a protest, his rejection of that idea instant and violent. The beast inside him still lurked too close to the surface, and that side considered Kasia his. His to protect. His to claim. Separating from her at Ladon's would be an exercise in willpower.

Brand took his time answering. *"Is that what the dark gray wolf told you?"*

"He offered me a choice. One that didn't involve mating."

Options.

Kasia had insisted options were always available, but Brand's entire life proved otherwise. Yet here she was, with options. Not good ones, but more than one.

"Dragons would be better."

"Duh."

He could just picture her rolling her eyes. *"You asked for my opinion."*

"Of wolves, not dragons. Don't compare them for a moment. How would wolves fare?"

Brand stayed silent as he considered her question. *"Dragons consider wolf shifters inferior, so most would tell you there's no way those mutts could protect you properly."*

"You said dragons, but what do *you* think?"

"I wasn't raised by dragons," Brand admitted. Not after his parents died, at least.

A bolt of unease stabbed through him. Other dragons knew he was rogue. The wolves did, too, apparently. There weren't many rogue dragons out there. Rogues didn't survive long—hunted by their own kind and not trusted by other species, which meant they had no place to go—but Kasia didn't know that, or so he assumed. So why was he admitting it now?

"What were you raised by?" she asked.

He should've known the question was coming. Brand remained silent.

"Fine. Don't tell me."

Her ire reminded him of a hissing kitten. She was kinda cute when riled.

"Do you think wolves are inferior?" she prodded.

He sighed. She wasn't giving this up. *"In many ways, yes. The wolves' strength lies in the pack and how it functions. They may exist in smaller groups, like the one we encountered today. But the entire nation of wolf shifters works together like a well-oiled machine. I'll admit they are relatively strong creatures individually, but there are bigger, stronger individual creatures…"*

"Like dragons?"

"And bears. Some of the bigger cats. But that's just shifters. I'm also thinking of creatures like vampires. A smaller pack will be able to do only so much against those bloodsuckers."

"I see."

"But you piss off one wolf, you piss off his pack. And if you come after a pack, you end up with the entire nation with their teeth at your throat. That's the biggest card they have to play in protecting a phoenix."

"That's a good card to play." She adjusted her hold on his spike.

"Yes."

"I hear a 'but.'"

"But wolves already live in peace, at least among themselves. My people have barely survived our infighting. We're not at war, technically, but the kings in charge have stripped their people of wealth, of livelihoods, of life sometimes, of mates. You name it. The colonies are dealing with uprisings already, and with Ladon's rebellion, the clans now face it directly. They haven't acknowledged it openly yet, but that's just a matter of time. You could end that, according to legend."

She let out a heavy sigh. "That's a heck of a thing to put on one person. So much responsibility." She paused. "But you said the kings were bad. *All* the kings?"

He could see where she was going with this. *"Ladon's different."* The only king Brand trusted.

"I see."

Damn. Again, he needed to see her face. That one sentence gave him no clue into her thoughts. Worse, what got to him about the conversation was his driving need to help her, not to manipulate her into the decision that benefited him.

When had he become someone who gave a shit about others? No one gave a shit about him. His survival depended on him, and him alone. And right now, his plans were directly tied to dropping her in Ladon's lap with a big fucking bow.

Screw helping her. He was too close to having the leverage he needed. *"I'm not risking my ass like this to give you to a bunch of mutts."*

She made a sound at the back of her throat that

sounded a lot like disgust. "Don't worry. I told the wolves I was going with you. If all you care about is what I can do for you with the king and what that earns you, then that's what you'll get."

VII

Kasia hung back as Brand confidently walked up to a questionable wooden structure situated, as far as she could tell when they'd circled it from air, on the side of the road in the middle of a Robin Hood–style forest in the low mountains between Manchester and the Scottish border. A bunch of mean-looking motorcycles, all leather and chrome, were parked outside in the gravel lot. No sign hung above the door, but she could hear music and the rumble of mostly male voices from inside.

She'd spent the entire flight here quiet, and honestly not paying much attention, because she'd been worrying about her sister the entire way. That wolf who'd talked to her…Bleidd, he said his name was…had given enough proof to know Angelika was with them. She still couldn't get over that. Their mother had sent Angelika to wolf shifters in the Pyrenees?

Gods, nothing made sense anymore. And now she was outside this dump with a man who thought a biker bar in the middle of nowhere was a good place for a pit stop.

"*This* is where you think we'll be safe for the night?"

Maybe he'd smacked his head during that stumble he took on landing when his still-healing leg gave out, though he did manage to keep from realizing her bug-squishing scenario.

Brand paused and turned back to face her.

Seeing her staring with open doubt at the building, he glanced over his shoulder, as if reassessing it. "It'll be fine."

"And saying so makes this place safe how?"

He ignored her and held out his hand. "Come on."

She refused to budge. "This is a biker bar, if I'm not mistaken?"

"Your point?" he asked.

"I've heard they can be pretty rough places." Granted, she'd been in plenty of rough places much of her life, but then she'd had her mother to watch over her and figure things out.

He set his feet and crossed his arms, staring her down. "I'm a dragon, and you can light on fire," he pointed out in low tones, like someone might hear. "Trust me."

Her visions told her that her faith in him would not be misplaced, and so far, everything he'd done was about keeping her safe, proving her point, even if he refused to admit it. But walking into this place, looking for all intents like a yuppie out for a stroll after not showering for two straight days, sounded like one of the dumber ideas in the history of her life. Not to mention, her red hair tended to act like a beacon to every asshole who wanted to see if she was a true ginger.

Somehow, she'd bet Brand had never dealt with that particular problem, but living in out-of-the-way shitholes with her mom and sisters on and off for centuries, Kasia definitely had. In most of those places, the good, down-to-earth folks of the world balanced out the asshole contingency. But not always. What were the odds of that happening here?

She sighed and closed the distance between them, pausing to stab him in the chest with her finger. "I hope this person you trust is a friend."

He snagged her wrist before she could pull back, and everything inside Kasia slowed and focused on that touch, hot against her skin.

"What?" Her brain had zapped out on her, short-circuited by the physical contact, and now her damn nipples were springing to buzzing life.

"I wouldn't call him a friend, exactly," Brand said.

Which meant what? More than a friend? Or not a friend at all? Did the man consider anyone a friend? No one could be that much of a loner. Sad to think of him that isolated. At least she'd had her sisters.

Not your problem. How many times would she have to tell herself that? This man was nothing more than a bodyguard transporting her to the UK.

"He basically raised me after my parents were killed. I'd holed up in the mountains, and he found me there."

She froze. What did one say to that? She suspected Brand would be uncomfortable with questions or sympathy. Kasia shook her head. "Even so, he's going down if one of those bikers so much as breathes in my direction."

She snatched her arm back, breaking his hold, and marched past him.

"Everybody has to breathe," he called after her.

Shoving through the rickety door that wobbled like it was about to come off the hinges, Kasia blinked as her eyes adjusted from the bright sunlight outside to the dim lighting indoors. Then she blinked some more, because she couldn't be seeing this.

"No. Freaking. Way," she murmured.

The bar on the inside was *nothing* like the dilapidated shack it showed the world on the outside. Inside was all polished chrome, freshly painted orange walls, top-of-the-line pool tables, and a mahogany bar, beautifully oiled and cared for. Even the mirror behind the bar gleamed, reflecting her own astonishment. It smelled nice in here, too—an underlying scent of cleaners below a stomach-growl-inducing waft of food. Not greasy bar food, either.

Kasia sniffed the air appreciatively. Garlic. Did they serve Italian food here?

This place was…classy.

"You have no idea," Brand muttered at her back as he stepped inside. "If anyone asks, you're a dragon shifter, like me."

"What?"

But he didn't answer, prodding her around the corner of the long narrow bar, which was empty of people sitting at the stools, and into the larger room beyond. Again, she slammed to a halt and stared, then scowled up at Brand.

What the hell was he thinking, bringing her to a place like this?

She'd been expecting tough customers—all tatted up and with a hardness that couldn't be faked. Instead, lounging around the matching tables and barstools, and some playing pool, was the strangest assortment of supernaturals gathered in one place that she'd ever come across.

At first glance, she wasn't able to identify all

the creatures. Most were in some sort of human or humanoid form. She bet a few types of shifters were in the mix, but no way could she miss the elf, almost beautiful with his pale skin and hair, delicate features, and pointy ears. Nor could she look past the man who had to be some kind of spider species. The extra arms, or legs, or whatever, sticking out of his back was a creepy giveaway. A vampire's eyes glowed red as she took in the scene, and she had to stop herself from stepping back. One encounter had been enough. And, of course, there was the massive creature in the back corner.

Was that a…? No way. So Bigfoot *did* exist.

Most of them wore matching leather jackets or vests sporting one word on the back in an orange that matched the walls. SLINGERS. As in gunslingers? With the collective powers in this room, who needed guns?

One by one, they stopped what they were doing to turn their attention to the man who could easily fit among them and the woman who stuck out like a cowlick that just wouldn't be tamed.

Kasia gave in and stepped back, closer to Brand, bumping up against his solid chest and staying there. Safe? Like hell. Every one of these guys would probably pay good money for her. Had Brand brought her here to sell her to the highest bidder? If not, she needed to worry that he'd lost his mind.

All she needed was one night of sleep and a shower without being attacked or struck down by a vision. Too much to ask?

One of the men, a djinn maybe, got up from the table where he sat with three others and moved toward them slowly. His bald head reflected the low lights of the bar, and a thick black beard obscured most of his face, making it difficult to tell if he was about to smile or start throwing punches.

The guy was massive, at least six foot three and heavy with it. Tossing a glance at Brand, Kasia consoled herself with the fact that he was taller, and his bulk involved impressive muscles rather than layers of fat. He hooked an arm around her waist and shoved her behind him so that he stood between her and Baldy. His arm muscles flexed, the bottom half of his tattoo moving with it, the pine trees along his forearm appearing to dance in the wind as his hands formed into fists at his sides.

"I think you're in the wrong place," Baldy said. "Clear out."

Kasia hid an inappropriately timed giggle probably brought on by nerves. But seriously, what other bar did he think they'd mistaken this one for? It wasn't exactly located in a thriving metropolis. The situation wasn't at all funny, but hadn't she watched scenes like this in every movie about rough-and-tumble bars? Only this one was more like on a drug trip, given the clientele.

"We're here to see Hershel," Brand said calmly. He was laying on a thick Manchester accent now, dropping the h's and sounding more like their new friend. She had to try not to do a double take at the sudden change. Did he do that everywhere? More importantly, why? Most paranormals didn't sport a definable accent. Too many years, too many places they'd lived.

The man was a damn enigma.

Baldy paused, giving Brand a more thorough inspection before moving on to her, what he could see of her behind her bodyguard, who kept moving to block her from view even when she moved to peek around him. The speculative light in Baldy's eyes did nothing for the butterflies throwing a party in her stomach.

"Who's asking?" Baldy demanded.

"Tell him Brand is here."

The biker sneered. "Brand? No last name?"

"Kind of like Cher," Kasia muttered behind Brand's back, soft enough that the other man couldn't hear.

But Brand caught it, she could tell by the way his shoulders stiffened.

He said nothing to Baldy, though, nor did his posture alter an iota, but he was laughing inside, she just knew it. She had serious doubts that he experienced the same nervous laughter she was prone to, which meant she'd made him laugh. Genuine amusement. A small glow of triumph, completely ridiculous at this moment, lit inside her.

Like predators sensing blood in the water, several more men got up and joined their bald compatriot facing off against them. Including the vampire who kept sniffing the air. "Oy. Problem, Oz?"

Oh, please tell me his name is Ozzie, because that would be adorable. Kasia paused that thought and gave herself a mental shake. Two days of nonstop action and not a ton of sleep had apparently muddled her brain.

She glanced down. Or maybe the fact that Brand hadn't let go of her arm was screwing with her ability to reason. What the hell was wrong with her? How could she let such a simple touch affect her so strongly?

"What did I say about throwing strangers out of *my place*?" The question was barked from behind the bar in a voice belonging to a man who must smoke a lot of cigarettes.

Strangers didn't run away screaming from here the second they got a closer look at the clientele?

Immediately Ozzie's shoulders slumped. "Sorry, Hersh. This feller's here to see you."

"I already know that, dumb-ass. He's a friend."

At that revelation, the vampire sucked his fangs back in with a scowl and skulked away. If anything, Ozzie's shoulders drooped even more, and Kasia suddenly wanted to give the guy a hug. He was only protecting his…errrr…people, after all.

"He didn't know us," Kasia offered.

Baldy flashed her an inscrutable look. Grateful? Irritated? That beard really hid a lot.

Brand's shoulders eased a fraction, and the pine trees of his tattoo stood back up straight as he unclenched his hands and let her go. "Yeah. S'all right," Brand added, still in fake accent mode.

"Don't do it again," came that gruff voice. Only Kasia couldn't see the owner, because Brand was in her way.

"Right, boss," Ozzie said. He nodded in Kasia's direction, and the three men wandered back to their seats.

Curious who, or what, considered Brand a friend, Kasia leaned around her overprotective shifter's broad form to find a man standing there, whom she took an instant liking to.

Totally unexpected, too.

Tall and lanky, the older gentleman had salt-and-pepper hair—more salt than pepper—which he kept short, and a thick handlebar mustache. All that white hair stood out against his dark, leathery skin, which spoke of countless hours in the sun, probably on a bike. Bright blue eyes, undimmed by time, twinkled, and crinkles that she could tell came from smiles easily given fanned out from the corners.

"He looks nice," she couldn't resist murmuring to Brand under her breath.

"Only when he wants to be."

If he kept this lot under control, she imagined that had to be true. Kasia had no doubts Hershel could handle himself in a fight. The guy was basically bone and muscle. He prowled around the end of the bar, moving in a way that reminded her of predatory animals, and held out a hand to Brand. The two did that manly shake-while-slapping-the-back thing that men did when they didn't want to seem girly with their hug technique.

"What brings you here?" Hershel asked as he stepped back, mustache twitching.

"We could use a place to stay for a night," Brand said. No smiles from him, though. Not even for an old…acquaintance…or whatever he considered this man to be.

Hershel glanced down at her and gave her the kindest smile she'd encountered in a long while. "You look like trouble."

Kasia grinned back and held out a hand to shake. "Kasia Amon."

Brand turned his head her way sharply enough that the action snagged her attention. Right. She hadn't given him her last name in the hospital. But that was when she thought he didn't know she was a phoenix. No need to hide it now—the proverbial cat had scrambled out of the bag days ago.

Hershel shook her hand. "American?"

She shrugged. "In a roundabout way." Hell, she'd been one of the first people to travel there after the Europeans discovered it existed. She had even lived with the land's indigenous people on a few occasions, but that had been over a hundred and fifty years after her birth.

"We all come from several somewheres," Hershel agreed. White eyebrows winged up as he assessed Brand. "Your mate?"

Brand shook his head.

Hershel glanced between them, as if trying to size up the relationship going on there.

Good luck, buddy. Let me know if you figure it out, 'cause I sure as hell can't.

"You runnin' from something?" came the next probing question.

"A lot of somethings," Brand confirmed.

"Bad?"

"I wouldn't bring her here otherwise." Brand didn't apologize, but somehow the sentiment was implied.

Hershel rested his hands on his hips, his glance going behind her to the strange assortment of bikers filling the bar. Then he gave a small nod. "They could use some action, I'm thinking."

Finally, Brand's lips tipped in the barest of smiles.

"I hope it won't come to that." He left the "but it might" hanging silently in the air between them.

Kasia's opinion of her reluctant rescuer crept up a notch or two.

He'd brought them here on purpose, to a place housing supernatural creatures who could fend for themselves if things turned ugly, but who, apparently, wouldn't touch her because of Hershel. Not instant victims, like humans would be, or immediate threats, thanks to their host.

He might not like to think so, but Brand Astarot was a decent man under all that tough guy bullshit.

"In that case, welcome to my five-star hotel, Kasia." Hershel offered her his arm.

After a quick glance at Brand's passive face, she accepted, tucking her hand in the crook of Hershel's elbow.

He tugged her along the length of the bar, through swinging doors into the kitchen, Brand following more slowly. "I'm going to take a quick shower, then I'll meet you in the kitchen," he said.

Hershel nodded an acknowledgment and turned to Kasia. "You hungry?"

"Starved." She hummed in appreciation as stronger scents of garlic and tomato swirled around her.

When was the last time she'd had anything to eat, anyway? On the plane? And Brand had to be worse off, because he'd flown them for hours across the English Channel and up to northern England, injured and on an empty stomach. How was the man still standing?

Food. Shower. Sleep. In that order.

Hershel settled her at what appeared to be his

personal desk, tucked back in a private office off the kitchen. Brand showed up while she waited, smelling of soap and fire, his hair damp from his shower. Obviously, he knew the place well enough to be aware of where to shower and change.

Shortly after, Hershel brought them steaming plates of hardy noodles covered in marinara and juicy meatballs as big as her fists, accompanied by a salad with all the trimmings and garlic bread. The food claimed her immediate attention.

After the first bite, she groaned. "You should be doing this in some big city, Hershel. This is fantastic."

"Nah." He waved away her comment, though his blue eyes twinkled. "Too many people."

Kasia didn't even try to be ladylike, shoveling the food in as fast as she could scoop and chew. Brand did the same. Their host waited in silence, obviously recognizing starving people when he saw them.

"I like a woman with an appetite," Hershel teased after she'd devoured everything but the plate and silverware and asked for seconds.

"Really?" Kasia mumbled around a mouthful of meatball. "I think men who eat are gross." She winked.

Brand choked on his drink.

"Was that…a laugh?" she asked.

He ignored her, but Hershel snorted, those crinkles around his eyes deepening. "She's got you pegged, son," he said to Brand, who ignored him as well.

"So, what's the story?" Hershel asked as they both slowed in their eating frenzy.

Kasia wiped her mouth with a napkin as she sat back and shared a long look with Brand, one she was strangely reluctant to break. Aware of Hershel waiting for an answer, she raised her eyebrows, deferring to the shifter. She had no idea what he wanted shared with this man.

For his part, Brand also leaned back in his seat, seemingly at ease. "Bad people are after Kasia. I'm trying to get her to someone who can help."

Hershel's thick mustache twitched. "Forthcoming as always."

Brand hitched a shoulder. "Forthcoming can get you killed."

"You brought the fight to my door," Hershel pointed out.

"Can't deny that fact," Kasia said around another bite of bread.

She glanced up to find Brand watching her with an indecipherable look that turned the food in her mouth to dust. She had to swallow hard.

"What?" she said. "He has a point."

Brand stretched out his long legs, tipping his chair back. "If I did my job right, the only thing at his door will be us. For the night. Then we're gone."

"*Did* you do your job right?" Hershel asked. His voice jolted even her—a mix of no-nonsense and "you better fucking answer."

Kasia did a double take between the two men. Brand didn't seem offended, but it was hard to tell with that indifferent expression of his.

"I did my job right," he said. "But if your people haven't heard the rumors of what she is yet, they will."

Again, Kasia glanced between them. Waited.

Nothing happened except a showdown staring match.

Another glance. Waited again.

As the staring continued, she gave up. "As fascinating as this conversation is, I could use a shower and bed." She pushed to her feet, her chair scraping across the tiled floor with a squeal of protest.

Hershel also got to his. "I'll show you to your room. Brand?"

The two held another one of those silent conversations. Eventually, Brand shook his head. "I'm going to have more to eat first."

He didn't look her way, and Kasia tried not to let herself feel oddly cut off from him. Without comment, she followed Hershel out of the office. Only she didn't like it, walking away from Brand. Strange how fast his mere presence had become her new normal.

"So how do you know Brand?" she asked as Hershel led her out the back of the building. She gave her head a mental shake as the scenery changed from fancy, well-stocked kitchen into a shack with worn-out wood siding, tires and barrels and other junk strewn about the grounds, and the stench of the large garbage bin permeating the air—the structural equivalent of Clark Kent versus his less-mild-mannered alter ego, Superman.

Actually, Clark Kent was in much better shape than the dilapidated outside of Hershel's bar.

"He didn't tell you?" Hershel asked.

"He said you raised him."

He huffed a laugh. "That kid practically raised himself. I just gave him a place to do it."

"Why?"

"You'll have to take that up with Brand." His long loping strides ate up the ground, and she hustled to keep up.

She cast him a sidelong glance. "You're not going to tell me anything, are you?"

"Nope. That's Brand's story to tell." He led her through a copse of tall trees, behind which stood an old cottage of gray stone with a steeply angled thatched roof, similarly banged up in appearance on the outside as the bar.

She sighed her disappointment that he wouldn't be a source of information, but relented. "I can respect that."

He flipped open a panel beside the door that had been hidden under a layer of old wood. As she watched with blatant curiosity, he punched in a code, and the door lock clicked with a soft snick.

"Your code is 0717," he said.

The old house had serious security. "Should I be concerned about all this?" She waved at the panel.

"Not really. Comes with the lifestyle." Hershel held open the door and ushered her inside.

This time, at least, she was prepared for the contrast. As opposed to the rickety front porch that protested with each step, the interior was a homey hideaway. Decorated in rustic mountain colors of browns, greens, and blues, with lots of natural wood, exposed beams, and comfy leather seating, it rivaled most luxury mountain cabins she'd seen in glossy magazine pictures.

"Okay. You have to tell me… Why the discrepancy between outside and inside?"

Hershel grinned. "Lots of reasons."

"Such as?"

"Keeps outsiders away. Thieves and looters are less likely to bother. Doesn't raise government suspicions more than any other pub. Taxes…"

"Taxes?"

He snorted. "You think I'm giving more than a token cent to those assholes in government? The key is an appearance of compliance."

Kasia shook her head, but said nothing. Her mother had insisted on paying taxes in order to keep *off* government radar. Centuries of life meant she'd met Hershel's attitude—to various empires, principalities, classes, and governments—with surprising frequency. What was that quote about the definition of insanity meaning repeating history with an expectation of different results? Not that dragons seemed to learn any faster than humans.

"And you're not afraid of the Slingers…doing stuff?"

Hershel glowered. "They wouldn't dare. I provide too much for them to screw it up—a place to meet, hide, and sleep, storage, safety, food—"

"They stay in your house?" She glanced around, trying to figure out what she'd missed. The structure hadn't appeared all that large from the outside.

"Nervous?" He grinned.

"A little. I have my virtue to consider." She gave a little wiggle.

He chuckled. "Not to worry. They stay in a building farther to the south."

"Quite a setup you have here." She didn't fail to notice the state-of-the-art media panel by the door, either, a bigger version of the one on the outside. She nodded at it. "What's that for?"

"Security."

Ha! So he wasn't as confident as he'd sounded

about the Slingers invading his space.

"For non-club-member contingencies," he added.

Kasia blinked, then looked closer at his face. Who was this guy?

"Because of Brand?" she asked.

"Because of a lot of reasons." He stepped around her. "Your room is this way."

In other words, question and answer time was over.

He led her down a short hall to a small guest bedroom with windows that faced the back of the house. An antique brass bed with a navy and white striped quilt graced the room. The only other furniture was a vintage bedside table in a rose-colored wood.

"You'll have to bunk up with Brand, I'm afraid."

Kasia sighed and shrugged, even as a small part of her perked up at the thought, and another part protested. All night in a bed with Brand… But she shoved that thought away with both hands. Brand wasn't interested. "I doubt he'd let me out of his sight overnight, anyway."

Hershel smoothed a hand over his thick mustache. "You in that much trouble?"

"Yes. But actually, last time he left me alone, I stole his car and left him high and dry."

Hershel stared at her for a long moment, then tossed his head back and roared with laughter. "Where was this?"

No harm in sharing. "Wyoming."

"The Hemi Cuda?" he finally calmed enough to ask, wiping tears from his eyes.

She grimaced, but nodded.

"Now *that* I would've loved to see." Hershel

chuckled some more.

Kasia grinned back. "He was pretty pissed."

"I don't doubt it. It's rare for someone to get the better of him." Hershel gave a few more chuckles before he sobered. "You're not trying to get away from him now, though."

"No. I guess you could say our goals aligned. He's taking me somewhere…safe. Or so he says. I'll make up my mind when I get there."

Hershel gave a slow nod. Then pointed to one of the two doors on the right-facing wall of the bedroom. "You said shower. Your bathroom is through there. Plenty of towels and soap and stuff for you to use."

A man with hospitality skills, now there was a rare find. "Thanks."

"My pleasure." She could just picture him tipping a cowboy hat, he gave off such an old cowboy vibe with his countenance and demeanor, despite living in Northern England.

He turned to go, but paused. "A word of warning?"

Kasia raised her eyebrows and waited.

"Brand's been a loner since he was a kid, by necessity. He's a tough man because he's had to be. A true rogue."

Everything inside Kasia paused, as she tried to suss out his meaning. He was saying something important, but what? "Why are you telling me this?"

"Not to frighten you. I would trust Brand with my life."

"But?" There was definitely a but in there.

"Not but. More like unless. I'd trust him with my life…*unless* a decision came down to my life or his."

VIII

"I'm surprised you told her I raised you."

Brand ignored Hershel's dry comment and took a swig of beer. He'd poured one for himself at the bar before sitting on one of the stools, back to the room, doing his best to give off "leave me the fuck alone" vibes. Because right now all he could picture was Kasia naked and wet in that shower she'd said she wanted to take, and the rock-hard state of his dick had him pissed as hell. He needed to kill this thing he had for her.

Fast.

"That's quite a woman you've got there," Hershel said next.

Brand lowered his pint of beer as Hershel pulled up the stool beside him.

"I borrowed your first aid kit," Brand said. "Hope that's okay."

He'd needed to pull the jeans out of his skin, the material having knitted into the wound as it healed while he flew, part of the trouble with his shift including clothing and the way it absorbed into his dragon form. That had opened up the bleeding again, but at least he'd be recovered in an hour or two.

Hershel glanced at his leg and shrugged. "I've seen worse from you."

Brand grunted.

"So…that's quite a woman you've got there," Hershel repeated. Only this time, he slapped him on the back to make his point.

Brand contained a sigh. Hershel was in his dog-with-a-bone mode, which meant he wouldn't let this go. "She's definitely something," Brand muttered.

"What's the story there?"

Brand glanced in the mirror over the bar, checking to see if anyone was paying a little too much attention. Most of them had enhanced hearing.

Hershel caught the glance. "I can vouch for them."

"Just a bunch of easygoing murderers and thugs?"

Hershel huffed a laugh. "Something like that."

Brand tipped his beer at his friend. "My kind of people."

The problem was, Brand's kind of people were the type who'd steal a phoenix the second her protector's back was turned.

Rather than get sidetracked, Hershel took a swig of his own beer and waited for Brand to answer his earlier question.

"She's…special."

Thick white eyebrows lifted. "No shit, Sherlock. How special are we talking?"

Another glance in the mirror and he lowered his voice. "A fire creature everyone wants a piece of, special."

Brand waited while Hershel mentally reviewed what Kasia could be. When the old man's blue eyes narrowed, Brand knew he'd figured it out.

"Nah," Hershel denied immediately.

"Yes."

"After all this time?"

"Seems so. I've seen her in action." Hell, he'd felt

her in action. His cock throbbed at the memory.

"I see." Hershel combed his fingers through his mustache, thinking. "Are you taking her to Ladon?"

He didn't need to answer. Hershel always was rattlesnake quick on the uptake.

"What the fuck are you doing, son?"

Brand curled his hands around his pint glass. "I'm taking her to people who can protect her the best."

Hershel's eyes narrowed. "You're still after Uther, huh?"

Dammit. He'd never been able to keep anything from the old man. "Yeah."

"And you're sure about her being protected there?"

Hershel gave him a hard stare, and Brand sighed. "What do you want me to say?"

"You're going to give her over to the kind of people who killed your family, hunted you from childhood, and used you when it turned out you had a specific set of skills that could benefit them. Those people?"

"You mean *my* people? I may be rogue, but I'm still a dragon shifter." Brand shook his head. "And Ladon may be brutal, but I've known him a long time, long before he took the throne. His plan for his clan is solid. Besides, no one can protect her like dragons can, given what she is."

Despite the errant schoolboy effect Hershel's questions were having on him, Brand was absolutely sure of that. Wolf shifters might come close, as he'd admitted to Kasia, but they wouldn't be able to deal with her fire, and they still weren't stronger than dragons. Not even the entire nation combined. Not against a full clan of dragon shifters.

He had no doubt Uther, or especially Pytheios, would bring an arsenal of them to capture Kasia.

His confidence in his strategy must've communicated itself to the old man, because Hershel backed off, holding up both hands in surrender. "You'd know better."

Damn straight, he would. Hershel may be a lot of things, but a dragon shifter wasn't one.

"So, what's your plan? I hope it's better than just dumping her there."

Maybe Hershel *hadn't* given up. "It depends on what Ladon needs me to do. I promised I'd stay until she decided for herself if it was the best place for her to be."

"And if she decides it's not?"

Brand shrugged. "I'm not worried. Kasia is a smart woman with strong survival instincts."

Like me.

He flicked aside that thought, not wanting to think of how he and she were alike.

"And she's agreed to all this?"

"Yes."

"With no concerns that might cause you problems?" Doubt filled every syllable of Hershel's question.

Just an inherent dislike and distrust of dragons, a small voice reminded him. When had he developed a conscience?

Worse, that same inner voice was pushing him to go find Kasia now. He didn't like her out of his sight. He gave the imaginary cricket on his shoulder an imaginary flick with his fingers. A conscience was not advisable to develop, given his line of work and life situation, and definitely not right now.

Hershel finished his beer and took the glass around the counter to clean it up. "One last word of advice?"

Brand waved him on when he didn't immediately proceed.

"I couldn't miss the way you look at her."

Denial slammed through him, and he pushed to his feet. "I don't look at her any way other than as a paycheck."

Hershel ignored him as he wiped down the counter. "I've seen need, son, and the way you look at her…" He whistled.

"What's your point?" Brand snapped.

Hershel paused in his cleaning and stared Brand dead in the eyes. "When you need a woman at that level, you have only two options."

"Which are?"

He held up a finger. "Fuck her and get her out of your system."

Brand's already hard dick twitched at the thought, eager to take what was behind door number one. Bad idea. "What's option two?"

Hershel held up a second finger. "Keep your hands off and get away from her as soon as you can."

Option two didn't sound any better than option one. A growl escaped Brand, one he clamped down on after the first noise. Where the hell had his legendary iron control disappeared to? That noise shouldn't have escaped at all. Subtly challenging a bunch of paranormal bikers who were already edgy sons of bitches was a bad idea. He should know. He'd done it before, on occasion.

"I was hoping you'd have some sage, old-man advice that was better than what I'd already come up with on my own."

Hershel snorted again. "Whoever called me sage?"

"True." Brand tipped back his glass and drained the last of his beer. He couldn't leave her unguarded another second, not with this lot around. Not even in that fortress that posed as a house. "Is she in my room?" he asked.

"Yeah. I figured you'd want to keep an eye on her."

"You figured right." Brand headed for the kitchen door.

"So what are you going to do?"

Hershel's question stopped him. Brand glanced over his shoulder. The other man was talking about those options that weren't really options.

Brand rubbed a tired hand around the back of his neck. "Hell if I know."

With that clearheaded thought, Brand stalked across to Hershel's house and punched in his own personal code to let himself inside. He paused, taking in some of the more recent changes, like the new leather couch in the family room, then made his way back to the bedrooms and knocked softly at his door.

"You decent?" he called, not wanting to wake her up if she was already sleeping.

No answer.

Frowning, Brand cracked the door and peeked

inside. Kasia's clothes littered the floor, but she was nowhere to be seen, and the bed remained undisturbed.

"Kasia?" He stepped inside and caught the faint hiss of running water.

Brand closed his eyes against a bombardment of images—her water-slicked skin, that red-gold hair hanging down her back, that impossibly lovely face tipped up to the spray. Brand clenched his fists against the driving urge to go in there and take her, sink into that glorious body, plunder those sassy lips. Over and over and...

"Fuck," he muttered. Through sheer force of will, he turned away, planning to return to the bar and get drunk, maybe even sleep it off in the barracks with the club. She'd be safe enough with Hershel here.

A small, feminine sob reached his ears through the door. *"Oh."*

Was she hurt? Was someone else in there with her?

On blind instinct—a need to protect her that he could no longer deny lived in his very bones— Brand spun on his heel and burst through the bathroom door, only to skid to a halt. Kasia stood in the shower, alone, the only thing separating her from him the glass door, every inch of her naked, wet...and perfect. Her hand between her legs was busy doing things to her body that he'd been craving since the first moment he'd held her at the clinic in Cheyenne.

And she didn't stop. He dragged his gaze from her hand, up her body, pausing at pink-tipped breasts thrust out, begging to be kissed and sucked and licked, to her face. Those chilly blue eyes were open, her gaze locked on his as she continued to try to pull an orgasm from her straining flesh. The bold heat of that gaze licked at his skin.

Instinct to claim warred with everything else inside him, ripping him apart as he struggled with the greater objective to take her to Ladon. Blood pumped through his body, pulsing through his now throbbing cock.

Still, he gathered enough of his shredded will to walk away, making it out of the bathroom and halfway to the bedroom door before her voice stopped him.

"Brand." The way her husky tones wrapped around his name had him biting back a groan. He tipped his head back, picturing that mouth, those lips, wrapped around his aching cock.

"Sorry about that," he forced between stiff lips. "I'll give you some privacy to…finish up."

But in his mind, he could still *see* her doing that to her body, reaching for pleasure, a pleasure he wanted to give her. Deliberately, he kept his back to her.

"I'd rather *you* finish up for me."

His lungs seized, deciding oxygen was of secondary importance. Did she just say…?

Slowly he turned to find her standing only a few feet away, her campfire scent now blended with the clean tang of soap, and a muskier fragrance that told him she was still slick and wet with desire. With need.

Pale blue eyes steady, she watched him closely

from beneath her lashes.

"We can't," he husked, the words dragged out of his throat.

"Who says?" With a flick of her wrist she dropped the towel she'd wrapped around her dripping wet body.

"You're about to be another man's."

She shrugged. "Maybe. If I choose him. But I'm not another man's yet, and right now I want…"

He tried a last-ditch effort to put a halt to his insanity. "I don't do virgins."

"I'm not a virgin."

Brand growled, unable to suppress the sound clawing out of his throat. What the fuck was wrong with him? But he'd used the last reserve of common sense and willpower he had left getting himself out of that bathroom. Now, no way could he walk away.

With purpose, he set his feet. "Then tell me what you want," he demanded.

"I want you."

Simple as three little words. Those combined with the strengthening scent of her desire swirling through his senses, and everything inside him contracted, as though a fist landed in his chest, while at the same time punching out with triumph. Heat slashed through him, and she gasped. Were his eyes ablaze? Dragon shifters in the grip of passion showed it with fire.

But he crossed his arms, trying to hold his shit together. Where had his fucking control gone, anyway? "What do you want me to do?"

She blinked. For a second he thought she was going to balk, but then she smiled and crossed the room, her breasts and hips swaying in a hypnotic rhythm.

"I want you to fuck me." Then she dropped to her knees, giving him little doubt as to where he should put his cock first.

Yeeeessssss.

He shouldn't have pushed her, because now the burn to take, and take, and take ignited in his blood. "You shouldn't have said that."

She smiled up at him, head tipped back and damp hair tumbling down her back in loose waves. Gods, she was the most gorgeous thing he'd ever seen. "You asked."

"You're right. I guess I'd better give you what you want." Brand whipped his shirt over his head as he toed off his boots, undid his buckle and pants, and shucked them off.

Only she didn't wait for a command or for him to take the lead. Kasia reached out and wrapped her hand around the base of his dick, pumping a few times. Brand shuddered at the soft feel of her skin and her firm grip. Then moist heat enveloped him as she wrapped her lips around him and took him deep.

Brand jerked his head down to see, to watch. Fuck, what a sight.

She released him with a pop only to lick him from the base of his balls to the tip of his cock before sucking him back into the torturous recess of her mouth.

Base need took over as blood roared through his body. Brand speared his fingers through her hair and held her head still as he started pumping into her, maybe a little too roughly, but beast and man were of one accord now, and that meant taking what was his.

Kasia hummed her own pleasure, the sound vibrating up his shaft and tingling in his balls. Shit. If she kept that up, he'd come inside that pretty mouth of hers and not where he wanted. Using the strength and speed of his dragon, he pulled her away from his dick and had her pinned beneath him on the bed in less than a heartbeat.

"Damn. Big men aren't supposed to move that fast." She laughed, and the delighted sound had his body tensing at the pleasure of it.

Brand grinned and leaned over to suck the lobe of her ear into his mouth, giving it a nip. "Wait until you see what that speed means when I'm inside you," he half warned, half promised. "And it doesn't mean we get there faster, just…harder."

The laughter faded from her eyes, and she groaned. "Show me."

Again, in a move too fast for her to track, Brand dropped down her body and put his mouth at the hot, wet core of her. She cried out as he speared his tongue into her tight channel, the spicy taste of her driving his own need higher. At the same time, he flicked his thumb over that bundle of nerves peeking out of her folds, begging for his touch.

Moans of pure, unadulterated pleasure tumbled from her lips, and her thighs clamped tight around his head even as she reached down to push back his hair. But he wasn't done. Gradually, he sped up the movement of his thumb until he acted like a vibrator against the sensitive nub.

Beneath him, Kasia thrashed, and every sweet moan made him harder and harder. Finally, Brand added fire to the mix. Not mating fire. That fire was different—deliberate, and pushed into her waiting body. The fire he used now was just for fun. Blowing a small flame into the recess of his mouth, he returned to her body, only now he slid two fingers inside her and started at her clit with his fire-heated tongue.

Kasia arched off the bed, tossed her head back, and screamed as the orgasm tore through her, her inner muscles gripping his fingers in a pulsating vise as wave after wave of sensation slammed through her body.

Brand kept it up, lapping gently, easing only as her body slowed. At her deep sigh, he raised his head. Satisfaction poured through him at the sight of Kasia limp and flush with satiated pleasure, spread across his bed, her chest heaving in the aftermath of what *he* had done to her.

Ignoring the clamoring of his own dick, he crawled back up her body.

Kasia lifted her head and smiled in a way that pierced his chest with both pleasure and pain. "Again," she shocked the hell out of him by demanding.

"Don't you need a minute—"

She hooked a hand around his neck and tugged him down sharply so that they were eye to eye. "I want to feel that again. Now. Only with your cock inside me."

Then she snared his lips in a kiss, sinking her teeth into his bottom lip, the small shard of pain traveling his nerve endings and every ounce of blood flooding south. He opened for her and played with her tongue, sucking it into his mouth, swallowing her soft moans.

As he enjoyed the give and take of their mouths, he repositioned their bodies, using his strength to come up to his knees and pick her up to straddle his lap. He held her with the tip of his cock at her entrance, but this time, instead of going fast, he waited and continued to claim her mouth over and over.

Her hands went to his shoulders as she tried to lower herself. When he grinned, she growled but kept kissing him. Only now one hand crept around to the back of his neck, under his hair.

Brand captured her wrist, pulling her touch away from the brand of his family there. She opened wide blue eyes, questions swirling in those pale depths. To distract her, he lowered her down his straining shaft with excruciating slowness, loving how her need replaced those questions, her eyes going hot and slumberous.

When he was sheathed, balls deep, inside her, he stopped, letting her adjust, reveling in the sensations of her body squeezing him like a vise.

Kasia tried to pull back from his kisses, but he didn't let her, tugging her lower lip with his teeth. Then she tried to wiggle her butt, so he gave her a light smack on the ass and then soothed the spot by rubbing his palm over it in slow circles.

"Brand," she begged against his mouth.

He smiled. "Damn you feel so good, sweetheart."

"Whatever. Fuck me, dammit."

A laugh burst from deep inside him at her eager insistence. "Don't light on fire," he warned. Because even though they weren't mating, just fucking, she was a phoenix. He didn't feel like risking her killing him if she flamed up during the act. Even if he didn't fill her with his own flame to seal the deal.

She nodded. Then he obeyed the command in her lust-dazed eyes. Taking her by the hips, he moved her slowly up and down, watching her face glaze over with ecstasy, and he forced them both to experience that slow slide together. A few times she tried to pump her hips, make him go faster, but he held off, waiting. For her. Allowing her body time to recover from that first orgasm and build into another, bigger one.

He took one pink-tipped breast into his mouth, alternately licking and sucking the puckered nipple, plucking at it with his teeth. Each action drew forth little sounds at the back of her throat. Still forcing himself to endure the agony of her slowly taking his cock, he switched to her other breast, ministering the same attention.

Her breathing started to hitch, then she let out a keening moan, tipping her head back, her long hair brushing against his hands at her hips. The sweet perfume of her need washed over his senses. She was ready.

The animalistic side of him wanted to flip her over and take her from behind, claim her in the way that beasts did, but Brand wasn't claiming her. Fucking her, yes. Claiming, mating, and branding her…no. Besides, he wanted to see her face when he tipped her over that glorious edge in the way that had nothing to do with her damn visions.

In a swift move, he flipped them over so that she was lying on her back with him between her legs. He released her hips for a second, trailing his hands over the sexy indent of her waist, up her ribs, pausing to knead those gorgeous pale globes, before continuing up to take her by the wrists. He moved her hands above her head to wrap them around the metal posts of the brass headboard.

Trailing his hands back down her body, he had to force himself not to pause at her neck, not to touch that sacred spot below her hairline where a mate's brand would one day be seared into her skin. A spot he'd already been fool enough to kiss in the motel when he held her through her vision.

"Hold on tight, sweetheart."

Her eyes widened, but she did as he asked. If anything, her cheeks pinkened. But she didn't look away, and she didn't ask why. Total trust.

A blackness plunged through his heart at that realization. *She shouldn't trust me like that.*

But he was too far gone to pursue that thought. He needed to bring them both the culmination of the pleasure they'd been building together.

He moved, resuming that slide, pumping in and out of her body with increasing speed, every sound from her driving him faster, higher. He waited, held off his own pleasure until her body gathered, tightening around his cock like a fist. With the first spasm, Kasia's body bowed off the bed, though she didn't release her grip on the headboard. She screamed his name as he pounded into her, pulsing around his cock as waves of ecstasy crashed over her.

Her orgasm pulled him down like an undertow. A tingle gathered at the base of his spine, then burst through his balls and out of his dick in hot spurts, pulsing in time with her body as she milked every ounce of pleasure his body had to give.

Spent and wrung out, Brand crawled up beside Kasia and did something he'd never done with another woman—he pulled her into his arms, holding her close, skin against skin. Strange, because usually Brand was eager to get whatever woman he was fucking out of his bed and out of his room as fast as he could.

He should be freaking the hell out and putting a stop to this right now, but he was too replete, too content as he lay there catching his breath. Too reluctant to re-erect those walls quite yet.

Kasia, unlike some of his past partners, didn't immediately start into inane chatter or uncomfortable questions. She snuggled into him, awake based on the sound of her heartbeat, but seemingly satisfied to simply lie together in a harmonious silence.

A balm to his soul.

Eventually, she gave a little sigh. "Tell me about Hershel?"

Not the question he was expecting after mind-blowing, off-limits, forbidden fucking.

"Are you asleep?" she prompted.

"What do you want to know?" he mumbled.

A small sigh. "He's not human, is he?"

Brand tensed, shock pinging around inside him. Kasia was way too perceptive. "Not my place to share his secrets."

At that, she turned in his arms, not to back away

but to face him. Her gaze sparkled with humor. "You two are made of the same mold, that's for sure."

Brand angled his head in silent question.

She reached out to push his hair out of his eyes. "He said the same thing when I asked him about you."

She'd been asking questions? Like what?

"I asked him how you two knew each other," she answered before he even asked.

Was the woman a mind reader now?

"I could see the thought bubble over your head," she teased.

"Huh." Apparently both his will and his poker face had deserted him. "I met Hershel when I was young. He gave me a place to stay when I felt like it; in exchange I did odd jobs for him."

She considered that. "Like the kind of jobs you do for…dragons?"

Brand was glad she hadn't brought Ladon's name into the bed with them. He wasn't ready to acknowledge that reality. Not while her skin was against his.

"Not at first. To start with, I helped him around the house."

She tucked an arm under her head. "That must've been an interesting way to grow up."

"The club is a relatively new element in his life, but yeah, he's always surrounded himself with what he calls the *people who get shit done*."

Kasia was silent a moment. In another highly distracting move, she traced her finger over the tattoo that ran the length of his right arm. "He must have something to hide if he needs to be surrounded by people like that," she finally commented.

Again, shock ricocheted through him at her level of perception. "What makes you say that?"

She hitched a slim shoulder, her breast moving against his chest in the most enticing way possible, yet another distraction. "We did the same thing."

Something about her words snagged his attention, and Brand managed to forget the naked body pressed against him for a split second. "We?"

Dammit. She'd almost given away her biggest secret of all.

"My mother and I," she blurted out, hoping he hadn't noticed her hesitation.

Two mind-blowing orgasms, better than anything she'd fantasized, and she was ready to spill her most precious secrets without a thought. But his unexpected revelation—she'd bet all the dragons' wealth that Hershel had basically raised Brand— had shaken her.

She had so many questions.

Oh, hell. When had she gotten invested in who Brand was as a person? Sleeping with him had started out as a bad idea, one she'd been fighting since the moment he appeared in her room at the clinic in Cheyenne, but now the consequences were steering toward the realm of dangerous.

"What things did you and your mother do?" he asked.

Kasia released a silent breath of relief. He hadn't caught her slip about her sisters. Thank the gods. "Well…my first memories growing up involve a band of gypsies in Europe."

"Gypsies."

"Yeah. Although they didn't call themselves gypsies. In fact, many consider that a derogatory term." She caught his expression—which landed somewhere between suspicion and curiosity. "What? You got a problem with that?"

"No. I'm just trying to picture you living with the Roma people."

She sniggered. "If you like that, try this on for size. We spent a few decades with an indigenous tribe."

"Which tribe?"

"Cherokee."

"With that hair and those eyes?"

She shrugged. "I've gotten used to standing out."

"I'll say. Were you captured?"

"No." She gave a fond smile at the memories of the close friendships with the other girls her age, tending the crops, helping with the younger children. "They made us part of the tribe."

"Through marriage?"

She shook her head. "Cherokee often accepted outsiders into their tribes after a period. But we had an advantage."

She paused, debating if she should tell him. Brand picked up a tendril of hair that lay over her shoulder and ran his fingers over it. "What advantage?"

In for a penny… "My mother did a little brain-washing, one of her minor skills as a phoenix. Each group of humans we lived with thought we'd been part of their clan, tribe, commune, or community all along."

That ability also handled many questions about their aging, a slow process as compared with humans. Although they usually left before those questions were raised.

"So that's how you hid from the dragons? Living with humans?"

"Sometimes. We also spent a lot of time in solitude, something I get the feeling you're quite familiar with."

When all she got was a noncommittal "hmm," Kasia figured they'd had enough of the serious talk. This was supposed to be about sex, not a relationship. So she switched her focus to his arm, tracing the tattoo. "I wondered what the upper half looked like."

The pine trees below, which wrapped around his wrist and forearm, were towered over by mountains with caves high above the ground, etched into the skin of his shoulder. And in the skies, flying from the mouths of the caves…dragons. Even in their small form in the artwork, she could feel the thrill, the exhilaration of flying, and the camaraderie of being together in the air in their animal forms. On the opposite shoulder stood a lone dragon perched on a rock, not flying like the others, wings outstretched as if to flag them down. No other tattoos graced that arm.

Given what she'd guessed about Brand being on his own a lot, her heart cracked at the sight of the dragon on the rock. Alone, abandoned, and so desperate to be…what? Found? Accepted?

Or was she spinning fanciful tales about his tattoo? Knowing a little something about being by herself, perhaps she was projecting her own experiences onto him. But she didn't think so. The artwork was part of Brand's soul, maybe the only part he'd ever let anyone see.

"Taking me to the Blue Clan…will it let you join them?" she asked.

She fully expected him to stiffen up or not answer. Instead, he surprised her by tucking an arm behind his head. "That's part of it. I haven't belonged to a clan since I was ten."

So young. Her heart ached for the boy he'd been.

"And a phoenix is your ticket in," she murmured. Unable, and a little unwilling, to put into words the emotions it stirred in her, she went up on one elbow and kissed that dragon on the rock.

Then she leaned back to find him watching her with guarded eyes, a wariness in those unique golden depths that added to that crack in her heart. Damn, she needed to put an emergency brake on these runaway thoughts. Sex and safety, that's all she could and should expect from Brand.

"What was that for?" he asked.

Instinct told her to play it casual, so she gave her best offhand smile. At least, she hoped it appeared offhand. "I like your tattoo."

He searched her gaze for a moment, and she stared steadily back.

"Thanks," he finally said. More like grunted.

Wanting to take away the wariness and the walls, she trailed her hand down his arm, over the ridges of his stomach, to the trail of hair leading to the promised land.

He caught her by the wrist. "What are you doing?"

She glanced up from under her lashes, hoping her attempt at femme fatale wasn't coming off vampy or silly. Either would be mortifying. "I should think that's obvious."

"We can't—"

She lifted her eyebrows. "Given that we're naked and snuggling after we just did…"

"That was a bad idea."

She tried not to let those words add more cracks to the walls of her heart. "I know."

That gave him pause. "You do?"

"Yes." She flopped onto her back and didn't bother to pull up the sheet when it dropped to her waist, exposing her breasts. The way he stared at her body was too mouthwatering to cover back up. "Getting physically involved is a horrible idea."

He didn't—or couldn't, she hoped—pull his gaze from her body. "Yeah…a horrible idea."

"And we should stop. Stick to the plan."

That seemed to sink in. He dragged his gaze up to her eyes. "You still want to stick to the plan?"

No.

Yes.

Who the hell knew what the best course of action was?

"As you pointed out, it's the best option available to me." Damn, it sucked to be levelheaded. "But…"

"But?"

"We already opened this can of worms, or let this cat out of the bag, or whatever. So maybe…just for tonight?"

She deliberately trailed her hand up over her ribs to squeeze one of her breasts, pinching the nipple between her fingers.

A fire ignited in his eyes, and she felt the heat of

his gaze fixated on her like a warm caress. The air in her lungs deserted her with a whoosh. He pushed away her hand to replace it with his own, and an answering tingle bloomed between her legs as he stoked the heat which hadn't completely dissipated after rounds one and two.

He glanced up at her, though his hand continued its hypnotic movements. "Tomorrow…"

"Back to reality," she agreed. "But for tonight…"

He leaned over and pulled her throbbing nipple into his warm, wet mouth. "Mmhmm?" he hummed his question against her.

Kasia tried to breathe, and think, and answer him. "I've had enough pain to last a lifetime, thanks to my visions. Maybe you can give me more pleasure?"

He grinned that lopsided, sort of adorable, sort of arrogant smile she might always associate with Brand. "I think I can help with that."

IX

Ladon was awake long before daylight broke over the mountain, so the ringing of his cell phone interrupted only a workout.

Sleep never reached any deep levels for him, anyway. Not since he'd overthrown Thanatos, the previous King of the Blue Dragon Clan, and claimed the crown, at least. These days he slept with one eye open—not the bad one—waiting for the assassination he knew had to be coming. He'd also gotten in the habit of giving up on sleep around the crack of dawn every morning, choosing instead to put his body through rigorous physical training in solitude.

Every day he observed his warriors for their daily rounds of training, skill assessments, and combat practice, followed by their assignments. However, he didn't do more than observe. He had Asher, his Beta, to run that, and preferred to keep his own abilities to himself.

Secrets got his ass onto the throne. Secrets would keep him there.

Chest heaving, he paused in his methodical and yes, brutal—he'd earned that reputation for a reason—work on the heavy punching bag that hung from the cavern ceiling in his suite.

A person calling this early could be bothering him for only two reasons: bad news or information that needed immediate action. Rarely did the second reason fall under the realm of good news. But that couldn't be helped. He was waging a one-king war on the five other clans, and losing ground daily. The White, Gold, Green, and Black Clans were each ruled by an old king, one who'd gained power thanks to the Red King, Pytheios, and owed him their allegiance. None would relinquish his throne or his ways unless his cold dead fingers were pried loose from the crown.

Fine by Ladon.

He stalked over to his bedside table where his phone sat and checked the screen. He raised his eyebrows at the number displayed. New information.

He picked it up. "Yes?"

"Your rogue found her," came a familiar nasal voice.

Ladon didn't even blink. So he hadn't been wrong about Brand's cryptic call a few days ago. His friend wouldn't have asked for that meeting if he didn't have her. "Where are they?"

"Unknown. They escaped a small pack of wolf shifters in France. Twice."

Shit. That meant her existence was known beyond the dragon community. Dragons were already a major concern—if any of the other clans found her first, he'd be screwed—but wolf shifters and gods knew what else threw an extra layer of complication into the mix. At least Brand had made it across the ocean.

"Headed a specific direction?" he asked, though he already suspected.

"My guess is they're coming to you."

Good, but Brand would need help. What he protected was too important to risk losing.

Ladon waited for the quid pro quo he knew

was coming. His informant, a man established deep inside Pytheios's organization, had come to him a decade ago—a relationship that benefited them both and had been a direct influence on Ladon's ascension to the throne.

When the typical request wasn't immediately forthcoming, Ladon shifted his phone to his other ear and checked his watch. "What do you want?"

"Your rogue."

"What the fuck does that mean?" The ice in his voice would give even his most hardened warriors pause, but not the man on the other end of the line.

"Pytheios is aware of her existence."

"And the wolves trailing her?" Ladon asked.

"Them as well. He had someone following them to try to track her, but the wolves have returned to their home."

"And my rogue? Does Pytheios know about him?" Brand had stayed under the radar of the other kings up to this point. The mercenary would be pissed if he were found out.

"Not yet, but it won't be long before that information reaches him."

"Thanks to you, I've no doubt."

A small pause followed the accusation. "If you want to continue to receive the type of information I provide to you, I need to retain my...usefulness... to the king I serve."

"And you think you can do that by sacrificing one of my best resources?" He chose his wording with deliberate care.

Dammit. Was he considering handing over one of the few men he trusted?

As king, he found he had to make these kinds of choices way too fucking often. He'd never been raised to rule, though he had a few drops of royal blood in his lineage. He'd taken this clan because he *had* to. A fighter at heart, not much more than a thug, the longer Ladon ruled, the more he despised the politics of the position—the constant give and take, particularly the giving up of things important to him personally.

For centuries he'd scraped to survive the lean years Thanatos had put the blue dragons through, suffering alongside his people while the wealth of the Blue Clan had been plundered, dwindling until they could hardly feed their own people, and their numbers had dwindled as more mates went to other clans.

He loathed the old kings, had even taken great pleasure in ripping Thanatos's guts out of his body. Not even a blip of regret to drag at him over that act.

The man at the end of the phone line gave a small hum, as if considering Ladon's question. "I think giving up the person who is bringing you the best lucky charm a king could have is a small price to pay to continue to receive information valuable to your crown."

Ladon gazed up at the ceiling, holding onto his irritation with effort. "To save your ass, I can see how you would think so."

"He's a rogue, and not of your clan. That makes him disposable. Now is not the time to go soft."

"There's soft, and then there's the matter of leadership and loyalty."

A small chuckle reached him. "Not something that used to concern you."

The thick scar that slashed through Ladon's left eye started to twitch, a sure sign of his fury. Guilt was not his problem with his past. He'd done what he had to. "I wasn't king then."

"And kings must make difficult choices for the greater good."

A reality Ladon was fast learning to resent. "This is one choice I won't rush."

Long pause. "I understand."

So did Ladon. If he didn't produce Brand for his informant, he'd lose his inside information that was critical to the war he was engaged in. He was gearing up to bring the fight directly to Pytheios's door—correction, to a back door in the Alps, a location that had belonged to the Blue Clan until recently. Time to take it back.

"One more thing and then I really must go." As though they were having a casual chat.

Ladon rolled his eyes. "What's that?"

"One of my king's most…valued…cohorts has been sent after your prize."

No surprise there. "Anyone I know?"

"Uther."

Ladon gripped his phone tighter. "You're shitting me."

"I don't…shit…my lord. Not in this sense, at least."

"Pytheios risked sending another king?" The Rotting King had lost his bloody mind if he actually trusted Uther. Granted, Pytheios had helped put Uther on the gold throne, but a phoenix was too tempting a prize to trust to another king, especially one that ambitious.

The man was ruthless, something Ladon had heard from Brand firsthand. Despite how Ladon had helped him, and years of working and plotting together, Brand never gave up much about himself. But he *had* divulged who killed his family, and many other families with royal bloodlines within the Gold Clan.

Was the Red King getting desperate, or careless, not to have handled this himself, instead sending a king likely to double-cross him? Ladon tucked that piece of useful info aside for later examination.

His informant continued, oblivious to Ladon's thoughts. "Uther has been given certain incentives to bring her back here. Unmated."

Those must've been some hefty incentives. "Is he close?"

"I don't know."

"I thought you knew everything."

His informant chuckled, an oily sound oozing through his cell phone. "Some things are even beyond me."

"Find out."

"The rogue." Now a demand.

Dammit. "I'll consider your request."

"Excellent. I'll see what I can find out about Uther."

Awkward did not begin to cover a morning after when the sex had been nonstop, mind-blowing, panty-melting, and maybe even soul-shaking…only to turn around and move forward with their plan of taking her the rest of the way to a different man who might become her mate.

Kasia pulled her jeans up over her hips and zipped them, conscious of how loud the rasp sounded in the heavy silence of the room.

"Nice of Hershel to wash our clothes last night," she commented, just for something to say.

Brand grunted what she assumed was supposed to be an agreement.

"I must've smelled like bad body odor to you after so many days without a shower." *Oh my god, stop talking.*

"You were fine."

Obviously, Brand was not a morning-after type guy. *Bet he has most women out of his bed before after-sex turned into a long cuddle.*

Which begged the question, would he have done the same to her if he hadn't been forced to watch over her all through the night?

Probably.

So yeah, keep your mouth shut and play it cool.

He pulled his black T-shirt over his head, hiding that fantastic set of abs as well as the top half of his tattoo. Kasia shoved a strange sense of discontent down deep as she plopped onto the bed and worked on getting her sneakers on her feet and tied. Only her fingers didn't want to cooperate, so it took several fumbled attempts. She blamed it on lack of sleep. That and Brand's golden stare—perceptive and disarming—which seemed to follow her around the room despite the fact that anytime she glanced over, he wasn't looking her way.

And now I'm imagining things. Stress was going to crack her up before her time.

A sharp rap at the bedroom door had her jumping, heart attempting a jailbreak up her throat.

"Breakfast." Hershel's gruff voice came through slightly muffled.

She tossed Brand a self-conscious smile. "Coming," she called. With what was probably a telling amount of speed, she hustled over, swinging the door wide.

"Good morning, Hershel."

"Morning." He glanced over her shoulder at Brand and nodded.

Kasia didn't turn to see if Brand nodded back, instead following Hershel out into the hallway and down to the kitchen where she plunked herself down on a stool.

The kitchen held the same rustic charm as the rest of the house with cabinets in warm woods. The center island, which included the stovetop, ended in a bar-height tabletop where she sat.

"Can I help?" she asked as he scooped eggs and bacon from frying pans onto a plate.

"No need." He set the plate down in front of her along with a fork.

Her hunger returned with a vengeance—probably thanks to the sexual Olympics she and Brand had engaged in all night—and Kasia shoveled the eggs into her mouth.

"Coffee?"

Embarrassed to be caught wolfing down her food again, she swallowed and sent him a sheepish grin. "Please."

Thankfully, Hershel didn't comment. He just

poured her a cup and set it beside her plate with cream and sugar.

"Hershel?"

"Mmmm?"

"I hate to ask, but…" She paused, trying to figure out how to ask this.

He beat her to it. "What am I?"

She nodded.

He leaned back and crossed his feet at the ankles. "You sure you want to know?"

Kasia swirled the coffee in her cup. "I find it's usually better to know."

"Don't say I didn't warn you." He grinned. "My name is Pazuzu."

Kasia frowned. Why did that sound familiar? Realization widened her eyes. "Isn't that the demon's name in *The Exorcist*?"

Hershel snorted. "Don't get me started on that movie. I'm neither demon nor god. I'm an ancient spirit. Like humans, I can bring both good and evil."

Dang. Brand had said Hershel was ancient. He meant it.

"So you're not going to take possession of my body and make me spew green vomit everywhere?"

"Not today."

Hershel winked, and Kasia laughed.

"What's so funny?" Brand asked as he came into the room.

"Just swapping backgrounds with your phoenix," Hershel said.

Brand took the stool opposite her at the island table. She tracked his movement but avoided outright eye contact. Eye contact was like being touched by the fire of his kisses all over again.

This was getting ridiculous. They were grown adults who'd agreed to a one-night fuck-buddy session. No future. She knew that with a painful logic that lodged in her throat.

So what if it had been the best sex of her relatively young life?

So what if she wanted to drag him back to that room and see what else he could make her body do?

So what if…lots of things.

As much as she touted having choices, she knew mating a dragon king was her best shot at surviving now that her existence was more widely known. No matter what Brand did for and to her body, she'd walk away before her heart was a total goner and she started making stupid choices.

Selfish choices.

Her sisters were still hidden, and she could keep it that way. As far as dragons knew, there was only ever one phoenix at a time. A mother had to die or deliberately pass on her powers to her daughter. Either way, only one woman held them at any time. Hell, she didn't even know if her sisters had any. As the firstborn of the four, maybe she was the only one, but that was neither here nor there. Their safety was the important part.

Maybe she should ask Brand to leave as soon as he delivered her to Ladon Ormarr. But the mere thought brought on a wave of despair, so she tucked it away, deciding to Scarlett O'Hara that shit and think about it another day.

"What's the plan?" Hershel asked around a steaming cup of coffee as he leaned against the farmhouse sink.

The man must be a mind reader. Kasia turned to Brand, eyebrows raised.

He shot her a quick, inscrutable glance. "We'll be leaving after breakfast."

Hershel's bushy eyebrows shot up to meet his hairline. "Flying?"

"Driving," Brand corrected.

Was he going to risk summoning the Hemi Cuda again?

The older man must've caught Brand's "don't bother with more questions" tone, because instead he turned to Kasia. "How do you like flying?"

A snort came from the brooder across the table.

"What?" Kasia asked.

"Nothing." But she swore Brand was smiling on the inside.

"I like flying fine," she answered Hershel's question.

"Just fine?"

"She hates it," Brand interjected.

"No, I don't," she protested. *Lies. All lies.*

He pushed his plate back, leaning his elbows on the counter. "No? I think my back has permanent bruises from your death grip on me."

Kasia rolled her eyes even as Hershel chuckled. "Dragons don't bruise."

Brand stood. "Want me to show you?"

Half afraid he'd pull off his shirt and give Hershel a firsthand view of the nail marks branding his skin after a particularly robust tussle in the sheets, she jumped to her feet, cheeks warming. "Nope."

The two men shared a grin, but she ignored them as she took her and Brand's plates to the sink and rinsed them off. Taking her time, she dried her hands on the towel before turning back. "Ready?"

At the question, the almost indiscernible spark of humor in Brand's eyes disappeared, and his lips flattened. "In a rush, princess?"

Before she could answer, he about-faced and headed for the front door, shaking his head as he walked. "Let's go."

She glanced at Hershel, who shrugged.

"Fine. I'd sure as hell like to get this over with," she muttered under her breath at her would-be rescuer's back, which stiffened.

Had he heard? Well…good.

On the front porch, Kasia wrapped her arms around Hershel's neck and gave him a solid hug. "I'm sorry we couldn't stay longer. I suspect you have some great stories to share."

He laughed as she stepped back, his mustache twitching from side to side with the movement. "What makes you say that?"

"You're a demon." She shrugged. "Just a hunch."

Before she could move out of the way and let the two men say goodbye, in whatever way that looked like, a shout rose up from a direction across from the bar but farther south than Hershel's house.

"What was that?" she asked.

It couldn't be the wolves. Despite the lead wolf telling her Angelika was waiting, Kasia had been crystal clear she wasn't going with them.

Please let this be some problem that has nothing to do with us.

A tendril of smoke rose up above the rolling hills of land between where they stood and the barracks.

Hershel yanked the screen door open. "Get inside."

"No." Brand grabbed her by the wrist and dragged her down the stairs behind him. "You get inside, hunker down. Whatever is out there, they're after us."

Hershel started forward, scowling in a way that would've made Kasia shake in her sneakers if she weren't already too focused on more sounds of shouts.

"No way should you risk Kasia's life—"

Brand cut him off. "I'll get her out of here. I'm not bringing this down on you. Get inside."

"I agree," Kasia added her two cents. "This is about me. I don't want you hurt."

"You're both off your rockers," Hershel grumbled through clamped teeth before stomping off inside.

Was that gratefulness in Brand's expression when he turned to Kasia? "Step back."

As swiftly as she'd ever seen him do it, Brand transformed into the massive creature she'd long feared. Only fear no longer filled her. Awe was there. Even faith.

Without waiting to be asked, she scrambled up onto his back as soon as he lowered his body to the ground, wrapping around her spike on his back. "Go."

The sound of shots rang out, joining the shouts of the men as smoke rose into the air in black billows. Brand angled away from the noise and pushed off, taking to the air with a few swift beats of his wings. Kasia turned as they rose higher, searching for the source of the commotion, and gasped as she spied a large rectangular two-story building going up in a violent fury of flame and smoke.

Dragon fire.

No other fire burned that hot that fast. Terror slammed through her, its icy cold talons piercing her heart even as they gained altitude and Brand leveled out.

A shadow passed over them, and suddenly Kasia was transported back to the night her mother died. A shadow had passed overhead then, too, preceding the red dragon.

Before she could duck, or look up, or even scream, something massive rammed into Brand from underneath. How the hell had it moved around them so fast? The momentum tossed Brand sideways as he wrapped his wings around their attacker to wrestle him.

Kasia tried her damnedest to hold on, scraping and clawing to keep her grip, but the violence of the fight raging beneath her and the wind trying to pluck her from her spot as two massive dragons plummeted through the air was too much for her puny arms. She slid up the spike until she dangled from the tip, her legs flapping around in the air, kicking and scrambling to return to the safety of his back. But the tip of that spike was razor sharp, unlike the smoother base, and sliced into her hands, spilling her blood and making the surface too slick for her to keep her grip.

Swallowing her scream, she was ripped violently from Brand's back. Relative to the dragons, she shot up in the air, her body lighter than their bulk and not falling as fast. Ridiculously, an old physics lesson from her human schools struck her right then about bodies falling at the same rate despite size. But was that in a vacuum? Because it sure didn't apply here.

Who cared? She was fucking tumbling toward the ground with no way to save herself from splatting when she hit.

For a strange reason she didn't have time to examine, that image of her body broken and smeared across the green lushness of northern England gave her the injection of calm she needed. If she was going to live, she needed to think, not panic.

First move, stop flailing.

She threw her arms out and aimed her belly at the ground like she'd seen in Skylar's videos. Who knew her sister being a licensed pilot and skydiver would come in handy in quite this way. Kasia tried to mimic the posture she'd witnessed. After a couple of tries, she managed to stabilize. Now what?

Her eyes blurred and teared up as the wind seemed to want to push her eyeballs out of her head, but she squinted and tried to keep track of the dragons grappling below her. If Brand could get to her before the ground…

Hard to tell through the distortion of tears, but it looked as though Brand was wrapped around a larger, amber-gold dragon, more orange in color than Brand. Another gold dragon fighting his own kind?

Oh hell, the ground was getting closer by the second.

"Brand!" she yelled, the wind greedily snatching the sound from her vocal cords even before it moved past her lips.

"Brand!" she screamed louder, already going hoarse with the effort.

But the dragons didn't part, and the ground was rushing up at her. She could make out details now, like trees, and the fire from the barracks and the bar and Hershel's house.

She was going to die. Right here and now.

A miniscule shard of logic pierced the overwhelming panic trying to flood her system. She might not fly, but she could teleport. *If* she could ignite. The last time she'd tried she'd messed up, and that had been only thirty feet. Not thousands.

Closing her eyes, to shut out the view of her imminent death, Kasia tried to light the fire inside her soul, willing the inferno to take over. But other than a small spark that the wind kept blowing out, she couldn't focus enough, her fear mounting with every second she plummeted.

This wasn't working, and the ground had to be so close now.

"Brand." She didn't scream his name or even yell it. She whispered it, like a prayer.

Even as she continued to try to burst into flame, she waited for the impact with the unforgiving earth and hoped her death would be quick. Like snuffing out a candle in the dark.

Unable to stop herself, she opened her eyes and threw her arms out as the ground rushed up at her. Then choked on the screech that clawed out of her throat as something huge snatched her from the jaws of death.

"Got you." Brand's deep tones penetrated the eerie acceptance that had settled over her about two seconds before talons wrapped around her body.

He flared his wings, slowing their momentum,

then adjusted his grip, effectively caging her in. *"Hold on, sweetheart."*

Kasia looked down and jumped into his grasp to find solid earth only twenty feet from her face. Damn, that had been close. Brand seemed to hover with her. As gently as a mother handling her newborn baby, he set her down on the ground, just outside Hershel's house.

"Run. Hershel will be waiting."

Then dirt and leaves flew up, coating her hair and clothes and lungs, as he flew away.

Uther.

The false Gold King himself had come to capture the phoenix.

A roar of challenge punched from deep inside Brand.

I'm going to kill this fucker here and now and end this once and for all.

As soon as he delivered Kasia safely to Hershel, who could defend her better than most, Brand took off into the dull gray of the cloud-covered morning sky, searching for a glint of amber-colored gold. If Uther was above him, he wouldn't know until the last minute. Damn the camouflage that kept them hidden from prying human eyes.

Brand's only warning was a flash, like seeing sun glint off glass from far away.

This time he had a better idea of how Uther liked to fight. The amber dragon was a grappler, wrapping around his adversary and clawing at the underbelly, trying to gut them. At the same time, Uther would dig in tight while they plummeted to earth, letting go only at the last moment in a maneuver meant to slam his opponent into the ground with all the momentum of two massive dragons, crushing his victim with the impact while he flew away.

Now that Kasia was safely on the ground, he wouldn't screw up again. No way was he going to lose this. No way was Uther going to get to her.

Only Brand's flying skills—he was big, but had taught himself to turn on a dime—had saved him the first time, allowing him to soar away before hitting the ground, though it had been a close thing. Barely in time to get to Kasia and save her. Fire and bile mixed in a noxious cocktail inside him. He didn't think he'd ever get over trying to reach her before she hit the ground, but he couldn't think about that.

Now he pretended like he hadn't seen the flash, still acting as though he were scouring the skies for any sign.

Ready. Waiting.

He gathered flame and fury in his belly. This asshole was dead.

The attack came from the side. Using his maneuverability, Brand sliced below the figure barreling at him through the air. At the same time, he flipped onto his back and managed to drag the lethal spikes of his tail along his opponent's underside, missing the belly, but striking a hind leg.

A low grunt of pain told him he'd hit his target. Now for the fire. Dragons might be impervious, but only when their scales were intact. Any wound was a weakness to be exploited.

Tucking and tumbling away faster than the amber dragon could pivot and dive, Brand put some distance between them, then stretched out his wings and swooped upward, all the while keeping his sights locked on his enemy.

No hiding anymore, fucker.

The dragon, rather than running, dove, thinking he was taking advantage of a tactical mistake Brand was making in coming up at him from below. Again, Brand waited until the heat from his adversary warmed his scales, then he changed the angle of his approach just slightly, going for that back leg.

He let loose a torrent of angry fire tinged with sparkling gold, the flames curling back in on themselves even as they shot from his maw and fought the wind. Brand's aim was true. Even as the amber dragon passed overhead and struck at Brand's back with teeth and talons, he howled in pain. The fire found Uther's weaker, exposed flesh, eating at the meat underneath, melting his leg from the inside.

Brand knew the slashing wound hadn't been big enough or deep enough for the fire to do damage that would be debilitating—or permanent, for that matter—but it would slow the fucker down.

Taking a lead from Brand's move a moment ago, Uther shot downward, using his plummeting momentum to drop away quickly. Brand knew exactly where the other dragon was headed. Cursing a stream of profanity in his head, Brand tucked his wings in, angling in a stoop that had him gaining. He couldn't let the other dragon get to the mountaintop in the distance first.

A dragon in the air was dangerous. One who commanded a peak was lethal if you tried to attack him. With no ground at the same level to find purchase on, Brand would be forced to fight from the air, presenting his softer belly to the dragon below as they brawled. He wouldn't be able to land, because he'd end up below the dragon, forced to scramble up the rock to get to the fight, in range of a swinging, spiked tail.

Tactically, the smart move would be to clear off, not engage. But if he did that, then he couldn't get Kasia out of there without putting her directly in the path of the brute lying in wait.

Only neither of them reached their destination. The distinctive roar of another dragon thundered through the air. Afraid his amber adversary had been holding on until reinforcements could arrive, Brand spun toward the source of the sound.

Smoke-tinged breath punched from his body at the sight of a band of blue dragons. Though still far off, they converged on his position. Ladon had to have sent them, or possibly brought them himself, though how he knew or found them was a mystery.

Relief didn't exactly flood Brand, because the outside possibility that they were here to take Kasia away from him was still in play. Ladon may not know the full story and think that Brand was trying to keep Kasia for himself, but at least he wasn't contending with that amber fucker alone anymore.

Turning back to search for the dragon he'd wounded, he found not a trace of him. The older, wiser dragon had taken advantage of Brand's distraction and disappeared.

Brand roared his frustration. He'd lost his shot at taking out the one man he hated more than any other dragon shifter.

X

Kasia watched the entire fight between the two dragons from the ground, despite Hershel tugging at her the entire time, trying to drag her inside.

"I'll go inside if Brand loses," she finally snapped at him, jerking her wrist from his grip.

"You're injured."

Kasia looked down at her hands, but was too numb to truly absorb what she saw. Man, that spike had sliced deep. She must be in shock, because the pain wasn't getting through. Either that, or that spike had severed nerves so cleanly she couldn't feel the pain yet.

Good. Then she could deal with it later.

"In a minute." She returned her gaze to the sky.

"Stubborn female," Hershel muttered. He ripped off pieces of his shirt and bound her wounds, at least stemming the bleeding.

She didn't pay him much attention, too busy watching the midair fight and trying to keep her breakfast in her stomach. At least he'd stopped trying to drag her away. No way in hell was she hiding inside while Brand was in the air, fighting to save her.

"Hershel. Give the phoenix to the dragon."

She jerked her gaze to the woods around the house to find them surrounded by a handful of the creatures from the bar, four or five she could see. She had no doubt others lurked about. Shivers cascaded down her spine at the vampire's glowing red eyes. He'd been the one to speak. Baldy was nowhere to be seen.

Fear and adrenaline spiked yet again, but she set her feet. The worst thing she could do was show that fear. Not to these guys.

She glanced at Hershel, whose mouth flattened in a grim line. "She belongs to one of those dragons, and not the dark gold one."

"With what he's paying us for her, we won't need to worry about money for a century," the vampire hissed.

The creature tensed and sniffed the air, then zeroed in on Kasia. Had he smelled her blood? He pulled his lips back in a snarl of a grin, and Kasia stepped closer to Hershel.

Given their long lives, supernaturals were frequently concerned about supporting themselves over time. A century was a good chunk. Hershel, however, didn't so much as twitch. "You know the consequences if you go against me on this. I'm telling you to let it go."

Though the lion shifter and the falcon sitting in the tree shared an uneasy glance, none left. "We have people of our own to consider," the vampire said. "And she's worth a gold mine. You can't ask us to ignore that."

A clash of sound reverberated from above, and they all glanced up at the fight going on overhead.

"I've promised her my protection. I'll give you one last chance to clear out." Hershel's warning made her shiver even more than the vampire's red eyes. He'd meant that.

The group before them shifted. The lion and the falcon left. Smart men. But everyone else stayed.

"Dammit," Hershel muttered under his breath. Then louder. "You had your chance."

With a wave of his hand every creature before them doubled over, screaming in agony. Bile rose up her throat as, one by one, they each dried up, as though the water was being leached from their systems—like watching them decompose in fast forward. Then skin shriveled to expose bone, then turned black, and each body slowly became ash, the fine dust blowing away in the wind. Reminding her of her mother.

"Holy shit," she muttered. She glanced at Hershel, who remained grim, but his back was straight.

"Hope I didn't scare you," he said.

He'd killed some of his people. For her. "Thank you," she murmured.

Another roar ripped through the air. Above them, the other dragon flew away, seemingly in disgrace, one back leg held at an awkward angle. Had Brand injured it? They'd missed a good chunk of the fight dealing with issues on the ground.

Brand moved to follow the damaged dragon, but paused, arching that long neck to look at something.

Kasia frantically searched the sky, but saw nothing. "What's happening?"

Then she winced as the nerves in that hand finally woke up and screamed in protest. She let him go and cradled that hand, blood leaving her head with the agony of it.

Before she could do more than whimper, Brand turned and dove in their direction. He didn't stop until he threw out his wings, slowing to land outside Hershel's home. *"Get on."*

"But—"

She cut Hershel off with a shake of her head and scrambled up Brand's back using only her wrists for balance. "What's happening?" she asked Brand.

He didn't answer her.

"Stay inside until we're long gone," he told Hershel, letting her overhear.

Then they took to the air.

Given her last experience, evidenced by the blood staining the tip of his spike—*her* blood—she wasn't exactly thrilled to be back up here, but she didn't see any other choice. Kasia ignored the pain in her throbbing hands and wrapped herself around him with a death grip.

What if that other gold dragon returned?

She didn't have time to ask as they launched into the sky, quickly leaving the earth behind. Then, seemingly out of nowhere, ten dragons, most smaller and leaner than Brand, and all various shades of blue—from pale sky to a deep navy—suddenly appeared in the air on either side of them. Each of the shifters took up a position, two below, two above, and three on both sides spaced out in protective formation.

Brand let loose a low growl of warning, practically twitching beneath her in agitation. The blue dragons around them shifted, giving him a bit more space.

"Brand?" she prodded.

He didn't answer for a long second, body still quivering. He'd said he had trouble controlling himself in this form, especially when he was angry.

"Brand? Please don't flip out on me. I can't handle another fall."

That seemed to snap him out of it. His chest heaved beneath her, but the quivering stopped, almost like he'd forced himself to relax. *"I'm okay,"* he finally answered.

Good. Because one of them needed to be, and she really wasn't.

"I smell blood that's not mine," he rumbled.

"I cut myself, but I'll be fine." Total lie.

Her hands were raw, but the more important thing was getting to Ladon and safety first. She'd handle the pain and pray to all things good and holy that she'd have full function, but at least her wounds weren't life threatening.

Not wanting the others to hear, but still needing to talk to Brand, she tried projecting her voice, doubting it would work, but worth the attempt. She stared at the back of Brand's spiky head, focusing her thoughts, trying to aim them. *"Can you hear me?"*

He bobbled in the air, and she gripped the spike with what would've been white-knuckled fear if she could use her hands.

"How the hell did you do that? Only shifters are able to do that."

Holy shit, it worked. The emotion in his voice alone told her how unusual that was. Again, she focused on sending her thoughts to him. *"I focused on your head. Did any of the others hear?"*

A long silence greeted her question. *"I don't think so,"* he finally said.

"Good." She was starting to shake—shock, and pain, and the deep cold at this altitude all combining

to bombard her system. Shouldn't she be going numb by now? Numb would be nice. Maybe if she could distract herself long enough, she could muscle through this whole freezing and pain thing.

"I think I've heard you before," Brand said.

That confession layered on the shock. *"You have?"*

"Did you whisper my name when you were falling?"

"After screaming it? Yes. You heard that?"

"I heard the whisper." A dark edge crept into his deeper tones. She couldn't quite put her finger on the emotion behind it.

"Let's not test that out again." She might not ever get over the plummeting through the air thing. In fact, Kasia suspected nightmares were in store for her tonight.

"Yeah," he agreed. Again, some harder emotion swirled, and the muscles under her shifted, not from the steady beat of his wings, more like he was tense.

"Who was that gold dragon?" She asked the question that had been burning in her mind.

"I can't be positive."

Now *that* emotion she had no trouble identifying. Pure rage. *"I'm not buying it. Who was he?"*

"Uther Hagan."

For the second time that day, Kasia had to fight to keep her breakfast inside her stomach. *"He helped kill my father."*

Brand's muscles tightened beneath her. *"Your father? Zilant Amon?"*

That's right. She'd mentioned her last name to Hershel. Figured Brand had caught that. *"The King of the White Dragon Clan. Yes."*

Brand was silent for a long pause, and her shaking

worsened while she waited. *"Uther killed a lot of people,"* he finally said.

That statement went deeper than generalities. *"People you loved?"*

Silence.

Not like she'd expected an answer. Brand didn't ever vocalize anything to do with emotions. She'd figured that out on day one. With a sigh, she leaned her forehead against his spike, eyes closed, suddenly exhausted in a way that had nothing to do with their nighttime activities or her visions.

"My entire family," came the sudden, low reply.

Kasia sucked in a sharp breath. *"Oh, Brand."*

Again, his muscles shifted under her. *"Don't go all mushy on me."*

She huffed a tired laugh. *"I'll tell you what...if I decide to mate Ladon, when I'm queen, I'll make sure we take that asshat Uther out first."*

"He's the King of the Gold Clan, so that might be tough."

Of course. Because you reward your coconspirators by putting them in power, which Pytheios had obviously done.

"With a phoenix in your corner? Cakewalk," she teased.

Though she secretly doubted her presence would do anything. Her mother hadn't even been able to keep her mate alive, let alone bring luck, or whatever, to the clans. How lucky could a phoenix be if that was possible?

Another long silence. Had she tapped out Brand's emotional threshold? Time to change the subject, because if she shook any harder, she'd shake herself right off his back. Her jaw ached with the effort of keeping her teeth from chattering. *"How'd the blue dragons find us?"*

Periodically, each of the creatures surrounding them would crane their necks to look over. At her? At Brand? Checking for attackers?

"According to Asher, that big navy dragon ahead of us who's missing part of his tail, Ladon got a tip from inside Pytheios's organization."

Brand was talking to the other dragons? Wait. Pytheios knew her location? And the wolves had found her. Who else? *Please let my sisters still be safe.* Gods, she wished she could contact them, check on them. At least she knew Angelika was still safely with the wolves.

For now.

"What will happen to Hershel? And the club?" she asked next.

"Hershel will sort it out."

She'd have to take that at face value, she guessed. Brand didn't seem concerned and, after Hershel's demonstration, she knew he could handle himself.

"Why are you jiggling around up there?"

Now he notices? *"Because it's freezing."*

And if I let myself think about falling again, or how badly my hands hurt, I might start screaming and never stop.

Hysteria lurked close to the surface, under control for now, but not by much.

"I can help with that." The strangest sound emanated from beneath her, like sucking and swirling winds. Then Brand's scales started to glow underneath her, lit from the inside as he stoked

his own fire and heated up. Her ass thawed first, followed by the rest of her.

"Thank you." The paralyzing fear and her hands were two things he could do nothing about, but at least the shaking had stopped.

"Brand? What happens now?"

Long pause. *"We get you to your king."*

That statement and the ice coating every syllable of Brand's words threatened to chill her to the bone. Regardless of the warmth he provided, her shiver competed with the altitude, shock, and a fear of flying that was now ten times worse than before. Dragon was not her favorite mode of transportation.

"Not my king yet." Even with every creature on the planet hunting her, she still refused to be pushed into a mating. Yes, it appeared to be the safest, and maybe only, recourse to keep her and her sisters safe, but mating was for life, and phoenixes lived forever. No way was she making that decision lightly.

"As far as I'm concerned, he is," Brand said.

Kasia swallowed. Words could cut deeper than dragon spikes, it seemed. He had to know she wasn't happy about the prospect. Why had he suddenly shut her out, slamming up barriers between them like that?

After that, she shut up, clung to that damn spike, and waited while they flew. Below, the earth gradually changed into craggy mountains, with fewer trees and more rocks. Every so often the dragon guard surrounding them would change positions, swapping out. Periodically, one or two would drop back. Patrolling? Watching out for Uther?

Suddenly, the dragon in the lead trumpeted—a blast of sound almost like a siren's call.

"What was that for?" she asked Brand, staring hard at the back of his head.

"Password for the sentries."

She looked around for the sentries, but saw none.

"Hold on," Brand said.

She obeyed and gripped her spike harder with her arms, still not using her sliced hands. Please let them be almost there.

A few seconds later, seemingly as one, the dragons dove. The angle wasn't so steep she couldn't stay seated, but steep enough that she felt the rush, and the fear of falling again tightened her stomach to cramping. Brand tucked his wings in closer, his body elongating to arrow toward the ground.

Kasia held in her screams. No way was she squealing like a sissy in front of all these flying shifters. Eventually, they got close enough to the ground that it seemed to be rushing up at her. If the wind weren't whipping all around her she'd think she was already in a nightmare about her earlier experience.

"Ummm, Brand…" Damn she hated how weak she sounded in her head.

He didn't speak and didn't slow. Kasia couldn't see around his bulk to know for sure where they were headed.

Unfortunately, the closer they got to the ground, the more panic crawled all over her. Just as a yelp crept up her throat, they leveled off, cruising above the thick forest of trees, the piney scent of the needles stirred by the torrent of air created by her own personal squadron of dragons. Then, as they neared mountains, the land rose sharply up.

In accord with the shift in topography, the dragons flew up the side of the mountain, then passed through a gaping hole in the rock—a natural canyon. Brand and the others followed, banking through the twists and turns of the canyon walls.

"Won't people see us?" She didn't think to keep the question to herself, voicing it aloud.

"Not here. Once we're inside the canyon walls, we're magically protected. Invisible to the human eye."

"Again with the handy tricks." How her mother kept them secret as long as she had, given all that dragons could do, was a miracle.

"Evolution. Humans once hunted dragons to the point of extinction. Only by hiding among them in our human forms did we survive. That and with the help of witches and other magic-wielding creatures."

"What? No unicorns? Maybe a leprechaun or two?"

"You have to catch one first," Brand deadpanned.

The dragon closest to them on her right, one almost a turquoise color, snorted, smoke trailing from his nostrils.

"Did he just laugh at me?" she demanded of Brand. And on second thought… "Did he hear you?" They'd need some kind of signal when he was on open mic channel versus just talking with her.

"You'll have to ask her. Arden is female."

Kasia looked closer. Sure enough, the dragon was smaller and sleeker than the others. A female-born dragon? Or a made mate?

"Sorry!" Kasia called across the expanse of nothing separating them.

The turquoise dragon rumbled a sound, and Brand rumbled back. *"And she apologizes for laughing."*

"That's okay." Kasia thought about it for a moment. "Is there an easy way to tell gender in dragon form?"

"Is my mascara not showing?" a female voice rang through Kasia's head. She winced but didn't say anything about the volume as the dragons around them all shared rumbling chuckles.

Great. She was a sideshow, the outsider among them. Not a dragon. Not raised in this strange world or even on this continent for the most part. In other words, a freak. Fantastic. What a moment to make that realization.

She kept that bit to herself and forced herself to laugh along with them. "Sorry if my questions are silly, but I learn fast."

So suck it.

Before anyone could respond, the two dragons above her and Brand swooped down to fly in front, forming a single-file line. Kasia watched in mute horror as they headed straight for the wall, but Brand followed them without hesitation. Then, to her astonishment, it seemed as though the canyon walls…shifted.

An optical illusion.

Rather than slamming into rock and plummeting to their deaths, they circled around what seemed to be a cylindrical curve in the rock, with only 10 percent or so open to the rest of the mountain. Below them, she caught a glimpse of a raised, circular platform formed out of the mountain walls and emerging from a large cavern. People stood at the edges, waiting.

After circling down, all eleven dragons, including Brand, flared their wings wide, slowing their forward progress to hover for a moment before landing softly practically in unison.

Each of the other dragons immediately shifted into their human form. Brand did not. Instead, he lowered his body so that she might climb down first.

Trying not to appear as stiff and awkward as her muscles—locked into position after hours of flight— not to mention her still-bloody hands, actually were, she swung her leg over and climbed off. Then Brand, too, made the transition.

Strangely, the others who'd flown with them didn't approach. She stood in a circle of the men and one woman who had escorted her to theoretical safety, but none of them stepped any closer. Did they think she was dangerous?

She turned her gaze to Brand. "What next?"

"Couldn't bring her here safely on your own, rogue?" The owner of the raspy voice, more a hiss, obviously intended his words to be a joke, as he followed them with a chuckle. But as Kasia turned to face him, she caught the sneer on his pale lips, the coldness in his blue eyes.

"I guess not," Brand replied.

The other man, the only one seemingly brave enough to approach them, flicked a glance toward Brand in a way that reminded Kasia of prey trying not to look a predator in the eye, then he stepped up to Kasia's other side, away from Brand.

Realization dawned. *They're not afraid of me, they're afraid of* Brand.

A glance at his face showed him to be totally closed off. Although that seemed to be his resting face most of the time. Was this how he got treated anytime he showed up here?

Was it because he wasn't a blue dragon, or because he was rogue? Come to think of it, had any rogue dragon managed to rejoin a clan, especially a clan not his own? Her mother hadn't covered that topic in detail. Rogues were unusual, as far as she understood, because mostly dragons killed, rather than banished, their criminals and opponents.

Maybe she was reading too much into this. The other man's greeting had been more a taunt than anything. The man turned shrewd eyes her way, and she held back a sneer of her own as he ran his gaze over her, as though inspecting chattel. Not that she looked her best—probably appearing pale and still shaken up, her hair in an almighty tangle. At least she'd braided it this morning, though the wind had still snatched at the strands so that loose tendrils stuck out all over her head, falling into her eyes and tickling her neck.

He might be a striking man, with a chiseled face and a powerful kind of grace to his body highlighted by the pewter gray power suit he wore, but he obviously knew it, if the strut was anything to judge by.

Please don't let this be Ladon.

"You must be Kasia." He bowed. "I am Chante, the king's Viceroy of the Reserve."

Translation, the guy in charge of the money. She

waited for more information, but he seemed to think his name enough to impress her.

"Nice to meet you." Was she supposed to curtsy? Use a title? "I apologize if there is some etiquette I'm unaware of. I wasn't raised among dragons."

"Of course." He stepped closer. "A phoenix. We haven't seen one in hundreds of years."

Was she mistaken about the greedy light in his eyes? *This* was what her mother had warned her about. Those who saw her only for the value she could bring them.

"I'm aware," she replied. At the same time, she stepped back to stand beside Brand, hiding a shiver of apprehension.

You're being an idiot, she told herself. Chante was probably a good guy underneath the show he was putting on. But instinct warned her that wasn't the case, so she made a mental note not to be alone with the guy. Ever.

A hush fell over the crowd of about thirty gathered on the platform. From the shadows of the massive cavern, a man appeared.

A man she'd seen before.

Dressed in utilitarian black pants and shirt instead of the tailored suit from her visions, the power he radiated wasn't for show. No, he practically screamed danger.

This had to be the king. Ladon Ormarr.

He was undeniably handsome in a hard sort of way, not unlike Brand, but dark in contrast with thick, jet black hair that had a curl to it, a cleft in his chin, and blue eyes, particularly striking against his deep olive-toned skin. A blue-eyed gaze that locked in on her like a laser.

Her first impression was one of brutality. This was a man who could unleash violence at any moment and feel nothing about it afterward.

Ladon said nothing as he approached, stopping directly in front of her. Chante stepped back with an obsequious little bow. She locked down the urge to roll her eyes and glanced at Brand for guidance. What was she supposed to do?

He gazed back with that closed expression. No help forthcoming.

So she drew herself up to her full height, tipped her chin up, and waited while Ladon Ormarr seemed to study her. Not in the calculating way Chante had, more as though he were looking for something within her.

Finally, he smiled, an act that appeared more forced than sincere. The people around her shifted on their feet.

"Turn around," he instructed. Demanded, more like.

His first words to her, uttered in a voice that matched his appearance—dark, gravelly, and dangerous. She didn't take offense; however, she wasn't one to blindly obey, either. "Why?"

A muscle twitched close to his eye, along the scar that ran the length of his face. Not a man used to being questioned. He didn't ask again, indicating with his hand that she should turn. A silent command.

She did as bidden only to connect with Brand's watchful golden gaze.

Ladon lifted her heavy braid away from her neck. Was he going to try to mate her right now?

Didn't there have to be sex involved?

She stiffened. So did Brand. Subtly. She doubted anyone else caught it. A low growl rumbled from him…only, she was pretty sure he hadn't made an audible sound. Had she heard a thought? No one else glanced his way.

With a small puff, Ladon blew a rush of fire over the back of her neck where a mating brand would show one day. Out of instinct, she tried to jerk away, but he held tight to her shoulders, and she watched in fascination as the blaze crawled down her arms and a faint glow appeared under her skin—a swirling design that grew brighter with each passing moment.

Feathers. Like a tribal tattoo with breathtaking, delicate markings on each.

A rush of heat bloomed inside her, pushing up from deep in her core. The sensation spread from her center outward until her own fire poured out of her to join the king's.

A gasp ran through the dragons gathered around them. Kasia raised her gaze to Brand, who watched in silence, his lips pressed together in a tight line.

"What does it mean?" she asked, irritated with the way her voice wouldn't quite work properly. It wasn't every day a girl sprouted fire wings.

Brand's gaze traveled over the flames consuming her, raising above her and swirling around her, forming wings of flame on either side of her. "You are the phoenix."

Brand trailed behind the procession of dragons as Ladon led Kasia through the massive cavern system the Blue Clan considered their hub and home base. Originally, this clan had used the natural caves already hollowed out by time and the elements, but over the centuries, they'd expanded them and built them into what equated to an underground city with the opulence of a French palace, complete with a system of mirrors which brought natural light inside, penetrating the dark, though only dimly today given the gray weather outside.

Riches had paid for the decor, thanks to millennia of dragons hoarding gold. The human myths of their kind got that much right. The Spanish explorers looking for El Dorado simply hadn't looked on the right continent or deep enough. Not that they would ever have gotten far enough to find the dragons' stash. These days, the Blue Clan's vaults were practically hollow—the legacy of Thanatos's betrayal—and their poverty was revealed through a general air of neglect.

"What do you think of your new home?" Ladon's question to Kasia floated back to Brand as they paused at yet another dragonsteel door, which required a scanned handprint or some other form of secure feature to unlock.

They'd added more security since he was here last. Higher tech, too.

"It's quite…impressive," Kasia answered.

Brand smiled at her polite response. He'd bet dimes to dollars that she wasn't all that impressed by the decor. While the caves were overwhelming on sheer scale, he doubted the uber-posh style of decoration was her style, though many of the valuable pieces appeared to have gone missing. He had no idea why he knew she wouldn't care. He just did.

Maybe the way she hadn't even blinked at the crappy motel he'd chosen, or the run-down beach house she'd woken up in after the motel incident, provided the clue. Or maybe because *he* considered it ostentatious.

Vague memories of a rougher, more rustic system of caves in another country, where he'd been born and raised—at least until his family had been taken from him and he'd had to run—felt more like home than this palatial grandness left over from kings before Thanatos. Though what Uther had done with Brand's home since then wasn't worth contemplating.

Of course, beyond wanting to restore his clan to its former glory, Ladon probably didn't give a rip. The king just didn't know that Kasia wouldn't be impressed, either.

A petite woman with thick black hair, dressed in body-hugging athletic wear in hot pinks with glitter, sashayed up to him. "So you found yourself a phoenix."

Brand kept walking. "I found her for the king, Arden."

A smirk graced her lips. "That's what I meant."

Sure, she did. He'd known Arden since she was a girl, and her favorite pastime was trying to get him to emote.

"Do you think he'll give you a place among us?" she mused.

"You tell me. He's your brother."

Up ahead, Ladon pointed out a room, and Kasia tipped her head to look inside as they passed, but then glanced quickly back, her eyes searching those around her until her gaze landed on him.

She quickly looked forward. No smile or acknowledgment, but she'd been searching for him, he knew it. And he shouldn't like it, dammit.

"Brand." Arden rested a hand on his forearm, pulling him to a stop.

He reluctantly paused, and together they waited as the entourage turned a curve in the tunnel, leaving them alone.

She pinched his arm.

"Ouch," he protested, rubbing the spot.

"I haven't seen you in ages. Talk to me." She gave a pout that he was sure worked on other men. Not sexy, more little girl lost in the woods. As a rare female-born dragon, Arden had grown up in the unusual position of having lots of male attention, but none romantically serious. Male dragons didn't bother to mate female-born. The fact that they were sterile made them a dead end.

As far as he could tell, Arden had made it her goal to compete in a male-driven society and used her femininity to manipulate the poor male saps around her. Only he saw her coming a league away.

Now a more speculative light glowed in those turquoise eyes of hers. What was she thinking? That as a rogue he might be desperate enough to mate her? Didn't she realize that, together, they'd be the lowest rung on the totem pole?

"It's not smart to get chummy," he reminded her.

Arden tipped her head, then laughed. "Ever the plotter." She backed away, lips tilted in a teasing smile. "How long do you intend to stay?"

"That depends on the king."

"Huh. Well don't leave without saying goodbye. And don't be a stranger while you're here."

He shook his head as she happily sauntered away. "Ladon needs to find you a keeper," he called after her departing form.

"He tried," she called back over her shoulder. "He says I'm so badass I scare them off." She kept walking, her black hair swinging in a ponytail, and flipped him off.

Following the sounds of low murmured voices, Brand made his way after the king and his soon-to-be queen. Only, when he got to a large common room, Ladon was there, but Kasia was missing. Like before, when Ladon had dared to bare her neck, a sacred spot reserved for mates, Brand had to fight back a growl.

The only thing that had stopped him was the lack of a mark that was supposed to show on her neck with the heat. When fire was applied to the back of a potential human mate's neck, a design would appear temporarily. Every male was born with the mark of his family already on his neck, which was why Brand wore his hair long. He didn't need other dragon shifters knowing who his family was. Not even Ladon knew.

The human women who showed dragon sign—smoke, small fires, or shifting small parts of themselves—would show the sign of their destined mate's house on their neck when dragon fire was applied. He wasn't sure what that meant for Kasia, who had shown no such mark; instead, only the feathers marking her as a phoenix had appeared. He'd heard that a phoenix had to choose her mate. Maybe that was true.

And he shouldn't give a damn. In a mere handful of days, he'd become way too possessive of her. He'd even hit a point where he didn't like her out of his sight, like right then when he'd expected her to be in the room. Brand shook off the feeling, one he was sure he'd get over quickly—he'd have to—and strode toward the king.

The space could not be described as a throne room, exactly. A massive fireplace and hearth were placed at each end—a feat of engineering in caves, but worth it for dragons. Groupings of couches and chairs and a few long tables with seats, all in shades of blue, of course, formed smaller seating and meeting areas throughout the larger space.

The few times Brand had been invited in, Ladon had preferred to conduct most of his business in that room. Something about the previous king holding too many secrets and, quote-unquote, not wanting to be like that asshole.

The mix of warriors, advisors, and hangers-on who'd greeted Kasia on arrival lounged about the room in packs. Those standing scattered out of Brand's path as he made his way across the room.

At least his reputation still had some clout. Between Kasia and Arden showing no fear of him, he'd begun to worry he'd lost his edge.

"Where's Kasia?" Brand asked as soon as he could do so without yelling it across the room.

Ladon slowly raised his eyebrows.

Damn, had that been too proprietorial? Too demanding?

"Resting," Ladon said.

It had been a long couple of days. Not to mention a long night. Unease on so many levels warred with a need that was all sorts of wrong. Something he acknowledged even as questions rang through his mind. Was she sore from his lovemaking? Did she want a repeat of last night? Because he sure as hell did, which was a big fucking problem.

That's all he'd had since he met Kasia. Problems.

"Plus, she needed to have her hands healed," Ladon commented.

Brand frowned. "She said she was fine."

The king winced. "Then she lied. Her hands were sliced. Said she cut them up on one of your spikes trying to hold on when you were attacked."

Inside, Brand laid down a string of curse words. She'd said nothing to him. Not even a whimper of pain during the long ride here. The tips of those spikes were lethally sharp. She could've cut off her fingers.

A dark anger—at himself, at Uther—surged through him.

Ladon studied him more closely now. "Don't worry. They were already starting to heal by the time you arrived, and Fallon will take care of the rest."

Brand schooled his features to neutral, an act which took more effort than normal. "I wasn't worried. I…"

What? Couldn't stand the thought of her in pain? Gods, he'd sound like an idiot. One with designs on the king's future mate.

"I wanted to deliver your phoenix in good health." Then Ladon's words registered. "Wait. Who's Fallon? What happened to Galen?"

"Fallon's also a healer, but he's been in the colonies for several hundred years. His brother runs the enforcers you visited. He was here meeting his new mate when I took power."

Brand vaguely remembered that Finn had a brother. "I see."

Ladon grunted and stood. "Walk with me."

The rest of the entourage must've known what that meant, because no one stood and followed. Ladon led them out of the great room through a side tunnel Brand hadn't explored before.

Like the other tunnels throughout the complex, this one was gray rock, its walls still roughly hollowed out with spiraling grooves but worn smooth over time. Most of the tunnels were large enough to accommodate dragon shifters in their full-sized forms as long as their wings remained folded back, but not this one. This one was human sized. In fact, as tall as he was, Brand felt like the rock was pressing in on him from above.

As soon as they were out of sight, they paused, listened a second, then Brand turned to Ladon right in time to get punched in the face.

He landed on his ass, then glared up at the king as he rubbed his jaw. "What the hell was that for?"

Ladon offered him a hand and pulled Brand to his feet. "You brought me a broken phoenix, asshole. Her hands were a bloody mess."

"So the punch was because...?"

"She was in pain, and you didn't notice."

Brand blew out a hard breath. "I'm already kicking myself that she hid it. No need to pile it on."

Ladon eyed him closely for a long second, then nodded. "Sorry."

"Whatever." Brand shook his head. "Asshole."

That earned him another hard stare until they both broke. Grinning, they embraced as brothers.

"Fuck, Brand," Ladon said as they stood back.

"I know."

"That was a big risk you took, bringing her here on your own."

Brand grinned. "Worth it."

Ladon clapped him on the shoulder, and they continued down the hall. "Who else knows about her?"

He didn't need an interpreter to figure out what his friend meant. He wanted to know how many creatures were already after their prize. Brand shrugged. "The doctor at the clinic who tipped you off had loose lips."

Ladon grimaced and ran a hand through his hair. "What'd you encounter on the way here?"

"Wolves. Vampires. Uther."

"Fuck." Ladon cocked his head. "That it?"

Brand laughed. "I'd say that's enough."

"Anything else?"

"A hellhound." It'd taken more than a day to separate that smoky scent from his and Kasia's, but the taint of death underneath, sour and rotting, had given it away in the end.

Ladon swore under his breath. "Dammit. Even Pytheios knows better than to mess with hellhounds.

How did *they* get involved?"

"No idea. Other than you and Hershel, I had no contact with anyone." He crooked an eyebrow.

Ladon took the hint and glanced around. "You already know about my source in Pytheios's camp."

Brand nodded. "He's remained useful?"

"Yes. What about the bar you stayed at last night? Any of them need watching?"

Brand shook his head at that. "Hershel's got it under control."

Ladon nodded slowly. "I know you trust him, but—"

"He practically raised me after Uther wiped out my family." Brand glanced behind them and listened for a second, but no one else was anywhere near them. "If you hadn't smuggled me to those caves and he hadn't found me after that and taken me in, I wouldn't be here. I trust him the same way I trust you."

Ladon held up a hand. "Okay."

A small amount of the tension riding Brand's body eased. At least one worry was off his plate. Not the biggest worry, and not enough to make him relax around here, but that had more to do with being surrounded by so many shifters at once. That and Kasia, and the next step in plans he'd been carefully laying.

"I know what you did for me out there," Ladon said.

Brand remained silent.

"You brought me the key to victory, the key to eventual peace."

A boulder of protest settled in his gut. "I brought

you a woman who, I should warn you, is determined to choose her mate for herself."

Now why the fuck had he felt the need to warn his friend? It couldn't be the proprietary surge of emotion that seemed determined to wreck his plans for how this was going down.

"I'll bear that in mind." Ladon grinned like he thought the idea of Kasia refusing him was amusing, and Brand tried not to knock the smirk off that scarred face.

"Bringing her to you serves my own purposes," he felt compelled to remind the man.

Ladon sobered. "I know."

Good.

Ladon turned left down another winding corridor. This one narrower with heavy wooden doors sporting numbers branded into the wood. He'd never been to this area before. Were they apartments? Guest suites? Large ones based on the space between doors. Ladon walked down to one and paused there to turn the iron knob. The door opened with a squeak of metal on metal as the hinges protested.

This place was run-down, a legacy from the previous king who'd been weak. Thanatos had given everything over to Pytheios. Riches, resources, warriors. Even mates.

Brand had worked with Ladon—providing intel, taking out minor players, and supplying resources like weapons and food from his non-dragon contacts—until Ladon had taken that pawn out of the chess game permanently. A better king sat on the throne now.

"This is your room for the time being," he said.

Brand pulled his thoughts out of the past and glanced around, taking in the room laid out by the natural terrain of stalactites and stalagmites forming a suite with a distinct bedroom, sitting area, and bathroom, decorated in blues and golds, though visibly faded and worn.

"Kasia is next door." Ladon nodded to the suite that was one more door up. "We're fairly full here since Pytheios took our Alps location."

Brand wanted to protest, but given the reason, knew he wouldn't get far.

"Until I figure out what the best course of action is with you," Ladon tacked on.

That caught his attention. Brand turned away from his inspection of the room, head cocked.

Ladon's mouth flattened, his jaw working, and he suddenly appeared older than his years, the weight of the crown resting heavily on his shoulders.

But what was there to decide about him? Brand had proved his loyalty publicly, which should have allowed them to move on to the next step in the plan—making him part of the Blue Clan.

"You've proved your loyalty a hundred times over. No other dragon would have brought a phoenix to another dragon without guaranteed payment of some sort, and especially not a dragon like you. Not unless you were loyal." Ladon held up both hands before Brand could speak. "As your friend, I already knew that, but now my Curia Regis know it, as do my warriors."

"But?"

"We have a problem."

Brand crossed his arms. "The clan won't accept a gold dragon who's been rogue for five centuries?"

Ladon snorted. "No. That would be *your* problem."

Okay.

Ladon leaned against the wall and crossed his arms. "My informant among Pytheios's people has demanded I turn you over to him as payment for his information."

Brand fisted his hands even as he kept his shoulders loose and his expression neutral. By habit, he'd already checked the room for smells or sounds that might indicate danger. No one else was anywhere nearby to take him away. "Why?"

"So that he may retain the appearance of unimpeachable loyalty to Pytheios. You know he's the reason I found you and Kasia in the first place. He risked his life to provide that intel."

Brand kept his fists balled tightly. "I see. What do you intend to do?" Because Ladon could swing either way. He did whatever got him results.

"I'm still working that out."

Would slamming his fist through the rock wall show too much emotion? After helping Ladon take the throne, and after what he'd just done, he was to be payment to someone else? Because he was rogue, that made him expendable? Even to the one man of only two on the planet he trusted?

Fuck that. Fury pumped through Brand's blood in heated bursts of adrenaline.

He'd take Kasia and—

"I'm not going to turn you over," Ladon assured. "Which is why I'm telling you this."

Anger continued to churn in him, though the heat

turned down to a slow simmer. Brand narrowed his eyes as he worked to steady his breathing. "No?"

"No. I'll figure out another way to help my informant. I would never give you up."

"Yeah?" The words came out as a low growl.

Ladon crossed the room and clapped a hand on Brand's shoulder. "I trust you more than any man in my clan. That makes you my brother."

Brand hissed as heat manifested in his arm, feeling as though a red-hot poker were being jammed through the flesh between his thumb and forefinger. He held up his hand to discover an insignia as the intricate lines that represented the house of Ormarr formed, glowing white hot.

Trying to keep things light, he glanced at his friend. "Ironic that my new king has an old Norse last name. There must be some gold dragon in you somewhere down the line."

Ladon shook his head at that.

The glow on Brand's hand faded, leaving the black design etched into his skin for all to see. After almost five hundred years as a rogue, abandoned by his people, Brand Astarot had a clan. Only now, unlike the day he'd been born, the mark on his hand did not match the one on his neck.

XI

They sure treat a phoenix well around this place.

Kasia had been escorted to a private room. The cave system housed deep within the mountain of Ben Nevis, where the Blue Clan lived, turned out to be a massive home for all the dragons, with suites built into the rock like a honeycomb network. Soft white lights, which gave the appearance of natural sunlight, originated from a balcony window she had yet to explore and lined the ceiling.

Built and designed into the natural caverns, her favorite part was the matching en suite bathroom that boasted a spa tub, large enough to swim laps in, sunk into the floor, lit from below like her own private pool.

After a long soak in the tub and changing into the clothing provided to her, she felt a million times better. Granted, the clothes they gave her were also frillier than her typical jeans and tank top. The most casual outfit she'd found in the closet involved slim fitting black capris slacks with silver embroidery along the hem and pockets, and a deep blue cap-sleeved silk blouse that displayed way more cleavage than she was strictly comfortable with. At least she'd found a pair of silver ballet flats among the collection of stilettos. No way was she torturing her feet with those contraptions.

She'd picked up a book from a pile that had been thoughtfully provided, but mostly to kill time until something else happened.

The sharp rap of someone knocking on her door disturbed the serene silence of her cave bedroom. Kasia gratefully hopped up to answer it.

No peep hole in the door. That seemed like a bad idea.

"Who is it?" she called through the heavy wooden door.

"Brand."

Finally. When he hadn't shown up while she was with the healer, or when she was brought to her room, she'd figured he was doing a download with the king, or Ladon as she'd been asked to call the man in line to be her mate.

But then she'd waited hours.

His room was next door, she'd been told, and Brand was the only person she knew here. While she'd been treated with kindness, she could use seeing a familiar face. With a smile, she swung the door open, doing her best to ignore the eager hopping of her heart. Harder to ignore when Brand ran his gaze over her and suddenly everywhere he'd touched her last night flared to strung-out life. Meanwhile, the sight of him in a new pair of jeans and black T-shirt was doing wicked things to her, heating her up.

"You combed your hair." He'd also pulled the sides back. She'd never been into longer hair on men, but she found Brand's worked for him. She grinned and resisted the urge to reach out and muss it back up.

Tawny eyes, a predator's eyes, stared back at her, but with a distance that hadn't been there before now.

Growing more irritated with his attitude, Kasia proceeded to have a conversation with herself, filling in Brand's part for him.

"What do you think of your new digs, Kasia?" she rumbled in a deep bass, her attempt at a Brand impersonation. She even pretended to have bulging muscles, lifting up her arms to pretend to stand like him.

In a falsetto, she answered her own question. "This place is intimidating and ostentatious, Brand, but I think I can look past that. Thanks for asking."

Another round of Brand in fake low voice. "I only want you to be happy, Kasia."

The real Brand half sighed, half growled. "Kasia."

She ignored him, continuing her part in squeaky voice. "Awwww. You're such a teddy bear, Boo-boo."

"Boo-boo?"

The disgust lacing his voice had Kasia bursting out laughing. "My imaginary Brand likes it when I call him Boo-boo."

Brand's jaw clenched. "No, he wouldn't."

"You don't get to dictate what my imaginary Brand likes or doesn't like. I've known him longer than you."

"But—" Brand cut off his own argument and shook his head. "I can't believe we're talking about this."

Kasia shrugged. "You brought it up. I was having a lovely conversation with you."

"What's your point?" Brand finally grumbled.

"My point is, whatever your problem is, don't take it out on me."

"I don't have a problem." But he wouldn't look

her in the eye.

"Right. That's why you've been doing your best impression of a silent stone statue since we got here."

"What do you want from me?" he asked in an even tone that implied some sort of patience, as though she was acting like a petulant teen and he was the righteous, put-upon male. Granted, antagonizing him on purpose sort of fell under the bratty teenager heading, but she just couldn't stand the distance he'd put between them.

It made her feel lost and small. She was fully aware how crazy and slightly pathetic that sounded, even in her head. "You promised to help me settle in."

Crap, I'm turning into a whiner.

He gave his head a single shake. "No. I promised not to dump you here, and I'm not."

A need to break that distance surged through her. Before he could say anything, Kasia stepped in to him, kissing those harsh lips, tasting him again.

Whoa.

She gasped and yanked back as a flutter of pain tinged the pleasure piercing her core. She stared at Brand with wide eyes.

Not now, dammit. She couldn't have a vision now.

"Are you—?"

Her sight blacked out, and she nodded quickly.

"I'll go get Ladon."

She shook her head. "I haven't explained my visions to him yet. It would be…" *Wrong.* "I need to figure out if I trust him first."

"But he should really be the one—"

She managed to whirl on one foot, ignoring how her head spun with the movement, and grope her way to the couch. "I'll handle it myself if you can't help. This place is flame retardant. Right?"

"Like hell." He followed her inside, slamming the door shut behind him.

Kasia winced as the noise only increased the ache gathering behind her eyes.

This one wasn't coming on as fast. More like brushes of tingling, followed by slivers of stinging. She may not have his touch—and no way would she ask, even after what they'd shared—but the pleasure he'd given her had helped with the pain, too. Maybe she could do that for herself? Urgency pressed into Kasia, driving away all inhibitions—not that she'd ever seemed to have any around Brand, anyway. With trembling fingers, she managed to unbutton her pants, shoving them off, baring her flesh so she could stimulate herself.

"*Fuck*," she heard Brand mutter.

She ignored him and focused on her mission, trying every trick that usually worked for her, but her own touch did nothing. The pain only grew faster and had begun to override her system, turning into razors along her nerves.

All the while, Brand remained in the room, watching but not helping. Waiting to contain her fire, she guessed. Dammit. He felt this, too, right? Why wasn't he helping her? Helping *them*?

Tears of frustration pricked her eyes, but the pressure only added to her misery, her head pounding with the rhythm of her heartbeat. The next wave pulled a yelp from her lips. She couldn't have held it back if she'd tried.

A low groan reached her ears from across the room.

Kasia sucked in a deep breath. "Help me," she whispered.

Another wave stole the sound from the last word, and she dropped her head back to the couch again, unable to hold it up.

"The hell with this." In two strides Brand knelt between her legs. The second his hands were on her knees, the worst of the pain ebbed.

"Gods help us both," he growled.

A rustle of movement and then pressure at her entrance. Kasia arched as Brand slid one, then two fingers inside her.

"Yes," she hissed as the sensations flaying her insides immediately turned intensely soft. Beautiful. Kasia pumped her hips. "More," she begged. "More."

With a groan, Brand leaned forward and set his mouth to her body. Hot, wet heat flicked over her clit as he used tongue and teeth and lips.

Warmth lit her entire body as her fire finally spread. The rustle of his wings sounded seconds before the odd feeling of being cocooned overtook her. Brand pumped those fingers and circled her clit with his tongue, the pressure just what she needed.

Not what she wanted. She wanted more of him, but that was impossible. She'd take what she could get.

A whimper escaped her as he removed his fingers, only to be followed by a long, low moan as he speared his tongue inside her. She spiked her fingers through his hair, holding him to her as she felt every stroke to the core of her being.

Now the pleasure built fast—orgasm racing her oncoming vision. As Brand increased his speed, the power intensified, slamming through her system as she moaned and gasped and writhed. He reached his other hand up under the fall of her hair, brushing a finger against the nape of her neck, and that simple touch triggered her. Finally, everything coiled tightly inside her only to blow outward.

The vision came on the heels of her orgasm, as though the culmination of pleasure had thrown open the door for the images. It hijacked her mind as comprehensively as desire had stolen her body.

Kasia stepped into it as though she were in a waking dream. She looked down and gasped at the sight of her belly rounded with child. Someone stepped up behind her, and a male hand caressed her stomach.

Was this her future? With Ladon? Before she could turn and see who held her, multiple images chased themselves through her mind's eye, but softly as butterfly kisses...

Brand waking her in the morning with a sweet kiss. Brand arguing with her. Brand sitting beside her at some kind of meeting. Brand holding her hand in the woods.

Kasia floated back to reality from the high. Tears ran down her cheeks in warm rivulets that evaporated even as she recognized them for what they were.

I'm crying?

A gentle touch feathered over her cheeks, and she opened her eyes to find Brand wiping away her tears as he shifted his wings, folding them back before absorbing them into himself. "You okay?"

Not hardly. She dreamed of one man, saw him in her visions so regularly she'd fantasized about him for a year. And yet, she had to mate another.

For all her blustering about choices, she'd known that the second she set foot in this mountain she had none. No way would Ladon let her leave or mate another, not with what was on the line for him.

High King.

So what the hell were these images about? Was fate taunting her with a future she could never have? Or showing her what she'd walked away from when she came here?

It doesn't matter. I've chosen my path. Now I have to walk it.

Shaken to her core, Kasia did what her mother had trained her to do well.

Lie. Cover. Misdirect.

"Of course." She pushed through the exhaustion that wanted to pull her down and stood, dragging up her pants. "Thanks for the help. I'm going to wash up. I suggest you do, too."

Before she could make it to the door, he stopped her. "Kasia."

She turned back, hand on her hip, and spoke before he could. "You know, the orgasm seemed to help the vision come easier, less overwhelming, without most of the pain." Just good pain. "Definitely better than how things usually go." That was for damn sure.

Brand scowled. "I'm not going to—"

"I wonder if it will work the same way with Ladon?"

That shut him up. Good. She didn't need him asking about what she'd seen. She gave a deliberately casual shrug, then turned and sauntered into her room. "Guess I'll find out soon enough."

Brand watched Kasia disappear with every emotion under the sun roiling inside him. He still physically ached for her after bringing that glorious body to completion, needing his own release. Meanwhile a cocktail of desire, frustration, and unjustifiable possessiveness warred with the fact that she was supposed to become another man's mate. His friend's mate. His new king's mate.

Fuck.

Not to mention how she'd thrown that fact in his face. *Guess I'll find out soon enough*, she'd said before shutting the door and closing him out. There was no way she knew the same question had been on his mind since the first time he'd kissed her. Was she trying to piss him off?

Brand stalked out of her room and was halfway down the hall to his own when he jerked to a stop.

He'd shown up at her door to take her to Ladon, dammit. His orders hadn't changed.

Hand on his hips, he dropped his head forward, staring, unseeing, at the ground. With a growl, he pivoted and slammed back into her suite. She wasn't out yet, so he pounded on the bedroom door. "Don't take too long. We have to go."

Silence.

"Kasia?"

"Give me a second," she snapped.

Brand went to the sink in the kitchen area to wash his hands and face of her so Ladon wouldn't suspect. Gods how he'd wanted to suck her taste from his fingers. He hadn't had sex with her, not right under the king's nose, because even a rogue had some honor. Not enough to keep from tasting her or touching the back of her neck, though. What the fuck had he been thinking?

His rock-hard erection taunted him with the answer.

He glanced at the closed door as the water in the bathroom turned off. Should he check on her?

He snorted the thought away. Definitely not. Besides, if he went in there, he might not come out without doing something he'd regret.

Brand frowned as a thought struck. Had she tried to piss him off on purpose, or at least throw him off balance? Why? What was she hiding? What had she seen in that vision?

He tossed a speculative glance at the door. Should he barge in and demand she tell him? No, that wouldn't work. She was as stubborn as he was. Maybe more.

Shit. He'd have to let it go. Didn't matter anyway, because this had to be over.

Kasia pushed through the exhaustion that came with her visions, not as bad this time, since this one had been gentler. Not in intensity, per se, but in content. Maybe that mattered?

She used to understand how the whole vision thing worked, but nothing had been right since Brand came along and messed everything up. Why did his touch obliterate the pain? And how did pleasure factor into it?

She paused at her door and took a deep breath before opening it to find Brand leaning against a wall messing with his phone like nothing had happened.

Those damn tears jumped back into her eyes.

"Where are we going?" Good. At least she'd managed to sound cool and collected.

He stood up from the wall. "The king would like you to join him for dinner. That's what I came here for in the first place."

And got waylaid by her visions. Kasia's heart stuttered and sank. Mr. Straight-to-Business. "And he sent you?"

"He thought you'd be more comfortable with me until you make a few friends here and figure out who you can trust."

In other words, he was not her friend or even someone she could trust. Just a stand-in. Message received.

Again with the dang tears. Kasia blinked. Focus. Next steps.

She needed to be adjusting her thinking about Ladon. Her soon-to-be-mate. Kasia considered her mental image of the brutal-looking man who'd greeted her at the landing pad. The one who looked capable of killing at any second.

He'd been a polite host, pointing out interesting or informative aspects of the dragon city to her as they walked through security door after security door to a massive common area. He'd also been kind—trying to make her feel welcome, making sure her hands were healed, and now dinner. Maybe Ladon Ormarr was nicer than his terrifying appearance and reputation suggested.

Well, damn.

Guilt dripped through her about the night she'd shared with Brand, not to mention what had just happened.

Her spine straightened. Wait. There was no reason to feel guilty. She wasn't his mate yet.

Tell that to the lump taking up residence in her gut.

Until she put a face and personality to Ladon, he had been an abstract. Now he was her reality. Better to deal with that fact square on and get to settling down. No more heart tripping up or blood fizzing around a certain closed-off shifter.

She waved a hand at the door. "Lead on, Mr. Astarot."

Brand grunted, then led her out to the hallway and waited while she locked up. As soon as she clicked the lock into place, without a word, he turned and strode off down the hallway at a rapid clip.

Kasia glared at his back as she hustled to catch up, then keep up with those damn long legs of his. "In a hurry?" she panted after several seconds.

He dropped an unsmiling glance her way and did his silent act, but did slow his pace.

The insufferable bastard. The words popped out before she could stop them. "That can't happen again."

Good one. Way to move on.

"No shit."

He stopped walking, so she did too. "I'm not trying to be rude. It's just that I have to..." The stupid tears clogged her up, so she shook her head. "Never mind. You already get it. No need to go on."

She kept moving down the hall.

A frustrated growl echoed off the stone of the hollowed-out hallway. She glanced at one of the framed paintings on the wall, worried it might shake off, but it didn't move. Then he was beside her, a hand on her arm to slow her down. "I'm sorry—"

Kasia shook her head and her arm, knocking off his hand. "Don't apologize. This is my problem."

"It is?"

"Yes. You were right. Ladon's going to be my mate." She hid a grimace. "I should learn to trust him, rather than rely on you."

She could feel Brand studying her as they walked together, but she meant what she'd said. No sarcasm. No hidden meaning. Because no matter what they'd shared, she and Brand were on the best paths available to them now, and those paths were not the same.

No going back.

They came to a T in the halls, and she glanced at him. "Which way?"

"Left." She turned that direction only to be stopped by his lowly murmured, "Kasia..."

She paused, her back to him, and sighed. "Seriously, Brand. Don't worry about it. I was acting like a..." Pampered princess? No way was she giving him that one. She rolled her shoulders as she turned to face him. "I'm just nervous and unsure, and you're the only person I know."

And I'm so alone, it scares me.

He searched her expression with those hooded eyes that gave away nothing. "Don't worry. What you'll bring to this clan...you'll be treated like royalty. You'll be fine."

Kasia wanted to toss her hands in the air, frustrated equally with herself and with him. After what they'd been through—what they'd done together—you'd think he'd know that being a princess was not her thing. And you'd think he'd have some kind of personal feeling about it, one way or another.

Slow your roll, Kas. Didn't you just decide to put that episode in the past where it belonged?

And now she was having conversations with herself again. Damn, she was losing her grip.

Brand broke eye contact first, tipping his chin in the direction they needed to go. "Your intended mate is waiting."

Right. Stop staring at another man, or thinking about another man, or fantasizing about another man. Just stop.

She turned sharply away and continued down the hall with him dogging her steps. "Don't call him that."

"Why? He *is* your intended mate."

"The way you say it sounds like a curse."

Silence as a response. Shocker.

God, she was being such a bitch. Brand had reasons for his decisions, too, and she was overlooking that. "I should've asked sooner... Did you get what you came here for?"

He opened his mouth, but paused, and she thought he wouldn't answer. "I have a clan now," he finally admitted in a gruff voice as he lifted his hand, showing her the mark there.

Brand was no longer a rogue.

Heaviness lifted from her heart. At least Brand had finally achieved a home. She was safe, and he had a clan. Their plan was working exactly as it should.

So why did she feel so empty? Like the tin man in the stories—hollow.

The hallway suddenly expanded as they approached a massive, dragon-sized set of wooden double doors. Brand stopped. "Hey."

That one word from the man at her side and she paused as well, letting her gaze trail over his rugged face as she waited for whatever he had to say. After a silent beat, he grabbed both her wrists and flipped her hands over. Then a low hiss escaped him, and her nerves pricked along her skin at the sound. Anger? Irritation with her? Kasia sucked in a silent breath as he ran a finger lightly over the slash of white scar tissue gracing her palms.

"Why didn't you say something?" he asked.

She tugged out of his grasp. "We needed to get out of there. I was fine." Then she gave him a bright smile. "Besides, Fallon was a revelation."

He nodded. "The new healer. He's a universal donor, I assume?"

"Yeah." The second the dragon healer had injected Kasia with his blood—just a little bit, since Fallon wasn't sure what it would do to a phoenix—Kasia's hands had started healing faster. In minutes the agonizing open slashes had closed, leaving angry pink scars that had continued to heal the rest of the day. Like watching a time-lapse video.

"Good. Let's go." Brand pushed one of the doors open and held it for her.

Guess that's that.

A few more twists and turns and the corridors opened up. They passed a few dragon shifters, none in their dragon forms, all of whom stared as they walked by, though Kasia couldn't tell if they were staring at her or at Brand. He did tower over them—a mark of a gold dragon, which tended to be larger and stronger than the others. Blue dragons tended to be smaller, leaner, and faster.

No one dared speak to them, though.

Royalty?

Yeah, right. She'd be a bug under a microscope with every naysayer just waiting to disprove her worth. Kasia inched closer to Brand, who thankfully didn't seem to notice.

Then she stopped dead as the hall opened up into what she could only term an atrium. The place was massive. Essentially, the mountain itself had been gouged out from the base to the top.

The ground level, where they stood, reminded Kasia of a busy downtown street in any human city, except round. "Buildings" lined the rim, the faces built into the rock itself and taking up maybe two stories. The floors above that point appeared to be suites like her own and rose up to the top of the cone.

Under every balcony a giant slab of rock jutted out. Dragons flew overhead, circling up to land on a perch where they'd shift then walk inside. No wonder the hallways had been relatively empty. She'd figured Brand was taking her the back way, and he was. Since she couldn't fly, the back way *was* her way.

Guess I'll have to work on the teleporting.

Kasia gathered her jaw off the floor where it'd dropped and moved forward to join Brand, who waited. She moved her attention to the first two levels, which appeared to be businesses of all types. Restaurants, shops, a bookstore, grocers, even a nail salon and a barber.

With whatever trick of lighting the dragons used inside these caves, she felt as though she were walking down any bustling main street in the late afternoon when the sun had dropped behind the buildings. The only thing missing was cars.

Stares and whispers followed the two of them as Brand led her past most of the shops to the glass-door entrance of what appeared to be a classy restaurant. Italian food, by the name—*Il Dragone*. He held open the door and waved her to precede him inside.

"But we just had Italian at Hershel's," she whispered as she sidled by Brand.

He didn't respond, but his mouth twitched.

Inside was all white linen tablecloths, gleaming silverware, and candlelight. A single intimate table for two was set in the middle of the room. However, she and Ladon weren't the only ones there. Six or seven men, as well as one woman, stood behind the king in a semicircle, their appearances reflecting a mix of the human side of their heritage. Her mother had once called it the most beautiful gift human dragon mates could give to the clans, and in the face of Ladon's group, Kasia had to agree. The only features they shared were the lean builds and blue eyes consistent with their clan, though even their eyes varied in shade.

Kasia hesitated. She recognized several of these dragons, and not just from the platform earlier today, but from her visions. Had fate always meant her to end up here?

Ladon waved her over. Brand, in the meantime, took up a position standing just inside the door. Could the others feel the tension rolling off both of them? All Kasia could think about was how he'd just helped her come an hour ago.

She tried to forget he was there and focused, instead, on her host. As she approached, the woman stepped closer. "Kasia, I'd like you to meet my sister, Arden."

The female dragon from her honor guard earlier.

Beyond the same jet-black hair and olive-toned skin, there was little family resemblance between the siblings. Smaller, and not just in height, Arden Ormarr was delicate, with chocolate-box pretty features made more exotic by eyes the color of the sea in the sun. Her smile—a real one that reached her eyes, unlike her brother's—was full of kindness that shined in a way Kasia had rarely experienced in her life.

Maybe she'd misjudged the female shifter?

What had Kasia flummoxed, though, was she'd seen this woman before many times.

Arden held out a hand to shake. "Pleasure to

meet you."

"I feel like I already know you," Kasia replied as she grasped her hand, having to resist the odd urge to hug her.

Arden raised her eyebrows and shot a quick glance at Ladon. "Oh?"

"Since I've come into my powers"—so much easier to put it that way than connect it with her mother's death—"I have visions. You've been in several."

Beside her, Ladon straightened, suddenly harder and less relaxed, like if she touched him he'd be hewn from stone. One or two of the men around him stiffened as well.

His eyes went hard and cold, revealing a hint of the ruthless ruler who'd taken his crown by force. "Visions?" Ladon asked. "Of what?"

Kasia shared a glance with Brand, but that was a mistake, only reminding her of other visions. Ones she wanted to forget. She jerked her gaze back.

She had spent the parts of the trip when they weren't being attacked or she wasn't going up in flames debating what to share with the king and his people, finally settling on telling them about anything Brand already knew. He would probably share it all, anyway.

She watched Ladon carefully and gave a small shrug. "The future is my best guess. I can't control them, I can't hear anything, and up until I met Brand I wasn't even sure what I was seeing was real. But he was in some of them, too. So were several of you"—she glanced at the wall of men behind him— "and a few others. Most haven't come true yet, but they're happening faster now."

Ladon looked to Brand, who didn't react. Neither did the men. "I'd like to hear more about what you've seen, maybe tomorrow?"

Kasia nodded—not that she'd be telling him about the latest one. Ever.

Arden also caught the shared glance between men and jumped in. "That's really cool."

Kasia grimaced. "I guess. When they come on, they come with fire that I can't control and a full-body migraine, but a vision is why we escaped some wolf shifters on our way here, so they have their uses."

"Maybe you'll get better at them, and they can help Ladon win this war." Arden's enthusiasm stood in stark contrast to her brother's suspicious reserve. Arden leaned in, curiosity shining from her wide eyes. "What was I doing in your visions?"

Kasia grinned now. "Usually nothing. Talking to me, but I can't hear what you're saying."

"Sounds about right," one of the men quipped. The tallest of the bunch, with his deep black skin, was one of the dragons she'd seen in her visions. She knew he was even more handsome when he grinned. She also happened to know he had a diamond-shaped tattoo over his heart.

"Yeah," the bald brute beside him jumped in. "She never shuts up."

He softened his words with a wink at Arden, who scrunched up her nose at him, then turned back to Kasia with a sigh. "Sounds pretty boring."

Arden tossed a glare at Ladon, who crossed his arms and glared back, though without any menace behind it. "What? You're blaming me for you being boring?"

"Yup." Arden tipped her chin up to deliver a stare that dared him to argue before she faced Kasia, rolling her eyes. "He never lets me do anything."

"But you came to get me," Kasia pointed out.

"Only because this lot was with me." She hitched a thumb at the men.

The guys grinned. Most of them, anyway.

"And Ladon thought a female might put you more at ease," Arden continued.

Kasia watched the exchange between the siblings as well as the men around them with a growing knot in her stomach. They reminded her of so many random conversations with her own sisters. Now she swallowed down the memories and focused on this moment instead, laughing at Arden's antics.

She shook it off. "Actually, if I had to hazard a guess, I think we'll become good friends."

Arden lit up at that, giving Kasia a truly delighted smile that brought dimples out to play in her cheeks. "Fabulous."

Ladon glanced between them, then sighed. "My intention was to have Arden help you settle in here, but now I'm wondering if she's going to be a bad influence."

Kasia chuckled. "Probably the other way around."

Brand would certainly think so. She gave herself a mental shake. She needed to stop thinking about him. Even if he was standing right there and they'd just…

"Terrific," Diamond Tattoo muttered, interrupting her thoughts.

Arden's hand was still on her arm, or Kasia would've missed how the other woman stiffened at the word. She gave no other sign, though; instead she laughed. "I like you already."

"Definitely a mistake," Ladon said. No smile, but no conviction, either.

Kasia liked this marginally lighter side to the king, making him more human and less of the bloodthirsty, politically hungry tyrant she'd built up in her head.

He placed a hand at her back. "I would also like you to meet my men. These are my personal guard, as well as my closest friends and fiercest warriors."

The men didn't make a sound, but they stood taller, shoulders back, heads held high—proud.

"Fallon you've already met," Ladon said.

Fallon winked at her, eyes twinkling.

She nodded at the healer who'd helped her earlier in the day. The shortest of the group—which wasn't saying much, since he was still at least six feet tall—he also had the kindest smile, one that invited you to smile back and join in his fun. Vaguely she wondered what his mate was like, probably perky and adorable, not to mention feisty to keep his fun-loving side in line.

The next man reminded her a bit of Brand in that he seemed the silent, observant type. Around the same age as Ladon, of Asian descent somewhere in his ancestry, possibly Japanese if she had to guess, he had a similar hard look in his eyes, which were so dark blue they appeared black.

"This is Asher," Ladon said. "He is my Beta as well as part of my Curia Regis, Viceroy of Security."

Asher nodded, and she returned the gesture.

Next Ladon stopped in front of Diamond Tattoo. "Reid is Captain of my Guard. He keeps this lot in line. He's also on my Curia Regis, as Viceroy of War."

A good-natured grumbling rose from the group as she nodded at the man.

So this guy is the badass of the group. Got it.

She didn't voice that opinion, though. The other men wouldn't appreciate the observation. The bigger question was, did she share the vision she'd had of Reid and Arden with her soon-to-be good friend, or not?

"This is Duncan. He's our other mated man of the group."

The loud, brash, bald one with skin so pale he could try out for the invisible man, grinned at her. He was missing a tooth. Shouldn't that have grown back? His mate must be something else.

The others were Wyot—a quiet, dark-skinned man who seemed to be the steady one of the bunch—as well as brothers Ivar and Rainier, one a dirty blond, the other with darker hair, but with identical grins to go with their bright blue eyes.

The men nodded, though some, like Reid and Asher, with more reserve than others.

"We'll make ourselves scarce," Arden said as she took a few sideways steps toward the door. "I thought a formal introduction would be helpful before we just start randomly showing up at your door."

"I see. And why would you all randomly show up?" She glanced at Ladon.

He took her hand, tugging her around to face him. "As my personal guard, they will take turns guarding you as well now."

Kasia scowled and let go of his hand. "I don't need babysitters." She glanced at the men. "No offense."

Duncan guffawed. "None taken."

"We're under a constant state of attack. Mostly small skirmishes, and none have made it inside the mountain yet. However, I expect that to increase as word of a phoenix leaks out, and I'm not taking a chance with you."

Kasia crossed her arms. "Am I a prisoner?"

"Your Grace." The quiet correction came from Asher.

"Excuse me?" Kasia said.

"He's your king. You address him as 'Your Grace,'" Asher clarified, expression not giving an inch.

A quick glance at Brand showed no help from that corner, so she turned back to Asher. "He's not my king. Not yet, at least."

Six glowers met those words. She definitely wasn't winning friends with that comment, but she refused to let them think otherwise.

Brand stood by the door and did his damnedest not to put himself bodily between her and the angry shifters forming a wall in front of her.

If he could, he would've turned his back to them. Hell, if he could, he wouldn't be here in the first damn place, especially not after the way he'd helped her climax in her room. But Ladon had asked him to stand as Kasia's personal bodyguard, taking the majority of the shifts with her until the mating. The idea being he'd bond with Ladon's other most trusted warriors gradually.

Just his fucking luck she'd get herself in trouble within five minutes of meeting them. She'd have to get herself out of this, because he needed them on his side as much as she did. Maybe more.

Brand focused on his job. Physical protection only. But not too physical. Dammit. He scanned the people passing in front of the restaurant, but no one stood out. No alarm bells went off, which gave him plenty of time to listen in to the conversation going on inside the room.

Kasia sighed.

But rather than address his men, Kasia turned to Ladon and put a hand on his arm. The men tensed, Asher's hand going to the knife at his belt, the hiss of the metal against the scabbard audible.

Brand turned and loosed a warning rumble of noise, and the room went dead silent, tension thick enough to wring out of a wet towel blanketing all inside.

Fuckballs. Not his best move.

Ladon gave a single shake of his head, and the men eased off. Sort of. Asher, at least, dropped the blade back into its holder. Brand, however, didn't relax. He waited.

Kasia slowly lowered her hand, clasping it behind her. "Can I be honest?"

Ladon regarded her unsmilingly. "Yes."

"Fancy isn't really my thing, and while I appreciate

you trying to put me at ease at this lovely restaurant, introducing me to your…closest friends, I suspect fancy is maybe not your thing, either."

What the hell? Was that seriously what she wanted to say so earnestly?

Ladon stared at her for a beat, clearly as surprised as Brand, then laughed. A rusty, unused sound Brand had certainly never heard before. "That is definitely honest."

Even some of his warriors smiled, though not Asher.

Kasia winced. "Sorry. It's just… Mother kept us under the radar my entire life, working menial jobs, blending in with humans whom dragons wouldn't notice. We had a garden and raised chickens and ate simply—"

"I think I understand," Ladon stopped her.

Really? Ladon understood?

She gave an apologetic grimace. "Yeah?"

Ladon chuckled. "Yes. Actually, it's a relief."

Kasia straightened, eyes brightening. "Really?"

"Yes. My family didn't have much, either. I may have come from a long line of upper-class snobs—"

"A lot o' wealthy arses, if ya ask me," Duncan said in his thick Scottish accent.

Arden looked heavenward with a shake of her head as the men chuckled. Brand guessed this was a common joke among them.

Ladon ignored the bald warrior. "But the previous king bled this clan dry, giving tribute to Pytheios to keep a false peace."

Everyone sobered.

He spat that last word, and Brand didn't blame

him. Pytheios's version of peace was merely fear holding people in a state of inertia.

"Most of the Blue Clan didn't have much. These shops were dying—a dragon version of a ghost town—mostly closed and people fending only for themselves."

She raised her eyebrows as she looked around the restaurant as if seeing it through a new lens. "What happened?"

Ladon shifted his stance, and her eyes widened slightly as realization must've struck.

"You happened," she guessed. "Is that what you're reluctant to say?"

The king spread his hands. "I don't know how much is me. We're not giving anything to the Red Clan now, which makes a huge difference but also makes us vulnerable to attack from the other five clans. And if they were to tap the colonies, bringing fighters from over there, we'd be in deeper trouble. We've already had to abandon all our other cities, the last in the Swiss Alps falling to Pytheios recently."

Kasia laid a hand over his, only this time none of his men tensed. Except Brand. "You should be proud."

"I fight for my people. When they're truly free, then I'll be proud."

Every single one of his warriors gave a murmur of agreement.

Kasia grinned. "Well, I'm proud of you now."

Ladon sobered and clasped his hands behind his back. The most self-contained, back-the-fuck-off man Brand had ever met, except maybe himself, suddenly looked down, uncomfortable with the praise.

Had anyone ever dared to tell Ladon something like that? Even Arden?

"I like her," Duncan said.

Ladon looked up. "Thank you. I'll take any help I can get courting you."

And there it is. Brand stared. He'd never seen his friend look unsure of himself. Ever. But he did now, and in front of his men, too.

Kasia also stilled. "You're courting me?" she asked quietly.

Ladon shrugged, appearing even more uncomfortable. "Someone told me you were a woman who wanted to make up her own mind. As a phoenix, you have to, but I can see that's true regardless. I'd like to make it easier for you to choose me."

Kasia knew that not just Ladon's rule over the Blue Clan would be impacted by her decision. Mating her meant he'd be High King. If Ladon could claim that title, he could shut down the threats from the other clans. Take out the old kings.

There was way more at stake than he was letting on. It was…admirable.

Kasia's glance drifted in Brand's direction. "I see."

"I don't want to rush you into something—"

"But your people are depending on you, and you need whatever luck I can bring."

Ladon nodded.

"Can I ask you a personal question?"

Ladon's dark eyebrows raised. "Yes."

"Are you in love? Or is there someone special in your life right now?"

Ladon blinked. "You're worried about taking another lady's place?"

"Yes."

"Let me put that concern to rest. There's no one special." Ladon grinned, and this time the expression was real, making him appear younger, more lighthearted than the almost frightening countenance that usually faced the world.

Brand could see the impact that smile had on Kasia. Immediately her shoulders dropped, and she gazed at the king with different eyes. Brand couldn't pinpoint how different, and he had no idea how he knew, but he was positive she'd just decided to like Ladon Ormarr.

Brand refused to explore the dark hole that formed inside his chest.

"What about you? Any men in your life?" Ladon asked.

Brand held still, though he wanted to turn away.

Kasia glanced at him with an emotion in her eyes he couldn't quite identify.

"There was someone," she said.

He should look away, break the moment, but he couldn't.

"But…" She shrugged and directed her gaze back to Ladon. "It can't work."

Brand let out a silent breath, though it didn't ease the tightness banding his chest.

Ladon studied her closely. "It's over now?"

"Yes."

The finality in that one word had a roar rising up Brand's throat, a sound he had to choke back, the effort searing his throat. They'd agreed. She needed safety. Ladon needed a phoenix. And Brand needed revenge. They'd chosen the right path.

Granted, that didn't mean he had to like it.

"Just so we're clear," Ladon said slowly. "You're open to being courted?"

"Can you give me some time to get to know you first, and vice versa, before I give you a final answer? And I would have some stipulations."

"Of course. Like what?"

Kasia took a deep breath. "I don't want to be some talisman or a pawn," she said. "I know what's on the line, but I'm not the good little girl who sits in her room and waits to bring you luck and has to be rescued and—" She flicked a glance over the men, ending on Brand. "Guarded."

Ladon followed Kasia's glance with a flicker of his eyes, and Brand couldn't tell from his unchanging expression if he was annoyed or impressed. "What *do* you want?"

"My mother taught me about dragon shifters and phoenixes. She taught me survival skills. I'm a trained mechanic."

Since when? Not that they'd had a chance to discuss education or trade, or really any opportunities for this to come up. He'd assumed she had none. Although, given her independent nature, he couldn't say he was all that surprised. Suddenly her comfort in his lap looking under the dash of the Hemi Cuda made more sense.

"Plus, I have my gifts. I *want* to participate. Let me train, show you I can fight for myself. Let me shadow you, possibly see where I can be of help to your reign. Let me be part of your decisions, even if it's just behind closed doors. If I were to mate you, I would want to present a united front and be a true partner."

Ladon studied Kasia. Did he see what Brand saw? A woman with strength, grace, and an iron will? Someone who could fulfill that promise to walk beside him, a partner in life, and not just in ruling the Blue Clan of dragon shifters?

"It won't be easy," Ladon finally said.

Kasia tipped up her chin. "Nothing worth fighting for ever is. My mother taught me that." She paused. "So did my father, in a roundabout way."

"Your father?" Ladon asked.

"Zilant Amon."

"The hell you say," Duncan snapped.

Ladon didn't speak, but took a step back, a flash of something mean crossing his features before he controlled it. "As in the previous ruling family of the White Clan?"

She glanced at Duncan. "Yes. And my mother was the daughter of the previous King and Queen of the Red Clan, before Pytheios killed them." She paused, letting that sink in. "I have as much reason to hate Pytheios as all of you. More maybe, because he killed both my parents. My father before I was born. Their mating bond hadn't fully formed."

She seemed to disappear inside herself a moment. "My mother always wondered what the brand would have looked like. A combo of the two families, maybe."

Then she blinked, coming back to them. "Pytheios found us and killed my mother last year. He took everything from me."

"I see." Ladon seemed to consider the implications

even as the men shifted on their feet. Then he took Kasia's hand, and Brand held back a growl.

"I hope you'll learn to trust me enough to tell me about them someday," Ladon said.

Brand's respect for his friend went up another notch as Kasia took a deep breath.

"I accept your conditions." Ladon went down on one knee, a gesture of honor and agreement. "If you choose me as a mate, then we will be partners."

XII

Pytheios made his way up the winding stone staircase, treading stairs worn into smooth concave dips by countless dragon shifters over the centuries.

The inside walls, like the stairs, were carved into the natural stone of the mountain. Any outside-facing walls, however, were a special glass made only by dragons. Generations before him had hewn those walls from the very mountain itself, turning it hard as diamonds, strong enough to continue to support the weight and designed to allow those inside an unimpeded view of what lay outside. Any being standing outside saw only the rock, snow, and ice of the most massive mountain on the planet.

Tonight, the weather was crystal clear, stars and moon shining brightly from the black skies above.

Merikh huffed and puffed behind him, disturbing the peace of the icy view. "We should look into moving the prisons to lower levels."

This tower was the highest point of the Red Clan's stronghold. The top of the spire sat just under the top of Mt. Everest and housed a series of jails where his prisoners could forever see the vast skies dragons were meant to rule.

See but never touch again. Never feel the wind against their scales. Never know the freedom flight provided. Even be able to see those who came to their rescue fly by but with no way to contact them.

"Oh?"

That one word had Merikh snapping his mouth

shut with an audible clack. If Pytheios turned around, he'd bet his crown that his son was reconsidering his words. Rash and holding no true convictions, Merikh was at least learning when to quit.

Still, my blood runs in his veins. He can be taught.

"I suppose," Merikh mused now, "a necessity to house our worst enemies and biggest secrets far from the rest of the clan population overrides the inconvenience."

"You only suppose?" This time, Pytheios couldn't keep his frustration from seeping into his voice nor out of his eyes as he glanced over his shoulder. Dressed in a purple silk shirt and matching tie today, Merikh appeared the entitled man his witch-mother had molded. That would change, too.

Once Ladon Ormarr was removed from the blue throne, Pytheios had every intention of filling that vacancy with his son. Until now, he'd helped dragons from within their clans take the thrones. In theory, the clans would submit more easily to one of their own kind, and in the meantime, those dragons owed Pytheios their allegiance.

But that theory had broken with the Blood King's takeover of the Blue Clan. Time to try a new tack.

Merikh held his gaze, and Pytheios gave a mental nod. Stronger.

This place, the magnificent supremacy of being a dragon, the spectacular power that belonged to them alone…it was a legacy he had to protect and grow at all costs. Even if it meant eliminating the dissenting few, which included Ladon Ormarr.

Like a piece of glass embedded in his heel, a

snake in the grass, an itch no amount of scratching would soothe, Ormarr represented a fundamental problem with dragon shifters. In order to survive as a species, they had to make hard choices, like ensuring the leaders mated before lower level dragons got the chance, like pooling the wealth to ensure it could be applied in the most appropriate ways, like eliminating those who disagreed. Harmony as a society required kings to be brutal, or it would never work.

With the light tread of Merikh's steps behind him, Pytheios ascended the final stair onto a small landing with a single door. Pytheios stepped through into a massive round chamber that housed the prison. New dragonsteel doors to each of the eleven cells were spaced evenly around the edges of the room.

Rhiamon, his witch, stood in the center of the room bathed in moonlight that streamed in from the glass moonhole directly above. Her hair glowed white in the contrast of dark and light, as did the flowing pale dress she wore, giving her an ethereal appearance as she held her hands to the sky, head thrown back, eyes closed. Her lips moved in a silent incantation.

Magnificent.

She was the one exception he made to his own creed of relying on no one. While he was careful that the part others played could easily be eliminated, and still he would reign, Rhiamon kept him alive. Until they syphoned off the phoenix's power, granting him immortality, he needed the witch.

Pytheios waited as she finished her spell, a nightly ritual, a necessity to cage the man who occupied the center cell directly opposite from where Pytheios stood—not just with steel bars, but with magic.

Merikh stood behind him, blessedly silent for once. Chanting complete, Rhiamon's hands shook as she lowered them. The dark shadows consuming her eyes seemed to bleed from the sockets to the skin below, then slowly dissipated as she let the magic go. He caught a glimpse of the black depths that took over when she performed her magic, silver irises seeming to float in the center of the void. Then she blinked, and her eyes returned to normal.

Seeing him standing just inside the door, Rhiamon smiled. "My king. Have you come for the failure?"

Pytheios didn't need to glance to his right to see the man waiting behind the barred cell door. "I have. But first, how is our other guest?" He allowed his gaze to linger on the heavy bars of the center cell. From this vantage point, it seemed as though nothing lived or breathed inside that space, but Pytheios knew better.

She followed his gaze, then slid him a sly smile. "A pussycat, my king. So biddable these days."

"Still alive, though?" Pytheios needed to know. Serefina's mother had spoken a prophecy over this man, a mere child at the time, one that made keeping him alive crucial.

Before Rhiamon could respond, Merikh stepped out from behind him. "After this long, how can you still question my mother?"

Pytheios watched in unimpressed silence as his son crossed the room to stick his face near the bars.

"This...*thing* has been broken since the day you

threw his scrawny ass in here and gave my mother the task of keeping him captive and alive," Merikh sneered, addressing his words to Pytheios over his shoulder. He shouted into the darkened cell. "You're not going anywhere. Are you?"

Now Pytheios could make out the faint outline of a man prone on the slab they allowed him for a bed, the chill seeping into his bones yet another cage. The shadow didn't so much as twitch.

"See, Father? You have nothing to worry—"

Faster than a striking snake, an arm shot out from between the bars. When had he moved from the bed to the door? Even Pytheios had missed it. Only Merikh's quick reflexes kept him from being choked to death. Instead of choking the life out of his son, the prisoner caught a fistful of purple silk shirt. With a sharp yank, he slammed Merikh's head into the bars with a ringing clang before releasing him to tumble backward to land unceremoniously on his ass.

After a few moments of stunned dazedness, fury rose inside Merikh, as evidenced by the red shade his face turned as he jumped to his feet. "You're going to pay for that," he snarled at the still-silent occupant of the cell.

Pytheios sighed. "I thought you would've outgrown tormenting him by now."

"Father, I—"

Pytheios held up a hand, and Merikh cut off the rest of his excuses, the venom in his gaze still churning until his eyes appeared more red than brown.

"We didn't come here for Airk," Pytheios reminded in a deceptively patient tone.

At that Merikh settled, pulling himself up to his full height, shoulders back. "Of course."

Better. Not good, but better. What he needed, though, was ruthless.

Rhiamon and Merikh said nothing as Pytheios abandoned his interest in Airk and approached a cell farther over to the right. "I hope you have healed satisfactorily," he said to its occupant.

The glow of golden eyes showed eerily in the dark of the chamber before the man inside moved out of the shadows, approaching the bars. "I have."

Pytheios clasped his hands behind his back as he took in the other man's appearance. Dark blond hair streaked with gray hung in limp clumps around a craggy face that had been harshly handsome in youth. "You failed me, Uther."

"I failed us both." This admission was delivered with zero contrition, spine straight, gaze direct. The dragon shifter refused to back down, even as he admitted his fault.

Pytheios expected nothing less from the King of the Gold Clan. "What should I do about that?"

"You make a deal." Uther's words sounded almost bored, only the light in his eyes was too eager for that.

"What deal?"

"Help me kill the rogue. In exchange, I'll dedicate my forces to helping you extinguish the Blue Clan."

Pytheios slid a surreptitious glance to Rhiamon, whose expression remained neutral. She gave a small shrug that could easily be interpreted as "up to you," but after years with the witch, he knew she approved.

He hid his own satisfaction behind a thoughtful frown. "And the phoenix?"

Uther waved him off, seemingly indifferent. "Do with her what you will, but once we take down Ladon Ormarr, the rogue and the Blue Clan are mine."

Interesting. "Who is he?"

Grim anger tightened the skin over Uther's cheekbones. "A loose end."

He would have to find out more about this rogue who'd managed to wound Uther in one-on-one combat, an unheard-of feat. "I'll accept your deal with one small adjustment."

Uther narrowed his eyes and waited for the hammer to drop.

"Your dragons take out the blue dragons without my help. A small price to pay for your failure to capture the phoenix when she was vulnerable. I get the phoenix. You get the rogue and a second throne. Everyone is…happy."

Uther took his time answering, although Pytheios had no doubts the other king knew there was only one acceptable response. As the clan located closest to the Gold Clan's stronghold in Norway, Uther was the most vulnerably positioned.

"Done," Uther said. "When?"

"Now."

Kasia carefully flowed through the movements that all the warriors engaged in prior to breaking out into groups for various forms of combat training. The smooth moves were almost a dance, performed in silence, allowing her soul to focus.

"How are you already so good at this?" Arden asked beside her as she also went through the movements. "Reid says I still suck at them."

Reid, only a few people over, couldn't have missed the whispered comment, but didn't turn or acknowledge them.

"My mother taught me," Kasia whispered, conscious of the handful of glares aimed their way.

Warriors were trying to focus as well. This was part of their daily routine of physical and combat training before they went out on assignment. She got the impression that, while Ladon's core group had accepted her, the wider fighting force resented their king for making them work with Kasia, a phoenix and not a dragon shifter like them.

But proving she didn't need to be protected meant honing the combat skills her mother had taught all her daughters and practicing, for now in private, her ability to teleport and her control over fire. She refused to be some poor, defenseless lump waiting for dragons to protect her.

The fact that Brand, whom she was pretty sure most of the warriors viewed as a usurper taking a coveted spot among Ladon's most trusted soldiers when he'd only just become part of the clan, stood off to the side, arms crossed, unspeaking and giving off serious *I don't give a shit unless you go near the phoenix* vibes, did not help her cause. He didn't train with the fighters. He trained on his own, as did Ladon, at least she assumed he did.

But the king was a different matter. Brand needed

friends.

"Do you think King Gorgon is coming for a truce?" Arden asked.

Kasia didn't absorb the question, still too focused on Brand. Meanwhile, his serious golden gaze scanned every nuance of the outdoor platform on which they practiced and trained.

Two weeks had passed. Two weeks of enduring the watchfulness of the dragon shifters as she moved through her days, those stares ranging from suspicious to curious. She spent her time training in the morning and in meetings with Ladon in the afternoons followed by private dinners with him in his chambers, after which she holed up in her rooms, practicing at controlling her powers. Teleporting was improving, though it drained her. She'd come to think of her power as a tank which held only so much fuel. No visions had come, which she considered a blessing.

She'd met Ladon's Curia Regis, his king's council. Asher as his Viceroy of Security and Reid as his Viceroy of War, she'd gotten to know best, as they were also his warriors and she spent time training with them. But she still wasn't sure she trusted the other Viceroys, especially Chante. Not that he or the others did anything she could point to. Her unease stemmed more from a gut feeling about the guy.

Besides, there had to be a reason Ladon hadn't included Chante or the other Viceroys the night he'd introduced her to his warriors, to those truly in his inner circle. Not wanting to incite suspicion without cause, she hadn't asked. Perhaps Ladon was a warrior at heart, more than a politician.

Meanwhile, two weeks of Brand's constant presence and silent watchfulness, as he was assigned to guard her most frequently—her own personal fucking ghost—was grating on her nerves.

She couldn't be mad at him. She knew that. Her logical brain told her that over and over. They were sticking to the plan. The damn plan that was ripping her to shreds, because Ladon might be bloody and ruthless, but he was also good and loyal to his people and meant to be a king, but somehow, she just couldn't picture herself with him. Those damn images of her and Brand together kept fucking with her head, muddying up her thoughts. Doubts plagued her along with an uneasy feeling of not-rightness.

She should be delighted that she'd lucked out to be mating Ladon. The alternatives could have been so much worse. Instead, as the days passed, the reluctant lump in her stomach grew.

She'd lost weight, unable to eat much, thanks to the worry. All due to the watchful, distant bodyguard who had his own uphill battle—earning his place among his new people.

Brand currently sported a massive black eye that had faded to a spectacular shade of green in the half hour she'd been down here. Courtesy of a night patrol, he'd said, then he'd shut up.

"Has Ladon said anything about it?" Arden interrupted her thoughts again.

"About what?" Kasia murmured.

"About the King of the Black Clan coming to visit. During your private dinners, has he said anything?"

Oh, yeah. The last few meetings had focused on

King Gorgon's imminent arrival. Kasia shrugged. "Just that he'd asked for an audience to discuss possible partnerships. I don't think Ladon trusts him, but you know your brother. He doesn't really speculate."

"True."

Thanks to her meetings with Ladon, she was more than aware that these two weeks under the mountain, while relatively peaceful for her, hadn't been easy on everyone. Warriors went out in groups of five or more due to the increase in attacks, just as Ladon had predicted.

But who had given Brand the shiner? One of the resentful blue dragons? Or had he been in a skirmish while on patrol?

Kasia shook him out of her thoughts and focused on her moves and her breathing, but it didn't help. Tension refused to leave her body. Soon, Ladon would expect a final answer from her.

Logically, she knew her answer had to be yes. He'd proven himself to be harsh but fair as a king and surprisingly supportive of her need to be involved. His heart, his purpose, was entirely for his people. She could get on board with that. And, as the true High King, he could finally bring down her parents' killer.

But her heart and her body were drawn to the rugged, bruised giant in the corner.

At some unseen, unheard signal, the warm-up ended, and the shifters broke into groups.

Arden, the only one who dared to spar with Kasia—the men all spouting crap about not wanting to hurt her—turned to her with a grin. Everyone paired off and went at it.

"What do you want to work on today?" Arden asked.

"Don't you want to work with one of the men?" Dragons were stronger and faster than she was, which meant Arden had to hold back when they worked out together.

A shake of her head was Arden's only answer. She flicked her black braid, so like Skylar's, off her shoulder and brought her hands up.

"Come on, phoenix. Let's go."

Before Kasia could agree or bring her hands up, Arden landed a punch, right in the breadbasket.

Kasia doubled over with a muffled *oomph* and tried not to look like a wuss as she struggled to suck air back into her lungs.

"Keep your guard up," Arden said, completely unapologetic.

Kasia straightened and jumped back from the next punch. She managed to get her arms up and tapped Arden's shoulder, though her strike hardly moved the dragon shifter. Then she ducked under Arden's counterpunch and blocked a kick.

"Good. Faster."

Kasia gritted her teeth. "I don't move faster."

"You can. Anticipate the attack and move."

They circled each other, both striking and blocking and ducking. Arden was still holding back, but Kasia knew she was getting better. They'd agreed to work on her defensive skills the most, since she'd never be stronger than her opponent. Better to protect herself and maybe surprise them long enough for her to get away.

Even then, her chances were slim. Still, better to be prepared.

Seeing an opening, Kasia maneuvered into a front kick, jab, roundhouse combo and for once, connected hard with Arden's face.

The men around them stopped as they heard the crack, and blood gushed from Arden's nose.

Arden held up both hands to her face. "Good shot!"

Before Arden could answer, Reid strode over. "You should've gotten the hell out of the way."

Kasia had to step to the side to see around Reid as his larger form dwarfed her friend's smaller body.

Arden glared at him over the tops of her hands. "If you're so worried about me getting hurt, then you train with her," she snapped.

Reid ignored that comment. "Let me see."

He tried to tug her wrists, but Arden only smacked his hand away then put hers back to her nose.

He glowered at her. "If it's broken, you don't want it healing crooked and messing up that pretty face."

Something in Arden's eyes shifted, almost like defeat. She lowered her hands. "Fine."

Reid took her by the chin, tipping her face this way and that. Thanks to a dragon's accelerated healing, the bleeding had already stopped. "Looks straight to me," he finally murmured.

Was it just Kasia, or had the temperature in the room turned up a notch?

Reid let Arden go. "Better have Fallon look at it."

She pulled her shoulders back. "Kasia and I aren't

done. I'll go later."

His jaw worked like he was holding back what he really wanted to say. "Suit yourself."

As he walked away, rejoining his sparring partner, Arden glared at his back.

"Are you okay?" Kasia stepped up closer to ask.

Like Reid had a moment ago, she got a glare for her trouble. "Don't you ever worry about your opponent. He or she is the enemy."

Kasia laughed. "You sure you don't want me to garner up some phoenix tears and heal that for you?"

Arden gave a bloody grin. "Better. Besides, you'd have to mean it for those crocodile tears to work."

True.

"You going to tell me the story there?" she asked softly, flicking a glance in Reid's direction.

Arden shrugged even as she had to drag her gaze away from Reid. "Nothing to tell. Female-born dragons are in a tough position. Too small to fight, at least according to all the big, bad males tromping around here. And sterile, so destined not to mate. Most remain at home, taking care of parents, or helping their brothers' mates take care of children, but"—Arden visibly shook herself out of her mood—"I refuse to play by the gender rules."

"Good for you." Kasia totally understood her friend's need to prove herself, though her heart broke at the same time. Arden was so obviously in love with Reid. And Kasia's vision of them together suggested that, in the future at least, he might feel the same.

"Let's keep going," Arden said.

Kasia didn't see the punch Arden shot at her, the attack coming closer to dragon speed than she'd seen yet, but she felt it, felt Arden's intent before it happened, and sheer instinct took over. Kasia disappeared and reappeared about ten feet back, knocking into Reid.

The shifter swore. "What the fuck?"

He had his hand drawn back to hit before he recognized his "attacker." Then lowered his hand.

Well, damn. There went that secret. A quick check showed Brand out of his corner, feet planted, hands on his lean hips, with a glare that threatened to singe her from across the room.

"You've been holding out on us." Arden sounded delighted as she rushed over.

"Yes, she has." Asher joined them. The Beta's face was arranged in his usual glower, but now she could tell the difference between his resting face and truly pissed.

Kasia sighed and shrugged. "Not really. I'm not good at the teleporting thing. I can go only short distances"—though that was improving—"and I can't control it well. I usually don't land in the spot I intended."

"Why didn't you tell us?" Asher demanded, obviously not impressed with her *no big deal* act.

His tone had her tipping up her chin. "You didn't ask."

He glanced across the room at Brand. "Did you know?"

Brand shook his head, jaw tight.

"I didn't tell him, either." Kasia mimicked Brand's posture, putting her hands on her hips, and addressed

Asher. "And the why is self-evident, I would think. Dragon shifters betrayed my family and killed my parents. I spent my entire life running from your kind. Do you think trust comes easily just because you think you're the good guys? *Everyone* thinks they're the good guys. Even the bad guys."

Several of the dragons around her growled, and out of the corner of her eye, she caught Brand moving, making his way to her.

But Asher merely cocked his head. "You don't think we're the good guys?"

The fight went out of her, and she dropped her hands to her sides. "You might be when it comes to dragons, but you're all still myopically focused on yourselves. You don't let anyone in. No one but dragons is worthy, and even then, only your clan. You think I don't see that in your faces? In the way you all avoid me?"

More of the warriors had gathered around her, but Kasia didn't stop. She was on a roll now.

She flung her arm at Brand. "Hell, you don't even let one of your own in when he's proved himself and your king has recognized him. And why? Because he isn't born of your clan? Because he was rogue? If I were you, I'd want someone with those survival skills on my side."

Brand's lips went flat, and he shook his head at her. She got the message. *Don't bring me into this.*

So she brought it back to her. "Other than what I could potentially bring you as the phoenix, have any of you, other than Arden, bothered to get to know me as a person? Perhaps I have something to contribute, beyond luck. Maybe you should make sure I *want* to save your precious clan, rather than expecting me to."

She took a breath to deliver another set of home truths and gasped.

With no warning, pain started at the back of her neck and rushed down her spine arrowing out to the rest of her. Dammit.

But I can still see. What the hell?

"You're right," Asher said.

That caught her attention. "I am?"

"Yes—"

Before he could go on, another slash of shuddering agony poured through her. Kasia bit down on her lip so hard, attempting to hold in a moan, that she drew blood. She put her hands on her knees, bent over and breathing in and out as the sensations lanced through her.

"Kas? You okay?" She registered Arden's concern but didn't answer.

As the moment ebbed, she raised her head, seeking the one person who knew what was coming. Brand no longer stood among the men with his arms crossed. Tightening at the corner of his mouth was the only indication that he might have felt the pain, too. He watched her with the same intentness he'd shown when they'd made love.

As if in direct response to that hot gaze, a burst of pure need washed through her, swamping the pain, swirling with it inside her. At the same time, everything went dark, leaving her vulnerable in a room full of dragon shifters.

"Brand," she whispered. Then with a groan she couldn't keep contained, Kasia fell to her knees.

She was vaguely aware of Arden's urgent voice calling her name before strong arms wrapped around her middle, pulling her against a hard chest.

"Breathe, princess. I've got you." The words, murmured against her ear, had her shivering, and the painful edge eased.

Brand wrapped his wings around them, accompanied by that feeling of being folded into a world of their own making. Ostensibly, he'd done it to contain her explosion, but maybe also to hide the fact he had to touch the king's future mate from the prying eyes of Ladon's warriors.

Brand kissed her neck, and that simple touch set her off. She opened her mouth, but before a sound passed her lips, fire erupted from inside her and shattered outward. Kasia's head slammed back against Brand's shoulder, and a scream followed the flames out of her throat.

"Holy shit," Brand swore.

All she could hear was the rush of the blaze all around her. Then the vision took over—the images moving too fast for her to see everything, a blur before her eyes that hurt her head more, only a few scenes pausing long enough to recognize anything.

Arden screaming.

Brand yelling something before running out onto her balcony and shifting.

The flash of golden scales stained with blood coming out of one of the royal suites inside the blue dragon city of Ben Nevis.

Chante meeting with men she didn't recognize. Men with golden eyes.

A gray sky filled with gold and green dragons.

A massive black dog, limping over a mountainside, trailing blood behind an injured leg.

Kasia came back into her body feeling like she'd dropped ten stories to land with a thud. Brand, meanwhile, had buried his face in her neck as he waited out the storm, murmuring meaningless words meant to soothe. Her body vibrated with the need to turn in his arms, but shifters waited for them outside the cocoon of his wings.

Unfortunately, or perhaps for the best, a familiar lethargy seeped through her bones and muscles. Her tank—how she'd started picturing the reserves of her powers—was down to fumes after that one.

Brand leaned back to search her face, his gaze almost concerned. "All right?" The most words he'd said to her in two weeks.

"Ouch," she croaked around her charred throat. "That was…forceful."

She put a hand to her head. "I…"

"Need to see the king?"

There went reality, butting its ugly head in again. An unaccustomed heat surged into her cheeks. Hopefully the darker light cast by his wings and the lingering smoke from her flames hid that from him.

His gaze dropped from her eyes to her mouth and lingered.

"Just one taste. One kiss. What's the worst that could happen?"

Kasia sucked in a sharp breath. Was that his thought or hers? She was pretty damn sure that had been Brand's voice just then, and granted, he was partially dragon at the moment, but no way would he have projected that particular thought on purpose. How had she heard that?

"Brand." Ladon's voice cracked through the room like the blast from a shotgun.

Inside their little bubble, Kasia jumped, and Brand's arms tightened around her, even as his expression spasmed with guilt.

Brand loosened his grip and folded back his wings. The smoke drifted away on the soft breeze blowing in from the opening to the outside. The sight that greeted them was chaos. Warriors weren't gathered around them waiting to see what the hell happened to the phoenix. Instead, they were scattering, purpose etched into the serious lines of their faces, their moves efficient as some shifted and flew outside and others headed back toward the cavern with the concourse of shops and apartments to usher people to safety.

Oh my god. Did my vision about the green and gold dragons already begin? Other than the wolves, nothing had come to happen that fast before.

Ladon pointed to the door that led back to the residence. "Get Kasia out of here," he yelled at Brand. "Arden, go with them."

"I'm coming with you," Arden called after her brother. She was already starting her shift.

Kasia's soon-to-be-mate ignored his sister. He sprinted to the edge of the cave and leaped into the air, his body plummeting out of sight. Kasia barely squeaked her shock before a sleek dragon a striking shade of indigo shot upward. Arden, Asher, Reid, and several other warriors followed behind.

Brand, still holding her, jumped to his feet and ran the opposite direction, while at the same time, a heavy metal barricade lowered over the entrance to the cave, shutting out the light. She bobbed up and down as he sprinted through a tunnel that would take them the long way to the residential halls, but avoid the main thoroughfare of the city.

Kasia pushed at his shoulders ineffectually. "Put me down."

His grip didn't budge, and he kept going.

"I can run on my own," she insisted.

However, the exhaustion from her vision was already starting to ooze through her body, belying her words.

She stopped struggling and crossed her arms. They made it back to her room in record time. Meanwhile, he'd kept his wings partially shifted, folded behind his back.

"Can you hear them?" she asked.

He moved to the window, peeping through a slit in the curtain. "Yes."

"What's happening? Is it Pytheios? Uther?"

"No."

"A different dragon clan?"

"No. It's not dragons."

Something else? They wouldn't be protecting her like this if they didn't think a threat was real. Dread dropped a chunk of ice into the center of the frustration that had been heating her up till this moment. But that one vision of the injured animal…

"Is it a dog?" she asked slowly, afraid of the answer.

Brand whipped his head around, and his gaze snapped down to her. "What did you see?"

That answered that. Panic made her frantic as she pushed against him trying to get to the balcony.

"Get me out there. Now."

Brand's jaw went so hard, she was surprised his teeth weren't cracking. "No."

Kasia struggled against him in earnest, kicking and flailing and twisting, trying to reach the door. "You don't understand. I have to get out there."

Brand grunted as he took a knee to the gut. "Stop it."

"I said… Let. Me. Go." She managed to twist to face him and slammed both hands into his chest.

A blast of fire spewed from her palms, giving her shove an extra kiloton of *oomph*. Her head rang as she flew through the air in a mass of twisted limbs before she hit a rock wall with a painful crack. She dropped to the ground with an equally painful thud.

Kasia shook the stars from her eyes as she forced herself to stay lucid. Holy shit. That was new. Both she and Brand ended up on the ground separated by about twenty feet of her room. But she didn't have time to think about it. She had to get outside.

She jumped to her feet and sprinted for the balcony. Despite having nothing left in the tank, especially after that blast of fire, she'd try to teleport herself down there and hope she didn't misjudge the distance and miss one of the dragon perches on the way down.

Brand caught up to her in less than a frustrating blink, only he didn't stop her. "You're going to have to fly."

Relief trickled through her panic. "Then you'd better shift fast."

To her shock, he ran to the perch and started the process, taking up more and more of the rock bar as the transformation took hold. She climbed onto his back, and he launched into the air, spiraling down to the first floor and through the large opening to the training room where they'd been before.

Only the steel door to the outside was down now.

"How do we get out?" Kasia tried to not let her desperation show, but it came out in her voice anyway.

Brand turned to face the back wall where a man sat in a glassed-in control room. She couldn't hear the mental exchange he must've had with the guy, but after a moment, the door cranked open, with a heavy *clunk, clunk, clunk* of massive metal gears turning.

The door couldn't move fast enough for her. "Go," she yelled as soon as the door was up. Urgency drove her past the point of fear.

Without question and with a running leap, Brand took to the air, pushing with those strong wings to gain altitude, even as he had to navigate around the twists of the canyon wall until finally they burst upward, above the mountain. From there he tipped his wings to aim them to the south.

Where were the other dragons who'd flown out with Ladon? She couldn't see any in the air around them. Were they high above? That would make no sense if the threat was what she thought. They'd be on the ground.

"Where are they, Brand?"

"Almost there."

That's when she spotted them. Ten blue dragons on the relatively flattened side of a mountain circled something large and black that snapped and snarled. She could make out the ferocious sounds even from above. None of the dragons had gotten close yet, as far as she could tell, giving the creature a wide berth. But she could tell by the way they were swinging their tails, they were working closer with the intention of killing it.

Faster.

"*I'm going as fast as I can.*"

Wait. She hadn't aimed that thought. Kasia shook her head. They'd have to figure that out after. "Tell them to stop."

In her head, she aimed her own thoughts at all the dragons below. "*Stop. Leave him alone.*"

One of them must've gotten through, because the warriors paused; all but the largest indigo-colored dragon turned their gazes upward as Brand spread his wings wide and landed outside the circle they'd formed. He hadn't even dropped to his forefeet when she hurled herself off him, shooting between the blue dragons gathered to the massive black dog snarling in the center.

"*Kasia. No!*" Ladon and Brand both boomed, but she ignored them and the pain of their combined voices in her head.

Instead, she rushed the beast, threw her arms around him, and buried her face in his bristly, smoke-scented fur. "Maul!"

A rumble ran through the warriors surrounding her, and she could practically feel the need to kill pouring off them. She lifted her face, grinning and probably looking like a total lunatic. Maul's hot breath puffed against her hair. He opened his mouth, and every dragon took a step forward, but then he gave her a long slobbery lick up the side of her face. With a tongue as big as her head, she came off soaked and gross, but too happy to see the mutt to chastise him.

Two human-sized shadows fell over her, and Maul pulled back his lips, baring his teeth in a silent growl. Kasia patted him. "It's okay, Maul. These are friends."

Understanding her perfectly, the dog moved out of his defensive crouch, standing to his full six feet, and appeared to grin at whoever stood behind her, black tongue lolling out of his mouth as he panted, red eyes glowing eerily. Kasia gave his shoulder another pat as she turned and faced both Brand and Ladon who, now human, stared with twin expressions of incredulity.

"You know that's a hellhound, right?" Brand asked.

Kasia lifted a single eyebrow. "No, Brand. I thought he was just a really big sheepdog."

Ladon coughed, covering up a laugh. "Is he… yours?"

Kasia shared an amused glance with Maul, who huffed a chuckle, the sound coming out more like a dry cackle. Both Ladon and Brand tensed. In their defense, the cackle came off a tad on the creepy side. Still, seeing the toughest men she knew warily watch the hellhound brought on a bout of giggles she had to choke down. "He's mine as much as a hellhound can be, I guess. Have you ever encountered one?"

Two negative shakes of the head.

"Hellhounds are warriors who died too soon. They're reincarnated in this form, forced to remain this way until they complete their unfinished business." She patted Maul's neck again. "This one seems to think his business has something to do with my family, but he's never shown us what."

"He's been following us for weeks," Brand said. "I scented him shortly after leaving the clinic when you stole my car."

"Awwww…" She gave Maul another hug, and he gently nudged the top of her head with his muzzle. "He sees it as his job to protect me. My mother found him as a pup and brought him home. We thought he was the runt of the litter and abandoned. Though who could abandon you?" She gave the dog a playful rub across the bridge of his nose, and he rumbled deep in his throat.

Brand, as tall as he was, basically looked the hound in the eye. "That's a runt?"

She shrugged. "I can't say—I haven't met any others—but that was our best guess. He tends to do his own thing, leaving for weeks at a time, but he always comes back to me."

She left out the fact that the night her mother died, she'd teleported Kasia to the hellhound for protection. In Alaska, he'd never left her side, but Kasia had to leave him behind when she went to the doctor. He must've decided she'd been gone long enough.

"Shite. She's a phoenix, and teleports, and has a hellhound. Can we keep her?"

Kasia recognized Duncan's accent coming from the gigantic beast to her left. The gigantic sky-blue beast.

"You're awfully pretty as a dragon, Duncan," she teased.

That shut him up. The dark navy dragon, which

she recognized as Asher, snorted a laugh, and she blinked. The Beta had actually laughed.

She turned to Ladon. "Anyway, his name is Maul."

"Maul?" Brand clarified.

She nodded. "Seemed appropriate."

Blank stares.

"Remind me not to let you name our children," Ladon muttered.

Denial too strong to ignore gathered in her heart like a lead weight, and realization that she'd been holding at bay too long finally broke through.

Oh gods. I can't mate him.

But the specter of High King and the fate of these people and other dragon shifters hung over her head like the blade of a guillotine.

To hide her reaction, she turned to Maul, and he lowered his head so she could scratch him on his favorite spot, behind his neck right in front of the large, leathery hump that sat atop his shoulders. "I can't believe you found me here," she murmured.

Taking comfort from her pet and bodyguard didn't help. *What am I going to do?*

"I assume you want him to stay with us?" Ladon asked.

She peered back at them. Brand said nothing. Apparently, he'd gone back into shutdown mode, resuming the same closed-off expression he'd worn since arriving.

Kasia ignored him and her dang heart. "Yes. Maul's a big teddy bear, as long as no one is messing with me."

"I think we might be out of a job, boys." Reid's muttered comment rang in her head. *"The*

bodyguard position is filled."

And I think I'm out of a home. She needed time to deliberate, to make plans. Only she had no one to talk to. Surrounded by an entire clan, she was still alone. "He can stay in my room."

"If he can fit down the hall," Brand said.

She sent him a glare that clearly said, "Butt out if you can't be helpful."

Maul gave a tiny rumble of a growl delivering basically the same message, and Brand snapped his mouth shut.

"We should return. How do you suggest we get him down there?" Ladon asked.

"Maul can take care of that on his own. He teleports." Sort of. He had to see where he was going first, but he had a way to deal with that.

The two men exchanged a glance.

Before they could tell her no, which she could tell they were building up to, she hopped up on the hound's back, wrapping her fists in his thick fur. "I'll go with Maul. We'll follow you, so he can see where he's going."

Another manly glance containing a wealth of decision-making that made her want to smack their heads together, then Ladon nodded. He and Brand both backed up and made their shift. Maul watched as the dragons took to the air. Then together she and Maul blinked out and reappeared in a different spot, a cliff at the edge of the mountaintop where he could see the dragons diving below.

Unlike her mother's or her own version of teleporting, Maul's was so fast there was no silent break or moment in darkness. Just a flash as your eyes adjusted to a different view.

Another blink and they stood on a ledge halfway down the canyon wall. They teetered on the tinier outcropping as he tracked the dragons' movements, and Kasia stared down at the river at the bottom of the canyon.

Maybe I should've flown back with Brand.

But she didn't have time to do more than have that one queasy thought before another blink brought them to the platform where she'd landed the day Brand brought her here, where the dragons were all standing, already shifted into their human forms, murmuring among themselves.

They tensed as soon as Kasia and Maul appeared, a few even taking fighting stances, though they slowly eased up as they realized who stood among them. Kasia hopped down, noting that all the fighters cast wary glances at the hellhound at her side.

As well they should. Legends and stories of the mysterious creatures were nothing short of terrifying and typically portended death. Good. She could use another advantage to balance out her side of the scales these days.

"Let's move inside," Ladon said.

As they started to walk, it became obvious that Maul was limping.

My visions. How could she have forgotten?

She jerked to a halt and turned to Ladon. "I saw gold and green dragons in the skies." She'd tell him about Chante later, and the golden scales she held back. What if they blamed Brand?

"What?" he frowned.

"In my visions."

That got his attention. His hands fisted. "How soon?"

Frustration pinched from the inside. "I don't know." She tried to picture it again. "The skies were gray. Not blue like today."

"How fast do they usually happen?" he snapped.

Again, she felt like a fool with a power that maybe hindered more than helped. "Only the wolves and Maul have been immediate."

Which brought back the details she'd seen concerning the hellhound. She whirled to face him. "Are you hurt?" she asked the hound. Immediately an image of his leg flashed through her mind—the way she and the hellhound had always communicated.

Hurrying around his side, she hissed through her teeth at the sight of the deep gash oozing blood on his right hind leg. "What did this?"

Another flash of an image, this one of a dragon so pale gold, it appeared almost white, except for a pale yellow around the edges, its scales flashing in the sunlight with blinding brilliance.

She glanced at Ladon and Brand. "A gold dragon."

Both men went grim, lips pressed together, jaws clenched.

"How do you know?" Ladon asked.

"He shows me images."

"He shows—" Ladon glanced back and forth between her and the hellhound, as if not quite believing her.

"Where did he attack?" Brand asked Maul directly.

Kasia raised her eyebrows, impressed. Of her sisters, only Skylar braved addressing the dog directly. Meira and Angelika had been too afraid of the whole "look in his eyes, three times spells your doom" superstition, despite Kasia obviously not succumbing to any ill effects.

Unless you counted losing her mother, being caught by dragons, and being forced into choosing one she didn't love as a mate as ill effects.

Maul answered Brand's question with a flash of an image of mountains—though not as craggy with rocks like here, and steeper, taller. In the background was a long lake followed by a lush green valley that fell away to the flatter lands beyond.

"I know that location," Ladon said as Maul projected the same image to both men.

Kasia closed her eyes as a new dread sank into her like poison. "So do I." That wolf shifter, Bleidd, had told her where to find them if she ever changed her mind.

Angelika.

But she couldn't tell anyone here.

XIII

Brand scrambled up over the craggy rocks of the mountain, careful to keep his head low, following after Asher, Reid, and Wyot. Of the three, he preferred Wyot. The man kept his mouth shut and didn't bother Brand any.

After Kasia's visions, Ladon had doubled the patrols around the mountain as a precaution. It was a good thing he had, because gold dragons had been attacking the Blue Clan's sentries with increasing frequency.

Ladon had later shared Kasia's vision about Chante, something she'd told only the king. The jealousy that arose at the realization that she'd trusted Ladon with the info, and not him, had not been one of Brand's finer moments. Which was ridiculous. The only thing affecting him was the increase in time spent with Ladon's men.

They peeked over the edge of the ridge they'd skirted to find four men below them, huddled together, talking in low voices. Despite his acute hearing, Brand could catch only parts of their words. The gusting winds over the highland mountains did not help.

"Can't hear them," Asher whispered.

"If we get any closer, they'll scent us," Reid pointed out.

True. They were pushing the limits as it stood. Brand studied the scenario, working through options in his head. Based on their eyes—varying shades of gold, glittering in the moonlight—the men were all gold dragons. Which gave him an idea.

"Stay here," he whispered to Wyot.

"Brand." Reid snagged him by the arm. "Where do you think you're going?"

Weeks of getting all chummy with these guys and he was still the mistrusted outsider. Kasia, with her speech about "good guys" and her hellhound, had somehow managed to earn Ladon's warriors' trust. But not Brand, despite bringing a phoenix and fighting with them side by side through several skirmishes.

He glanced at the hand on his arm, then back up at Reid, who clenched his teeth but let go.

"I'm going to see if I can get more info from those assholes," Brand said.

"How?" Asher asked. The Beta, at least, respected Brand's tactical skills.

Brand pointed to his hair. "By blending in."

Before they could argue him out of it, he scurried away. Confident his form was blocked from view on the far side of the peak, he shifted then flew over to where the men were still gathered, his enhanced hearing allowing him to pick up their conversation.

The Norwegian lilt to the accent was familiar. Slightly English sounding, but with more *R* and *V* sounds mixed in. He'd spoken that way once, but that was over five hundred years ago. Dragons lived a long time, and he'd learned to adapt, to blend in wherever he went.

He landed and shifted back to his human form, hoping the fact that he was gold would keep them from checking the mark on his hand.

No bullets struck him in the chest, and none of the men shifted to confront him. So far so good.

Keeping his hand out of view, Brand approached with his gaze lowered submissively, not a natural position, but he'd learned long ago that acting weak got you closer to your enemies.

"Brock sent me." He tossed out Uther's son's name with the confidence of a practiced liar. At the same time, he deliberately switched to the more generic, slightly lilting accent he'd acquired as a child. Before Uther. Slipping back into that old way of speaking was like putting on a jacket. Comfortable. Easy. If you were going to trick someone, commit.

Besides, based on the intel they'd gathered lately, Brock was in charge of these patrols. Spies, trying to infiltrate the mountain or take out a few more of Ladon's warriors, killing the Blue Clan like a slow bleed.

The question was, when was the bigger attack coming? And when would the green dragons get involved?

"I don't know you," the shorter, stockier of the men challenged.

Ah. The one who thought he was the boss.

Brand raised an eyebrow. "I don't know you, either. Your point?"

"I know every warrior under Uther's command, and I do not know you."

Shitballs. Time to borrow a past. The healer, Fallon's, story would work nicely. "I've been in the colonies for a while. Part of an enforcer crew over there."

That at least gave the stocky one pause. "You

don't sound American."

Brand shrugged. "I can when I want." He pulled out the inflection just for effect.

Stocky sniggered. "What're you here for? Did the crew kick you out?"

"I'm here to meet a potential mate." Yup, borrowing Fallon's story helped give the lie truth.

That shut the leader up. In the last hundred years, mates seemed to go only to the richest, most loyal, strongest dragons, though the process was supposed to be dictated by the fates.

"I see." Stocky eyed him with new respect. "Our clan could use new blood. I hope you plan to fuck her hard and get her pregnant quick."

Unbidden, an image of Kasia popped into Brand's head. Yeah. He would have no trouble killing this guy. Instead, he grinned and made a lewd gesture, giving Stocky and his buddies a good laugh.

In like Flynn, he approached. "I'm Bjorg."

"Erling," Stocky said with a nod. He indicated his companions. "Magni. Sigrun."

Brand nodded at each in turn. "Brock didn't tell me much. Only to find you."

"We'll fit you into the plan," Erling said.

"What is the plan?"

Erling narrowed his eyes. "Eager to fight?"

Careful. "More like I have something to prove." Again, that edge of truth.

That had Erling nodding, suddenly the sage leader. "Brock's a hard man. Would you like advice?"

"Sure."

"Don't try to impress him. He hates flatterers."

"I'll keep that in mind."

Erling eyed him closely. Had his sarcasm leaked out? "Let's get on with it," the shifter finally said.

He pulled out a phone, and they gathered around the device to look over a schematic of the Blue Clan's city in the Ben Nevis mountain.

Fuck. They have most of the security measures mapped out. They seemed to be missing only the far interior of the structure. Most evident was the vulnerability laid out by the hollowed-out atrium. If their enemies breached any of the layers of doors to get to that section of the mountain, he and his newfound people were royally screwed. That could only mean Kasia's vision had to be imminent if they were that close.

"Tonight is recon only. Do not get caught," Erling said.

"Yes, boss," one of the guys—Magni?—replied.

"We need to determine access points here and here." Erling indicated the spots.

Good. They were still figuring out how to get through security measures at the first layer of doors. Which begged the question, how did they know the rest? Inside info?

Chante, or whoever the insider was, would be up to Ladon and Asher to figure out. Time to flip the switch. Brand snagged the phone from Erling's hand. "Thanks for that."

He tucked the device in his back pocket as he backed up.

Erling didn't even pause to do the typical "You betrayed us" line. He rushed Brand, slamming into him, shoulder connecting with stomach, and flipping Brand over.

The back of his head smacked into solid stone, and black and white spots burst into his field of vision. Even as he couldn't see, Brand used their combined momentum to roll them over so he came out on top.

He got in three or four solid punches before the other two grabbed him by the arms and dragged him off Erling. Blood coated the man's face, whether from his mouth or Brand's knuckles was questionable, but Brand didn't give a fuck either way.

Erling pulled out a wicked-looking knife.

Most dragons didn't bother with weapons, their animal forms more than enough and impervious to puny knives or guns, but the smart ones kept something on them for times like these, when you fought human.

Erling was smarter than he'd given the guy credit for.

"Any time, fellas." He shifted his nails to talons and signaled the waiting blue shifters watching from their vantage point above.

But no hint of a dragon showed up. Which meant they were waiting to see how he handled himself in a fight. Again.

Bastards. He'd get this done on his own.

Brand waited for Erling to move closer, then struck. Whipping out his tail, he knocked the knife from the man's hands. In less time than it took for all three of the shifters to react with exclamations of shock, he used his tail to wham each of their heads into the rock. They crumpled to the ground, out cold.

Asher was the first to reach him, flying in on silent wings, then shifting just as quietly. Brand pulled Erling's phone out of his pocket and threw it at Ladon's Beta as Reid and Wyot joined them.

"I'll leave the cleanup to you, ladies."

He didn't wait for a response as he shifted and took to the air. While he hadn't expected to be welcomed with open arms, being constantly shunned, made to prove himself, and tested had gotten old weeks ago.

He should take Kasia and find another way.

A thought that had been building inside him—one he'd managed to lock away—looked better with each passing day.

She hadn't chosen yet. Ladon was getting restless, but she'd put it off. A selfish part of Brand wanted her reason to be because of him.

You're just tired, he told himself.

Throwing away years of planning and maneuvering when he was so close because his new clan were jerks was senseless. Falling for a woman so off-limits and doing what he wanted with her would not only cancel his plans, but likely end one of the few friendships he had, not to mention *end* his life. Even the idea was plain idiotic.

He'd get some solid sleep. His shift guarding Kasia didn't start until noon.

Eight hours later, Brand couldn't say he was any less twitchy about the entire situation, but he'd committed, for the thousandth time since arriving, to stick with the plan. Rather than go out on his balcony and fly down, as the part of him eager to see Kasia urged him to do, Brand forced himself to walk the slower route, spiraling down through the human-sized tunnels.

Being away from her was getting strangely uncomfortable the more time they spent apart—like a muscle stretched beyond its limits. She was more relaxed with her other guards now. Maybe he should ask to be taken out of the lineup.

"Nice one!" Arden's exclamation reached Brand all the way down the last bit of tunnel leading to the training room.

"I think I finally got it," Kasia's reply floated back to him.

He came out of the tunnel to find Kasia standing in the center of the room, completely on fire, and grinning from ear to ear.

Regret punched through him. Had she had a vision without him there?

Brand pushed that feeling down, stuffing it inside with all the other inappropriate feelings he had about Kasia, and stepped up beside Reid. Maul, who'd lain down beside Ladon's Viceroy of War, lifted his head.

The shifter stood, arms crossed, watching over both women. "Brand," he acknowledged.

"Dickhead," Brand acknowledged back.

Instead of a growl or ignoring him, Reid actually chuckled. "I deserved that, I guess."

Brand didn't respond.

But Reid didn't let it go. He turned to face him. "Seriously. You've more than proved yourself. You're all right in my book, and I'd fight beside you any day."

He held out a hand.

Brand glanced at the hand, then back at Reid's face, but could detect no sign of insincerity.

He clasped Reid's hand. "About damn time."

He got a grin in response. "I think you'll find the rest of the team feels the same way." Then he glanced over at Kasia, who'd stopped burning and was talking quietly with Arden. "You got her?"

The man meant as a bodyguard, but suddenly every thought Brand had had about flying away with her reared their ugly heads and laughed in his face. "Yeah."

Reid nodded and left.

"Are you on duty now?" A feminine voice brought his attention down to the two women in the room. Only the question came from Arden, not Kasia.

Brand nodded, then glanced at his watch. "Time to get ready to meet with the Black Clan."

Kasia barely looked at him as the three of them walked back to her room, Maul padding along behind. Instead, she chatted with Arden. "That last time was the farthest."

"You cleared the entire room," Arden agreed.

"What are you talking about?" Brand asked.

The women exchanged a glance. "Kasia's been working on her teleporting," Arden explained.

He glanced at Kasia, who shrugged. "It's coming along. Maul showed me how he does it. That helped."

So she'd work on it with Reid and Arden, even the damn dog, but not him? "Good. You'll need it to get away from an attack."

"Yeah."

He definitely had to get off bodyguard detail,

because all he wanted to do was grab her and kiss her. Not an option.

Arden paused at her door, a floor under theirs. "I'll see you guys down there? I hear the Captain of Gorgon's guard, Samael Veles, is hot." She waggled her eyebrows.

King Gorgon of the Black Clan had sent his captain in his place today. For what, Brand had yet to determine. Ladon's best guess was Gorgon wanted confirmation of the phoenix. Ladon probably would've liked the meeting better if he were already mated to Kasia.

He walked Kasia the rest of the way to her room in uneasy silence. Could she feel the tension between them, too? Did she want…

Brand forcefully cut off the thought.

He glanced at the hellhound. "You should stay here." Then he moved his gaze to Kasia. "Knock on my door when you're ready."

"Fine," she said. Then closed her door in his face with a final-sounding *thunk*. Shutting him out.

That was the way it had to be, but that didn't make it suck any less.

To pass the time, he went to his room and flipped on his laptop, reading through the dry translations that he'd been pouring through for weeks when sleep eluded him and he had way too much time on his hands.

"What's that?"

Brand swallowed a snarl as he spun to face Kasia, who was coming in through his balcony door.

"What the hell, Kasia? I could've taken your head off."

"I wasn't exactly subtle coming over. I figured you'd smell me." She crossed the room to look over his shoulder and frowned as she read the words. "What has you so focused? Are you...researching phoenixes?"

Brand hid his discomfort behind his own questions. "How'd you get over here?" He refused to let his gaze linger on the red dress she'd changed into—the way it hugged her curves, the cleavage on display thanks to the deep *V* of the dress, how much leg was on display, despite the ankle boots.

"I teleported," she casually tossed off.

Brand grabbed her hand and tugged her to a stop. "You what? What if you missed?"

"I didn't."

Her casual attitude was not helping that protective instinct inside him from rearing its ugly head. "You could be a splat on the ground, and I wouldn't even know it."

Kasia gave him the patient look that reminded him of his mother from long ago, then reached up and patted his cheek. "I've been practicing. I'm much better."

He snatched her hand away. "I'm not laughing."

Her calm faded in the face of a fierce frown. "I wasn't joking. I'm terrified of heights. I wouldn't hop around out there if I weren't 110 percent confident I'd make it."

The rumbling growl of his dragon close to the surface dropped a decibel or two. Brand stared at her but got only total confidence back. Not even a hint of doubt.

"After the meeting with the Black Clan, I want

you to show me."

Kasia rolled her eyes. "Fine. Now, mother hen, what's this all about?" She waved at his computer screen.

He still didn't want to talk about it. "Why are you so dressed up?"

She blinked and glanced down at her outfit. "I was told meetings with other clans are more on the formal side."

"I'm surprised Ladon would risk showing you exist before he's finalized your mating."

Her lips pinched. "I told him I wanted to be there. Not a pawn, remember?" She looked pointedly at the computer and raised her eyebrows.

She wasn't going to let this go, apparently. "Research."

"I can see that. Why?" Brand stayed silent, and she sighed. "Why am I not surprised that you don't want to share?"

"We should go. You'll want to be down there before the delegation from the Black Clan arrives."

Before he could stop her, she picked up a stack of pages he'd printed out and flipped through them. He watched each page carefully, tension coiling inside him as she got nearer the bottom of the stack.

Then she paused.

Her mouth fell open slightly, and she cocked her head as she studied the document closer. "What is this?" The words came out softly, more a whisper, but he caught them.

"I'm not finished with it." He went to take the pile of papers from her hands, but she stepped back.

"You looked up the Amon and Hanyu insignias?" She glanced up finally, searching his face. "Why?"

Brand clamped his lips over the answer and looked away.

"Brand?" His name on her lips brought his gaze back to her. "Why?"

He couldn't look away. "You said your mother never knew what her mating mark would look like."

Confusion darkened her eyes as her pupils dilated. "Okay?"

Brand leaned over to tap the keyboard a few times, bringing up a screen. "I was going to give this to you when I finished." As a mating present. Or at least that had been the excuse in his head.

He stood back so she could see. Kasia pulled her gaze from him to the computer and sucked in a small breath. "Is that…?"

"I combined the two marks, so you could see what it might have looked like."

Kasia stared at the image on his screen for a long time. Long enough that Brand shifted on his feet. He wished she'd say something.

"You did this for me?"

"As a mating gift." For her mating to Ladon. He should have said to Ladon, because the way it came out sounded like he'd meant the gift one mate gave another.

She raised her head and stared at him, seemingly searching his face. Brand stared back, unwavering and giving nothing of himself away. Except that if she looked at him like that much longer—as though he were someone worthy—he wouldn't be able to hold himself back.

"I don't know what to say," she murmured.

She didn't look away. Neither did he.

"This must've taken you hours."

He could've shrugged it off or tossed out some sarcastic comment about her making a big deal out of nothing. But he didn't.

He was tired of forcing up walls between them, forcing a distance that didn't feel natural. The process was exhausting. Every instinct that had been dragging at him to claim her rose within him. To hell with dragon shifters and taking down his family's killers and any bullshit about High Kings.

Brand leaned forward, heart pounding as she reciprocated, closing the distance, her heart beating in time to his, music to his ears.

"Kasia, I—"

The boom of an explosion preceded the reverberations that rocked the very foundation of the mountain.

Brand and Kasia jerked back. Her eyes went wide, as dread swirled in his gut.

Fuck.

Together, they ran for the balcony, looking over into the atrium. Another explosion rocked them, and black smoke rose as the second steel door, the one leading from the training room to the heart of the mountain where the busy shops stood below them, was blasted away. A glittering of golden scales appeared in the billows of smoke as screams arose from the ground.

Kasia scrambled over the balcony to the perch, but Brand dragged her back, holding her against his chest. "Where are you going?"

She pushed against him. "I can help them."

"And I'm supposed to keep you safe."

Stubborn fury gave her eyes an almost dead look. "Then I guess you'll just have to follow me down there."

In two seconds flat, she went up in flames and disappeared, leaving him holding an armful of nothing.

Fuck me.

Brand vaulted the railing, shifting as he traversed the perch. As soon as his wings were formed, he dropped off the edge, letting the rest of his shift finish up as he dropped. Forget circling down, he tucked his wings in and rocketed to the chaos below, zipping past dragons, both gold and blue, in his need to find Kasia.

Billowing smoke obscured his vision, so he had to slow his descent earlier than he would've liked, circling until he reached the ground. The heavy scent obscured any way to track her by smell, which meant he'd have to see her. What had she been wearing?

Red. Red dress.

Brand scanned the ground. Some of his people had shifted, but many hadn't. Those who weren't fighters most likely. In their human forms, they were weaker. Why weren't they shifting for protection?

A flash of red caught his attention. There she was, inside the Italian restaurant. Only he blinked and she was gone, along with the owner of the shop. She was helping people get out?

A familiar snarl sounded close by. Swinging his head around, Brand located Maul, happily ripping into the delicate wing membranes of a gold dragon who screamed in agony.

"Maul. Find Kasia."

The dog let go of his victim and disappeared.

Another explosion shattered through the cacophony of chaotic sound.

"You won't take me alive." A small woman ran out of the smoke, straight at him, brandishing an ax, of all things.

Brand braced himself, not wanting to hurt a person who was part of his new clan, but who obviously mistook him for another gold dragon attacker.

Kasia suddenly appeared between him and the fierce woman. "That's Brand, Mrs. McGovern."

The woman paused, glared suspiciously at Brand, then lowered her weapon.

"Let me get you out of here." Kasia offered her hand.

"Kasia—"

"Not now," she snapped. Dammit. She was already gone.

Maul popped in and flashed an image of her—in the red dress, which meant he'd seen her.

"She's come and gone. Stay here. We'll pin her down together."

Even if it meant knocking that stubborn woman out.

Before he could search for her, a dragon so dark gold it almost appeared bronzed landed in front of him and blasted a torrent of fire at his head. Brand charged, running directly into the flames. When the fire stopped he was only feet away, but recognition slapped him in the face, and he hesitated.

"Geir?" He probed the other dragon's mind.

The dragon blinked, then spun and flung his tail

at Brand, catching him in the shoulder with a spike.

The need for retaliation—both for the blow and for a long-ago betrayal when Geir's family watched, doing nothing as Uther murdered Brand's family—burned into Brand, who let out a roar.

But Ladon's voice sounded in his head. *"Find Kasia and get her out of here."* A shadow passed overhead, and Brand caught the flash of an indigo wing as the king barreled into the bronze dragon in front of him.

Brand started after his friend; the only thought in his head was killing that bronze bastard, but Maul jumped in front of him, shaking his head. Then Kasia popped up between them. Maul growled then let up with a funny whine as he recognized her.

The cloud of fury swirling through Brand abated as the greater need of protecting this woman took over. *"Kasia, we have to go,"* he urged.

"But the people." She glanced over her shoulder, concern pulling her away from him even as he willed her to listen.

"If Uther gets his hands on you, those people will have many worse things to worry about."

She didn't turn back, but she didn't disappear, either. "I could help them."

"Help them by staying safe."

Maul suddenly flashed an image of a woman with long black curls and reddish-brown eyes. Kind eyes. Worried eyes. Kasia's mother?

Must be, because Kasia sucked in a breath, and when she let it out she disappeared only to show up on Brand's back, the weight of her slight but noticeable. "Go!" she shouted.

He took off, shooting out through the damaged door into the training chamber then out the second destroyed door that led from the training area to outside. They burst into clean air, blue skies startlingly brilliant after the black smoke inside.

Dragons of green and gold.

Brand caught her thought and looked up to find the skies swirling with them. *"Then we go down."*

No black dragons, though. Had they been part of the ruse, or had the other clans used their visit as a convenient distraction?

Regardless, he dropped away under the cover of the smoke pouring from the gaping wound in the mountainside. Maul popped up on cliffs and rocks along the way, following them closely.

"We'll never get out of there without them seeing." Kasia gripped his spike tightly even as she watched over her shoulder, her shifted weight throwing him slightly off-kilter.

"I know a place in the mountains. Hold on."

As soon as she righted herself and had a better grip, Brand tipped his wings, circling back and shooting through a gap into a smaller canyon. He hadn't been this way since he was a boy, and smaller.

He just hoped the back door he'd made centuries ago hadn't caved in over the years, and that he could fit.

XIV

"Where are we?" Kasia climbed down from Brand's back and looked around the obviously dragon-made tunnels, now dark and cold with lack of use.

She'd hardly been able to tell, he'd flown so fast through that narrow canyon—one she'd never noticed the few times she'd been outside—followed by a sharp cut into a long, tight tunnel that had been pitch black.

"My home."

That generic accent he'd been using slipped, the American tones coming through again. Who was she dealing with now? The rogue mercenary or the king's trusted warrior? She had a feeling she knew.

She jumped a little as Maul suddenly appeared beside her. Following them in the dark had probably made his teleporting a bit tougher. She put a hand on his side, grateful to have him there.

Brand sucked in a breath, and his belly glowed, warm and golden, with the fire he was fueling inside. With a concentrated blast from his maw, he spewed a stream of gold-tinted flames into a hole in the wall she hadn't even noticed. Immediately, the flames traversed a small channel built in behind the walls with rectangular cutouts every ten feet or so—fireplaces apparently, all interconnected. Immediately the room was awash in light cast by multiple fires burning in each pit.

She could see better now, making out different

rooms beyond the main one in which they stood—a bedroom, a kitchen, a bathroom—built into the natural formations of the cavern, similar to the dragon city.

Brand took her momentary distraction to shift, and she turned to find him standing close, gaze intent and pissed as hell. At a guess, because she'd teleported herself into danger and ignored him when he'd tried to stop her. He was supposed to be her bodyguard, and she hadn't exactly made that easy on him. Plus, he was a big, bad dragon shifter, a breed of male she realized took Neanderthal to a whole new level.

Damn. What was the best way to deal with a furious dragon shifter?

"Maul," he said. "Any way we can get a little privacy?"

The hellhound glanced between them but must've decided Brand wasn't a true threat to her, because he disappeared. *Traitor.*

Kasia swallowed but refused to show her nerves. "Your home?" she asked, proud of how steady her voice came out.

He didn't take his gaze from her, not even a blink as he started to slowly stalk toward her. "I made this place when I was a young dragon."

A young dragon? She had so many questions but suspected now wasn't the time to ask them. Besides, how could she engage in casual conversation when he looked as though he were going to devour her any moment, only she couldn't tell if he was only furious or massively turned on. It kind of looked the same to her.

Still, maybe a casual chat would give him time to defuse. So rather than hold her ground, or back up and trigger his predatory response, Kasia casually turned and walked toward the kitchen, sort of sideways from his trajectory. "You made this place all by yourself?"

"I had some help."

Yeah, he wasn't biting or budging.

She could feel him closing in as she kept her profile to him and pretended to wander. Or maybe you weren't supposed to turn your back to a predator? You definitely weren't supposed to run, but wasn't there something with bears about facing them? What were you supposed to do? Get big and yell? Would that work with an angry dragon?

"Who else has been here?" He hadn't pounced yet. Perhaps the banal conversation was working. Worth a shot to keep it up.

"Kasia."

That one word came from beside her ear, a low growl, and goose bumps feathered down her arms. She jumped and spun at the same time. How the hell had he gotten that close without her knowing?

The second she faced him, he yanked her into his arms and kissed her—a fierce, claiming kiss that shot through her defenses in less than a heartbeat. As though some part of him called to some part of her, like their souls recognized each other on an instinctual level. The part that needed him. Pleasure arrowed straight to every erogenous zone in her body, heating her up from inside.

Weeks of denying every urge her heart and body had flung at her, and she was lost. With a small, needy sound she tried to get as close as she could, and he obliged, wrapping those big arms around her to plaster her against him from head to toe.

Even with her up on tiptoe, he had to lean down to reach her. With a grunt of frustration, he cupped her backside and hauled her up. She wrapped her legs around his hips, his hard length pressing exactly where she wanted it, but with too many layers of clothing in between.

He pulled back, but only barely, and only long enough to berate her. "Don't you ever do anything like that again."

She would've sniped back, only he sealed his mouth over hers and stole her breath and her mind.

He pulled back again, and she sucked in air and beat him to it. "I'll do whatever I damn well think is—"

"Wrong answer."

Hot, hard lips crashed back down on hers. Vaguely, she was aware he was walking them somewhere else, but she was too busy shoving her tongue down his throat and vice versa to pay much attention.

Frustration edged his touch as he kneaded her backside with his hands, grinding her into his erection in the most delicious way. She knew now where that frustration came from—a concern for her. He cared. Instead of making her want to run, it added an edge to her own need.

She grabbed a hank of his hair and pulled back. "You can't tell me what to do."

"Wrong again."

With that he tumbled her back on the bed she hadn't even realized he'd taken them to. He leaned over her, hands on either side of her face, golden eyes feverish, sparking with desire, his jaw working as though he were holding himself back. "This isn't going to be slow and gentle."

Almost an apology.

In response, she whipped her red dress over her head and reached back for the snap on her bra. "Who said anything about wanting gentle or slow?"

Brand's neck muscles worked as he swallowed hard. Then he reared back and started stripping. Kasia shimmied out of her bra and panties. In short order, all that annoying clothing was no longer an issue, and Brand stood above her, unashamedly naked and proud.

And hers. Hers in a way that felt real.

Damn, he was magnificent—hard in all the right places, making her wet in all the right places.

She squealed as he whipped his hands out to snag her by the ankles and pull her ass to the edge of the bed. He wrapped her legs around his hips, then moaned as he inserted a finger into her, sliding deep and true.

She went stock-still, bombarded with a longing triggered by one simple touch, as though he'd finally staked a claim on her body, as though he wanted her for his own as much as she wanted him.

"Touch yourself," he demanded.

Compelled to do as he bid, with eager hands, she smoothed over her breasts and belly to where his finger still remained embedded inside her. He slid out, and she bit her lips, waiting for him to take his hand away, but then he slid back in before she could take his place with her own hands.

She raised her confused gaze to his, and he cocked his head. Then slid out and back in. Realization dawned—he wanted them both to play together—and heat flooded her cheeks even as it arrowed straight to her clit, wet warmth seeping out over his fingers.

Brand watched her, his eyes molten gold.

Trapped in that sinful gaze, she moved her fingers to the nub of hidden nerves above where he pumped in and out of her, circling it with her fingertip. Then she began to move in time to his touch. In and out. Circle and press. Like a dance.

Beneath both their hands, her body turned electric, pulsing and throbbing with each stroke, each brush, until she was panting, her eyes half closed, but still on his, captured by his compelling stare. Driven higher by the desire tightening the skin over his cheekbones, his gaze drew her in. The connection almost tangible. Her nipples beaded under that gaze. Unable to help herself, Kasia brought her free hand up to tweak and twist those rosy peaks, shooting sparks to her clit.

"Fuck," Brand muttered. Then his free hand went to his cock.

At the sight of the swollen purple head, thick and angry, in his strong hand, another gush of wet heat poured out of her, and a stuttering moan rose up her throat. Her breath punched out in panting bursts.

A build of pressure and pleasure started deep in her womb, pulling a wanton moan from her lips, and suddenly, Brand stopped, pulling his fingers out of her and grabbing her hand, pulling it away from her clit.

"Not yet," he commanded.

Her body screamed for release.

"Brand." She tried to come off the bed; the only idea in her head involved forcing him to finish what they'd started. "I need you."

He pushed her back down, gently, but pinning her in such a way that she couldn't move, eyes all wicked intent. "You have me."

Those words sent a charge through her.

But he didn't move, just stared at her, as though entranced.

She wriggled under him, trying to pull him closer by digging her heels into his butt.

"Please." She was begging now. "I need you inside me."

Something in her words, or the hitch in her voice maybe, released something within him. She saw the control snap in his eyes, felt it in the tension in his muscles.

He sucked in a deep breath. "You want me inside you?"

She nodded, perhaps a little too eagerly, but pride was no longer an element in this situation. She was almost frantic by now.

With a low rumble of sound deep in his chest that had her heart hammering, he loosed a stream of fire aiming downward, the hot flame licking that most intimate part of her, stoking her need to fever pitch.

Then he grabbed her by the hips, hitching her higher, angling her, and impaled her in one hard stroke. He must've used the fire on his own body, because heat seared her from the inside. Pleasure slammed through her, along with a feeling of deep-seated rightness.

"Is this what you wanted?" he asked.

But she wasn't backing down from him. Not anymore. "Yes," she cried. "I want you. All of you."

With a roar of primal satisfaction, he pounded into her, but she was so wet, so ready, that all she knew was the ecstasy of his possession. He filled her to the point that she didn't know where she ended and he began, their bodies linked by more than touch.

He set a driving rhythm, his face harshly beautiful as he watched his body move in and out of hers, almost as if his claiming of her body was driving him harder and faster. With each stroke, he pushed her closer and closer to the edge of bliss, building a pressure so incredible, she was sobbing his name. Living in a hazy place where only the two of them existed.

Somewhere down deep she had a vague notion that they shouldn't be doing this. But she was too far gone, every corner of her mind and body focused on one thing only.

Another wave of pleasure crashed into her, and she moaned as an electric charge sizzled along her nerve endings. She was close. Gods, she was so close.

"Harder," she whispered.

He did as she asked, moving harder, faster, grunting with each thrust.

She gasped as her skin suddenly lit up, golden flowers of fire that reminded her of Brand's, but these were her flames. She tried to hold them back, terrified she'd kill him, but the inferno blazed off of her.

Fire during sex could kill him if he wasn't her mate.

Oh, hell. She was going to kill him.

Only…the flames didn't consume Brand.

Truth blazed through her, reflected back at her in his eyes.

Did he see it, too?

"Kasia?"

She tried to focus through the sting of pleasure still buffeting her system. Her fire rose around them, and his muscles tensed, his body shaking, his face tightened, agonizing pleasure and awe visible in a way she never would have believed possible. What was he asking her?

"Kasia, do you want this?"

She thrashed under him, moaning through crests of sensation. Then reconnected with his gaze, drawn in by a reflected need. More than that, by desperation in his eyes that she felt to her bones. This was *right*.

To hell with supposed-tos, and the world outside, and what logic should tell her was a bad idea. She didn't want to stop this, to fight it any longer.

"Yes." She frantically nodded. *Yes, yes, yes.* "I choose you."

Relief filled his golden eyes, followed by blazing possession.

Her one final small worry whispered away. He wanted this, wanted her, as much as she did him.

Brand's chest lit with an inner fire. Linking their hands, he lifted them above her head. Then he sucked in a deep breath and kissed her.

As soon as she opened to him, he pushed his fire

into her. Kasia warmed from the inside out as she accepted her destiny, accepted her mate.

Heat spread through every part of her.

Need consuming her, she basked in the searing warmth and almost screamed at the pleasure. With the flames came sensation like she'd never experienced before. Like euphoria was just within her grasp. Her heart soared, and everything inside her strained toward him.

"That's it, Kasia. Gods, you're so gorgeous."

The flames flowed out of her as sensation built inside her.

"Let go," he said. "I want to see your face as you come."

That beautiful pressure built and built. At his words, she allowed her body to relax into what was coming. The glow beneath her skin brought out the design of feathers over her shoulders and arms, and the surge of power that came with them flowed through her like sparks in her blood.

Brand continued to slam into her, also aglow as her flames surrounded them both. Fire consumed her both inside and out.

"Kasia." Command laced the single word. "Come now."

Flame and ecstasy exploded inside her and all around them. As she pulsed, Brand's cock grew thick inside her, and he threw his head back, shouting as her pleasure tipped him into his own, more fire pouring from his body into hers in a new rush of joining, mixing with everything already swirling inside her.

"Mine."

The word blasted through her mind so clearly, at first she'd thought he'd spoken aloud, or she had. She still couldn't tell which of them it came from. She didn't care, either, too swept up in the magic of what was happening.

With each crest of the most incredible pleasure came a different kind of vision—pristinely clear, with audible sounds and vivid colors. Vision after vision, all of them skirting through and out of her mind. She couldn't bring herself to care or to drag her still-seeing gaze from Brand's face and the sensations flowing through her body. The beautiful completion in his eyes as they shared the intense climax. Riding it to its end until they'd pulled every ounce of pleasure from it.

Brand collapsed over her, chest heaving, and she relished the weight of his body on hers, his still semi-hard length inside her.

He gazed down at her, looking freer and some-how younger than he ever had since she'd met him. "So glad I invested in fireproof bedding."

Kasia could feel herself sinking into oblivion, her body completely wrung out. But she didn't want to think about reality yet. After a few beats without getting a response, he kissed his way up her shoulder and neck to her mouth where he lingered.

She was more than happy to oblige, forgetting the outside world and worries about what had just happened as they exchanged sated, sweet kisses until he finally raised his head.

With a shaking hand, she pushed back his hair, damp with sweat. "We shouldn't have done that."

He shook his head. "Yes, we should have."

Kasia rolled her eyes. His cocky confidence was a part of him—be that good or bad. Mostly good, she decided sleepily, as the lethargy crept over her body, stealing her thoughts as well as her ability to keep her eyes open.

Even through her struggle, she felt the press of his lips against the back of her neck. "You're mine now."

Kasia snuggled into his warm body, content that she was in his arms. Later they could figure out what would happen next.

As soon as Kasia's breathing evened out, Brand pulled the covers up over her and slipped into the bed beside her.

He stared down at her face—devastatingly lovely, so soft in repose, her hair spread out over his arm and pillow like a slash of flame.

My mate.

He hadn't meant to mate her when they started. He knew doing so would end in death, and if it didn't, it certainly cocked up their plans and put them both in several crosshairs. But he'd wanted her so much. When she'd loosed her own fire without burning him up, a total sense of destiny had settled over him—an odd peace in the middle of the storm of sensation.

He would have stopped if she'd said no, though the gods knew how, he'd been so far gone. But no hadn't come from her lips. She'd said yes, and everything inside him had eased and escalated at the same time. He'd completed the process, experiencing only a moment of terror as he'd poured his flame into her.

He frowned and brushed a finger over the nape of her neck. No brand had shown up on her yet, the delicate skin still a blank slate. The mating process was inevitable now. It had begun. He'd wait for that, for the day he'd see his brand on the back of her neck.

They'd mated. No one else could have her now.

He should be calling himself all kinds of fool. With that one action, he'd killed his place among the Blue Clan. Hell, he'd burned that chance at the stake. Worse, he'd taken away Kasia's chance at safety. Mating Ladon would have guaranteed her not only a king with the strength to protect her, but an entire clan to surround her.

Although, given today's attack, perhaps not.

Still, Brand was just one man.

I'm not enough. Not to protect her.

He had to set this right. He'd mated her and survived her fire. Fate had chosen him, not the king. Brand couldn't be angry about that, but he had to figure out how to fix this. Now.

As he lay there memorizing every curve of her face, the sweet campfire and chocolate scent of her skin, the vivid coloring that made her glow with heart-stopping vitality, he mentally sorted through and discarded every possible scenario for how they should move forward in such a way that wouldn't end up with her dead.

Enlist Hershel's help?

See if Maul could surround them with other

loyal hellhounds?

Ask Kasia what that wolf said to her?

But none of the options he considered were truly viable. They needed the support of a clan of dragon shifters.

Or…was another option open to him? An option he'd never let himself consider, revenge being the only future he focused on. What he was thinking now might be the only way to protect Kasia and keep her at his side.

Brand tensed enough that Kasia frowned in her sleep. Dropping a kiss on her forehead, he eased away from her body to sit at the edge of the bed, head in his hands.

What he was contemplating could blow up in his face. Ladon would smell Kasia on Brand's skin, recognize how their scents mingled. The guy could summarily execute him without a hearing, regardless of their long history. Friendship covered only so many sins.

But of all the bad choices available to them, this was the only one he could see working.

Two outcomes were possible. Either Ladon agreed with Brand's suggestion and they took the next steps together—fuck the whole "High King" thing—or…the king executed him. Since the mating bond wasn't solidified yet, Kasia wouldn't die along with him, leaving her free to be with Ladon. Not that they could mate, but he could still make her his Queen, force her to stay with him, give the illusion of mating a phoenix. If that happened, at least she'd still be protected, although she'd be miserable.

A searing pain stabbed through his hand. As he

watched in silence, the Ormarr mark, linking him to the Blue Clan, disappeared from his skin, leaving it blank for the second time in Brand's life. No shock there. Disloyalty to the king and the decisions he'd made tonight were enough to cut those magical ties, technically unmarking him as a traitor. He was a rogue again, but hopefully not for long.

Would Ladon feel Brand disconnect from the Blue Clan? Some kings claimed they could feel their people like that, but who knew if that was just a way to keep people loyal.

It didn't matter. His decision was made.

A future he'd never allowed himself to contemplate, let alone envision, lay just out of his grasp. One that involved taking back his birthright, rather than destroying the people who stole it in the first place. If he reached out to take it, would he lose everything?

He wasn't risking Kasia's neck to find out. He'd have to leave her here. She had Maul to keep her safe.

Careful not to jostle the bed, Brand jumped to his feet and hastily pulled on his clothes. In the living area, he grabbed paper out of a kitchen drawer and scrawled a quick note. Across the room, Maul lumbered to his feet from where he'd been sleeping on the floor. Brand had no idea when the hellhound had returned to them, but was grateful to be able to leave Kasia with protection now.

"I have to go talk to Ladon. Keep her safe, Maul."

The hound gave a soft huff of agreement.

Kasia's safety taken care of, he returned to the bedroom and left the note on the pillow beside her. If he woke her to explain, she'd only insist on coming with him.

He curled his hand into a fist at his side, resisting the urge to touch her, kiss her, one last time. He had no idea if he'd return, if they'd ever get a chance to work through what they'd just done. Hell, she might kill him herself when she had a chance to think through the consequences.

Too late now. He'd known in his soul that she was meant to be his.

With a grunt at the tightness in his chest, he forced himself to turn away, leave his mate sleeping in his bed, and go present the king with a plan.

Brand didn't return to the canyon. The king and clan would no longer be there. The last installation of the Blue Clan had fallen. Most would have scattered. Ladon would gather his advisors at one of the several emergency points and decide where to go from there. Thankfully, Brand had been given a list of places to memorize and then burn. He just hoped he wasn't too late and the clan hadn't already scattered to the four winds.

The first location south of the mountain was a total bust. A small contingency of the clan gathered there, but not the king, so Brand tipped his wings east to Cairngorms National Park and another mountain. Ben Macdui.

No sign of dragon shifters had him thinking through his path to the third location in France long before he got to the mountain. He'd have to go back for Kasia, because France would involve days of travel.

But before he could formulate a plan, the hint of a smoky scent reached him. Dragons.

He'd found them. Now how to approach without getting torched?

They might not be able to differentiate him from the gold dragons who'd attacked earlier despite fighting side by side with him, so he started broadcasting his identity.

After a moment, two blue dragons dropped from above, flanking him. The light blue dragon with a darker stripe down his back was immediately recognizable, as was the slightly smaller turquoise female. Reid and Arden.

"Follow us," Reid said.

The two dragons guided him around the back side of the mountain to land near a copse of evergreen trees. When they shifted, he shifted. From there, they made their way to a human-sized cave. Arden placed her palm against a seemingly innocuous rock that lit up as it scanned her palm. With a soft click, another rock slid back noiselessly, revealing it to be a door with a corridor beyond.

Another three layers of security, and at least two stories underground later, they entered what appeared to be a standard conference room—boring table and chairs in the center, TV projection unit on the wall at one end of the long, skinny space.

Ladon looked up from his computer, deadly serious. "Is she safe?"

Brand nodded. "For now."

"Where?"

"You know where. Maul is with her."

Ladon sat back and rubbed his eyes. "Thank the gods for that." He paused, took a moment, then angled a shrewd glance at Brand, and his nostrils flared.

Damn. The king had just scented the difference.

"May I have a second alone? Please?" Brand asked.

Not usually one for begging, he had zero problem with the word now. Finding a way to protect his new mate was too important for pride.

Impossible to tell Ladon's reaction behind those hard blue eyes. "What did you do?"

The others in the room must've taken that as a signal and quietly vacated the space. Ladon stood slowly, coming around the table to face him directly. Brand braced himself.

After a long hard stare, Ladon snaked out a hand to grab Brand's wrist and flipped his hand over, finding the marking gone.

"She's my mate." Brand winced. He hadn't meant to lead off with the bald statement, but he knew Ladon already suspected.

Ladon looked down at the floor, still giving no hint as to his reaction. "Why'd you do it?"

"Fate."

Ladon shook his head. "Not good enough." He didn't yell. If anything he got quiet. A bad fucking sign.

"It should be," Brand said.

A bitter smile twisted Ladon's mouth, the scar through his eye twitching. "Yes. It should."

Shock at the agreement had Brand pausing. What did Ladon mean by that?

"But I have bigger considerations than fate and your dick." He didn't say the words. He didn't need to. High King. A chance to take out Pytheios by removing the illusion of his power.

Shit. This was going sideways fast, and Brand had never been a smooth talker. "I know she's important to your cause," he tried.

"*Our* cause." Ladon's voice snapped as he slammed a fist down on the table, his rage finally visible, reflecting in eyes glowing iridescent blue. "Our cause, Brand. You are one of my warriors. You were the one who convinced me to fight, to kill my king and take his place. Did you forget that? Did I accept you, confide in you, trust you, only to have you stab me in the back?"

No apology would settle Ladon or make this go away, so Brand didn't even try. "There's a way to make this right."

"I'm not interested." Ladon stalked around him to the door.

"You have to listen to me."

Ladon swung the door open, then turned toward Brand; under his skin dragon's scales shone through, moving as though a serpent lived inside him. Fuck, the man was as furious as Brand had ever seen a shifter. "I don't listen to traitors."

The king turned to Ivar and Rainier standing outside the door. "Lock him up. Before I kill him."

At least Ladon hadn't taken his fucking head off. Maybe there was still time. Every instinct inside Brand screamed at him to fight, but doing so would seal his path to death, so, despite vibrating with the need to shift, he walked calmly to the guards.

"There's a way to fix this," he repeated.

"You mated her," Ladon spat. "There's no way to fix that. You've condemned your people to fight without the one element that could have turned this riptide in our favor."

The guards grabbed Brand by the arms, but he jerked out of their grips. "Touch me again and I'll rip your arms out of the sockets and beat you to death with them. I'm coming peacefully." Brand stalked off down the hallway, forcing the guards to scurry to keep up.

Brand tried one last-ditch effort, pausing where the tunnel turned to look back at the man watching him with cold, dead eyes from the doorway to a mundane conference room.

"My given name is Branek Astarot Dagrun."

Ladon stared at him for a long beat, absorbing that information. "The sentence for treason is death."

The king, a man Brand had thought a friend, turned back into the room, closing the door with a soft click, his judgment final.

The brothers didn't touch him. Brand turned to them and nodded. They exchanged a glance, then continued on in silence, leading him to his prison until Ladon could carry out his execution.

Kasia. I've failed us both.

XV

Kasia groped her way out of a dead sleep slowly and groggily. It took her a moment to focus her gaze on the panting, drooling snout in front of her, blowing her hair into her face with muggy dog breath.

"Maul," she groaned, her voice all crackly. "Back up."

The hellhound gave a pathetic whine but did as she asked, removing the sauna from her face. But he still sat beside the bed panting.

"If you need to go pee, just teleport," she mumbled into her pillow.

Maul made a noise—the doggy version of *"What the hell are you talking about?"* Then he pawed at her back, which, given his size, felt more like being whacked by a two-by-four. A two-by-four with sandpaper.

She knew he wouldn't quit, so she peeled her eyelids—which seemed to have taken on the consistency of flypaper—off her eyeballs.

"Fine. Fine. I'm getting up." She rolled to sitting and clasped the white sheet that had been covering her to her chest as she realized she was naked.

Wait. I'm naked.

Naked and sitting in the middle of an unfamiliar bed—

The night came rushing back with the force of a tsunami—the attack, their escape, and what had happened in this very cave. Kasia squeezed her eyes shut.

Oh shit. Oh shit.

What had she done to Brand? They'd…mated. She'd been so consumed with need, and how they fit, and the sensation of sheer completeness in his arms. She'd wanted it. Said yes.

At least she hadn't killed him. Thank the gods.

Still, they'd mated, which royally fucked up his place with his new clan. He'd waited so long.

Kasia dropped her head into her hands with a groan. *What have I done?*

She rubbed a hand around the back of her neck. No brand raised the skin there, but that was only a matter of time. A small spark of excitement ignited in her chest at the thought of wearing his mark. Only reality was something she couldn't ignore in the cold light of… She glanced around. Was it day or night?

Didn't matter. She groaned again. *I've ruined everything for him.*

Not to mention for herself. She didn't spark to life under Ladon's touch like she did with Brand, but there were other, more important factors to consider. Like Pytheios. Like her sisters. Like the fate of dragon shifters, though she still had her doubts a phoenix would have much impact on that disaster.

Still, Brand seemed to have faith, and given his general sourpuss attitude, that was saying something.

Speaking of which, where was he?

"Brand?" she called out, then listened. Silence. Maybe a blind cave cricket or two chirped, but no sound of him.

Maul gave a soft rumble, then flashed her an image of Brand dropping a note on the pillow beside her and walking away, disappearing into the darkness of the tunnel leading up and outside.

"Oh," she murmured, trying to keep her heart where it belonged in her chest rather than allowing it to sink to her feet.

She glanced down at the pillow, but saw no note, so she flopped to her stomach to check the floor. There it was. Hastily scrawled in nearly illegible handwriting, she still managed to make out the words.

I've gone to ask Ladon's forgiveness and try to fix this.
Stay here with Maul until I return.
—Brand

He'd left to go try to fix things with Ladon? How? Did he regret what they'd done? Dread plunked through her. Had he gone to sacrifice himself? The second Ladon knew, he'd kill Brand on the spot. Was Brand trying to get that out of the way before the connection solidified so that she could still go on?

Kasia expected her heart to protest with pain, but an odd numbness settled over her. The same way she'd felt right after her mother had died. For weeks, Kasia had walked around her tiny cabin like a zombie, Maul watching over her. The pain hadn't come right away.

Was that what this was?

A strange heat had her opening her eyes. Kasia gasped. She was on fire.

Before she could decide what to do, the vision tumbled through her, soft, like bubbles, but beautiful nonetheless, and with it came images she'd never seen before. Uther—though younger—executing a family of dragons inside a gleaming golden throne room. Slitting the throats of the three children before taking the lives of both mother and father. Their blood staining the golden floor crimson.

A boy with dark blond hair and familiar golden eyes watching from behind a massive gilt throne, then running through a corridor tucked behind that chair.

The same boy alone and scared, making his way to other dragons, blue dragons, and being turned away by the king—Thanatos she assumed, because the man in the vision wasn't Ladon—shunned.

Now the boy was hiding in a cave. Alone. Except another boy—one with dark hair and blue eyes— brought him food. Ladon. They'd known each other all this time?

The scene jumped years, to a teenaged Brand, recognizable as the man he would become, training with Hershel, living in this cavern, meeting with Ladon in secret.

As fast as the vision came on, the images faded, leaving her reeling from the fact that it had come with pleasure instead of pain, and without Brand's help. Even more so, from what she'd discovered.

Brand was the rightful King of the Gold Clan?

No way could she be wrong about that. Suddenly so many things about him clicked into place—the changing accents, why he'd been a rogue dragon, his insistence on doing Ladon's bidding. Uther had murdered his family, taken the throne, and somehow Brand had escaped, turning rogue rather than being killed alongside his parents and siblings. Like her, a usurper had destroyed his family and taken everything from him. Only she'd had her mother, her sisters. He'd been cast out alone.

Kasia put a hand over her mouth as the reasons driving his decisions, including mating her, sank in. Brand had mated her for a purpose.

Revenge.

All this time, he'd said he needed a clan to get it. She'd been leverage when he first found her, something she already knew. Leverage to gain not just the Blue King as an ally, but Ladon's entire clan, he'd said. Like the wolves, one dragon was dangerous, multiple even more so.

But *mating* her... That gave him the kind of leverage that would enable him to exact the biggest form of revenge—taking back the gold throne and forcing every other king to submit to him.

Brand wanted to be High King. Needed to be. Finding her had given him that opportunity. And somehow, she'd fallen for him and given him exactly what he wanted.

So why was he fixing things with Ladon? The king would have to bow to Brand soon enough. Maybe he wanted to keep his alliance with the blue dragons.

Even the High King needed allies. Or, more

accurately, pawns.

That was it… I'm nothing more than a pawn.
Used, just like her mother warned her.

Numbness gave way to pain, sort of like having
her chest ripped open with a dragon claw. Tears
burned the back of her eyes, demanding she give
in and break down, but Kasia sucked in a harsh
breath, holding them off through sheer will. Crying
never helped a damn thing, and she wasn't into pity
parties.

Her mother had taught her that, too.

I've been such a fool.

She shoved off the bed and made her way to the
bathroom, where she turned on the shower and got
under the spray of blessedly hot water. How he'd
managed to pipe and heat water down here was a
vague secondary thought. She really didn't give
a shit as to the hows and whys. Hot water was the
important factor.

Okay.

The way to deal with this mess was to put one
foot in front of the other. Even if that led to tying
herself to Ladon. She couldn't mate him, or she'd
kill him. But she could still be his Queen. That didn't
require mating. She'd just spend the rest of her days
with a man she could never love like the one she'd
already given her heart to.

I love him.

The abruptness of that realization sucked air
from her lungs, even as she acknowledged what
she'd already known. Hell, he'd asked her to choose
him last night, and she had, gods help her. Of course
she loved him.

But finally letting herself face that truth broke something inside her. Because facing that truth meant facing a future without him. A long, long future.

A keening wail forced itself from her mouth, and the tears she'd been holding back joined the spray of the shower running down her face. Kasia couldn't stay upright under the onslaught of pain, doubling over, wrapping her arms over her middle, and finally sinking to the floor. She pulled her knees up and wrapped her arms around them, then let the emotion wash over her, sobs shuddering her entire body.

Even after her despair was spent in the form of headache-inducing tears, and the water had long since turned cold, she still sat. Quietly. Not wanting to face the world or any more truths.

Eventually, she started to shiver. Her ass had long ago lost feeling on the rough stone floor, and she was aware of Maul, making worried little cries on the other side of the bathroom door.

Exhausted and defeated, she reached up and turned off the shower.

"I'm coming, Maul," she assured the hellhound.

She forced herself to her feet and stepped out from behind the stone partition. Kasia glanced around through puffy eyes. No towels.

With a sigh, she ignited her own fire, allowing it to flow over her skin, drying and warming her better than any towel could have, anyway.

Then she glanced in the mirror. And froze.

The sight of herself, naked and aflame, triggered a memory of one of the visions she'd had last night. This exact moment in time. An image of herself looking in the mirror, flames covering her body and lifting her hair, eyes red and swollen from crying. Even the emotions of the moment. She had seen this moment.

Why?

Because I've changed. Something has changed.

The way she'd gotten there was different, the racking pain gone, and more vivid and with sounds and color.

Kasia closed her eyes and did what Brand had made her do last night. Let go. She let the flame take over her body, opening herself to her power, and reached for the memories. What had she seen?

A vision of Skylar dressed all in black, her long hair pulled back in her customary braid, standing beside a familiar tree. Though Kasia couldn't quite place it, she knew she'd seen that twisted pine somewhere.

A man inside a cell high in the mountains. So high the sky was more black than blue. Was it at night? She couldn't see much of him as he sat on a long stone bench and stared out at the stars.

Gods. Why was any of this important?

A flash of Chante letting a group of five men into the Blue Clan's mountain through a side door she'd never seen.

A tall, skinny man in an ornately embroidered suit. Skinny to the point of appearing emaciated, with his bones jutting out from under his skin, and pale almost to the point of being albino. He was speaking. "I can save your sister, my queen, but you must act fast."

With a gasp Kasia's eyes flew open, and she lost

her concentration, the flames turning to smoke as they died.

Save her sister? No one else knew about her sisters. Which one? And something about that "my queen" reference felt off. Was this yet another vision that revealed a more distant future? Either way...

I have to keep my sisters safe.

She'd spent enough damn time wallowing in that shower. Too much. Kasia summoned the fire and closed her eyes again. She needed to watch that vision more closely.

To her shock, she returned to that exact image, which she then watched over and over, searching for any sign, any clue. But nothing jumped out at her.

Before she could end her own personal rerun session, another vision followed.

Uther, leading a squad of golden dragons, flying over what looked to be a small town. Kasia frowned as that image settled in her mind, as though she were flying not with the dragons, but what? Above them? Then movement on the ground caught her attention, and she narrowed her focus. Did the people below see the dragons?

Wait.

Those weren't all people walking among the buildings. Those were...

"Wolves," she whispered. The shifters from the woods. She was too high to recognize any, but she was certain of it in the same way that she'd known she'd lose her mother the night she died. The second her mother's voice had sounded in her head, telling her the time had come, she'd known. She knew now, too.

Angelika. I have to warn them.

Thank the gods the lead wolf, Bleidd, had told her where to find them if she changed her mind.

Kasia snapped her eyes open and shut off the fire like flipping a switch. "I'm coming out, Maul. Go into the other room to wait for me." Ignoring Maul's worried whines, she yanked on her dress from last night. No way would she fit into Brand's shoes, and his clothes would swamp her. At least her boots were semi-practical.

Dressed, she hurried toward the door, only to pull up short when Maul jumped in front of her, blocking the exit with his bulk. He gave a low growl and shook his head.

"We have to go, Maul."

Another shake of his head, then an image of Brand popped into her head, Maul's memory of his leaving. Brand's face was drawn, almost gaunt with worry. "*I have to go to Ladon. Keep her safe, Maul,*" he said.

So now her hellhound was listening to Brand? Fantastic. "I understand Brand is trusting you, but I have to do this."

Even alone in this cave, she refused to speak her sisters' names aloud.

Something in her voice must've caught his attention, because Maul eased from his crouch and cocked his head.

"Dragons are about to come down on top of a group of wolf shifters. I have to warn them." *Warn Angelika.*

Maul's fur rose on his back, releasing the scents of smoke and death heavily into the air, but still he shook his head, projecting an image of Brand.

Kasia shook her head. "We can't tell any of the dragons. They despise wolves." Not to mention being in the dark about Angelika. She wouldn't risk exposing her sister. "Helping them is up to me."

He regarded her for a long moment, then pulled back his lips to expose his teeth as he gave a low rumble. Kasia wasn't bothered, she knew his show of aggression was his way of saying, "Let's fight."

Her shoulders dropped, relieved she wouldn't have to try to get past him. "We have to get to France, the Pyrenees near Beget. Fast."

Maul turned his back to her, their childhood signal for her to climb on. Kasia allowed her tight lungs to expand a little more freely. At least she had a hellhound on her side.

She scrambled up onto his back, sitting on the giant dog like a horse, holding on to the leather hump at his shoulders. "We can take turns teleporting."

B rand lay on the cot in his cell, the only furniture provided, arm flung over his eyes. To his guards, he probably appeared as though he were sleeping. In actual fact, he was plotting.

He needed to get Kasia away from this place. Ladon would never forgive her for mating another dragon. He probably wouldn't try to mate her himself, even after dispatching Brand, because of the whole burned to ashes thing if she didn't choose him, but he'd hold her here anyway. Even against her will. That was no kind of life, especially not for Kasia.

Ladon had already set off to bring her back. Brand could do nothing about that now. But could he get them both out of here once Ladon returned?

A ruckus—the pounding of running feet and the low rumble of raised voices—filtered down the long, drafty hallway that led into the cells.

Brand stopped bothering with his pretense of sleep and levered up. Just in time for Ladon to burst into the foyer-like room where Ivar and Rainier sat, watching over their prisoner.

"Where the fuck is she?" Ladon demanded.

Brand jumped to his feet, fear surging. "What do you mean?"

"Don't pretend you don't know," Ladon scoffed.

Panic spiked, riding in on a crash of adrenaline and fear for his mate. Brand grasped the bars of his cell. "She has to be there. I left her there with Maul."

"The place was empty."

"Let me out." A command, not a request.

"So you can scurry off to meet your lover and fly off into the sunset? You're a traitor and awaiting execution."

Brand shook the bars, not that they budged, desperation fueling the futile attempt. "You have to let me out. She could be in danger."

"No," Ladon spat. He stalked away.

Impotent fury and the need to find and protect his mate tipped Brand over the edge of a rational-thinking man to release the caged beast inside him. With no thought of doing so, Brand started to shift. These prisons had been built to hold dragons, including magical wards and steel strong enough to hold under an attempted shift. He'd probably kill himself trying, but his mate was in danger. Rational thinking was beyond him now.

As his body expanded, he pushed against the walls and bars of his prison until the dragonsteel dug into his skin. Still, he didn't stop the shift. Couldn't. The dragon inside him was in control now. The bars became knives slicing through the rough hide of his scales along his left hind leg. Brand howled his pain but didn't stop. Next his leg would snap; he could feel the bone bending under the constriction of the space.

"Stop!" Ladon's shout pierced Brand's fevered mind. "I will release you."

Brand's head was jammed into the corner of the room, so he could no longer see Ladon or his men, but the telltale *beep*, *beep*, *beep* of a combination being keyed into the lock panel, followed by the snick of the lock releasing, reached his ears.

Even in his dragon form, as feral as he could turn, he had enough sense to obey. Brand stopped and reversed the shift until he stood before the open door. The bigger concern was the three gashes in his thigh. His wrist, which he hadn't noticed in the crush, ached, but he could deal with that. He suspected the steel bars had reached the bone on his leg, but he didn't have time to stop and see Fallon for faster healing.

Ladon stared at him, his expression a cocktail of fury and incredulousness. "Dammit, Brand. I should've just let you kill yourself. Over a damn woman."

"That damn woman is my *mate*," Brand growled, his dragon still ready to break loose and plow through anyone who intended to get in his way. "You never deserved her."

Every warrior in the room growled, but not the king. Ladon's brows drew down in a frown, patently confused. "Do you love her?" His tone implied that possibility would be sheer insanity.

Brand almost felt sorry for the guy. Hell, he'd been the guy, but he didn't have the fucking time to answer this shit. "My mate is in trouble."

"There's no trail to follow. She's in the wind."

"Get my phone," Brand snapped.

They'd taken it from him when they locked him in here. Ivar snatched it from a drawer in the wall and tossed it over.

No signal. Dammit.

He needed to get out of these dungeons. Now. Urgency drove him to ignore the blood trailing behind him in a splatter of red on the stone floor.

"You should put a tourniquet on that before you bleed out," Ladon observed conversationally as he followed behind Brand.

"Fuck off."

A snort sounded behind him. "I knew you were holding back with me all this time."

Brand ignored the man. Watching his phone for the signal bars. As soon as he had four, he stopped. Pulling up short, he tapped the screen to get to the app managing his home security system. After inputting his fingerprint and password, he checked the feed from his cameras backing it up until he found footage of Kasia still in his home.

What the hell was she doing on the floor of the shower? Was she okay? Had someone taken her? Hurt her?

"Why is she crying?" Ladon asked over his shoulder.

Gutted didn't begin to describe the pain slashing through him. She was crying? He tapped the screen to bring up the audio. Sure enough, his mate was crying her eyes out. Bile burned up his throat. He'd broken his mate.

Brand clenched his teeth and forced himself to move forward in the feed. He needed to find her before he could fix whatever was broken. As he watched in fast forward, she got out of the shower, then seemed to stare at herself in the mirror for a long moment before lighting on fire. A vision without him there to help her control it?

"Was my place burned all to hell?" Brand asked.

"No."

As they watched the black-and-white image, she closed her eyes, and the fire remained under control.

She whispered a word, stood still for a long while, then seemed to freak out over something, running back into the bedroom to dress.

"What'd she say?" Ladon muttered.

"Wolves," Brand muttered through grimly set lips. "I knew that fucking wolf shifter said more to her than she let on."

He could practically feel Ladon's speculative gaze burning a hole into the back of his head. "You think she's running from you?"

Asshole. "Given the crying? I'd say that's a fair bet."

As soon as she'd dressed, she ran for the tunnel, trying to leave, only to be stopped by Maul. She and the hound engaged in an argument, but what caught Brand's attention was when she said, "Dragons are about to come down on top of a group of wolf shifters. I have to warn them."

She's not running from me. A small trickle of relief dropped into the pit that had taken up residence in his stomach. *Dammit, she's running to where dragons are headed.*

"That girl has a bleeding heart," Ladon snarled.

"Or a death wish," Brand tacked on.

"Wait, back it up. I think she just said where she's headed."

Brand fiddled with the controls on the screen.

As soon as she repeated the location, Brand started moving. "I know that town."

Then her other words sank in. Uther. He pulled up and turned to Ladon, who took a step back with a scowl. "What?"

Brand ignored the scowl. "We have a narrow opportunity here. One that can fix the problem for both of us."

"How?" One word, growled low. Ladon's dragon was close to the surface. Again. The guy had serious control issues. Not that Brand could say anything about dragon control.

Brand had only a few more minutes, maybe even seconds, to convince him. "I kill Uther."

Ladon's eyes narrowed to blue glowing slits. "And, other than making my day a little happier, that helps both of us how?"

Brand raised an eyebrow and waited. He'd already

told Ladon his name once. He wasn't going to do it again.

Thick black eyebrows raised as realization dawned. "You were serious?"

As a drug lord with a habit.

"Dagrun," Ladon finally said, doubt lacing every syllable. "As in the previous ruling family of the Gold Clan?"

Brand didn't back down, standing on the truth. "I told you I had more reason to hate Uther than anyone."

"You've been dead for centuries."

"A little over five centuries," Brand pointed out with a grim smile. The same amount of time since he'd come here begging the previous king, Thanatos, to take him in.

Ladon leaned back and gave a low whistle. "You want the gold throne?"

"I was born for that throne." He might have been born to it, but after Uther he hadn't wanted it. Not until Kasia.

"You didn't answer my question."

Brand stared him down.

Ladon's lips flattened, forbidding reality staring back from those eyes along with a wealth of weariness after only a few years of leading himself.

"You're doing this for Kasia?" Ladon asked.

"It's complicated." Because Kasia wasn't the only reason to try to take back the throne, but she was the only reason that mattered.

"Good." Ladon let that one word hang, and Brand got the message.

Heavy the crown and all that bullshit. Yeah. He

knew. Better than the young king before him, even.

"What're you thinking?" Ladon asked.

"I kill Uther. We form an alliance. With your help, I take back the gold throne. With my help and my phoenix, you keep yours. At the very least, killing that bastard should get you back inside Ben Nevis. They won't hold it without a king and may even follow me if I show up with his head and my brand marking their hands."

Harsh words. Brand waited for Ladon to try to ram them down his throat. Instead, Ladon smoothed a palm over his jaw, the rasp of skin against the stubble of his beard loud in the heavy silence surrounding them. Ladon's men didn't move by even a twitch of a muscle. "*You* kill Uther."

"He killed everyone I ever loved and took away my home, my clan, turning dragon shifters against me." Brand's voice dropped as his dragon pushed to be out, riding the wave of helpless fury that Brand had buried long, long ago. "And the new king must kill the old, or it'll never work. You know that."

A king became king either by killing, or by the old king deliberately stepping down and choosing his successor.

"What about High King?" Ladon asked.

Brand grunted. "No one gets that title until the clans live in peace, right? Let's take this one step at a time." Because he sure as hell didn't want that dubious honor.

Ladon tipped his head back as he considered the ramifications. Suddenly, he relaxed, blowing out a long breath. "You know the first time I met you I thought you were an arrogant asshole."

"Gee, thanks."

"One who could get shit done, even when you were ten."

Brand tipped his head. "And I've proved that." So if he said he'd kill Uther, he'd do it. Or die trying.

"You have." Ladon huffed a laugh. "I also thought that if anyone would take my crown, it would be you."

Those words, from a man who'd had his loyalty even when Brand didn't realize it himself, were like a fist rammed into his gut. "Then why make me a leader in your guard?"

Ladon's lips tipped up. "Ever hear the phrase, keep your friends close…"

"…and your enemies closer," Brand finished for him. "Cliché, but apt." He shook his head. No wonder Ladon's men had continued to test him. "I was never your enemy. I don't intend to start now."

"No." Ladon stepped closer. Brand watched him warily but did not prepare to defend himself, keeping his stance loose. He'd take whatever decision the king made.

"I accept." With a harsh laugh, one full of cynicism, he clapped Brand on the shoulder. "You're all sorts of fucked up. Over a woman no less."

Well, holy shit in a handbasket. He hadn't expected that to actually work. "I'd like her to stick around. Mind if we go save her now?"

A dark light lit Ladon's eyes. Brand had seen that look before. Bloodlust.

The other dragon gestured down the hall. "By all means."

Brand limped off up the tunnel leading to the exit,

Ladon striding beside him, his warriors behind them. He'd just have to heal on his way.

"Don't forget," Ladon tossed over. "Uther has a son."

"Brock?" All that came with those words was purpose. "I'll kill him, too, if he gets in my way."

XVI

Kasia stood on the gray granite peak of a mountain five miles from where her vision told her she'd find the wolves. Just a small peak, but enough to give her a good vantage point to teleport.

She glanced at the hellhound at her feet. Granted, even lying down, his back still came up waist high. The sound of his panting joined the rustle of the wind through a copse of aspen trees not too far below. Teleporting this far, this fast, had taken it out of him, and he had to rest longer between each leap.

"You have to stay here, Maul."

He lifted his head from his paws and made a small chuffing sound, red eyes glowing. Then he lumbered to his feet, exhaustion evident in every move.

Kasia leaned into him, rubbing his shoulder, her palm tingling from the bristled texture of his fur. "I can't take you in there with me. The wolves won't like it, and I need to go in without them feeling threatened."

Maul shook his massive head, his jowls flapping.

"No choice, buddy, but I'll come get you when I'm done." She'd figure out what her next step was from there.

Instead of responding, Maul tensed under her hand, his muscles bunching. He lifted his head to the air, sniffing.

"What is it? The wolves?" She thought they'd

stayed out of the zone where the wolves might smell them or sense their presence.

Maul cocked his head. Why wasn't he growling?

"Not wolves." Brand's voice sounded softly from below her, rather than above, where Maul had been looking.

Kasia sucked in a sharp breath and whirled to find him leaning casually against a pine tree a little way down the slope of the mountain from her, arms crossed, feet linked at the ankles, and an expression she couldn't identify.

Too many thoughts smacked her in the solar plexus at once. Mostly the question of what to do about his presence. She couldn't go to Angelika with him on her tail. Underlying the practical, an ache that formed in the center of her chest—as the tug on her heart that always happened when she got anywhere near his lying, arrogant ass—hadn't gone away like she'd hoped it might.

Kasia ignored the tug and aimed a glare at him that should've skinned him alive. "What are you doing here?"

His expression shifted, but she didn't catch the emotion flashing in those golden eyes. Brand levered off the tree. "I'm protecting my mate."

"You *used* me," Kasia spat. "Another man can't have me, but I refuse to be your mate."

Brand froze, jaw clenched. But he didn't seem surprised.

Another piece of her heart shattered. She was right. "Feel free to go crawl back into whatever hole you came from."

Brand held up his hands in a conciliatory gesture.

She almost expected him to treat her like a spooked horse and say, "Easy." Instead, he took two steps closer. "I can't leave you. You're my ma—"

"Stop calling me that." Kasia couldn't go anywhere. A wrong step could have her tumbling down the rocky face of the mountain that dropped sharply away behind her. She stoked the fire inside her that would allow her to teleport away.

"No." He spoke the word softly, and her insides quivered at the refusal to leave her. Where was the bullying, brutish, easily irritated man she'd been dealing with all this time? She was prepared to deal with that guy. Not this calm, sort of knowing one.

He took another few steps forward.

Kasia tipped her chin up and snapped her fingers, letting him see the flames dancing from her fingertips.

He shook his head, gaze never leaving hers. "I'll only follow."

Kasia's jaw ached from clenching her teeth together. "I won't be used."

She'd seen his story in those visions. She knew the motivation driving his actions, and she was merely a pawn in that bid. Hadn't Hershel warned her of just that?

Brand frowned, and she told herself the confusion darkening the gold to amber in his eyes was all a show. "You think I used you last night?"

Kasia gathered her anger and hurt and heartbreak around her like a cloak. "I had a vision. I saw what Uther did to your family."

That stopped him. Brand pulled his shoulders back. "And?"

Are you kidding me? "All I am to you is a tool to get you on your throne. The ultimate revenge, right? To become High King? You can stop the Neanderthal 'you're my mate' bullshit."

Now Brand scowled. "It's not bullshit. It's fate."

"Fuck fate." She flung the words at him with all the force of a cannon.

Brand went dead still and dropped his head, hands on his hips, staring at the ground. If she didn't know better, she'd swear pain had lanced across that usually stony face of his and defeat weighed on his shoulders. She took a breath and hardened her heart.

Lies and schemes. She couldn't trust him…or her damn heart.

After a long moment, Brand lifted his gaze. "It's not bullshit."

"I don't have time for this."

"Dammit, Kasia. I mean it. I love—"

He stopped mid-sentence as she slammed up a hand.

"Don't. You. Fucking. Dare," she choked. She gave an inward wince that her voice refused to come out stronger.

Beside her Maul shifted and gave a small whine, bumping her shoulder with his snout. Kasia put a hand on his neck, curling her fingers into the fur, trying and failing to find comfort.

Brand stared at her long and hard, jaw working. Then he rolled his shoulders and gave a jerky nod. "You're not ready. I get that."

"I'll never be ready to believe anything you say again."

Dead calm wiped every other emotion from his eyes. "I understand."

He was going to give in? Let her go? The five feet separating them might as well have been the Grand Canyon.

"But I'm not letting you go into that wolf shifter camp alone."

Shock followed that moment of weakness that had nearly driven her to ask if he was giving up so easily. "How did you know?"

"Video feed from my place."

"Ah." How did she save Angelika now?

"Let me help you."

He couldn't have shocked her more if he'd slapped her. "Help me? With wolves? Why would you do that?" She expected him to make sure she wasn't damaged or try to make her come with him, yes. But help her?

His lips quirked in that familiar cockeyed smile, though a sadness now tinged it. "You won't let me say why."

Don't let yourself get sucked into the charm.

Brand and charm in the same thought. She was losing it. "The wolves won't want you there," she pointed out.

"Too damn bad."

Shit. He wasn't going to back down on this. Of that, she had no doubt.

"At least let me go ahead and smooth the way," she said.

And get Angelika out of sight, not that they looked anything alike. But her sister didn't smell like a wolf shifter, and Brand's sense of scent would pick that up in a nanosecond.

"I'll give you ten minutes. Then I'm coming in."

"You and none of the others, right?" She hadn't missed how Maul kept glancing to the sky. Besides, she could feel them now, the dragons, sense their presence in some weird way. "Who's up there, anyway?"

"Ladon, Duncan, Reid, Wyot, Fallon, and a few others. Asher stayed behind to watch over the clan."

Ladon. Figured. The two had certainly put on a show, fooling everyone around them. "I'm surprised he didn't kill you, taking away his chance to be High King and all. What'd you do? Flip a coin to decide who got me, and you won? Promise him all the Gold Clan's wealth?"

"I claimed you, and you chose me."

"Forget it." She held up a hand, already regretting going down that conversational path. "Ten minutes, then only you. Right?"

"To start with, yes, just me."

That was the best offer she was going to get, and she knew it. "Fine."

"Fine."

She glared for a moment longer.

Brand lifted one eyebrow. "You'd better get going…mate."

If she threw a rock at his head, would he get the message? Rather than give in to that childish urge, she turned her back to him, facing the direction of the wolf shifter camp. Closing her eyes, Kasia allowed the fire from her fingertips to spread over her body. She pictured the town she'd seen in her vision, in particular, the grassy field over which several stone and wood buildings were dotted. Then she let go. A beat of silence and darkness as she pulled her body through the blank landscape that existed between the planes of the physical and spiritual realms.

She opened her eyes to find herself hovering over the grass. Gently she lowered, turning off the fire with a thought, the flames slithering back into her skin as she dropped gently to the ground... to face a crowd of wolf shifters in varying forms— both human and animal, all with their teeth bared, hackles raised, ready to defend their people against this threat. Not exactly her idea of a fun time. *Please let someone keep them from ripping me to shreds.*

"Peace. Everyone calm down."

She would recognize that gravelly voice anywhere, even though she'd heard it in her head only that one time.

Bleidd. The leader. Alpha of this pack. In human form, the man appeared older, with dark hair graying at the temples and a gray beard. He moved like his animal, all predatorial grace.

Excellent. She wouldn't have to waste time explaining who she was to some overzealous guard. The crowds parted to let Bleidd through, and she moved forward to greet him. Unsure of the protocols, she held out a hand to shake. "I'm sorry for appearing so suddenly."

He encompassed her small hand with his own— his skin warm and rough. "I assume you have a good reason."

Straight to business. She liked him more already. "We need to get Angelika out of here. Now."

He frowned. "Why?"

"Dragons from the Gold Clan are on their way. I saw them in a vision."

"Do you want to see her?"

More than anything in the world, but Kasia forced herself to shake her head. "There's no time. My…bodyguard"—because to hell with calling Brand her mate—"is right behind me, along with members of the Blue Clan. They've come to help."

Bleidd didn't even blink. He turned and looked to a stocky man, all muscle and grit, with red hair that sported a white streak by his temple. The rust-colored wolf from the woods?

"Tell Jedd," Bleidd ordered.

The red-haired man pivoted and stalked through the crowd, who skittered out of his way.

Bleidd turned back to her. "Anything else?"

"Brand is a gold dragon, but he's with me, and he will have a hellhound with him."

He gave his head a shake and huffed a laugh. "A dragon and a hellhound are coming to help a pack of wolf shifters? There's got to be a punchline in there somewhere, but damned if I can see it."

She didn't have time for humor. "Don't kill the dog."

Bleidd raised his eyebrows but didn't comment further. They waited in silence, Kasia looking to the sky. She wouldn't call Brand, needing to give Angelika every second to get clear. As they stood and waited, more men arrived, gathering to stand behind their leader. She thought she recognized the one with brown hair, his nose slightly askew.

The red-haired man strode back into view and

murmured in Bleidd's ear. Bleidd looked to her.

"She's safe?" Kasia asked.

Bleidd nodded.

"Good. Don't tell me how or where." She couldn't know, not with dragons surrounding her.

Bleidd's eyes softened, almost like he understood what she was getting at. Kasia's job was to protect her sisters. She'd been found, and that had set her life on a path that could no longer intersect with theirs. If they were safe, then she'd done her duty. That's what love did. Love was about sacrifice.

Not like Brand. Not taking. But giving.

"You look nothing alike, if you don't mind my saying."

Kasia smiled and tried to keep it from being a watery one. "I know."

"Hope you're ready." Brand's voice interrupted the moment and allowed her to suck those unshed tears back in.

"He's here," she said to Bleidd.

"Clear the green." He put out his arms and backed up. All the shifters around them did the same.

Only the sudden violent bending of the trees warned them of the dragon coming in low and fast, and then Brand appeared. Several people around her dropped to the ground, instinct of avoiding a large predator kicking in. Brand swooped overhead, then pulled up sharply, seemed to float for a moment, golden wings stretched wide and shimmering in the late afternoon sunlight, before he landed nearly silently. Immediately, he started to shift, his body compacting back down to his human form.

"You didn't mention your bodyguard is the same

bastard who snapped my leg in half," the red-haired man snarled.

"Rafe," Bleidd spoke just the one word, a low warning in the name.

Kasia tossed Rafe an unimpressed glance. "Given he was the one guarding me when you attacked him, I'd say logic should've helped you figure that out."

Before Rafe could respond, Maul appeared at Brand's side.

Rafe gaped. "Fuck me. That really is a hellhound!"

Kasia grinned. She didn't think she'd ever get tired of how her pet's appearance made these big, bad shifters cower in fear, or at least exclaim in shock.

"He's the observant one in your pack?" she asked Bleidd, nodding to Rafe. The red-haired shifter glared while his leader tucked a secret grin behind a bland expression.

Maul sniffed the air. Thankfully, he didn't snarl at the wolves. Rather, he turned his massive head and searched for her, then stalked over, watching the shifters around her with wary distrust. Kasia smiled and patted his side as he stood beside her.

Brand approached, almost as wary as the hellhound, face like the granite of the mountains that surrounded them like silent sentinels. Only now she noticed a slight limp. He was favoring his left leg. Had he been injured? When?

She kept her questions to herself as he stopped beside her, invading her space in a way he knew she wouldn't protest with all the shifters watching. However, he didn't look at her, keeping his gaze trained on Bleidd. Then he gave a deep nod, a show of respect to the wolf shifter leader. "We haven't been formally introduced. I'm Brand Astarot. I hope we can put that previous incident behind us."

Beside Bleidd, Rafe snorted. "You want to be friends now?"

Brand didn't even glance his way. "Dragons are coming for you. You could use a few friends."

"You're the only dragon I see around here."

Again, Brand didn't bother to look at Rafe. "Whatever my mate saw in her vision had her rushing to help."

Bleidd glanced at her. "Mate?"

Kasia gritted her teeth. "Only on a technicality."

Rafe sniggered.

Bleidd ignored him. "I thought you were going to mate the King of the Blue Clan."

"I'm still going to offer to align with him." And Brand could choke on that thought for all she cared.

"Ladon and nine of his best warriors are circling above," Brand interrupted. Only the new tense set of his shoulders showed any reaction to her words. "They've come to help. May I tell them they have permission to land?"

Bleidd didn't answer. Instead he turned to her. "You're certain these gold dragons are coming?"

She nodded. "Led by Uther himself."

Brand stiffened beside her. "You shouldn't stay here."

She faced him, hands on her hips. "Stop trying to protect me."

He crossed his arms. "Never. I'm your mate, and I love you."

Kasia wanted to slap that smug expression right off his face. "Stop saying that."

"No."

"Perhaps we should take this somewhere more private," Bleidd interrupted.

"Fine." She and Brand both snapped the word at the wolf while continuing to glare at each other.

"I'll let Ladon know they can land," Brand added.

"I'll have them brought to us when they arrive," Bleidd agreed. "My name is Bleidd Roark, by the way. Follow me."

The leader of the pack strode away, down what appeared to be the main street of sorts. She and Brand followed, then several of Bleidd's people, with Maul bringing up the rear.

"You're adorable when you get angry," Brand tossed at her out of the side of his mouth.

Kasia cracked her neck she swung so hard to glare at Brand. "Quit it."

"I'd love to see what all that aggression looks like in bed."

Wolf shifters and dragon shifters all had phenomenal hearing. Kasia mentally reviewed the list her mother had made them memorize of all of a dragon's most vulnerable places, because she was going to kill him after this was over.

"What happened to your leg?" she asked sweetly.

Brand audibly snapped his mouth closed. He got the point. A dragon was most vulnerable where wounded. "I tangled with dragonsteel when I heard you weren't where I left you," he gritted out. "Turns out that metal is harder than a dragon's scales."

Now was Kasia's turn to snap her mouth shut. What did that mean? She frowned up at him. "Were you caged?"

He shrugged. "Just in Ladon's dungeons."

"Ladon's dun—" Kasia cut herself off and held up a hand. "Forget it. I don't want to know."

Stubborn woman.

"Suit yourself," Brand said, rather than do what he wanted to do, which was pin her body between his and a hard wall somewhere and kiss her into submission, kiss her until she stopped looking at him with those wounded, mistrusting eyes that were slowly gouging a hole in his soul.

Bleidd led them to a two-story building in the center of the long line of old stone buildings topped with thatched roofs that made up the main street of the town. Inside, they made their way up narrow stairs.

"What is this place?" Brand asked.

Bleidd glanced over his shoulder as they moved down a long hallway, their footsteps echoing off the stone floors and walls. "This was a medieval village. But it's inaccessible by anything but mule, and even if roads were built to it, the streets are too narrow for cars or machinery, so the people abandoned it in the early 1920s. We moved in around 1940. Human roads still don't make it here, which means we are sheltered."

"And you kept it looking the same all this time?" Kasia asked.

"Not entirely. The place was falling apart when we moved here, so we had to bolster everything, fix a lot of collapsing structures. We have running water and electricity that we pull off the human grid, but otherwise we live fairly simply."

Bleidd ushered them into a room furnished with two long leather couches and several tables scattered about. Comfier than Ladon's conference room, if that's what this was.

Bleidd sat and waved to the couch opposite. "Unlike dragons, wolves don't have hordes of gold. Besides, anything more than what we can do with our own hands would require human involvement and attract attention we don't want."

Smart. Maybe wolf shifters had more to offer than dragons thought.

Bleidd's lieutenants moved to stand behind the couch, presenting a united front of aggressive male shifters. Get a photographer in here and they could make a calendar—the wolves of summer.

Brand ignored them. He didn't ignore how Kasia chose to sit at the opposite end of the couch. A smart man would give her space, but no one had ever accused him of being smart. Brand moved over a cushion, not touching, but definitely crowding her.

Kasia stared ahead, stone-faced, and crossed her leg away from him, doing her best to make friends with the arm of the couch, which she was now plastered against.

No one spoke as they waited for Ladon and his team to join them.

The door opened, and Ladon stepped in, followed by Reid, Wyot, and Duncan. The king's sweeping glance took in the room, landing last on Brand and Kasia. "I see I've arrived just in time to break the tension."

Bleidd's neutral expression broke, and he tossed his head back and laughed, then he stood, offering a hand. "I am Bleidd Roark, the leader of this pack."

Ladon shook the wolf shifter's hand. "Ladon Ormarr. King of the Blue Dragon Clan."

Intros done, Ladon joined Brand and Kasia on the couch, and his men stood behind, mirroring Bleidd's men's postures. Nothing like interspecies tensions to kick off an unlikely partnership.

Bleidd turned to Kasia. "You said a vision showed us under attack?"

She nodded. "I saw a group of about thirty gold dragons circling overhead. Below, several people are out in the street. They seemed oblivious."

"Any clue as to timing?"

"Beyond a gut feeling that this is coming soon…" She glanced around, then shook her head.

"You recognized Uther, though?" Brand prompted. She'd said Uther.

"The dragon who attacked you at Hersh—" She cut off mid-name, and he knew she'd caught the warning twitch he'd given. "At that bar when we were on our way to Scotland," she continued.

Right. Hard to mistake that beast for anyone else.

"Anything else?" Ladon prompted. "Time of day? Season?"

"The beech leaves were golden, like they are now. No snow on the ground yet. The sun is about to lower over the western horizon. And…"

Kasia frowned, her eyes going sort of glassy, as though she were seeing, but not seeing. Without warning, a flame leaped from her fingertips, jumping to Brand's jeans. The wolves all tensed to scramble, but Brand simply put it out. At the same time, he watched her closely for any sign of pain or a need for his help. No ache entered his own body.

Kasia, however, didn't budge, still caught in whatever review of the scene was happening in her mind's eye. Finally, she blinked, then gasped and shook her hands, her finger smoking as she willed the flames away. She indicated with a jerk of her chin a tall, lanky shifter with rich sable skin, black hair, and blacker eyes. "You're standing close to that building with the green roof."

Bleidd twisted to see who she indicated. "Hunter?"

"Yes. And his digital watch reads tomorrow's date and 3:07 p.m. as the time."

Brand held still, doing his best not to react. When had she learned how to go into a vision at all, let alone apparently zoom in and pick out details?

"Holy shit," Rafe exclaimed. "That's a fantastic advanced warning system you've got."

Brand didn't miss the shuffle of shifting stances of the wolf shifters. All except their leader, who sat in calm thought, his gaze firmly on Kasia.

Brand knew why. Kasia was gnawing at her lower lip like it was a meal. "Hey," he murmured, pulling her attention his way. Yup, that was serious doubt in those frosty blue eyes. "What's wrong?"

Kasia blinked, and he thought a flash of something akin to trust warmed the deep oceans of those eyes for a heartbeat before she shut him out, turning to Bleidd. "You should know I've never had a vision like this. It's possible my actions, bringing all these dragons here, may have changed the outcome, the timeline." She gave a helpless shrug. "Anything. I honestly don't know."

Bleidd nodded slowly. "Then perhaps it's time you leave. You've warned us. We can take it from here."

Brand exchanged a glance with Ladon, then cleared his throat. "All due respect, you could use our help."

No way was he missing this opportunity. If Kasia's vision was correct, they could match Uther and his forces dragon for dragon. Add in the wolf shifters and Maul, and this might be his best shot at Uther without risking the lives of every one of Ladon's warriors.

"Dragons are going to help wolves?" The guy called Hunter narrowed his eyes. "Bullshit."

Ladon and Brand both stood, and a snarl arose from the group of wolves gathered, only to be answered with rumbles from the dragons at his back.

Bleidd raised a hand, and they all silenced.

Brand nodded at the leader. "The dragons who treated you as beneath them are the old guard. The kings we are trying to remove from power. We're—"

"What? Different?" The youngest of the men stepped forward. With his light brown hair and crooked nose, Brand had a decent guess as to who this was.

"You broke my nose and his leg." Crooked nose waved an arm at Rafe.

Definitely one of the wolves from his earlier altercation with them. "To be fair, you guys attacked me."

The young wolf bared his teeth in a half grin, half snarl. "We were rescuing Kasia."

Brand cocked his head. "That's funny. So was I."

"By bringing her into the heart of a dragon clan so you can use her as a phoenix?" Crooked nose had a thing about dragons. What had caused that?

"Enough, Cairn." Bleidd rose to his feet as the guy named Cairn stepped back, though he continued to glare.

Bleidd glanced between Brand and Ladon. "You fight with us, and I'm in charge. We know these mountains better than you do."

Ladon nodded. "Agreed. One request?"

Bleidd raised his eyebrows in question.

"We kill the king. Uther is ours."

Uther is mine, Brand silently swore. The final step toward the revenge he'd been slowly, meticulously plotting for over five hundred years. He just had to kill him to claim the throne.

He caught Kasia's small gasp and glanced down to find her glaring up at him. What had he done now? "Problem?" he asked.

She clamped her lips shut and rose from the couch with a controlled grace that told him more about her anger than punching him in the face would have.

Kasia turned to Ladon. "I had another vision you need to know about."

She paused, and Ladon nodded for her to continue.

"Chante let the gold dragons into the mountain. My previous vision wasn't proof positive, but I'm sure now."

Never liked that fucker. Brand glanced at Ladon, whose lips were white.

"You're certain?" the Blue King asked.

She nodded.

"I'll take care of it."

Before more could be said, Kasia turned to Bleidd. "Do you have somewhere I could sleep? Maul and I took turns teleporting, but I need to rest if I'm going to be ready for tomorrow."

Bleidd flicked Brand a glance but nodded. "Of course. Cairn?"

Pretty boy with the crooked nose stepped forward, and Kasia went to step around Brand to follow, but Brand moved into her path. "After you rest a few hours, you're going back to Ladon's camp."

She tipped her chin. "No. I'm staying here. I can help."

Again, she moved to pass, but Brand caught her by the arm as she stepped away. "You're not going anywhere near that fight."

She jerked out of his gasp. "The hell you say."

"I forbid it."

She snorted. "Who put you in charge?"

"I'm your mate."

"That doesn't mean a damn thing, lizard boy."

Ladon and the other dragons stiffened, but the wolf shifters lost it, their laughter rolling over Brand's tattered patience. "Kasia…" he warned through gritted teeth.

Not the least intimidated, she rolled her eyes and turned to Bleidd. "Between my visions, which may or may not be of use, and my ability to teleport, I can help. Plus I have Maul to protect me, so none of your men or Ladon's need to babysit."

To give Bleidd some credit, he did consider Brand's thunderous expression. "The phoenix stays."

XVII

Kasia flipped over in the twin-sized bed they'd found for her and stared out the window at the moonshot landscape. The fullness of the glowing orb in the sky cast the small town, the surrounding pine trees, and the mountain peaks in varying shades of dark blue, gray, and black.

She'd left the window open, enjoying how the snap in the fall air cooled her fire-warmed skin. Out of sight, hidden beyond the line of trees, she could hear the content gurgle of the river. What had those watchful mountains witnessed over the passage of time? Human wars, dragon wars, shifter wars. What about love? Had the towering peaks seen that, too? As an immortal, what would she see?

Her chest rose and fell with yet another deep sigh. Sleep had eluded her tonight. Probably didn't help that she'd taken a long, needed nap in the middle of the day.

When she'd woken earlier, she'd sought out Bleidd—convincing herself that Brand being with him made no difference to who she was looking for. She discovered Brand, Ladon, and Bleidd still in that office with the couches, only they'd pulled out a map of the town and surrounding areas. In the hours she'd been asleep, they had devised a plan.

"They will already have smelled our presence," Ladon said. "So I am going to take my team and make a show of us flying back to Scotland."

"How does that change the whole scent thing?"

she asked.

"The strong scent leading away from here will make them believe we've left," Ladon said. "When we're far enough out, we'll double back, behind Uther's position. No dragons can camouflage like blue. He won't see us coming."

"Meanwhile, I have already evacuated those of our people who can't fight to a secret location where they'll be safe," Bleidd said.

Angelika?

Bleidd must have recognized the question in her gaze, because he gave an almost imperceptible nod.

Kasia let out a silent breath. Thank the gods for that at least. Her sister would stay protected and secret.

A small movement snagged her attention, and she glanced at where Brand stood in the corner of the room, arms crossed, gaze on her intent and unreadable.

Was he still pissed about Bleidd letting her stay and fight? Too damn bad. Kasia raised her chin.

"Who's Angelika?" The thought came across as clear as day. Only no part of him was dragon.

Panic and shock widened her eyes. He'd heard her? *What have I done?*

Brand frowned.

Gods. Had he heard that, too? Kasia could feel the blood drain from her face. She must've looked awful, because Brand straightened off the wall he was propping up and made as if he was going to come to her side.

She shook her head, and he stopped. Thankfully. With sheer force of will, she turned her gaze back to Bleidd. The wolf shifter, seemingly oblivious to her and Brand's silent interchange, continued. "We plan to set up some of my wolves in the town, positioning them where you saw them in the vision, but making sure they are in locations easily defensible once it starts."

Kasia managed to nod. "I can tell you who I saw and where they were standing. Even what they were doing."

"Excellent."

"They'll start with a fire run," Ladon explained. "Go for the buildings and the trees close by, as well as any people or wolves they can see on the ground. Two or three of Uther's people will make a sweeping pass over the area, one right after the other."

The idea obviously being to burn most of the wolves alive and smoke out the rest.

"Only we won't be there," Bleidd said.

He pointed to five locations on the map, forming a circle around the town. "We'll be here, waiting."

"For what?" she asked.

"Us," Ladon said. "We will attack from the sky, driving them to the ground. Then the wolves come in."

"Where will I be?" she asked next.

"In this building." Bleidd pointed to the map. "You and Maul can handle the fire. Wait for Ladon's attack to start before you show yourself, then your job is to get the injured out of the fight and the outnumbered out of danger."

"Got it."

"We need Maul to contain any fire being created, to allow the wolves to come back in and join the fighting," Ladon said. "Can he do that?"

The hellhound waited for her out in the street, unable to fit in the small building, but she knew his abilities. "Yes."

"The objective is the king," Ladon said. "If Brand takes out Uther, then the other gold dragons will be more likely to stop fighting."

Right. Uther. The main reason Brand had mated her in the first damn place. His revenge would be easier to take, to finally fulfill that lifelong goal, with a phoenix tied to him by that bond. She didn't need the reminder that she was just a stepping-stone. "Anything else?"

Brand narrowed his eyes. "Keep Maul at your side at all times."

No doubt in her mind that was an order, but one she was willing to concede. "Yeah."

"I mean it, Kasia. No sending him off to help one of us or one of the wolves. He's your protection."

She crossed her arms, mimicking his own posture. "I can protect myself. Besides, they're not going to hurt me. I'm too valuable."

His jaw set, and she knew whatever was coming out of his mouth next, she wouldn't like. "Maul stays with you…or I do."

She was right, she didn't like that.

"And miss out on your revenge?" she scoffed. "Yeah, right."

"Revenge?" Bleidd narrowed his eyes, glancing between them.

Kasia raised an eyebrow at Brand. He could bloody well explain it. His expression remained blank, but she could still tell by the twitching muscle in his jaw that she'd struck a nerve. She got it. He didn't talk about his life. Hell, his life and her life were two sides of the same coin—lost a family and their place in the world thanks to a conniving, backstabbing dragon who wanted the throne, not to mention being abandoned by every other dragon who'd turned their backs, unwilling to stand up to bullies.

That didn't make how he'd mated her to further his goals any easier a pill to choke down. She'd dedicated her life to protecting—her sisters, her secrets, even those dragon shifters caught up in a power struggle that boiled down to a few self-centered assholes. Brand included.

"I'm a bit lost here, guys," Bleidd said.

She glanced his way. "Brand is the rightful heir to the Gold Clan's throne. Uther killed his family and sent him into a secret exile of sorts. Now he intends to kill Uther and take it all back. And I'm the icing on the cake, because mating me makes him the High King." She crossed her arms and swung to face her mate. "Isn't that right?"

Brand leaned his knuckles on the table, a dark energy coming off him that just fueled her own anger. "I guess you have it all figured out."

She gave him her best bored look. "Did I get anything wrong?"

"Yeah." He shoved off the table and stalked toward her. "You."

Kasia set her feet and held her ground. "Oh?"

"I didn't mate you to become High King. I don't want that position." He stopped just shy of touching her.

If she breathed in hard, the tips of her breasts would brush his chest. Her traitorous nipples pinched, almost as if her body were reaching for his. "I don't believe you."

He barked a laugh that held no amusement. "No shit."

Ladon interrupted their staring match. "Maybe we should give you two some privacy."

Kasia stepped back. "No need. I have nothing else to say to him."

Three hours had passed since she'd walked out and Brand had flown off with Ladon. They couldn't have dragons here, but Uther and his people would expect to smell a phoenix, since they were coming for one, so she stayed. Maul was a different story. He'd teleported to the underworld where he could wait undetected and return at the appropriate hour.

She'd spent a quiet evening with Bleidd and the men who would be in the town when everything happened tomorrow. One of those men stood outside her room now, guarding her.

"I promised to protect Serefina's daughter," Bleidd had said when she protested. "Just because there are two daughters doesn't make that promise any different."

She'd shaken her head but accepted. Even now, if she flipped back over to face the door, she could see the shadow of two resolute boots in the light sneaking in under the rickety wood door.

Dammit, she should be asleep.

She shut her eyes tight, but her mind refused to stop spinning like a windmill in a tornado. Not about what would happen tomorrow. They were ready. Her vision had given them time to prepare. No, her mind wouldn't quit going over every moment with Brand.

Every look, every word, every touch.

How had she gotten him so horribly wrong?

Gods forgive her, she'd chosen him. His mark might not yet grace her neck, but her heart had chosen him or he'd be a heap of ashes right now.

The hand that closed over her mouth was the first clue that anyone was even in the room with her. At the same time, a strong arm banded around her waist, and the heavy weight of a body came down on top of her.

A scream bubbled up her throat, only a cloth was shoved into her mouth, followed by duct tape.

I can't breathe. Her panicked mind wouldn't process anything else.

Roughly she was shoved to her back. Even in the dark, she'd recognize that face above hers from her visions.

Uther. The false king of the Gold Clan.

The shifter straddled her body. She thrashed in the bed, trying to somehow shove him off or wiggle out from under him, but he was bigger and stronger, and everything happened so fast. Even as she struggled, he managed to tie her hands to the bedposts with rough rope using knots he tightened to the point of pain, bringing tears that leaked out of the corners of her eyes.

He's going to kill me.

A quick glance showed shoes no longer at her door. Instead, the light under the door was entirely blocked by something large, and a pool of dark liquid oozed its way across the rough wooden floorboards of her room. Her breath audibly hissed through her nostrils in sharp bursts, along with little whimpers in her throat, as she struggled to force air into her lungs and to think.

He'd killed her bodyguard.

A handsome face stared down at her—rugged with high, prominent cheekbones. His dark blond hair showed the early signs of age. He had to be nearing that point when desperation would become a factor. Find a mate or start to rot.

He smiled. "You're mine. Time to make that indisputable."

Oh gods. He's not going to kill me, he's going to try to mate me. Is he crazy?

He didn't know. She and Brand may have started the process, but no claiming mark branded her skin yet.

For less than a second, she considered letting it get to sex, just so she could take this asshole down, consuming him in her fire, but bile stung her throat at the thought. Fuck that.

She kicked out, and he put a hand to her throat and squeezed hard enough that she started to see stars. The pounding of her heart thundered in her ears as adrenaline and terror mingled in her mouth, adding a metallic taste to the cloth.

If Maul were here… But he wasn't. He was in the underworld, waiting for the timing they'd arranged based on her visions. She didn't even know if he could see her from there or not.

Fire. She could burn the ropes.

As the first rational thought penetrated the haze of terror, she called up the flames inside her, trying to ignite them. She needed them to teleport.

Uther squeezed harder, and her vision went patchy. "Light on fire and I cut off your air long enough to kill you."

She couldn't breathe, not just from his hands but from her fear, couldn't find her fire anyway.

One hand remained at her neck as the other traveled down her body, pushing back the flimsy sheet to expose her body. She'd slept in only a T-shirt she'd borrowed from Angelika's clothes and her underwear, providing no barrier, no protection.

With one hand, he fumbled with his pants. Hysterical laughter burbled up and out of her before she could stop the sounds, mingling with the tears and the terror. This was not how she thought she'd go.

"Psycho bitch," he muttered as he struggled to pull his dick out of his pants.

"Brand!" Her mate's name screamed through her mind, but she knew he'd be too far away to hear her. He was with Ladon, and they wouldn't have circled back yet.

Suddenly, all the fear settled. It didn't leave her, merely retreated to a corner of her mind where it couldn't touch her, as cold resolve settled in her heart.

Brand was her destined mate. She'd made her choice, no matter his path to her. No fucking way was she letting this man take that from either of them.

Through the frozen core of pure rage an inferno slammed outward, outward from her. The resulting explosion ripped her from the bed, jerking one bound arm so hard against the restraints that she cried out at the pain. Not from her hands, like last time, but from every part of her. Everything disintegrated around her as the force flung her up and out.

Kasia flew through the air, along with flaming shrapnel, and slammed into the wall of another building, cracking her head against the stone siding before she dropped to the ground with a thud. She had no fucking clue how that happened and was pretty damn sure she'd dislocated her shoulder. Kasia managed to use her one good arm to yank the tape off her mouth and pull out the cloth, sucking in smoke-laden air.

Her body wanted to quit—to fall into the oblivion of trauma-induced sleep. But while her involuntary pyrotechnic folly had been explosive, it hadn't been hot, not hot enough to affect a dragon, at least. Which meant Uther was still close by.

She forced herself to her feet, despite the nauseated dizziness swamping her senses, and gaped at the scene around her.

Her fire must've gone off like a bomb, because the building where she'd been sleeping was demolished, flattened in an instant, with a massive hole carved in the solid mountain below.

At least it had raised the alarm. Shifters ran out of all the other buildings, most already turned into wolves or making that transition as they ran.

The ruckus of voices all around her suddenly raised a notch, howls of warning passing through the village. Through the red haze of fire, she saw them. Golden dragons descended upon the wolf shifters, wings tucked back as they set up for the fire runs that Ladon had warned them about. They were going for the buildings and the trees. Only the wolves weren't hiding in the woods yet, they were here. And Maul wasn't here to control the fire; neither were Brand and Ladon's men.

A terrible bellow, the blood-curdling screech of a wild animal, raised the fine hairs on her arms, the sound piercing. Kasia put her hands to her ears, only to feel a wetness seeping from them. When she pulled her hands away, crimson slashes of blood stained her palms.

My ears are bleeding?

To her right, a massive creature raised up into the dark, the fire from her explosion casting it in a golden glow. Uther had shifted.

A roar preceded a gale-force wind as Uther, now fully formed into his monstrous self, lifted from the ground, wings cast wide, forcing his body higher with each push against the air, his giant head swinging back and forth as he searched.

For her.

Kasia frantically glanced around, but there was nowhere to hide with the building at her back surrounded by a treeless mountainside and only the burning rubble of her little hovel in front of her. She raised her gaze just in time for Uther to find her, his head snapping as he zeroed in on her location.

He seemed to hover there for a moment, as if debating. Why? But then he angled his body, intent on her and her alone.

Likely, his next move would be to pick her up in those massive talons and take her away.

The hell with that, too.

Fight.

Kasia pushed past the fear and exhaustion and pain beating at her from all sides. She closed her eyes and summoned her power. And this time, she found it, found her strength, letting the soothing heat wash over her. As she pictured the lick of each flame, her body consumed by the conflagration, she held out her arms.

Rather than run, she opened her eyes. Thankfully, her sister's borrowed clothing also appeared to be fireproof, remaining intact. Later, Kasia would have to ask how she'd gotten some. Flames now starkly illuminated the town as she faced the creature bearing down on her. Uther extended his legs, claws reaching, ready to pluck her from the ground. Kasia waited like she had that night—when another monster had tried to take her away while her mother tried to save her life.

At the last second, Kasia teleported, disappearing only to reappear less than a heartbeat later ten feet to her left.

Uther's tail whipped by her with the sound of a freight train as he pulled up.

Kasia smiled grimly even as she allowed a shard of annoyance to pierce her newfound calm. Mental note to practice her skills in the middle of a personal attack if she survived this night.

Uther gained altitude and circled back around, clearly reassessing his options. Meanwhile, Kasia got ready to do it again. And again. And again. But she needed to save the wolves as well, and her reserves of power were already depleted because of what she'd used on that uncontrolled explosion. Rather than waiting for another attack, she took a moment to evaluate the chaos surrounding her, searching for wolves who needed help.

In a blink, she teleported to where Rafe—his red fur and white patch over the eye a dead giveaway—circled another grayish-brown wolf pinned under a jagged piece of lumber. From her explosion?

The second she appeared, he rounded on her, teeth bared. A snarl ripped from his throat.

Kasia held up her hands. "It's me, Rafe."

He held his defensive position for a moment as he stared at her intently. She didn't blame him. Even her voice sounded different, raspy. Finally, he relaxed his position and gave her a nod.

"Can you help?" his voice growled inside her head.

"Let's get you out of here," she said.

Kasia pulled the flames back from her functioning hand, her other dangling limply at her side. She left the rest of her body on fire, but this allowed her to touch, not wanting to seriously burn the wolves, who, unlike dragons, were not immune to flame.

She knelt and touched the wolf under the debris then opened her mouth to tell Rafe to touch her as well.

"Watch out!" Rafe yelled just before he shoved a shoulder into her, forcing her to the ground.

Pain spiked through her as her dislocated shoulder jostled. Kasia looked up just in time to see golden talons outstretched, feet away.

A scream rose, unbidden, then choked off when, from out of the darkness, another golden dragon barreled into Uther from the side.

Brand.

XVIII

In the split second before he'd struck, it seemed as though every emotion under the endless black sky had flown with him. Terror for his mate. Even a little pride as she'd faced down Uther, a dragon most other shifters, even dragons, wouldn't mess with. Relief that he'd gotten there in time. Triumph. The time had finally come to take out the man responsible for his entire fucking life.

Got you, you son of a bitch.

Brand managed to sink his fangs into Uther's shoulder as they tumbled down the slope of the mountain, crashing through trees, the trunks snapping under their weight and momentum like dry twigs in a drought.

All those emotions didn't let up, mixing inside him, swirling with the bottomless hate he held for the creature whipping around in his grasp.

They slammed into the ground, hard, ploughing a deep trough in the earth as they slowed to a stop. Wedging a back leg between their bodies, Uther gave a hard shove, ripping himself out of Brand's teeth and hold.

They both flipped over, gaining their feet to stare down their opponent across the small field separating them.

Uther turned so that the open wound on his shoulder was shielded by the rest of his body. Brand couldn't see the damage he'd done.

I wish I ripped the entire leg off.

But he knew he hadn't. Meanwhile, Brand did the same, keeping his injured leg out of sight, still healing from the dragonsteel bars of Ladon's dungeons. Neither tried to take to the air. Other than mid-shift, a dragon was most vulnerable on takeoff, which took a few precious seconds to get their bulk moving. Another dragon close by on the ground could gut them while they tried. Flying was out.

For now.

Off in the direction of the town, the sounds of dragon battle and the blue glow of fire indicated Ladon and his team had arrived on the scene. Wyot, scouting ahead, had found Uther's trail, indicating the timeline was off, and they'd already turned back early to follow, but as soon as Brand heard Kasia's cry—a sound he'd been too far away to hear with his ears, but had felt with every part of his soul nonetheless—he'd shot ahead.

Thank the gods he'd beat them there. He prayed Kasia had gotten herself out of harm's way, or Maul had. But right now, he couldn't think about that. She'd have to watch her own back while he took care of the monster before him.

They circled each other like sharks testing the water, wings tucked in so they could use all four legs to move. Rather than watch Uther's eyes, Brand studied his body. Eyes could be used to deceive and misdirect, but the body telegraphed physical intentions.

Sure enough, Uther's scales rippled as he gathered himself. He lunged, jaws snapping for Brand's neck, but Brand moved too fast, pivoting out of the way and curving his neck to snap back. Uther jerked out of range before he could land the bite.

A slower, weaker, less seasoned dragon wouldn't have been able to move out of the way that quickly. Damn, the king was fast.

Let's dance, old man.

Brand tuned out every other thing around him—the noise of the battle, the growing fire, even Kasia—as he focused solely on his opponent.

They continued to circle, trading jabs and snaps, lunging and counterlunging and retreating. Brand managed to get in a solid swipe with his talon, landing it across Uther's back, but couldn't dig in to wrestle the beast to the ground as Uther spun out of his grasp, whipping around to catch Brand across the bridge of his nose with one of the spikes on his tail.

The metallic tang of blood registered as it dripped down his face into the corner of his mouth.

Uther opened his mouth in a grin and blasted a jet of fire at him, trying to melt the open wound on Brand's face. Brand managed to cover the gash with an arm, protecting it from dragon fire. He also had to close his eyes, which were the only parts of a dragon susceptible to flame. A direct hit could blind him.

At the same time, Brand tried to move backward. As soon as the stream of heat ceased, he opened his eyes, bunching his muscles to move fast. Sure enough, even as he'd spewed fire, Uther had run straight at Brand.

He had barely a second to brace himself before they collided with a *crack* like thunder resounding around them.

They grappled, grunting and snorting, smoke rising around them as they tried to find purchase, both attempting to slash open their opponent or to topple the other in ways that would leave him vulnerable.

Trees and boulders and dirt flew as they drove with their back legs, pushing and shoving each other across the already torn-up landscape. Uther, bigger and stronger, not to mention more experienced at fighting dragons, had the advantage.

But Brand was no idiot. He'd trained all his life for this moment, as much as he could. Human classes in martial arts had given him moves Uther may never have seen. As a king who eschewed all things human except their possible mates, Uther might have a blind spot to Brand's fighting techniques.

However, those techniques in dragon form, hampered by wings that served a purpose only in flight, might not work, anyway.

Brand's muscles burned, and not with his inner fire, as they maneuvered, and scrambled, and flipped, and grasped, and shoved. This needed to end before exhaustion took over, and—after the skirmish at Ladon's, mating Kasia, and several cross-country flights, not to mention the gashes in his leg from the dragonsteel cage—his body was already shaking with the effort of the battle.

But Brand's craving for this man's blood burned inside him, stoking his fire. He'd waited centuries for this moment, each small step moving him ever closer to when he'd take his revenge.

Uther's death would be the sweetest revenge.

Their wrestling rolled them along the path of earlier destruction, from when Brand had tackled Uther out of the air and into the town. A blue dragon and a gold dragon facing each other down over the smoking remains of what had once been a building had to leap out of the way or be crushed by the forcing of their entwined bodies.

That distraction was the opportunity Uther needed. Brand hadn't even looked away, but his attention had, for just a millisecond, wandered. The dark gold dragon gave his wings one pump, hauling them up into the air, and then snapped his wings straight over his head. With Brand underneath him, Uther slammed them both into the ground. Brand's head struck the solid rock with such a crack that the blast echoed through the peaks around them.

Brand lost consciousness for half a beat—falling through the blackness even as he tried to claw his way out of it. If he went out, he was dead.

Sounding far off, another dragon roared, and suddenly a great weight lifted off Brand's chest. He sucked in air, choking and coughing, even as his vision returned like coming to the end of a long, black tunnel with the light of the world far away at first and then closer and brighter with each step.

"Don't just lie there," Ladon's voice echoed in his head.

That brought him back to the fight with a *whoosh* of sound as every sense returned to him.

Uther had taken to the air, the deep gold of his scales glittering up above in the dark, reflecting in the gold and blue firelight around them.

Fuck me.

At least Ladon had bought him time. Forcing his body to cooperate, Brand flipped over and launched himself into the sky after the false king. No way was that asshole getting away.

The time it took to get airborne meant he lost sight of his enemy. Brand carefully circled, searching with every sense at his disposal, waiting for the attack that had to be coming. No damn luck.

Had Uther returned to the fight?

He tipped his wings to pass back over the town in a low sweep. Ladon's forces were outmatched in numbers but so far were holding their own. How long could they last? The wolves weren't fighting yet.

Where was Kasia?

A potentially debilitating cocktail of terror for her mate and relief that he'd come assailed Kasia, except she had a job to do. Wolves to get out of the dragons' paths.

With her one good arm, she shoved back to her feet, bobbling a bit as the useless arm pulled at her, weighing her oddly down. She reached out and took hold of a hank of the pinned down wolf's fur.

"Take my hand," she yelled over the noise of fire and screams and roars of dragons. "I'll get you both out of here."

Rafe didn't even hesitate. He shifted, turning from wolf to man so much faster than the dragons that she blinked. Then he took her by the wrist. "Go."

She cast an image in her mind of the clearing beside the river, then pulled them through that dark silence between physical planes to end up beside the cool bubbling water.

"I'll get the others," she said as she released her grip on the wolf struggling to his feet.

Rafe didn't let go of her wrist. "Not with your arm like that."

"Even if I'd lost both my legs, I can still teleport." She glared. A smile actually kicked up the corners of his mouth. The damn shifter was smiling? She scowled. "I mean it."

"I believe you. Let me fix the arm first."

A collective howl rose from the town, a sound so eerie the fine hairs raised on her arms. "Do it fast."

Rafe wasn't smiling now. "Turn off the fire."

She took a deep breath and pulled the flames inside her body, though she kept the fire stoked inside, her skin glowing golden with the effort, the feathers usually invisible to the naked eye showing in stark relief in the dark.

Rafe faced her square on, took her by the wrist, and placed his other hand over her collarbone beside the empty socket of her shoulder. "On three."

"If you pull on two I'll already see it coming—"

He yanked her arm forward with a hard jerk, using the unique strength shifters claimed, and the shoulder popped back into place. Kasia cried out. Pain—like someone had just jammed a red-hot poker into her shoulder—radiated through her. She doubled over, one good hand on her knee, and breathed through the hurt, waiting for it to recede.

After a second she righted herself, gritting her

teeth as the poker sensation eased. The shoulder was still sore, but she'd heal. "Stay here."

Rafe nodded.

Kasia pulled the waiting flames back over her body like a cloak of living light, feeding off the magic the fire fizzed through her blood. With a thought, she popped back inside the town, aiming for a spot by the trees at the edge, since she didn't know what structures had moved, fallen, or were on fire.

She spied Cairn, sprinting for the woods fifty yards away, five other wolves in tow. Another thought and she appeared before them; fatigue washed over her, dragging at her like hands reaching out of the underworld, trying to pull her down to hell.

How long can I keep this up?

With them unable to touch her flaming body, other than her hands where she'd pulled back the flame, she could transport only two wolves at a time. If she pulled back more of her fire, she wouldn't be able to teleport—the two were linked.

She managed to get Cairn and the other four wolves to safety, then headed back in. She found Bleidd squaring off against a dragon the color of sunglow who'd landed in front of him. At his nod, she transported him back with the others. After that, she brought three more individual wolves to their people. Fatigue weighed down her movements more with each jump.

The battle continued to rage overhead, on the ground, the dragons seemingly everywhere, their battle deafening. *Deafening*. She caught a flash of

Ladon as he'd gutted one dark yellow beast, blood spraying across his face, giving him a terrible, dread-invoking appearance, living up to every inch of his name as the Blood King.

With every trip, she frantically searched for her mate, but Brand continued to remain out of sight. Uther also didn't show. Were they somewhere fighting? A bone-deep knowledge that he still lived throbbed through her, allowing her to continue her job.

She found another group of five using the buildings as cover as they skirted the town, only they were close to where they'd have to make a run through a wide-open field. The combination of moonlight and the blaze from the fires all around would make them easy target practice to any gold dragons not engaged in the fight.

Two successful back-and-forths and dark spots were trying to hijack her vision. *But I can still see.*

Just one more. Just one more.

"Faster," Cairn yelled after her second teleport.

He pointed over her head to a pale, glittering yellow dragon circling above where she'd just left the last shifter. The winged creature prepared to pounce on the wolf like the predator he was.

Kasia gritted her teeth against the lethargy stealing through her limbs and forced her body back through the void. She arrived in the right spot, only to find her final passenger hadn't waited. Wind feathered her face. She glanced up only to suck in a gasp as she simultaneously dropped to the ground and used her ability to take herself thirty feet away.

She came out of the teleport lying on her stomach

on a bed of pine needles, gasping, and frantically checked her back for gaping, gushing wounds, then rolled over and collapsed with a relieved groan.

Shit, that had been close. She could still feel those talons raking through her even as she'd faded away.

Brand watched that pale fucker go after his mate and just about lost his mind. With determined focus, he tucked his wings back, streamlining his body as he flew, planning to attack the shifter—who'd risen into the sky—from below.

As he shot past the tallest tower in the town, blazing with flames forty feet in the air, Uther exploded out of the fire and rammed into him from the side, wrapping him up with a harsh grip. Ribs cracked with the force of the impact, immediately shooting pain through his body.

Wind whistled around his head, and Brand knew Uther was going to try to slam him into the ground again, only this time from higher. He thrashed in the king's grasp, but talons dug in deep, pierced his scales, burying deep into the flesh underneath.

Brand roared his pain.

He had seconds.

Kasia.

That bastard wasn't getting his mate, even if Brand had to kill himself to ensure that.

Brand kindled the flames inside his belly, ignoring the pain of his ribs to suck in air, feeding the fire with more oxygen. Then, with only death in mind, he let loose the torrent, knowing the blaze would find his own wounds.

Pain worse than any he'd ever known screamed along the nerves in the gashes in his leg and his face and where claws had dug deep into his sides, but he kept going. He blasted the fire until Uther screeched above him, an ungodly sound that would strike fear in the heart of every warrior below, but still Uther didn't let go.

And Brand didn't let up.

His nostrils filled with the putrid scent of charred flesh and blood, and still he didn't stop. He was melting his own body, but if he was melting Uther's then he didn't give a shit. He'd learned to live with pain long ago. He doubted the same could be said of the gold usurper.

As suddenly as Uther had attacked, he released his grip, using his leverage to shoot up, escaping Brand's fire.

But as he moved, his tail whipped by.

You're not getting away that easily.

Brand snapped his jaws around that lethal tail. He managed to avoid most of the spikes, but one drove through the bottom of his jaw. Another form of agony joined the rest. With this many injuries, shock couldn't be far off.

Uther convulsed above him and then turned, beating at him with wings and powerful back legs. He even tried to whip his tail, dragging Brand around.

Brand waited, watching the ground. He had one shot to get this right. Somehow, he blocked out the pain and Uther's struggles and kept his jaw from being dislocated as he held on to that thrashing tail.

And still, he waited.

At the last second, he let go of Uther, using his front talons to pull the long spike out of his own jaw. Then he flared his wings, popping up above his adversary's body. Uther also tried to flare his wings, but he didn't have the extra seconds Brand had.

With a satisfying boom that reverberated through the air, Uther hit the ground hard, just at the edge of the burning town.

Brand wasn't far behind him. He hit hard, too, his debilitated leg crumpling as he struck, but he pushed back to his feet, his gaze on Uther.

The gold dragon managed to lumber to his feet before Brand could attack. With a hiss, he fished his tail back and forth behind him.

Damn. He was a hard fucker to kill.

"You'll never take my throne," Uther snarled.

"It was never your throne, asshole." He gathered himself, ready. *"Let's go."*

They threw themselves at each other, moving slower than when they'd started, but still deadly. One of them would die tonight. Or they both would, if it came to that. Hell, he was knocking on death's door as it stood. But Uther was not walking away from this.

The thundering clash of two dragons nearby had her backing up and searching, moving slowly now, as if quicksand had taken hold of her body, dragging her under. Every step, hell, every twitch, took effort to push through. She could rest later.

That pale asshole was still above her—she hadn't gone that far away—and she had at least one more wolf to ferry to his people.

A quick search of the area showed him limping quickly along the edge of the tree line as he circled the worst of the fighting. Kasia focused on his location and teleported. Only, mid-leap through time and space, she shorted out. Like electricity in a thunderstorm, her flames blipped on and off, and she stumbled to the ground only halfway to her objective—and out in the wide open, exposed like a live wire.

Fuckballs.

A small part of her almost laughed, something she chalked up to impending hysteria, but obviously she'd picked up one of Brand's swear words. Figured *that* would rub off.

Tuning out her returning panic and the deafening noise of the fight, she concentrated on the fire inside her. Like striking flint to stone over damp tinder, it took several attempts, and a whole lot more energy than she thought she had left, just to light up.

But she did manage to ignite again.

Rather than go long distances, she teleported in short hops, trying to zigzag so her destination wouldn't seem obvious to any dragons monitoring her progress from above. She made it to the wolf and got them both back to the rendezvous point.

Kasia dropped to her hands and knees, pine needles and rocks digging into her skin, but she didn't care. Chest heaving, she sucked in air, doing her damnedest not to pass out. Thankfully, many more had gathered there than she had transported.

Bleidd knelt beside her. "I think the fight is winding down."

"Who's winning?"

His eyes went flat and grim, even in the semi-dark of the firelit night. "No idea."

Dread sank like a man with cement boots to the bottom of the river. She almost didn't want to ask. "Anyone else?"

"This is everyone."

"But…"

"But Maul's still out there."

She jerked her head up to look at Bleidd. Her hellhound had shown? When? "How long?"

"He appeared here five minutes ago, then disappeared. I think he went out for you."

Despite the urge to rush back and find her faithful pet, Kasia's mother's voice sounded in her head, memories of the times—so many times—Serefina Amon had drilled into her daughters, Kasia especially, one basic premise. "No matter who is in danger, don't rush in, or you'll make a stupid mistake. Wait and think."

"Wait and think," Kasia whispered now. She nodded, still sucking in air. "He'll come back. Let's give him a second."

Bleidd held out a hand and pulled her to her feet, then caught her when she swayed. "Whoa. Hold on, little dove."

She barely had the energy to pull one corner of her mouth up in a smile. "I'll be fine after I've had a chance to sleep—"

An unmistakable howl broke through the lowered din of the dwindling fight.

She knew that howl. "Maul."

"Stand back," she told Bleidd.

He didn't budge. "No. You're too weak. He'll teleport back."

"He can't, or he would have already."

Bleidd still regarded her with stubborn concern.

"Move," she boomed at him.

Lips flat, he released her arm and took a step back. "We'll be right behind you."

Kasia nodded. The pack as individuals couldn't do much against a dragon. But as a solid unit... Killer bees took down much larger creatures for a reason.

She sucked in a breath, reaching for anything left of that spark inside her. Like a lighter out of fluid, nothing happened at first. Then another howl pierced the night, and from down deep, she found a small reserve.

Flame trickled over her, again lighting the world in an eerie glow. Before she lost it completely, Kasia pictured the town as she'd last seen it, trying to angle herself toward where the howl had seemed to originate, and forced her body to go. This time the darkness and silence dragged at her, as though hands reached out trying to keep her in the void forever.

With a cry—silent in the cavity, but agony filled when she reappeared—Kasia made it to the town, only to find Maul surrounded by three golden dragons who seemed to be toying with him like cats batting at a bug. Blood pooled beneath him.

Off to the side, she spotted Brand and Uther engaged in a knock-down-drag-out fight.

"No," Kasia cried out as one of the dragons lined up to swing at the hellhound with his spiked tail.

From the gods knew where, she dredged' up enough energy to run headlong between the massive beasts. Maul bared his teeth and shook his head, obviously wanting her to stay away, but she couldn't. Kasia made it to his side.

"Look what we have, boys."

Kasia winced as the dragons let her hear their piercing thoughts.

"A little phoenix girl and her pet."

Kasia reached for her fire again, but the well was dry, every last ounce of it used up to get to Maul. She looked at the hellhound. "I'm sorry."

The dog whined a reply, his body trembling under her touch.

Brand was vaguely aware of Kasia's shout somewhere nearby but couldn't stop to look for her, as he and Uther struggled to find that opportunity to strike, neither letting go of the other.

Her cry hadn't sounded scared—she'd sounded pissed. She had to be okay. That strange connection screamed at him that, other than exhaustion, she was okay.

The instinct to protect his mate clawed at him, even as centuries of the need for revenge scorched his blood with purpose.

He wrapped his upper arm around Uther's neck, but he didn't tuck his wing back far enough. Uther managed to rend a decent tear in the elastic membrane of Brand's wing, but he didn't even feel it. Too many parts of his body were in agony for it to register. He managed to get Uther in a choke hold; he stood up on his hind legs and threw himself backward, twisting in the air as he did, so he came down on top of his opponent.

At the same time, he managed to force the false king's head back, exposing his neck.

"Brand." Kasia didn't scream. She didn't even cry out audibly. She simply whispered his name in her mind as though he were the last thought she'd ever have.

His mate was in trouble.

Suddenly the dragon beneath his talons didn't matter at all. The only person who mattered was Kasia. Fuck Uther. Brand's life would be worth less than nothing without his phoenix. How could he have ever thought of leaving her alone in this world, even to kill Uther?

Something snapped in place inside his body, like all systems coming online, followed by an instant burning sensation at the back of his neck—the mating bond solidifying as the mark of his house copied from his neck to hers. Suddenly he could feel her—her exhaustion, her pain, her fear.

She'd given up.

Without a second's hesitation, Brand extended his wings and heaved off Uther. Thanks to the tear in one wing, he dipped in the air, which meant he couldn't fly. But, like most flightless birds, he could hop. In a flash, he hopped over the dragon closest to him, coming down on top of Kasia and Maul. He didn't have enough time to pick them up and get out of there as the three dragons attacked. Instead, he cocooned his mate and her pet beneath his bulk, careful not to crush them, but covering them with his body and bracing his weight on his forearms.

Protecting her with his life.

"Brand?" Kasia's voice broke.

The three dragons blasted triumphant roars, and blows rained down over him. Every spike striking true, digging through scales, rending flesh from bones. He managed to raise his spikes on his neck, so none of them could attempt to snap it. Otherwise, he held still and telegraphed a need for backup to any blue dragons who had survived the night.

He grunted, smoke snorting from his nostrils, as a particularly vicious blow snapped his already cracked ribs, one possibly puncturing a lung as it became harder to breathe. Then a roar blasted from him involuntarily as one of the dragons found the charred injury on his leg and tore into the weakened spot, like a predator tearing the flesh from its prey.

"Brand, stop." Panic filled her voice now. She pushed at him with puny, ineffectual shoves. "Stop. Get off us. Get away."

"No way am I leaving you." He managed to communicate through a blackness that was descending. His body was shutting down on him now. Too many injuries, too much blood lost. Shock would come first, followed by black oblivion…then death.

"They're killing you!" she screamed. She stopped pushing at him and leaned into his chest. "One phoenix is not worth your life," she pleaded.

"My mate is."

"No." She was sobbing now.

Suddenly, the violent attack stopped. Just in time, because he couldn't have held out much longer.

Kasia sucked in a watery breath at the sudden silence. "What's happening?"

"Don't know." Brand grunted. Now that his mate was out of danger, a deep trembling took up residence in his muscles. He rolled off of her even as she reached for him.

"Brand?" Her voice seemed to come from down a long tunnel.

As soon as he knew he wouldn't crush her or Maul, Brand collapsed to the ground and let darkness consume him.

"Brand!" Kasia yelled his name as she dragged herself across the short distance to where his head struck the ground when he collapsed. She fell to her knees beside him.

He didn't move, didn't open his eyes. Was he even breathing?

Vaguely the sounds of wolves and dragons fighting around them registered, but all she could do was lie beside her mate, his blood pooling beneath her legs from the multitude of wounds crisscrossing his back. His leg and a few other spots were charred lumps of meat, and his lungs were making a godawful gurgling. He was drowning in his own blood.

Tears poured down her cheeks, the salty liquid slipping in the corners of her mouth and running down her neck. She didn't care.

From where he lay on the ground, Maul gave a pathetic whine, which only made the tears come faster.

She shook Brand's head, not that she could move an unconscious dragon. "Brand Astarot, open your eyes," she yelled at him. "You are not allowed to die. Do you hear me?"

But he showed no sign that he was alive, let alone obeyed her commands. Kasia slumped forward, her hand on his cheek, and sobbed her heartbreak.

Gradually the noise calmed, leaving a screaming silence in its wake, punctuated only by the sounds wrenching from her throat as she poured out her sorrow in heaving gulps.

"Kasia." Ladon stood behind her, a man, not a monster.

She didn't look up. Couldn't.

He knelt and placed an arm around her shoulder. "He's gone, Kasia."

She shook her head, ignoring how the action made her sway. "No."

"He's gone."

She lifted her head to glare at the Blood King of the Blue Clan through her tears. "He can't be," she choked out.

"I know it's hard—"

She lurched out of his grasp. With jerking movements, her muscles no longer interested in functioning, she yanked her hair away from the back of her neck to show him the mating mark branded there. No way could she have missed that burning, even through exhaustion and fear. "If he's dead, then so am I."

She turned back to Brand and shoved him again. "So wake up, dammit. I can't go through this life without you."

Only he didn't move.

"He's not breathing, my king." Kasia caught Fallon's words to Ladon. "He's gone."

Ladon said nothing.

But Kasia still heard. Perhaps the bond hadn't solidified in time, and that's why she was still alive?

With nothing left to give and nothing to hold on to, she crumpled. Sobs so violent her muscles clenched as her body and her soul grieved. Wrung out and unable to hold herself up any longer, she lay across Brand's head, cheek to cheek, and wept.

Everything poured out of her into those tears. The loss of her mother. How much she missed her sisters. The worry over her future. Most especially her incomprehensible, soul-binding love for this man that had snuck up on her even as it had always been there between them—a connection more real than any she'd ever known or would ever know again.

"I only just found you," she whispered and kissed the tear-soaked scale beneath her cheek.

"What do we do with Uther?" Reid asked Ladon behind her.

They'd captured the Gold King?

Ladon sighed. "I'll do it."

"No," Kasia said. She lifted her head and wiped the back of her arm across her eyes. "I'll do it."

Several men exchanged glances behind his back, but Ladon watched her steadily. Then he nodded.

Kasia stumbled to her feet.

In an instant, Ladon was at her side, holding her steady. "This can wait until you're stronger. Brand left him barely alive as it is."

"No." She took a deep breath. "That bastard needs to pay for what he did to Brand and his family. Now."

She didn't even think about the how. Ladon would tell her. To her right, Fallon already leaned over Maul, working to heal the hellhound.

A small pinprick of relief pierced the numb sense of purpose now replacing her grief. "Where is Uther?" she demanded.

Wolves and men and a few blue dragons parted as Ladon practically carried her over the charred, smoking remains of the wolf shifter's village to where a massive golden dragon was pinned down by three of Ladon's warriors.

"I thought he was near death already," she said.

"He is. Brand saw to that. But we're not taking any chances."

Despite all that, the false king continued to struggle, his muscles bunching and twitching, smoke rising from his nostrils. No one dared put themselves directly in front of that maw.

Ladon led her to stand beside the beast's neck. She glanced at the king beside her, eyebrows raised. What next?

Ladon searched her face then drew back his shoulders. "Uther of the Gold Dragon Clan, you are found guilty of the murder of the Dagrun family, rightful rulers of the Gold Clan. In tandem with that heinous act, you are also found guilty of treason. Your sentence shall be immediate death by fire."

He turned to Kasia, and she bit her lip. "How?"

"Enough fire into any one of those wounds and he'll burn from the inside."

Gruesome, but appropriate.

Just one tiny problem. She slumped forward, hands on her shaking knees. "I'm all out."

To her shock, Ladon dropped to one knee before her. "Then take mine."

The Blood King of the Blue Dragon Clan cupped his hands and blew into them, then offered her his hand, palm up, a pale blue flame dancing there.

Kasia's mouth dropped open in a silent gasp.

"Take mine, too," Asher offered.

"And mine."

One by one, all the blue dragons in human form followed their king's lead, dropping to their knees to offer the phoenix their fire.

For her.

For Brand. Her dead mate.

Kasia choked back the tears scalding the back of her throat. She reached out to scoop up the fire still flowering in Ladon's hand.

"If we're killing kings today, can I join in the fun?" Brand's voice rang through her head.

Kasia lost the fire as she whirled to where they'd left him, Ladon catching her as she pitched to the side. The body of a gold dragon no longer lay in the ashes behind them. Instead, a man, whole and alive, limped through tendrils of smoke and those still kneeling, his gaze trained solely on her.

A shaking started deep in her core, even as she flung herself into his arms. Brand winced and swayed. "Gently."

Oh hell, all those gashes. She tried to let go and jump back, only he wouldn't let her, tightening his grip around her. "You're not going anywhere," he growled.

"But your wounds—"

His mouth tipped up in that infuriating, perfect lopsided grin of his. "Almost done healing."

Kasia frowned. "Almost done? You were… dead." Her voice broke over the word. "How is that possible?"

He leaned his forehead against hers and inhaled deeply. "You."

"I don't understand."

"Phoenix tears, when truly meant, have healing powers. Or so I've heard." He shrugged one shoulder, although a soft grunt of pain accompanied the movement. "Guess it's true."

Kasia gurgled a half laugh, half sob of relief. Then reached up to cup his face with her hands, pushing his hair back from his forehead. She gazed into those blazing eyes. Gods, the way he looked at her.

He reached under the heavy fall of her hair to trace the brand on her neck with a finger, and she gasped as pure aching need swamped her senses.

"My mate," he murmured. Satisfaction lingered in those low tones, but she caught something else as well. Awe. "I used to think fate was as cruel as dragon shifters, but now…"

She couldn't look away from those golden eyes. "Now?"

"Now I think fate set me on a path to you." He nuzzled her hair. "I've loved you since the moment you stole my car."

Then he caught her laughter in a breath-stealing, heart-pounding kiss, and Kasia's soul took flight, finally home…with her mate.

A polite cough had Brand pulling back. He glanced over her head, presumably at Ladon, and nodded. Then he dropped his gaze back to her. "We have something to do."

Right. Uther.

She moved to turn away only to be tugged back. "Not yet," Brand said.

"What?"

"I just told you I love you. We're not making another move."

Realization dawned, and she cast a nervous glance around at the hardened warriors around them, trying not to laugh. "Right now?"

"Yeah."

She could see the stubborn resolve in the set of his jaw, the focus of his gaze. And something else. Somehow, she could feel him, feel her mate's emotions beneath the teasing surface, and he was… unsure of her. Even now.

She went up on tiptoe to place a sweet kiss on his lips. "I love you, Brand."

Again, he pulled her back when she went to move away. "I heard you earlier, when I was bleeding and dying, and those are possibly the sweetest words I've ever heard."

"Possibly?"

Brand sobered. "I need to hear you tell me what you want from me."

Without his telling her more, she knew where he

was going with that. "I want you as my mate."

Through that strange connection, she felt his relief and his elation. Ignoring their audience and the task that he'd been waiting centuries to carry out, Brand kissed her again.

"That's sweet and all, but we can't hold this bastard down much longer," Wyot, one of the dragons on top of Uther, grumbled.

Brand lifted his head and grinned. "Shall we kill a king, my queen?"

She laughed, pure joy erupting from the blackness that had consumed her. "By all means."

EPILOGUE

Ladon gritted his teeth as Brand and Kasia entered the war room, Maul limping in behind them. They weren't giggling or making goo-goo eyes or anything, but they gave off this vibe. They were right together, and every cell in their bodies knew it, trusted that bond.

In the weirdest way, that tangible connection made him want to chuck something hard, with sharp corners, at their heads. The biggest reason for that, though, was how they prioritized their relationship over the practical steps that needed to be taken right now.

"I received a new piece of information," Ladon started as they joined his warriors and Curia Regis at the table.

Minus Chante, of course. Ladon's informant in Pytheios's camp had been happy to take Chante, one of Ladon's Viceroys, rather than Brand. The needed intel that man provided would continue, which was crucial if they had any chance of taking down Pytheios and cutting off the head of the snake.

He hit a key on his keyboard to project an image of a man—a younger version of the king recently executed.

"Despite the Dagrun insignia that now marks Brand's hand and every other golden dragon's hand of those we captured or who have joined him, Uther's son, Brock, has taken over leadership of the Gold Clan. However, because of the branding, there is unrest at Brock's leadership. The rumors we've managed to circulate among that clan that you killed Uther are also helping. Like the Blue Clan with Thanatos before I took power, most of the gold dragons are too scared to rise up against their king. But with you in the wings, a new king of royal bloodline, I think they'll rally behind you once you take out the remaining leaders. Now is the time to attack."

Brand and Kasia shared a long, unspoken look, communicating through a link they claimed allowed them to know the other's feelings. "What if Kasia and I go there alone? Does your informant's evidence lead you to conclude that my claim to the throne would be accepted?"

Ladon gritted his teeth again but gave the question due consideration. "Asher?"

His Beta cocked his head. "We killed all of Uther's main supporters at the wolf shifters' camp."

Reid leaned forward. "Those occupying Ben Nevis have either left, are in our dungeons, or asked for asylum to pledge loyalty to their new king." He nodded at Brand.

Ladon eyed his ally and friend. "Brock is your biggest roadblock to the throne."

"But?" Brand asked.

"I would rather not lose my only true allied king, or the phoenix, or both. It's too dangerous. You're both too valuable."

"What do you suggest, then?" Brand demanded.

"We take the throne."

"Killing more of my people?" Brand asked. "Why would they accept me as king after that?"

"There has to be a middle ground," Kasia insisted.

"Such as?" Ladon asked. This aversion to spilling blood coming from one of the more ruthless dragons he knew was perplexing. Perhaps a destined mate was not a desired relationship for a king, making the man weak and soft.

"I'd love to hear this myself," an unfamiliar female voice interrupted.

Ladon jerked around to find a woman standing just inside the door, glaring at Kasia and Brand.

The men around his table all jumped to their feet, low rumblings of warning filling the room.

Interest stirred inside Ladon, and his dick responded. She was the type of woman to make an instant impression. Tall and slender, an oval-shaped face with gloriously fuckable lips, raven black hair, and ice-blue eyes. Eyes that were a hallmark of a white dragon shifter. Add in a hostile gaze currently blasting the room with an arctic chill.

"Skylar?" Kasia choked as she rose unsteadily to her feet.

Brand, usually so unmovable, couldn't hold back an exclamation. "Holy shit." The man had to reach out to keep his chair from tipping over as he stood beside his mate.

Even Maul, still healing from the fight but never far from Kasia's side, raised his head from his paws and whined.

Ladon stood, too.

"Who's Skylar?" Arden asked, looking back and forth between the woman and Kasia.

Meanwhile, Ladon turned to the woman, sniffing the air. Shock mingled with confusion as a familiar scent washed over his senses. "Who are you?" He reiterated his sister's question, but directing it at the woman.

"What are you doing here?" Kasia overrode his question before Skylar could answer.

"I'm here to save you from yourself." She flung the words at Kasia, like an accusation.

Now Kasia scowled. "Dammit, Sky. I mated Brand by choice."

"Not what I heard."

"I don't give a shit what you heard. We're supposed to stay apart—"

"We were supposed to stay apart so we could be safe from dragon shifters. You went and *mated* one."

Another rumbled warning filled the room as his warriors took offense to the words and the venom in her voice.

Skylar advanced into the room—stalked, more like, with the predatorial grace of a jungle cat—her intent to do harm to Kasia telegraphing through her balled fists.

Ladon stepped into her path.

With a sneer, she ran her gaze down him, sizing him up. Then she lifted a single eyebrow, obviously having found him wanting.

Ladon shoved aside the irritation that unusual reaction drew from him. "You're not going near her."

She crossed her arms, clearly unimpressed. "You're not going to stop me."

"Who the hell *are* you?" He didn't like repeating himself.

Skylar smiled, those fantasy-inducing lips tipping up in grim delight. "I'm Kasia's sister."

"Fuck me," Duncan muttered.

The rest of his people stirred. He could practically feel the shock reverberating through the room. Everything inside Ladon froze as multiple implications hit him at once, but one came front and center.

Another phoenix. Impossible.

On the heels of that realization came another.

Mimicking her posture, he crossed his arms and smiled back. "You shouldn't have revealed your presence to me, little firebird."

Narrowed eyes shot sparks at him. "And why not?" she challenged.

"Because now you're *mine*."

ACKNOWLEDGMENTS

As always, I have a ton of thanks that I owe to a wide support network of fantastic folks.

To my fabulous readers... Thanks for the support, and hugs, and interest, and being awesome. (And especially for reading my books!) Kasia and Brand's story started as a novella, but as I wrote, their world and their story just kept getting bigger, until this became one of my favorite stories ever. I hope you love them as much as I do! If you have a free sec, please think about leaving a review. Also, I love to connect with my readers, so I hope you'll drop a line and say "Howdy" on any of my social media!

To my amazing editor, Heather Howland... You believed in my voice and this series from the get-go. You supported me through edits, and brainstorming, and rewriting, and more edits, and more brainstorming until we got it just right. I am so happy and grateful to have you in my corner!

To my Entangled team, you've made everything about writing and publishing romance fun and exciting. Because of you, I know I'm publishing the best book possible and that it will get the best support. Y'all rock!

To my agent, Evan Marshall... Thank you for everything—your wonderful guidance, your belief that I will do great things, and your patience as I sign up for, well, everything.

To my writing partner, Nicole Flockton... You

make this gig fun, day in and day out, with your support, love, and straight talk.

To Anna Stewart... Thank you for loving these stories as much as I do. Your edits, and support, and squeezing me into your schedule, have been huge for making these stories great!

To my support team of beta readers, critique partners, writing buddies, reviewers, RWA chapters, friends, and family (you know who you are)... I know I say this every time, but I mean it... You're the best and make my days brighter by being part of them.

Finally, a huge THANK YOU and I LOVE YOU to my happily-ever-after husband and my incredible kids, who laugh and shake their heads as I wander around in a daze 90 percent of the time, living in the worlds in my head. You are my inspiration and my heart. Because of your support and love, I get to live my dream.

On the other side of the world,
the clan kings have tasked elite dragon
enforcers with keeping order among the
American colonies...

THE BOSS

from the companion Fire's Edge series
by Abigail Owen

Finn Conleth leads his team of enforcer dragon shifters with an iron fist and a cold heart. Every dragon seeks his destined mate, but the process to turn the woman he once thought was his killed her and devastated him. He will never risk his heart again. His team is his family now. When his body eventually gives out, he'll leave, living his last days alone.

Delaney Hamilton moved across the country to escape the freak fires that plague her. But when another suspicious fire erupts and rapidly escalates around her, her hopes for a new life go up in smoke. She has no choice but to turn to the mysterious men who come to her aid.

Finn knows the fire is dragon-caused, which puts Delaney's problems directly in his jurisdiction. No matter how her wounded grey eyes call to every part of him, he refuses to risk her life in the mating process.

Until another dragon threatens to claim Delaney for his own, and Finn has to sacrifice everything to keep her alive...

*A team of elite military hackers who will
do whatever it takes to protect their country
and the women who enter their dark and
dangerous world...*

DEADLOCK

by *NYT* bestselling author Cherrie Lynn

Ex–Air Force hacker Jace Adams is the best at what he does. There isn't a system he can't infiltrate or a country his team can't topple. But when he finds Lena Morris,, the woman he hates most in the world, on his doorstep, the last thing he wants to do is help her.

Lindsey Morris can't believe her twin sister Lena is missing, with only a cryptic text to find the man Lena once betrayed. But as easy as Jace is to look at, getting him to agree to help her find her sister is a lot harder. He refuses to put his team at risk, until they find out the enemy they're facing may be one they have in common...

As Lindsey and Jace race against the clock to save her sister, their shaky truce begins to morph into a fire they can't control. But their lack of trust might be exactly what gets them killed.

Northern Exposure meets *Two Weeks Notice* in this new romantic comedy series from *USA Today* bestselling author Amy Andrews.

nothing but trouble

by Amy Andrews

For five years, Cecilia Morgan's entire existence has revolved around playing personal assistant to self-centered former NFL quarterback Wade Carter. But just when she finally gives her notice, his father's health fails, and Wade whisks her back to his hometown. CC will stay for his dad—for now—even if that means ignoring how sexy her boss is starting to look in his Wranglers.

To say CC's notice is a bombshell is an insult to bombs. Wade can't imagine his life without his "left tackle." She's the only person who can tell him "no" and strangely, it's his favorite quality. He'll do anything to keep her from leaving, even if it means playing dirty and dragging her back to Credence, Colorado, with him.

But now they're living under the same roof, getting involved in small-town politics, and bickering like an old married couple. Suddenly, five years of fighting is starting to feel a whole lot like foreplay. What's a quarterback to do when he realizes he might be falling for his "left tackle"? Throw a Hail Mary she'll never see coming, of course.

ALSO BY ABIGAIL OWEN

AMARA
an imprint of Entangled Publishing LLC